# On the Wings of Dragons

# On the Wings of Dragons

Terrie M. Scott

On the Wings of Dragons

Copyright © 2019 by Terrie M. Scott

ISBN 9781652883111

Printed in the United States of America

# Dedication

To my children – Ashlee and Rachel

To my grandchildren –
Judah, Elizabeth, Everett and Isaiah

To Ashlee and Rachel – I began this book when you were very young. You are both grown now with children of your own. We had a wonderful journey together but it was not always easy. From that, we learned strength and perseverance. Being your mother has been the greatest blessing of my life. Thank you for the laughs, the love and the memories we have shared over the years. I love you both dearly.

To my *Gang of Adorables* – One day you'll read this book. I hope you'll be proud of your Gammy. You are loved more than words can say. I can't wait to see you mold the world into your own creations! I see my children reflected in your eyes. I hear their voices when you laugh. You carry my hopes and dreams with you. Come ride a dragon with me!

To my parents, my family and Tim – Thank you for your unwavering support throughout the years. I appreciate everything you've done for me. Love you all.

To my grandparents – Love you, miss you and Uff da!

To all my dogs. Thanks for making me smile. To my Mick for sitting next to me when I wrote this. To my Frodo for dogs in sweaters. Miss you.

To Rutger Hauer for inspiring the character of Martin, with his depiction of Navarre in *Ladyhawke*.

This is a story about finding strength and courage in the face of adversity, and forging unbreakable bonds. The path is different for everyone. We have a responsibility to learn from our past and be caring human beings to all. The power lies within us, as it does with Emily, to move beyond our own pain and doubt, and to become a light in dark places.

# Acknowledgments

I was greatly influenced by Philip K. Dick's *Do Androids Dream of Electric Sheep*, J.R.R. Tolkien's *The Lord of the Rings* trilogy, Ray Bradbury's *The Martian Chronicles*, Isaac Asimov's *Robot* series, Larry Niven's *Dream Park* and Richard Bach's *Illusions*. I spent a lot of time in libraries, reading books on the Middle Ages, the Elizabethan and Napoleonic eras.

My first book was called *The Bobbles*, which I wrote when I was nine. It was about a family living in outer space. It was in our school library and checked out 23 times.

In 1976, I went to see *King Kong* with my family. I looked at a poster on the theater wall, which read, "A long time ago in a galaxy far, far away..." The words *STAR WARS* were at the bottom. No release date was given. I was twelve and intrigued.

I was there opening day, May 25, 1977. *Star Wars* was like nothing any of us had ever seen before. My friends and I saw the film 42 times that year. My transformation into total geek was complete. My room was adorned with posters, models, books, t-shirts and vinyl records based on *Star Wars*. My Grandma Olga gave me a *Star Wars* comforter for Christmas that year, which I still have to this day.

Our other obsession was Tolkien's *The Lord of the Rings* trilogy and *The Hobbit*. We'd write notes to each other in our own elvish language, so the teachers couldn't understand them. We wrote countless stories based on Star Wars and LOTR.

I had wonderful teachers that encouraged me to write – Mrs. Ford (Honor's English) and Professor Swafford (CCM),

This book is a reflection of my younger self. My head was always in the clouds! My mind always somewhere else – dreaming of distant worlds full of knights, dragons and castles. My main character, Emily, is much like I was at that age. And, as I watched my daughters grow, Emily came to life.

*On the Wings of Dragons* is the world I created.

Welcome to Aquila! I hope you enjoy it!

# Part I

## Distant Memories

*We forget because we must*
*And,* **not because we will.**

~Matthew Arnold

1825

# Prologue

Run. Run as fast as your feet will carry you, until your lungs feel like they will burst. To stop running is to die. The sound of her feet pounding the ground beneath echoed in the dense forest as twigs and branches snapped underfoot. She could hear it, closing the distance between them, crashing through the brush somewhere behind her. It was gaining ground. She could almost feel its hot breath on her back.

She dared not look behind her for fear of what she might see. The dragon closed in on her with fierce determination. She made a calculated move to dash into the forest in hopes of losing the loathsome beast, bent on making her its next meal. Had she made a fatal error in doing so?

The brush was only slowing her down, constantly snaring her cloak in the thorns, while the beast had no difficulties plowing its way through the underbrush. She tore off her cloak in hopes of increasing her speed and maneuverability. She cast a fearful glance over her shoulder, alarmed at how dangerously close the dragon was to her. As she turned forward again, a branch tore across her face. A silent tear of blood trickled down her cheek, stinging momentarily.

"Faster," she told herself. "I must run faster!"

Her heart was beating incredibly fast. With each passing moment, she breathed heavier and heavier. She could feel the air being pushed out of her lungs faster than she could take it back in.

Is it possible that this foul beast had tricked her? Had it intentionally driven her into this tangled brush knowing full well it would spell her doom? Could it be that cunning? Had it herded her exactly where it wanted to? She pushed the thoughts out of her mind, refusing to believe that a dragon could have outwitted her. Nonsense!

Yet, the dragon showed no signs of slowing down, while her legs felt like they would buckle at any moment. She drew her sword and swiped to no avail at the intertwined branches blocking her escape route. She stumbled and fell to her knees, pushing herself up while hearing the snap of the dragon's jaws within inches of her skull.

She urged herself to move faster. She dove headfirst under a massive grove, clawing her way through the thickets, feeling her skin being torn to shreds as she did so. She saw the darkness up ahead turn to light and for a fleeting moment thought a clearing must be in front of her. If she could make a break for it on open ground and perhaps find a cropping of rocks to conceal herself under, before the dragon freed itself from the thickets? Maybe, just maybe she'd have a chance.

With renewed hope, she pushed onward. She crawled as fast as she could until she could stand upright once again. As she did so, her heart sank.

She had in fact been duped. It was not a clearing as she had hoped for, but instead a sheer cliff wall with not even a ledge to get a foothold on. The dragon had driven her there knowing full well she would have no way out. No chance for escape. Behind her lay the thicket she had just freed herself from, while on the three remaining sides of her she was flanked by sheer rock cliff that rose high into the sky.

She quickly spun around, with her sword drawn, to face her opponent. Panic now consumed her. She steadied her weapon as the beast crept slowly towards her. She could hear it smashing down the ground in front of her but could not see it yet. She pressed back as close to the wall as she could get, once again looking frantically around her to see if there was any possible escape route that she had overlooked.

She saw none. The sound of the dragon's heavy breathing was upon her now. She placed both hands on her weapon, preparing to battle for her very life. Just then, the thickets parted, and the dragon's nose slowly pushed out from beneath it. Seconds later, she saw the cold blackness of its eyes. Had she not known better, she could have sworn it was grinning wickedly at her, boasting at how easily it had acquired its prey.

As if to warn it otherwise, she said angerly, "Think not that you have captured me so easily. You will find me a worthy opponent and I plan to gut you before you take your first taste of me!"

The dragon tilted its head sideways, as if it were amused by this tiny warrior's protest. It pulled its head back slightly and then slowly nudged forward until it was almost completely above the girl. The size of it this close was terrifying, even for her, a trained soldier. She swallowed hard and fell to her knees, sword still raised in front of her. She began to tremble, but held steady. The dragon's breath blew her hair away from her face in torment.

She silently said a prayer to herself for courage and wished for a swift death, if that be the case. She stood up slowly, cautiously raising her eyes to meet the gaze of the beast.

She looked up to the heavens. "Give me courage," she said. She then turned her attention back to the dragon and shouted, "Go ahead, be done with it!" She held her sword bravely in front of her prepared for whatever fate was to come.

The dragon raised its head and let out a roar that sent chills down her spine. It opened its mouth and lowered its jaws over the girl to enjoy its midday snack.

"Damn you to hell!" she screamed at it. She tightened her grip on her weapon, ready to strike when suddenly she heard it…

*With hands held high into the sky so blue, as the ocean opens up and swallows you…*

The dragon pulled back, closed its mouth and tilted its head in confusion.

"Darn it!" the girl said, fumbling in her pocket while the familiar chorus continued somewhere within her clothing.

*With hands held high into the sky so blue, as the ocean opens up and swallows you…*

The dragon stepped back two paces as the girl lowered her sword, shaking her head in annoyance.

"Excuse me," she said to the dragon, "I have to take this call." She pulled out her cell phone and flipped it open.

The dragon eyed her curiously. Not sure of what to do next. This was not part of the day plan.

"Maaaaaa! This is really *not* a good time," she argued.

A woman's voice could be heard on the other line and she did not sound happy.

"But, Ma…"

More scolding could be heard. The dragon shook its head slightly from side to side, realizing its meal was about to be taken away. It was not at all pleased by this turn of events.

"But, Ma, you don't understand!"

The girl could tell where the conversation was going. She looked back up at the dragon and gave it an apologetic shrug.

"Okay, Ma. I'll be right there. Promise." She hung up the phone and studied the beast resting idly in front of her. "Well, you heard what she said. I have to go home right now. Sorry, perhaps another time?"

With that the dragon faded away right before her eyes, leaving her alone in the clearing not far from her home.

# Chapter One

This was not the first time Emily found herself lost in her imagination. She should not have wandered off again but it seemed as if the forest kept beckoning her and she could not resist the urge to explore it. It was the only place she felt free. Free to be a mighty warrior princess. Free to slay dragons and monsters of all description. From her viewpoint she could see the entire groves spread out before her. Her kingdom awaited her. She jumped down from the boulder only to catch her knee on a fallen limb. Ma would be angry, she sighed, as she looked down at her torn jeans.

Emily was a wisp of a girl, a tomboy, who took great pleasure in being able to outrun, outwit and outlast most of her male counterparts, a loner by choice. Emily had no idea just how beautiful she really was. She was a rare songbird with flaming red hair, usually pulled back. She was always pushing the bangs out of her eyes that flowed freely around her oval face and flawless complexion. She had fierce green eyes and a penetrating gaze that left many boys at a loss for words, always smitten by her beauty and quick wit. When pressed Emily would admit that she liked the attention, but she had no time for boys. She was unusually tall for her age, slender and athletic. She was confident yet shy. She was almost thirteen, as she would boast, nearly a teenager.

She was socially awkward and preferred books to people. Her mother was always pressuring her to use more tact when she spoke to others, but Emily just couldn't seem to stop herself from being brutally honest with people. She was too smart for her own good her father would tell her. How can one be "too smart for their own good" she would ask? He would just frown and sigh.

What few friends she had were the other brainiacs in her class. They were a close circle of friends as socially inept as she was. While other kids her age attended football games, Emily and her friends spent their time on computers or playing video games. They enjoyed role playing as their favorite book characters and often wrote letters to one another in their own elvish language to avoid detection from a teacher's prying eyes. There was always a spirited game of *Dungeons and Dragons* in progress. Nerds to the core and proud of it.

Emily gazed up at the sky and could tell another storm was fast approaching. She hurried home before she added rain-soaked clothing to her list of offenses for the day. She quietly opened the back door hoping to sneak in. She could smell dinner in the oven and was reminded of just how hungry she actually was. Chips and gummy bears were a pitiful food for a warrior princess, but alas she always made do. Emily tiptoed through the laundry room hoping to quickly change and bury her torn jeans deep within the confines of the hamper when she heard the giggles of her young sister bellowing through the hallway.

"Mommy!" Sarah shouted, "Emily's trying to sneak in the house!"

Emily stopped dead in her tracks. She heard the steps of her mother fast approaching. She'd been had. Her mother placed her hands on her hips and surveyed her daughter from the doorway of the laundry room.

"Well, it's about time. Dinner is almost ready, young lady."

"Hi, Ma," Emily said sheepishly, trying to cover her ripped jeans with her hand.

"Emily has a tear in her jeans," Sarah offered.

Her mother exclaimed, "Did you ruin another pair of jeans?"

Emily shot Sarah a threatening glance. Sarah only giggled from behind the protection of her mother's legs.

"It was an accident," Emily tried to explain. "I was running from this dragon, you see, and…"

"Oh, Emily, at least have the decency to tell me the truth about it. This is the second pair you've ruined this month. We're not made of money, you know," her mother reminded her.

"Yeah, we're not made of money," Sarah piped in.

Emily shot her another glance. Sarah ducked behind her mom again amidst her own giggles, enjoying her sister's predicament.

"I'm sorry. I'll work to buy a new pair," she offered.

"Take them off and let me see if I can mend them. If not, you'll have to do some extra chores around here to help pay for these. This is becoming a bad habit of yours, coming home late from school, filthy or torn clothes," her mother pointed out.

"I'm sorry, I'll try to do better," Emily promised.

Her mother frowned at her doubtfully. "In the meantime, go to your room and get cleaned up. Then come down and set the table for dinner, understand?"

"Yes, Ma."

Her mother shook her head and returned to the kitchen. Leaving Sarah alone in the doorway smiling gleefully at her sister. The little girl stuck her tongue out at Emily.

"Rat," Emily scolded her. "You know they used to kill people for betraying someone. You might want to remember that."

"Mommy! Emily said she's going to kill me!" Sarah yelled to her mother.

"Emily!" she heard her mother call.

"I was kidding, Ma," Emily called back to her as she ran upstairs.

In the privacy of her room, Emily pulled out the note from her Honor's English teacher and thought it best to wait till later that evening to break the news to her parents that she had once again failed to complete her assignment. Mrs. Forester made it perfectly clear that this was her last chance. She'd lose her spot in the class and was already lectured on what that would mean to any possibility of her earning advanced placement classes in high school.

Heaven forbid, what would that do to her chances for a full academic scholarship? Seemed like a lot of unnecessary pressure just because she failed to finish her report on Albert Camus' *The Plague*. Would the sky open and the ground split apart? Would she be cast down with the other students that failed their higher learning opportunities?

"Oh, ferryman of the river Styx, take me away!" she announced dramatically in her room to an invisible audience. Shudder the thought!

Emily loved to write, but rarely loved writing her assigned readings. She preferred to let her pen indulge itself in her flights of fancy and create worlds of her own. This love affair with fantasy had gotten her into trouble time and time again. It seemed that her parents and teachers appreciated her vivid imagination, but not at the expense of her other school assignments, an unreasonable request, at best, thought Emily.

She wasn't interested in the Cold War or politics. Yawn... Give her a castle and a sword in her hand any day or some far off planet where weary people needed to be saved. Those were the things that held her interest. However, for the time being, she would have to answer to her parents and those henchmen at school.

Ugh. Her father would have a fit when he learned that she was close to losing her coveted spot in Honor's English because she had neglected her school responsibilities. She could already hear the lecture formulating in her mind about the colleges that would pass her by due to her "lack of effort" and her "inability to apply herself."

Ugh again.

Maestro, cue the music - as the sad melody begins to play, showing her destitute and scooping ice cream cones at the Skippy Dip Ice Cream Parlor for the rest of her life. That would be her lot in life. Her father would drum that into her head all night long, lucky her.

"Father, dearest father? Would that be one scoop or two?" She grinned and shoved the note down into her book bag for safekeeping.

Sigh. She flopped onto the bed and rolled on to her back and let her head hang over the edge, looking at her room upside down. She felt like she viewed everything upside down from the norm.

Quite frankly, she was perfectly fine with being different. She let her gaze linger at her overpacked bookshelves and smiled warmly at her worn out copies of *The Hobbit* and *The Lord of the Rings* trilogy.

"Dear Frodo, what must we do? These mere men do not understand our burden. Quick, give me the one ring! Let me carry the load!" she said out loud.

She loved her parents deeply and was smart enough to know they only had her best interest in mind. After the torn jeans, she could do without a second lecture today. She pulled out her writing journal to see where she had left off. Sarah stuck her head in the door and frowned at her older sister.

"Mommy told you to get cleaned up and set the table," she reminded Emily.

Emily gave her a look, walked over and closed the door.

"Mommy!"

She heard Sarah calling downstairs, tattling on her once again. One day, she'd have a very long talk with Sarah about the values of loyalty. No one liked a tattletale.

Emily heard her mom yell from downstairs, sighed and did as she was told. There would be time to escape into her latest adventure again soon enough.

~~~~~~~~~~~~~~~~~~~~~

Dinner came and went. Emily was relieved that her mother didn't feel the need to tell her father about the torn jeans. Her father took a phone call in the next room while Emily helped her mother clear the table. Emily stood over the sink rinsing the dinner plates only to overhear her brat sister telling her father that not only had Emily torn her jeans, but she was also three hours late coming home from school.

Emily lowered her head in aggravation, wishing that she could exercise her divine right of justice on her betrayer. Her father walked over to the sink, looking very displeased. Then she saw the anger on his face and knew this was more than lecture mode and wondered what more damage had been done. Much to her demise, that wicked teacher had phoned him, informing him of his daughter's precarious situation in Honor's English.

Is there no end to this evil? Could this day end up any worse?

"Where is it?" he demanded to know.

"What?" Emily asked, knowing full well what he was referring to. She could see her mother standing in the background, shaking her head in disapproval and that little rat Sarah grinning from ear to ear.

"I'll get you, my little pretty and your little dog!" Emily thought to herself with visions of pulling Sarah's stuffed dog's ears off as a lesson to her sister to keep her trap shut or pay the penalty.

Her father put his hands on his hips. "Don't play dumb with me young lady – the note from the teacher."

Oh, that note... Emily pretended to have forgotten all about it. "I'll get it," she said.

He followed her up to her room. She could feel his stare on her back and wondered what her punishment would be. He stood in her doorway, waiting for the precious teacher's note. He looked at the disarray around her room. Books and video games galore littered the floor. Emily rifled through her bag, pulling out the crumbled piece of paper. She smoothed out the wrinkles and handed it over to her father.

"Do I need to tell you what will happen if you get kicked out of Honor's English?" he scolded.

"Yes, I will scoop ice cream for the rest of my life," she thought to herself, but didn't dare say it, least she would never set foot outside the house again, grounded for all eternity, like those pathetic children from *Flowers in the Attic*. Instead of the snide remark, she opted for a simple dutiful nod, wisely trying not to upset her father further.

"Emily, I am sorry, but this is really the last straw. You've been warned repeatedly. You've left me no choice but to punish you."

Uh, oh. Here it comes.

"I'm taking your journals away until you can demonstrate to me that you are capable of doing your schoolwork. I'm all for the creative side of life, but not at the expense of a solid education. I'm taking your Xbox too. Once you bring your grades back up to where they should be, we'll discuss you spending time in your fantasy world again."

Huh? Emily couldn't believe her ears. He was joking right? Hand over her journals? Turn over her Xbox? This was cruel and unusual punishment. She blinked hard to focus once again on what her father was saying.

"Until such time that your teachers and I are satisfied that your head is in the right place and you are committed to your fundamental education, there will be no more writing exploits unless they have been assigned by a teacher. And, no more mindless video games. Understood?"

He walked over to her bed, picked up her journal, and tucked it under his arm. Then he proceeded to yank the connections from her Xbox and toss the handful of games that laid scattered around the floor into a box that sat near her bed. Emily's mouth dropped open in disbelief. He gathered up the box and her game console then turned back towards her again.

"And, don't think you can just find something else to write in because I will be checking your work every day. Don't make me hire a private tutor to supervise you. If it comes to that, it will come out of your allowance money. I won't let you throw away your future just because you can't get your head out of the clouds! You like to tell us you're not a child anymore and almost a teenager. Start acting like one. Time to grow up, young lady!"

Emily felt numb.

She had always been given a wide margin to spend time on her stories. Her parents had never balked before. As a matter of fact, they had always indulged her whims, until now. She could tell by her father's demeanor that he was not to be swayed. She had truly pushed the envelope too far this time and it had come back to bite her hard.

She had never intended to fall behind in her work, but one thing led to another and her own interests always seemed more important than what her teachers expected of her.

Honestly, why did she need to learn Algebra? She wasn't going to be a NASA scientist, as much as she loved the idea of space exploration. Complex math was just a concept she failed to grasp, nor did she care. Was it necessary to learn the life cycle of the fruit fly? Was it important that they be given a forum?

Emily was going to be a writer. Maybe, she'd even write screenplays for movies one day. The rest of that junk was just...filler.

It seemed she underestimated her father's tolerance for neglecting her education. He rattled on about how she must be committed to academics, if she ever planned on making her dreams come true. Emily only heard half of what he said. Her eyes drifted down to her beloved journal still tucked beneath his arm and the box of her beloved games in his hands.

What if she grabbed them and made a mad dash out the door? And went where? She could hear Sarah laughing at her stupidity now. Not many college prospects from behind juvenile detention bars.

She pictured herself wearing stripes or worse – a bright orange coverall, picking up trash by the side of the expressway. Bright orange? Wow, won't that be a hoot with her bright red hair? She should just stick a clump of grass on her head and make her transformation into a carrot complete.

Emily's father handed her mother the box and took the book from under his arm, pounding his fist on it. Emily's eyes widened. She could hear the dragons within it, asking that the crazy man stop thumping them. It was giving them a headache. He told her to do her homework immediately and left the room in a huff.

Emily walked slowly to her desk and sat down. She could hear her mother and father arguing in the next room. Her mother, bless her heart, thought her father's reaction was a bit over the top. He cut her off with "spare the rod, spoil the child" or some other nonsense from the dark ages. Emily had clearly caused a rift between them and she didn't like being the cause of discord within her own home. That was generally Sarah's place to do so.

Emily opened the music box, which sat on her desk next to her dragon piggy bank and fumbled through it. She took out her most prized possession, a necklace passed down from her grandmother. The necklace held two dragons with their wings wrapped around a purple jewel on a long silver chain. She held it up to the light, admiring its beauty. It made her hand tingle slightly. It was almost pulsating in the warm glow of her bedroom. She had always felt a strange connection to the necklace, as if it was beckoning her from far away. She dismissed the stirrings from within as just another figment of her imagination and placed the necklace safely around her neck.

The arguing continued for another hour. How could she concentrate on her homework with all the shouting coming from down the hallway? Sarah walked past and frowned at Emily.

"See what you did?"

"Not now, Sarah," Emily told her. Sarah hugged her stuffed dog and went into her own room across the hall. Emily heard her father say something harsh to her mother and then slam the door. She listened to his angry footsteps stomping down the stairs, followed by the sound of his office door slamming. Looks like someone is sleeping on the couch tonight. This was followed by the sounds of her mother sniffling.

Mom was crying. Oh, no. Emily felt awful.

I caused this, she thought to herself. Not cool. She stood up and thought of going down the hall to see her mom and apologize, then thought better of it. She had caused enough trouble for one day. It was best if she made herself scarce.

"I've made a fine mess of things," she said to herself. She felt bad that they were fighting, but angry that her father had taken away her things and banned her from writing stories until her sentence was lifted. She'd go nuts if she couldn't write. It was like asking a fish to live out of water.

She walked across the hall quietly to check in on Sarah, who had drifted off to sleep. Emily pulled the covers over her sister and gently gave her a kiss on the forehead. She could still hear her mother sniffling and decided to do the right thing and look in on her. Emily stuck her head in the room to see her mom wiping her nose with Kleenex.

"Sorry, Ma."

Her mother looked up, eyes puffy and red. "It's okay, hon. You need to do what they say. This is serious. I don't agree with your father taking your belongings away from you, but Mrs. Forester threatened to drop you from Honor's English, and we can't have that."

"I know," Emily said, although she really didn't care if she took the course or not, but she knew the best and brightest took it. If she wanted to succeed, she had to do the time. "I just wanted to make sure you were okay," Emily added.

"Yes, just go back to your room and finish your work."

"Okay, sorry again. I'll try harder. Love you."

"Love you too, hon."

With that Emily went back to her room to sulk. She'd give anything to be back fighting that dragon. This day had taken a horrible turn for the worse and she was not at all happy about it. She tapped her pen on her spiral notebook, not even slightly interested in the work in front of her. She closed her book without doing one single assignment, vowing to get up early in the morning and finish it before the bus came.

She got washed up, changed into her pajamas and climbed under the covers. She stared out the window at the full moon looking back at her, wishing she could be that warrior princess of her dreams. A teenage girl with too much schoolwork to do and chores to boot left much to be desired.

Emily listened to the wind outside for quite some time. She touched her necklace and thought fondly of her grandmother. She finally drifted off to sleep only to find herself in the groves again pursuing some nasty beast. Her dreams overtook her. She tossed in her sleep.

In her dream, she was surrounded by a heavy fog and felt a cool mist on her skin.

*Annadune adelth mirash tonagoden...*

Strange words from a language she did not know flowed through her mind. A dragon, unlike any she had ever seen, circled her. She did not fear it.

*Annadune adelth mirash tonagoden...*

It was communicating with her, speaking to her mind. Repeating the same words over and over again. What did it mean?

Suddenly, an image of a woman kneeling near the water's edge appeared to her. Around her neck dangled the same necklace that Emily wore. From behind her a figure, basked in shadow, approached, striking the woman on the back of the head, shoving her into the water. The shadow reached for the necklace only to break its chain.

Emily thrashed in her bed. The vision of the woman drowning was replaced with an image of the necklace floating slowly to rest upon the soft bottom of the riverbed.

*Annadune adelth mirash tonagoden...*

The dragon spoke to her mind. The words cleared in her thoughts.

It said, "Protect the keystone."

"Is that what you ask of me?" she asked the dragon.

"She is coming for you..." It whispered to her mind.

"Who?"

"She murdered once to possess it and she will do so again."

"Who?" Emily asked again.

"She is coming for you…"

With those words of warning, the dream faded away.

# Chapter Two

The rickety stagecoach raced across the plains. The driver wore goggles to protect his eyes from the dust and harsh light. Inside a man gazed briefly out the window and sighed deeply. The passenger was in his late twenties – tall, ruggedly handsome, muscular build, blonde with striking silver-blue eyes, wearing a light tunic over dark pants. A finely tailored hunter green cloak was folded on the seat beside him. He was well educated and reserved.

His name was Martin Stewart – Doctor Martin Stewart to be precise. Martin had finished medical school in Pedora, a northwest province on Aquila. He was a man of science and cared not for the ways of magic that ruled much of his planet. He preferred the well adorned halls and upper crust snobs of Pedora. To his dismay, he was assigned to a clinic located at a remote outpost along the southern rim of the light side.

He swore to himself. Of all assignments he could have drawn, why this one? He never thought he'd return to this province but here he was traveling in a dilapidated transport, when a man of his stature should be hob knobbing with Aquila's finest citizens.

There were no fancy halls or bustling marketplaces where Martin was going, and the clinic was far too isolated for his liking. The thought of being stuck so far away from the lifestyle he had grown accustomed to had put Martin in a very foul mood.

It was nearly impossible to sleep on the stagecoach. The breaks were few and brief. Just long enough to stretch his long legs and check on his horse, tied to the rear. Martin stared out the window as the hours dragged slowly by. The closer they got to their destination; the more Martin was filled with dread. There was a nagging in the back of his mind that he just couldn't ignore.

From his vantage point, he could see the snowy mountains in the distance. Martin watched the landscape race by. Thoughts of his lost childhood crept into his mind. The bond between he and his dragon friends had never left him, but those fond memories were overshadowed by darkness. Crippling darkness that he was reluctant to face.

Aquila was a beautiful planet, with its own sun serving as a fiery beacon in the sky. Two magnificent moons, nestled behind the tallest mountain peaks, could easily be seen during the day. It was blessed with an abundance of natural resources – lush terrain, rolling valleys, endless forests, a bountiful supply of sustainable food, clean air and water. Thanks to the plentiful water sources, the skies were full of clouds, helping regulate the heat generated by the sun. The temperature was moderately warm. Rain was frequent and the cloud cover caused the temperatures to fluctuate drastically on an hourly basis. In the higher elevations, one could expect cold and even frigid conditions.

Most lifeforms inhabited one large land mass, surrounded by ocean. The smaller land masses supported life but were sparsely populated. Aquila was comprised of several provinces in various regions, with their own governing bodies, adhering to an agreed upon set of rules and principles for all to abide by. The governors of those provinces worked together to maintain order and to enrich the lives of their citizens.

Aquila was no longer under the rule of one banner. The days of a singular ruling body – a king or queen – had long passed. Occasionally, an overzealous governor would try to assert his or her own agenda, causing squabbles among provinces, but nothing serious enough to escalate to a show of force. No such army of men existed on Aquila anymore.

Trade and a rudimentary form of currency existed but no one went without, no one. If someone lacked the means to pay for something, they could merely offer their services or trade items for what they needed. Even if someone fell on hard times, due to a death in the family or sickness, they would be cared for, regardless of ability to trade or pay. The people took care of their own, for the most part.

Aquila was not a technology driven society. Its citizens adopted a simpler kind of life, for the good of the present and future generations. They had the tools and means needed for life's comforts, opting to harness the sun's power and the planet's resources for solar energy, wind energy, hydro energy – sustainable energy – preserving Aquila's beauty with minimal environmental impact. It was their way. It was the only way.

It was a utopia where inhabitants thrived and grew, basking in an abundance of light and warmth, unspoiled by man. There was no poverty or injustice. Freedom and individualism were encouraged. They were a civilization in perfect harmony with nature. Days were spent in pursuit of arts, academics or activities that fancied any interest. They embraced a peaceful and a carefree lifestyle. It was an age of enlightenment.

At least, this was true for half of the planet.

Aquila was divided in half by a great mist wall, the product of powerful magic set in motion ages ago. There were those on Aquila that were not content with what they had. They wanted more and craved it all. When black magic threatened to destroy Aquila, and wickedness nearly consumed them, the wisest among them intervened. At great risk, Aquila's elders joined forces with the Council of Dragons to contain the threat – to stop the spread of hatred, cruelty and greed. Guided by the power of the keystone, their efforts to protect those in the light succeeded, but forever altered the face of Aquila.

Evil was contained.

The darkness was pushed back.

Hope prevailed.

The mist wall trapped unfortunate souls within perpetual darkness. No one dared speak of its origins. No one questioned its existence. It was merely an accepted part of life. Most that knew the truth had long since passed on. Despite the elders' best efforts, the dark arts were still practiced and continued to slowly seep across the light side of Aquila. Those that practiced black magic, and craved its power, remained hidden in the darkness, avoiding detection.

What the elder's failed to realize is that evil never rests. Evil cannot be truly contained, for it always lurks in the shadows waiting to strike. Darkness always sought a way to penetrate the light, no matter how effectively the mist wall kept it at bay.

The mist wall forever splintered the land and sea into two distinct territories – one side of the wall was darkness and the other side was light. There was no dawn, nor was there dusk. There was only light or darkness. Few lived that remembered the days when both light and dark coexisted together.

Most of Aquila's inhabitants lived in the light, comforted by warmth, surrounded by hope and prosperity. Others struggled for survival in the dark, infected with fear, drowning in suffocating despair. There was no middle ground, no gray area. Aquila's inhabitants simply accepted the separation and wallowed in their own prosperity or lack thereof, caring nothing for what transpired on the other side of the wall, unless it directly impacted them.

For those on the dark side, the bleakness of their existence crushed any fleeting thoughts of hope. Left only to wallow in pity and despair, every moment was a fight for survival. The very air they breathed was putrid. Their surface water was contaminated from the ash that fell from the skies. Fresh water from deep underground caverns was brought to the surface through irrigation systems to sustain life. Predators ravaged the land, forcing inhabitants to take shelter underground or in close proximity to the fortress for protection. If you wanted morsels of food? If you wanted to live? If you wanted anything on the dark side? You were at the mercy of those in power. You did their bidding. You were alive because they allowed you to be so.

Geothermal energy drawn from active volcanos regulated the temperature on the dark side. It was cold but not unbearable. Crudely built greenhouses grew potatoes, cabbages and other vegetables to feed and sustain them. Those that could fend for themselves bartered or worked for their rations. Those that could not, resorted to thievery or violence to obtain what they needed. Fossil fuels provided oil to keep their torches and lamps lit, and the two giant moons shining down upon all of Aquila provided

28

soft light across the dark side. They had adapted. What choice did they have? They had enough to survive, but barely.

The inhabitants of the dark side resented the good fortune denied to them by those on the light side. Because of this resentment, Aquila was prone to violent raids from those residing in the darkness, desperate for resources, protected briefly by black magic or they risked being absorbed by the mist wall, as they had long been led to believe. Fighting seemed like the preferred method rather than civil negotiations. Raids were frequent closest to the mist wall. Although it seemed from time to time that a peace accord could be reached or a humanitarian supply chain agreed upon, they would ultimately fail.

Too many had come to profit from the misfortune, misery and suffering of others. There were plenty of riches for all but those on the light side were not eager to share their good fortune or give up power for the betterment of all things. Rumors of war grew stronger. A dark storm was rising, countless years in the making. The complacency of the light side would soon be tested. Their very way of life would soon, once again, be threatened.

There was no real peace on Aquila, only the illusion of such.

Martin suspected that his family was somehow at the center of that storm. Somehow the root of its cause. The tragic loss of Martin's mother years ago had driven his father mad from grief. His father abandoned all that he once knew, leaving his kingdom in ruin and despair.

As soon as Martin was old enough, he too left everything and everyone behind, with no regard for the consequences of his actions. Martin pushed aside any thoughts of regret and stared out the window. He would soon learn, however, that you cannot run from your past, no matter how hard you try. You can only pretend for so long and then your past catches up to you, whether you are prepared for it or not.

An evil grew within Aquila. It fed off the fear and ill will of men and creatures alike, sustaining their pain and fueling their hatred. For countless years, it endlessly hunted for the keystone.

The keystone had been present on Aquila since all recorded time. It was the most coveted artifact in all the lands. It stood as a bridge between all worlds, all knowledge, a key to all things. In ancient times it was used for wise councils to travel between worlds, a measure of peace between civilizations and beings. Those days had long passed.

Kept safe, the keystone protected order. However, in the wrong hands, the keystone could be used to control, corrupt and destroy worlds. If the delicate time stream that linked known worlds together was disrupted, the damage could be catastrophic and irreversible.

The keystone itself was forged in the deep chasms of Aquila, by the breath of dragons, and was said to be the rarest of all gems, harnessing unimaginable power, with even the means to restore life or take it away. It connected all life and knowledge, all time and space, all energy and all elements of the natural world. This made the keystone the greatest peace keeping tool or the most dangerous weapon in existence. The keystone was the greatest power Aquila had ever known. For this alone, it was kept hidden. Few knew what had become of it and those that did know, remained silent.

~~~~~~~~~~~~~~~~~~~~~~~~~~~~

The sorceress Miranda of Aquila desired the keystone all of her natural life, wanting nothing more than to possess it and wield its power for her own bidding. Not content to live in the shadows of men, she secretly sought to bring all to their knees and demand they beg for mercy at her feet.

What she failed to realize was that for the longest time the keystone was right in front of her. She just could not see it. Keepers of the keystone were chosen by bloodline to protect and defend it at all cost. They alone could wield its full power. They alone were bonded to it, called upon to do its bidding, becoming one with it.

Miranda's obsession with finding the keystone drove her to madness. Her black magic garnished her unnatural long life. Some thought she had dwelt on Aquila for a thousand years. Miranda corrupted the minds of many, stripping them of their will. Her dark riders hunted for the keystone throughout all corners of the lands and across time. Her black magic revealed little as to its true location, much to her frustration.

She spent countless hours reading over ancient prophecies, desperately trying to decipher their hidden riddles, occasionally uncovering a piece of information. She wanted only to change the world to her liking. She had been banished to the dark side of Aquila long ago, forbidden by the great leaders to ever set foot upon the light side again. Miranda was deemed a danger to herself and all others.

A binding spell held her at bay within the dark side, but exile had only made her resolve stronger. It had poisoned her mind. She would have her keystone and see the fall of men. Why would one desire peace, when there existed a way to rule over all living creatures? She planned to lay waste to the fruitful lands of Aquila and destroy its kingdoms, claiming all for herself.

She prepared to unleash an ancient evil upon the land. A winged beast of such pure evil, that its existence was believed to be a myth. Driven by hunger, fueled by the blood of innocents, Miranda kept the beast well hidden, deep in the caverns of Aquila, until the time to strike and devour all in its path had come. It was larger and stronger than all other dragons. It was said that nothing could defeat it. None had survived that ever tried, so the legend was told.

There were plenty of dragons on Aquila. The wisest among them had stepped aside as the true rulers of the realm eons ago. They once played a vital role in the stability of the kingdoms. However, the Council of Dragons had not been called upon for hundreds of years and preferred the isolation and solitude of the misty mountains rather than get tangled up in the affairs of men.

Although, most dragons were harmless, rogue dragons did exist that occasionally killed men for food and sport, hoping to snare the lonely traveler. These dragons were easily recognizable by their darker appearance, a stark contrast to the brightly colored dragons that had grown accustomed to the presence of men.

~~~~~~~~~~~~~~~~~~~~~~~~~~~~~~~~~~~

The stagecoach slowed and turned down a tree lined road, opening into a vast valley with snow covered mountains as its backdrop. It came to a rough stop outside of the clinic, jolting Martin forward in his seat. He moved towards the door to exit, then hesitated. He looked worse for wear. He stepped down from the coach and walked to the rear to check on his horse.

The black horse nuzzled its nose into his master's hand. Martin reached into the feed bag strapped to the horse's saddle and pulled out a handful of oats.

"There, there Thunderbolt. I promise we will not be staying long," he said, trying to convince himself of this truth.

Martin quickly let his gaze scan the area around him as his horse eagerly ate the food. He sighed deeply again and brushed off his hands when his horse had finished.

He gazed up at the clinic with its shiny tall spirals reaching into the sky. Solar panels, strategically placed among the glass of the towers, captured the sun's rays, providing a never-ending supply of power to the structure. The clinic was a beautiful building, glistening in the sun, like a brilliant diamond protruding from the ground.

Martin spotted a young dark-haired boy watching him from a lower window. His eyes locked on the boy momentarily until Martin heard the sound of his luggage trunk thudding to the ground, tossed off the stagecoach by the driver. Martin frowned in disapproval at his finely crafted bags, now covered in dust.

He looked around and closely scrutinized his surroundings. A group of children laughed nearby, running happily through the giant maze made out of tall flowered hedges. The trees were full of birds chirping. A massive wall of water, at least one story tall, gently flowed down the side of the clinic, emptying into a marble reservoir, filling the courtyard with the sound of rippling water. Wind chimes smacked together in the cool breeze, creating music of their own.

An elderly man, who did not bother to speak, waited patiently at the double glass doors leading into the clinic. Finally, he motioned for Martin to follow. A stable boy walked forward and took the reins of Martin's horse.

"Take proper care of my horse or you will answer to me, understand?" Martin warned the stable boy. The boy nodded but said nothing. Martin patted the horse on his hindquarters as the stable boy led him to the nearby livery yard.

"Behave yourself, Thunderbolt," Martin called after his horse before turning his attention back to his escort, standing dutifully at the doorway.

Martin dragged his luggage trunk with one hand and tucked his other bags under his arm. One of Martin's bags slipped from his grasp and landed on his foot. Martin swore under his breath.

"See here, can you give me a hand with these?" Martin asked, struggling to carry all his bags at once.

The old man ignored his request and stepped into the building, motioning for Martin to follow.

"Thank you for your help. You are too kind," Martin snapped sarcastically. "Has no one here any manners?"

Martin stepped into the building, known by all as 'The Clinic', and was escorted down a long busy corridor to his quarters on an upper floor. He hauled his luggage up several floors and dropped his bags to the marble tiled floor when the man stopped outside of what would become Martin's quarters.

"Finally," Martin uttered, annoyed and out of breath.

Martin quickly looked around the room. It was not at all like Martin was accustomed to, much smaller than his previous quarters, quite drab actually but it was adequate.

The old man walked stiffly to the heavy drapes and threw them open, allowing the full force of Aquila's sun to consume the living quarters. Martin winced briefly at the sudden assault to his visual senses but then quickly adjusted to the brightness.

33

"Doctor Pernell will want to see you at your earliest convenience, sir," the old man said in a low gravelly voice.

Martin threw his hands up in exaggerated surprise.

"He speaks!" Martin declared sarcastically.

The old man cast a disparaging glance at Martin and left the room without another word.

"Nice chatting with you too, kind sir. Please do stop by again soon," Martin called after him.

He situated his luggage on the nearby table before stepping out onto the balcony. He rested his hands on the railing and letting the reality of his situation sink in.

"I cannot believe I am here," he said to himself.

There was no denying the beauty in front of him. Shafts of sunlight bathed the meadow. The twin moons dipped over the snow-covered peaks, looming larger than life in the distance. A purplish hue colored the sky. The air was crisp and refreshing. To his immediate right, he could hear the sound of the babbling brook, leading to the river. It was hidden behind the mighty pines dotting the outer perimeter of the clinic. Butterflies within his reach floated gently above the flowered vines, climbing up the side of the towers, a pleasing blend of manmade structure and natural elements.

If he were to be honest, Martin could appreciate why so many liked to venture here. It was a utopia within a utopia. Even at this level above ground, he could hear the sounds of the harpsicord and wind instruments softly filtering through the clinic hallways. He sighed and stepped back inside his quarters.

He just wanted to finish this assignment and get back to Pedora, leaving all the past unpleasantness behind him. He had already requested a transfer back to Pedora before he even left. He wondered what condition he would find his old home in. He stopped and allowed those words to take root – his former home was here, quite nearby actually.

He caught a glimpse of his reflection in the mirror.

He was a grown man now. There was no sign of the young boy that pretended to slay dragons in his youth.

Once settled in, Martin headed down to the garden adjacent to the courtyard and waited for his meeting with the Chief Medical Officer. Children ran past him giggling happily.

A nurse approached Martin and announced, "The doctor will see you now. Please follow me."

She led Martin down the main corridor filled with patients and visitors. Martin looked up at the vaulted ceilings reaching high into an open central gathering place. The blend of mirrors and stained glass, combined with ample sunlight, filled the space with an array of colors, playing off the sunbeams. The effect was quite remarkable. Natural vegetation was woven inside the clinic to provide an aesthetically pleasing aroma and calming visual. Visitors felt like the interior was merely an extension of the outdoors. It was impressive, even to Martin.

The clinic met the emotional, mental and physical needs of residents of the southern region on the light side of Aquila. Often times, special cases from other regions were sent to this clinic as well. Cases that other regions deemed far too difficult or challenging to manage. No one was ever turned away from this clinic and some patients never left. Great thought and detail went into making the clinic as comfortable as possible for all who entered through its doors, regardless of circumstance.

As they continued deeper into the patient wings, the sounds of the harpsicord were drowned out by sounds of patients coughing. They passed by a large glass door leading to an atrium.

The boy Martin saw earlier was watching them from the doorway as they passed by. The boy's eyes bore down on Martin, with contempt. Martin gave the boy a curious glance but continued to follow the nurse.

"Who is the boy?" he asked.

"A patient," she answered without pause.

"He looks well enough. What is wrong with him?"

"There is nothing wrong with him," she replied curtly.

Martin frowned. "Then why is he here?" he asked.

Martin looked back over his shoulder. The boy had moved into the hallway and continued to stare at Martin.

"He shifts," the nurse told him.

"Shifts?" Martin replied, surprised to hear this.

Shifters were rare. To his knowledge, Martin didn't believe he had ever actually met one.

"Fascinating," Martin said under his breath as he looked back at the boy again, eying him intently.

The boy tilted his head slightly to the right and Martin felt a sudden pain in his left temple. He stopped walking and turned back to the boy. The child was grinning at Martin. The pain in Martin's head intensified. The child's grin grew wider.

Martin started walking towards the boy. "You there!"

The boy lowered his head, allowing a long cropping of dark hair to fall across his face. He slowly raised his chin and lifted his eyes to Martin with such a sinister grin that it literally stopped Martin in his tracks. A cold chill ran down Martin's spine.

From this close proximity, Martin could see that the boy's eyes were black, completely colorless, like those of a doll. Another grin slowly crept across the boy's face, as a high-pitched ringing began in Martin's ears. It was painful but not unbearable. Martin locked eyes with the boy intently.

The nurse tapped Martin on his shoulder, causing him to break his stare. "Let's not keep the doctor waiting."

Momentarily perplexed, Martin nodded at the nurse and then looked back one last time at the child, standing menacingly in the corridor, seemingly daring Martin to challenge him.

"Are you certain that shifting is all he does?" Martin asked with genuine concern.

The nurse ignored his question.

Martin followed her, rubbing his temple once more.

She stopped outside an office door, knocked and entered. "Sir? Doctor Stewart is here to see you."

Doctor Quinlan Pernell was a distinguished dark-skinned man of average build, who appeared to be in his late sixties. He was Chief Medical Officer and head administrator of the clinic, and had been so for years. He wore a long white tunic with gold trim over dark pants, with a multicolored braided belt around his waist. A pocket watch with no face sat on his desk, along with a pitcher of water and cups. Paperwork was scattered in front of him. His black rimmed glasses rested on top of his bald head. He was a warm, jovial man, a well-respected cleric and physician, who had devoted his life to helping others.

He waved at Martin and motioned for him to take a seat. Doctor Pernell's office was modest, given his status, but he certainly had the best views. One wall of glass overlooked the courtyard and gardens below. Another wall of glass overlooked the indoor gathering place. A third glass wall, directly in front of him, featured a breathtaking view of the snowy mountains. The doctor could watch over all activity from his vantage point.

The only solid wall was located behind Doctor Pernell's desk, where shelves were lined with books and medical journals. The same wall was adorned proudly with artwork from his patients. The clinic was his home. It had always been his home.

He motioned again for Martin to take a seat.

Martin grinned at one picture depicting Doctor Pernell holding a big bouquet of flowers and wearing a floppy hat. He then noticed a sketch in colored pencil of the misty mountains, with dragons flying overhead, that was actually quite beautiful.

Martin pointed at it. "This one shows some real talent."

Doctor Pernell nodded enthusiastically.

"Indeed, that is from one of our special children, Thomas," he smiled warmly, looking around the room at the many paintings and drawings adorning the walls. "As you can see, I am a blessed man."

Martin examined the drawing more closely. "It is actually quite remarkable, the detail. Does Thomas have dark hair and dark eyes, by any chance? If that is the case, then he and I have already met," Martin frowned.

Doctor Pernell chuckled, "No, he does not. Thomas has red hair. You can't miss him."

Doctor Pernell reached out to shake Martin's hand.

"Rejoice! Doctor Stewart. It is nice to see you again. It's been far too long. How was your trip?"

"Horrendous," Martin admitted.

Doctor Pernell laughed, "I bet."

"I dislike traveling such long distances," Martin told him.

"And, yet here you are," Doctor Pernell replied. "Welcome back, Doctor Stewart."

"Thank you," Martin said as they shook hands again.

Martin looked around the office. "This clinic is much smaller than I remember," Martin commented with a touch of arrogance in his voice.

Doctor Pernell crossed his arms and leaned back in his chair, studying Martin. "Really?" he asked. "It is actually the largest clinic in all of Aquila."

Martin frowned. "Perhaps it is the isolation that makes it appear smaller."

"Perhaps," Doctor Pernell replied, looking curiously at him.

"I shall give you this, though," Martin said as he looked out the window. "It is charming, in its own way. Although, I do not intend to be here long enough to enjoy it. I already put in a transfer request back to Pedora. I expect to be leaving soon."

Doctor Pernell nodded, opened his desk drawer and pulled out a single piece of paper. "Are you referring to this?" he asked, turning the paper towards Martin.

Martin leaned over and looking at the letter. Doctor Pernell reached over to point at two words stamped on the bottom.

"Request denied," he said with a slight grin.

"But wait. this cannot be correct," Martin said confused.

"Request denied," Doctor Pernell repeated, tapping lightly on the paper. He slid the document closer to Martin and pointed at the two words again.

"I can see what it says," Martin snapped, somewhat annoyed. "No need to keep repeating it."

"Perhaps you should hold on to this, Doctor Stewart," Doctor Pernell smiled pleasantly.

Martin looked at the paper and then back at the doctor.

"It cannot be so," he uttered quietly.

Doctor Pernell chuckled, "Oh it can be and it is so. I guess you'll be able to partake in our lovely clinic after all. Happy to have you here."

Martin looked defeated. He continued to stare at the paper as he sat back in his chair, saying nothing.

Doctor Pernell drummed his fingers across his chest, grinning at the young physician. "We are in much need of your services, doctor. Much has changed since you were last here," he told Martin.

Martin remained silent.

"The raids have increased in frequency of late and rumors abound that a major attack may be imminent from the dark side," Doctor Pernell revealed.

Martin dismissed the doctor's concerns and shook his head no. "I have heard this before. How is that even possible?" Martin asked skeptically. "They cannot crossover."

Doctor Pernell interrupted him, "Oh, but they do. Dark powerful magic assists them."

Martin rolled his eyes. "I do not believe in such nonsense."

"That does not make it any less true, young man," Doctor Pernell pointed out.

Martin leaned forward, "Look, I am a doctor, not a wizard wrangler."

Doctor Pernell chuckled, "Wizard wrangler? That is quite clever. I might use that again if you don't mind."

Martin sighed. "I do not want to be here."

"I sensed that," Doctor Pernell countered. "Yet, you are here and we do need a good doctor." He studied Martin for a moment. "I think you'll find that you'll be greatly needed here. May I suggest you try to make the best of it?"

Martin sulked and looked away.

Doctor Pernell smirked. "Welcome home, Doctor Stewart."

"Please do not say that," Martin said quietly.

"But you are home," Doctor Pernell reminded him.

Martin just looked away and shook his head no.

"I do not want to be here!" Martin said in a raised voice, pounding his fist on Doctor Pernell's desk.

The nurse immediately opened the door and peered inside. "Is everything alright, Doctor? I heard raised voices," she said, looking disapprovingly at Martin.

Doctor Pernell unphased by Martin's outburst, shooed her away. "Everything is fine. Please close the door. Thank you," he smiled at the nurse.

She closed the door once again but not before giving Martin a harsh glance. Martin rolled his eyes again. Doctor Pernell caught the look and laughed.

"My, my Doctor Stewart, I see you are already making friends here."

Martin ignored the remark and stared at the floor.

Doctor Pernell scratched his head and watched Martin in silence. The last thing he wanted was animosity between himself and his new doctor.

"I understand this is not where you want to be. I understand we do not have all the trappings of a place like Pedora. Things move at a much slower pace here but we are literally right at the doorstep of the mist wall itself. Things do happen here. This place, whether you like it or not, is the heart of Aquila. You might find that this is exactly where you belong. Please keep an open mind," Doctor Pernell asked gently.

Martin rested his forehead in his hand and then looked back up at the kindly doctor, wisdom exuding from his eyes. Martin sighed deeply.

"It would appear I do not have much choice in the matter," Martin conceded.

"I'm afraid not," Doctor Pernell agreed cheerfully.

"Fine, I shall try to keep an open mind," Martin finally said.

"Excellent," Doctor Pernell replied.

# Chapter Three

Far within the plains of Aquila, a giant oak tree stood beside a modest homestead. A man placed baskets into the back of a wagon, some full of produce while others were empty. It was market day in the nearby town and there were goods to be traded.

The man would not be traveling alone on this day. His young daughter, Rebecca, eagerly awaited the journey. She climbed up into the wagon and sat next to her father.

"Let's go!" she said happily to her father.

He laughed cheerfully at her enthusiasm.

"Child, you're likely to burst if you don't settle down," he smiled.

"There is so much to see and do," she reminded him. "And, Momma said I could get a new hair ribbon, remember?"

He laughed again, "Yes, how could I forget? You've reminded me several times."

Market day was her favorite day, besides her birthday. She loved strolling down the main street, smelling all the breads and pies.

Rebecca had hazel eyes and long blonde hair, braided down each side. Her cheeks had a touch of a sunburn from being outdoors too much the previous day. She was wearing a light rose patterned dress with a matching satchel to carry a small brush, mirror and extra hair ribbons. She was at an age where she fussed over her appearance quite a lot.

Her mother had given her five coins for her to buy whatever she wanted with. Twenty-five cents was a lot of money for such a young girl. She was anxious to add to her hair ribbon collection.

"We're going to be late," she complained to her father.

"Late?" he laughed. "The market will still be there when we arrive, young lady. Patience." He looked over his shoulder and back towards the front door.

"Mama," Rebecca called out, "hurry up!"

Her mother ran out of the house carrying two sack lunches. She handed them to the little girl.

"Don't forget these. My, don't you look pretty," her mother smiled proudly.

"Thank you," Rebecca replied sweetly, smoothing down her dress with her hands.

The man winked at his wife and slapped the reins on the horses to propel the wagon forward. "We'll be back before supper. Off we go!" he yelled out enthusiastically.

"Goodbye!" called out the mother, "Have a wonderful day! Have fun! I love you!"

The girl looked over her shoulder and waved back happily to her mother, "I love you too!"

The mother watched them until the wagon disappeared behind the bend in the road and out of sight. She turned to go back into the farmhouse but stopped when she heard a strange noise behind her. She looked around but saw nothing. She had an uneasy feeling that she was being watched. She quickly returned indoors. Living this close to the mist wall, they did come across raiders from time to time. She hoped that was not the case.

Her husband and daughter continued on the country road with not a care in the world, casually talking back and forth about the adventures the day would bring.

The wife went about her morning chores when she heard another strange noise, a creaking sound on the porch perhaps? She put down her dust rag and stepped gingerly on to the front porch and surveyed the area. She walked from one side of the porch to the other, but still saw nothing unusual. She stood with her back to the front door and sighed heavily.

All was strangely quiet when suddenly she was pulled forcibly inside with a knife held to her throat. She didn't even have time to react but let out a gasp as the wind was knocked out of her. The intruder loosened his grip and she let out a scream, but there was no one near to hear it. He dragged her roughly back into her kitchen and forced her to sit down in a chair.

"What do you want?" the woman gasped. "We have nothing of value here."

The intruder just laughed and stroked her hair.

"Please, please don't," she begged in a trembling voice.

A second intruder, a female, walked in the front door. She looked around the small house. She had dark hair and a visible scar running down her cheek. She barely paid attention to her partner and the woman he held captive. She was looking for something.

"So pretty," the male intruder said, as he continued to play with the woman's hair. A sinister grin crept across his face.

The female intruder finally spoke, "Stop messing around. You know what we came for. Let's get on with it. I can't stand being here in all this light."

Her partner grunted in protest but released the woman.

"Stay put," he ordered.

The woman did as she was told, nervously fumbling with her hands. She turned her head towards the female intruder, "What do you want? I-I can assure we have nothing of any real value. Is it food you want? I can give you some food."

The female intruder walked around the home casually. She turned and came towards the woman sitting in the chair. She leaned into her, "The girl. We want the girl."

The woman struggled to get free, but the male held her down, pinning her arms behind the chair and pushing her back down into the seat. "My daughter? But, why? I don't understand."

The male backhanded her in the head, "Shut your mouth," he ordered, holding her firmly in place with his hands.

The woman in the chair began to whimper quietly, shaking uncontrollably.

The female intruder walked over to a nearby shelf and picked up a sketch in pencil of a young girl. She studied it carefully.

"Is this your daughter?" she demanded to know. The woman in the chair shook her head yes. The intruder tossed it on the ground. "She's not the one. Another dead end," she informed her partner, as she exited the home. "Get rid of her."

43

"Gladly," her male companion said, as the woman struggled to free herself. Moments later, a scream shattered the silence.

~~~~~~~~~~~~~~~~~~~~~~~~~~~~~~~~

Rebecca reached down into her satchel to make sure she had her five coins. She felt nothing. She frantically began digging deeper into her satchel.

"Oh no!" she cried out.

"What's wrong, Rebecca?" her father asked.

"They're not here. The coins Mama gave me for the market. They're not here!" she said, tears forming in her eyes.

"Are you sure?" he asked.

"I'm sure. I thought I put them in my satchel," she hesitated. "Oh no. I took them out when I put my hair ribbons in and forgot to put them back in. Daddy, we have to go back!"

"What?"

"We have to go back, please?" she cried.

He looked down at the disappointment on his daughter's face and the tears streaming down her cheeks.

"Okay, okay. We haven't barely got started but for you. We will go back and get your coins," he smiled down at her.

Rebecca let out a sigh of relief and hugged her father's arm. Her father turned the wagon around and headed back to their home.

"You must think I'm silly," she said to her father, somewhat embarrassed.

"Not at all. Your mother gave you those coins to spend today and you can't very well do that if the coins are back home, now can you?" he winked at her.

"I cannot," she smiled up at her father.

They rounded the bend with their home just in sight when they heard a blood curdling scream. The man pulled back hard on the reins to stop the horses. His eyes wide with concern.

"Daddy, what was that?" his daughter asked, scared.

The man smacked the reins on the horses and hurried back towards his home. As he approached, he thought he saw multiple movements inside, but he couldn't be sure. He looked back into his wagon. The only weapon he had was a shovel. It would have to do. He pulled the horses off the dirt road and turned to his daughter.

"Rebecca, you listen to me carefully," his voice urgent.

"Daddy?" she asked, frightened by his tone.

"Remember that hiding spot we have in the grove when we play hide and seek?" he asked as he climbed down the wagon and motioned for the girl to follow him.

"Yes?"

"Go there now, through the trees at the ridge there and stay put. Do not come out until I come get you? Do you understand?" he said with alarm.

"Yes, Daddy, but…" Her voice quivered.

"Do as I say, be a good girl. Daddy loves you. Now scoot!"

She nodded, wiping away a tear.

He hugged her quickly, turned her around and gave her a light shove towards the tree line. He waited until she was gone and then he grabbed the shovel from the back of the wagon and sprinted towards his house.

Rebecca did as her father instructed. She ran into the trees. She didn't stop running until she heard shouting. She stopped and turned back, ducking behind a tree close enough to see the commotion at her home.

She gasped. Her father was struggling with a man far bigger than he was. The other man punched her father repeatedly until her father staggered backwards and fell off the front porch.

Rebecca fought back the urge to run and help her father. She cowered behind the tree and continued watching in horror, waiting for her father to get up. He was moving slowly on the ground. The other man approached him and kicked him repeatedly. He had something in his hand. The blade caught the sun and Rebecca saw the reflection of a knife in the man's hand. He stabbed her father repeatedly until he no longer moved.

Rebecca covered her mouth with her hand to avoid screaming out, to avoid detection. Daddy said to hide and she must do what he said. She leaned back against the tree, peeking around it, waiting for the bad people to leave. Wondering if her Daddy was alive... Wondering if her Mama was okay... A sickening feeling swept over her and she was overcome with fear.

She didn't know what to do or where to go. She waited and waited, too frightened to move. Finally, she saw the bad people leave. She watched them disappear into the woods behind their home and heard the sound of horse hoofs beating on the ground.

When she thought it was safe, she slowly crawled out of her hiding place and ran down the hill towards her home, towards her father's lifeless body. She threw herself to the ground and wrapped her arms around her father's badly beaten head.

"Daddy, wake up, please Daddy," she wept uncontrollably.

He was dead. She knew that. She knew what death was. She had pets that had died before. Their dog Tessie had passed away last year. She watched her Daddy dig a hole and bury her beloved dog.

Her father was dead now too. She stood up, covered in his blood and looked down at her red stained hands. She desperately tried to wipe the blood off on her dress.

She slowly turned her head towards the front door. From where she was standing, she could see her mother's legs, partially visible in the kitchen, in a pool of blood.

Rebecca inhaled sharply and wiped tears away, streaking her face with blood. She moved on shaky legs and stepped inside the kitchen. Her mother was lying there, motionless. Murdered by the bad people.

In a daze of disbelief, Rebecca stepped over her mother's body and walked into her small bedroom to collect what she had come for. It seemed like such an ordinary thing to do in such a tragic moment.

Rebecca's mind was racing. She had to get help. She looked back towards the horses. Sometimes Daddy let her hold the reins and steer the wagon. She had to do it alone now. She had to get help. She ran towards the wagon as quickly as possible and climbed back in and smacked the reins on the horses. They didn't move. She smacked them harder.

"Go please, go," she cried.

She smacked the reins a third time and the horses reluctantly obeyed. She pulled as hard as she could and got them back onto the dirt road and headed towards their nearest neighbor's farm.

The husband working in the field spotted her first. A tiny girl trying with all her might to control the wagon. He threw down his hard rake and called out to his wife. She stuck her head out the door. He pointed towards the girl as he ran towards the wagon. She was covered in blood. They both could see that.

Even Rebecca's blonde hair was soaked with blood. They reached her quickly. The woman threw a blanket over the little girl and tried in vain to wipe the blood off of her.

Rebecca told them as best as she could what had happened, but by this time, she was in shock. The farmer called out to his son to join them. Together, they made their way back to the little girl's home to discover the massacre.

Not knowing what else to do, they wrapped the bodies in blankets and placed them on the back of the wagon. Rebecca stopped speaking at this point, too overwhelmed by it all.

Frantic and hushed voices all around her, but she heard none of that anymore. She looked down at the dried blood on her hands and wept silently.

The farmer and his family brought Rebecca and her deceased parents to the clinic. They didn't know what else to do. They pulled up to the front door and were immediately surrounded by orderlies and nurses ushering them inside. The frantic cries for help barely penetrated Rebecca. Everything seemed to be so far away from her right now and nothing seemed real.

Someone picked her up and carried her inside the clinic. Rebecca felt herself slipping away. Her eyes fluttered before darkness overcame her and she passed out. Her life would never be the same again. All she knew was lost.

The door to Doctor Pernell's office opened abruptly and the nurse stepped inside. Both men turned to look at her. They could tell from the panicked look on her face that something serious had happened.

"Sir, we have an emergency. A homestead on the outskirts of the southern glen was attacked. There have been casualties and…a child is involved," she said with alarm.

Doctor Pernell's facial expression changed immediately. He stood quickly and rushed out the door. Martin followed close behind. They swiftly made their way towards the emergency room, past concerned patients and visitors, many of whom had seen the wagon arrive outside.

When they arrived at the intake room, Doctor Pernell and Martin saw two bodies lying on tables, both covered with blood-soaked sheets. Doctor Pernell quickly examined them. Martin hesitated, then slowly lifted each of the sheets to inspect the deceased.

A man and woman lie beneath the sheets, brutally murdered by all appearances. Martin winced and covered them back up. It was a gruesome sight. He had never seen this kind of savagery before outside of battle. His mind raced back to the days when he carried a sword in his hand instead of a medical bag. He lowered his eyes and wished the unfortunate souls safe travels to the heavens. No one should die like this. Martin slowly backed away from the corpses.

He turned his attention back to Doctor Pernell, who was having a very animated conversation with another man and a nurse. Doctor Pernell looked visibly upset by what he was being told. He looked over and motioned for Martin to follow him.

They exited the intake room and walked quickly down the hallway. Martin listened carefully to Doctor Pernell.

"The husband and wife owned a homestead a few miles from here, near the mist wall," he explained.

Martin nodded.

"They were attacked, raiders. The mother was killed first and then the father was killed, trying to save his wife. Their daughter…," he continued.

Martin interrupted, "Is the child alive?"

Doctor Pernell put up a hand to silence him, "She's alive, but in shock. The neighbor said she witnessed the murders."

"Dear heavens," Martin whispered.

"This way," Doctor Pernell pointed down a corridor. "In here," he said.

They stepped inside the examining room to see nurses tending to a little girl, still partially covered in her parents' blood. Martin stopped in his tracks.

Back in Pedora, Martin didn't see brutality like this. Accidents, natural deaths or the occasional squabble but not murder. They were far from the mist wall and raiders never ventured that far north.

Seeing the child lying dormant on the table, covered in blood, triggered something within Martin, a painful memory from long ago. He leaned against the wall to steady himself and swallowed hard, regaining his composure.

Doctor Pernell quickly examined the little girl but found no wounds. He sighed with relief.

"She's not injured, not physically anyway," he said to Martin.

Martin approached the table and assisted in stabilizing the child. It took quite some time to get her cleaned up and into fresh clothing.

"There is nothing more we can do for her at this time. She'll need a great deal of help when she finally wakes up," said Doctor Pernell. "Keep her warm, hydrated and her feet elevated. Come get me the moment she wakes. Is that clear?"

The nurse nodded and continued to monitor the child.

"Yes, doctor."

Martin looked down at the blood-soaked dress and hair ribbons on the floor. Noticing his gaze, Doctor Pernell added more instruction.

"Get her a nice dress with hair ribbons. And, have someone swing by her home to collect her belongings. She's not going back there," Doctor Pernell said firmly.

"Yes, sir," the nurse complied.

"And, notify the marshals at once. They're supposed to be patrolling that wall," Doctor Pernell said angrily. "This should not have happened."

The second nurse nodded and hurried out of the room.

Doctor Pernell moved his hand gently across Rebecca's forehead. He closed his eyes, bent over and whispered softly into her ear.

"Rest easy, little one. We will take care of you. This I promise you."

Martin saw Doctor Pernell wipe a tear from his eye. He began to turn away from the table when he looked down and noticed the little girl's hand was clenched shut. He gently pried it open.

"What is that?" asked Martin.

Doctor Pernell took the objects away from the girl and examined them in his own hand. He turned to show Martin.

"Coins," he said. "Five coins covered in blood. How curious. Make sure these are cleaned and she gets these back," he ordered the nurse.

"Yes, sir."

With those words, he turned on his heel and left the child in the capable hands of the nurses. Martin looked back quickly at the girl and followed Doctor Pernell out of the room.

"I will see you later this evening," Doctor Pernell spoke quietly and entered his office, closing the door behind him.

Martin sighed and looked back at the little girl who had just lost her parents, remembering his own past trauma. He didn't realize he was clenching his own fists. He shrugged off the painful memory and headed towards the stable to take his horse for a ride.

Martin needed to get away from the clinic for a while. He had more than his fill of death this day. Martin rode his horse far beyond the clinic grounds. He had not intended to go back to his home, certainly not on his first day, but he felt himself being drawn there. Perhaps, it was the tragedy he witnessed back at the clinic. It affected him deeply.

His eyes were fixed straight ahead as the terrain grew more familiar. He was close now. He sensed it.

Storm clouds rolled over the mountains, rumbling overhead. Martin glanced up as the sun slowly disappeared behind a massive cloud. The wind picked up and bent the trees around him. There was a chill in the air as the forest grew dark.

Martin was keenly aware that he was unarmed. He felt foolish for journeying to this place without a weapon. Perhaps, his time on Pedora had made him soft, made him careless. He would rectify that by commandeering a sword as soon as possible. Being this close to the mist wall was a dangerous situation and he should have considered that before leaving the clinic.

Martin brought his horse to a full stop when he neared the edge of what was once the heart of his family's kingdom. The castle grounds were long abandoned and now in ruin. The massive gate had toppled over and rusted beyond recognition.

Martin heard the rustling sounds of dry leaves blowing across the once pristine stone pathway, now covered with overgrown weeds. His horse whinnied in protest, unsettled by their environment.

Martin patted his horse on the neck, "Steady boy."

A massive structure loomed in the distance. Martin felt uneasy but continued forward. His senses awakened by the sights and smells around him, some familiar and others not. The overgrown vegetation hid hungry eyes.

Small shadows darted from one twisted tree to another. With no one left to properly care for the estate, his once grand home had fallen prey to the undesirables of Aquila. Those that lived among the shadows, feeding off the dead.

The heart of the family, his mother, had died and the richness of the land died with her. The decay around him was unsettling.

How could it have all gone to hell so quickly, he wondered. Had it really been that long?

He saw the bench where he and his mother spent countless hours reading enchanting stories together, now crumbled to bits. The white gazebo and arbor where music and merriment rang out were reduced to a pile of debris.

The pond to his right, where many a day were spent swimming to avoid the sun's heat, was now covered with a thick green slime. The putrid stench of rot assaulted his senses. He could hear the river's violent protest nearby as its water raged towards the ocean, flowing hundreds of miles away. The river where his life changed that fateful day. The same river that robbed him of his childhood and the family he loved.

Martin climbed down from his horse. The forest was alive around him and not in a friendly way. He walked carefully into the crumbling remains, tying his horse at the entrance.

The moment Martin placed his foot inside the castle he was struck by the eerie stillness of it. The once bustling home was silent. He peered into the darkness but could see very little. Dried leaves crunched under his boots. The castle had been left to the elements and nature had claimed her.

A rush of wind from the darkness directly before him pushed Martin back a step, kicking up the debris from the stone floor. Cobwebs reached hungrily towards him in the darkness, flicking past his skin. Martin swept his hand in the air to brush them away. He thought he heard the sounds of children laughing but knew his imagination was getting the best of him.

The laughter reminded him of the little girl he had seen earlier at the clinic. Her childhood stripped from her. The sight of her parents butchered invaded his mind. He thought he was done with that kind of brutality. He thought he had escaped it long ago.

Martin felt suddenly apprehensive. He didn't like that feeling and he knew fear all too well. Violence by those on the dark side had not been exaggerated. He scolded himself for being so flippant earlier at the clinic.

He had traded in his combat training for the more refined life of a physician, as far away from the wall as possible. It was painfully obvious to Martin that he could not be complacent here. He would have to reach deep within himself to a part he had closed off long ago.

Martin heard the faint beating of a dragon's wings nearby and glanced back over his shoulder.

"Martin?" a haunting voice whispered from within the darkness.

He spun around, staring hard into the castle, straining his eyes to see. A figure stood in front of him, hidden in the shadows.

"Martin?"

The hushed voice sounded like his mother.

Startled, he called out, "Who is there? Reveal yourself."

When the figure stepped into the light, Martin's face turned to one of shock and dismay.

"Mother?" he spoke softly in disbelief.

She smiled and reached her arms out towards him.

He took a step towards her but stopped suddenly when he saw her more closely. It resembled his mother, but the figure before him was filthy and the gown it wore was shredded at the bottom. Pieces of moss were intertwined in its long hair. Its skin was smeared with sludge and mildew. Insects crawled in and out of its vacant cheekbones.

"I have missed you so," she said softly, reaching out for an embrace.

As the figure shuffled towards him, the sound of water sloshing on the floor and dripping from its gown echoed within the chamber.

"You are not my mother," he said bitterly, taking a step away from the grotesque figure.

She crossed her bony arms and looked around curiously. "Have you seen your father?" she asked, "I have been looking everywhere for him."

The woman turned back towards him and smiled sweetly, showing rotted teeth.

Martin did not answer but looked cautiously around for any more ghoulish figures.

"Where have you been, Martin? You have been gone for so long. You left us, without a word. You should not have left us. We needed you," she said to him in a monotone voice.

"You are not my mother, vile creature!" he shouted.

The figure stopped shuffling towards him and spoke.

"The ancient power, bridging all time and place...find it and find her..."

"What? I do not understand. Find who?" Martin asked, his voice laced with annoyance.

"You cannot allow any harm to come to her..."

Martin stepped back and took a defensive posture.

"Stay away," he warned.

"Find it and find her...," the raspy voice replied back.

"I am in no mood for riddles," he snapped.

The ghoulish figure stared blankly at Martin momentarily and then stepped back, engulfed by the darkness.

Martin shook his head, "What in heavens."

He turned on his heel and exited the castle ruins, mounted his horse and pulled the reins sharply. The horse responded by turning around and galloping back towards the entrance of the estate.

"I should not have come here," Martin uttered angrily under his breath, without so much as a backwards glance.

His horse raced across the plains, back towards the clinic, leaving Martin's family home far behind, and the memories dead and buried where they belonged.

Back at the clinic, the dark-haired boy sat alone in his room, crossed legged on the floor, deep in concentration. One might have thought he was sleeping, if it were not for the wicked grin on his face. He was pleased with himself for frightening the newcomer but also annoyed that someone had invaded his playtime to send the stranger an ominous warning. He would have to let Miranda know of this intrusion as soon as possible.

# Chapter Four

Emily overslept. She heard the sounds of her family hurrying about their morning. Her mom tried to rouse her from her sleep three times before heading out to take Sarah on her school field trip. Emily buried her head under her pillow, drifting back to the imaginary dragons that occupied her mind.

When she finally woke up, she gazed at her alarm clock through sleepy eyes only to learn that she had missed her first class. She jumped out of bed, scrambled to get dressed and off to school before she missed the day completely. She grabbed her backpack and raced out the door. She came to the edge of the forest and stopped, contemplating whether to take the shortcut through the groves or stay out on the main road. She could make up some time if she took the shortcut, maybe even make it by third period. She glanced down at her watch. It read 10:17 a.m. She ducked into the woods and ran as fast as she could.

Thunder clapped overhead. She looked up and could see more storm clouds rolling in. She hoped the rain would hold off until she made it inside the school. She didn't want to spend the day in her gym clothes, if she got soaking wet. Oddly enough, she didn't remember seeing a cloud in the sky before she ducked into the woods. Maybe she was just in too much of a hurry to notice, she mused. With that thought, light rain began to fall down on her.

She paused under the protection of a tree to pull her hood over her head. Raindrops fell on her from the leaves above. A crack of thunder startled her just as a heavy rain began to fall. She pushed her bangs out of her eyes and surveyed the area looking for a better shelter from the pounding rain. A clump of trees to her right seem to offer the best protection. Emily let out a battle cry and leapt into action, darting from cover to cover.

She lost her footing on the slippery wet leaves beneath her, hitting her head soundly on a low hanging branch

"Ouch!" she yelled to no one in particular.

This is pointless, she thought to herself. Emily was drenched. There was no way she would make third period at this pace. Emily ran out from under the tree, letting the rain hit her face. She did her best impression of *Singing in the Rain*, laughing to herself. Lightning hit somewhere close by and she ran quickly back under the cover of the trees. Not the best place in the world to be during a lightning storm she realized.

She rifled through her backpack for any snack that might be buried in there. She found an apple on its last days and half a bag of Starburst candies. She ate them hungrily. Emily looked over her shoulder and saw a cropping of large bushes that appeared to be relatively dry underneath. She sprinted for the bushes and crawled on all fours until she was well under their protection.

"Ahhh, once again, I'm muddy and wet! Another stellar day!" she chuckled.

She felt something damp on her forehead and reached up to touch it. She pulled her hand back to reveal blood. Ugh. She must have struck her head harder than she thought. Her head was starting to throb, and she knew she'd have a wonderful headache for the rest of the day from it. She wiped the blood away with her sleeve.

At least this spot seemed to offer some protection. She looked behind her and noticed that her little pocket of dry ground reached further back under the brush then she had first realized. Curious, she crawled deeper into the brush, twenty feet, thirty feet. Emily noticed that her surroundings appeared to be changing. The sound of rainfall seemed to be fading, as if it were somewhere in the distance rather than right above her. The foliage seemed thicker too and she struggled to clear a path.

A drop of blood slowly trickled down her forehead again and she stopped to wipe it away before continuing further. She blinked hard, fighting off the pain that was growing increasingly more severe. Don't be a baby, she thought to herself.

She continued back under the brush. It smelled differently here. It was not the musty smell of the forest ground that she knew so well, but there was a fresh pleasant odor which she could not quite identify. It reminded her of the lavender her mother had planted one time. She smiled, sensing she was about to uncover some incredible mystery and kept crawling forward on her hands and knees. A wave of pain swept over her from the gash in her forehead.

Darkness engulfed her momentarily and she hesitated, considering whether she should turn back. She looked back but could no longer see the path that she just crawled through. It had been swallowed up by the brush around her. That's odd, she thought. She had no choice but to continue moving forward and hoped she would find a clearing soon. She was getting slightly worried because it seemed to her that she had been crawling under these bushes for an eternity. She hit the light on her watch to check the time. It wasn't working. She must have broken it.

She pulled out her cell phone to verify its time, but it was dead. That didn't make sense to her either, because she knew it was fully charged when she ran out of the house. Maybe she was in some weird vortex where time and space stood still? She chuckled to herself and wondered when the aliens were going to beam her up to their spaceship.

Still, she could not deny that this was getting weird. She continued moving forward, finally seeing a break in the thick foliage. She quickened her pace as she saw a ray of light spiraling down through the dense vegetation around her.

She crawled through the opening, stood up and looked at her clothes. She was soaking wet, covered with mud, debris and bloody. She brushed herself off and knew she'd be grounded for sure once her parents took one look at her and found out she missed school. Tearing her jeans was one thing, but she looked like she'd been rolling around in the mud.

Emily squeezed the water out of her long red ponytail and pulled the last of the leaves and twigs out of her hair. She heard something to the right as the ground beneath her feet began to shake. She turned towards the sound just in time to see a man on a horse charging towards her. Startled, she stood frozen in place.

The man on the horse didn't have time to steer around her. He pulled back on the reins, causing the horse to rear up in protest, throwing the rider to the ground. He moaned in pain.

Emily looked back in the direction she had just come from and considered making a run for it, but the hole she climbed out of had disappeared. The man gathered himself upright, brushed the dust off his clothes angrily and scolded his horse. He then turned and looked so sharply at Emily that it sent a chill down her spine. She instinctively took a couple of steps back.

"What in blazes are you doing standing in the middle of the road?" he demanded, rubbing his shoulder.

She had nearly been trampled. It took her a moment to notice how the man was dressed. She studied him curiously.

"What are you staring at child?"

Emily just stood there, gawking at the stranger. He sounded British to her and looked like someone from the medieval days. She had books in her room about the Middle Ages and this man definitely looked like he belonged there. Pretty authentic looking costume, she thought to herself. The man raised his voice, forcing Emily to pay attention to him once again.

"Speak child, what province are you from?" he ordered.

Emily slowly smiled, "Are you for real?"

"Of course, I am real," he snapped. "What kind of an absurd question is that?"

"Are you okay?" she asked. "That looked like it hurt."

"Yes, I am quite alright, no thanks to you," he said angrily.

"Hey," she replied defensively. "It was an accident."

"What province are you from?" he demanded.

"What province are you from?" She mimicked his accent.

"Are you mocking me?" he asked.

Emily realized she had offended him. "No, I think your accent is cool," she explained.

"Cool? I am not cool. It is actually quite warm. What province are you from?" he demanded to know.

"Province?" she asked.

"You are wet, unwashed, unkept and wounded," he pointed to the blood smeared on her forehead.

Emily raised her fingertip to feel the dry crusted blood over her nicely sized bump. "This? I'm okay. I just hit my head when I was running to get out of the storm."

The stranger looked in the sky and then back at Emily. The storm clouds had long passed and the sky was clear.

"There is not one storm cloud in the sky, child, as you can see," he corrected her. "And, yet you are soaking wet."

Emily frowned at him. "I don't know where you've been, but it's been raining nonstop, for the past hour. And, stop calling me a child. I'm almost thirteen. Why are you dressed like that?"

"Dressed like what?"

She waved her hands in the air, gesturing towards his clothes. "You know, dressed in that get up."

"Get up? I am up."

"Your clothes." She spoke slowly, enunciating her words. "Why are you wearing those clothes?"

"How else should I be dressed?" he asked with irritation.

"Geez, stop answering every question with a question. What planet are you from?" she complained.

"What planet are you from?" he quipped sarcastically.

Emily laughed. "Okay, I get it. You're messing with me."

The stranger eyed her with annoyance. "I beg your pardon?"

Emily thrust her arms in front of her stiffly and walked dramatically in circles. "Take me to your leader," she said in her best robotic voice. She waited for a reaction.

"Why would I take you to my leader?" he asked, perplexed.

"It's just a joke," she laughed. "Get it?"

"I do not," he replied, extremely annoyed.

The stranger gave her an odd look and frowned.

"Are you sure you didn't hurt yourself when you fell off your horse?" Emily asked.

"I did not fall off my horse," the man said angrily.

Emily made a face at him, making her eyes go cross eyed

"Looked like you fell off to me," she said with sarcasm.

"I was thrown from my horse because you were standing in the middle of the road!" he reminded her again.

Emily stepped back. "Whoa, you have some anger issues."

"I most certainly do not," he snapped, brushing the rest of the dirt from his trousers.

She walked past him, attempting to touch his horse.

"Please leave Thunderbolt alone," the stranger said, stepping between the girl and his horse.

Emily looked up at the tall stranger and grinned.

"Thunderbolt? You named your horse Thunderbolt?" she said with a laugh.

"Yes, not that it is any concern of yours," he snapped.

She stretched her arms into the air, palms facing upwards and sang, "Thunderbolts of lightening, very very frightening."

The stranger stepped back, pulling his horse with him.

"Please go away," he said, rubbing his temple. "You are giving me a headache."

"It's probably from falling off your horse," she smirked. "You should really be more careful."

The man inhaled deeply, his silver blue eyes piercing into her. He was trying hard not to lose his temper.

"For the last time, I did not fall off my horse," he corrected. "I was thrown from my horse because you were standing in the middle of the blasted road. Do you understand?" He turned his attention back to his horse, trying his best to ignore the girl.

"I understand you have anger issues," she pointed out, with a healthy dose of attitude.

The man's shoulder stiffened and he turned back to face her.

"Who are you?" he asked. His voice laced with frustration.

She crossed her arms in defiance.

"My mother told me never to talk to strangers, so I'm not going to answer that," she countered sarcastically.

"Good, that is truly the wisest thing you have said thus far. Do as your mother advised and stop talking. Off you go," he said, motioning her away with his hands.

Emily was quite tall for her age, actually the tallest in her class, but this brutish man towered over her and she was acutely aware of that fact. She stood as tall as she could and stared right back at him, making direct eye contact.

He shook his head in disbelief at her tenacity.

"Quite strange," he muttered, turning away from her again.

"Look who's talking, Mister Renaissance Festival," she snapped back.

He looked back over his shoulder at her, "What?"

Emily nodded, "Am I right or not? Taking your part, a little too seriously, don't you think? Chill out."

He ignored her and adjusted the saddle on his horse.

In the distance, a piercing screech rang out in the air. Both jerked their heads towards the direction of the sound.

"What the heck was that?" Emily asked with genuine alarm.

"That has done it. We are in the thick of it now. I best be off, and I advise you to do the same, child, unless you plan on being a dragon's dinner. The dragons in these parts are not of the friendly variety."

The strange screeching noise rang out again. Emily spun around towards its source and covered her ears. When she turned back, the man had already mounted his horse. He gave a quick nod and sped up the path. Dust flew behind him as his horse's hooves hit the ground.

"Hey wait!" she called after him.

She felt the bump on her head. It was really starting to hurt. Emily looked around, but she didn't recognize anything. Where was she? She'd spent most of her life exploring the woods. How could she have missed this clearing before? She looked back at where the man rode off on his horse. He was long gone.

"A dragon's dinner? What the heck does that even mean?" she asked herself.

She began to worry that she had somehow got herself turned around and was now lost. The sky looked different to her. It was now a light purple in color, with no signs of the ominous storm clouds she had just escaped. Tall, thin trees stood side by side in neat rows like toothpicks. She didn't see any buildings or houses anywhere. No airplanes in the sky for that matter either.

There was no sign of the man she had just spoken to. She had no idea why he would be dressed that way. Unless, the Renaissance Festival was in town and he was one of the performers, she reasoned. That explains everything – the clothes, the weird speech pattern, the dialect. He was good, she thought approvingly. Very authentic. Never broke character. Emily was impressed.

And, yet…

That still didn't tell Emily where she was. Certainly, she couldn't have wondered so far off that she was no longer in Glendale. That would be bad, she thought. A sudden feeling of unease crept over her. Emily had to find someone that could help her make it back home. With neither her watch nor cell phone working, Emily had no idea what time it was either. She was trying to be brave, but she was growing increasingly worried that she was indeed lost.

She looked around but wasn't sure which direction to go. Nothing looked familiar.

"Gandalf? Left? Or right?" she said, kicking the ground in frustration.

# Chapter Five

The blood curdling sound rang out again. Emily turned, scanning the trees and skies, searching for its source. It was getting closer, that much she was sure of. She had no idea what could be making the noise, but she wanted as much distance as possible between her and whatever it was. She decided it was safer to walk closer to the tree line rather than stay out in the open where she felt completely vulnerable.

The sound was getting louder. Emily cautiously peered around a tree and looked out into the clearing, hoping to catch a glimpse of whatever it might be. Something in the sky was heading straight for her. It was huge, like nothing she had ever seen before. Transfixed, Emily stepped out from the tree. She couldn't allow herself to believe what her eyes were seeing. She'd seen it in her mind and in drawings so many times before, but never like this…

"No way," she said in awe and disbelief.

A dragon…

As clear as day…

A huge, powerful dragon was soaring through the air and it was coming straight towards her…fast. Emily could not have moved if she wanted to. She was fixated by the sight of it. She stood there with her mouth open, watching the creature's heavy wings beat as it moved through the air gracefully, yet with so much power. Her eyes were wide with wonder.

Had her imagination conjured up this beast? She marveled at its strength and beauty.

The dragon closed the distance between her, screeching that awful sound once again. Could it possibly be real? What had that man said? From somewhere in the back of her mind she heard his voice say… dragon's dinner.

Dragon's dinner? The meaning of his words finally dawned on her. Emily turned and ran as fast as she could. The irony of this moment did not escape her. She had literally just written about a similar encounter with a dragon in her own story yesterday and now here she was today being chased by one. She was, however, lacking the use of a sword like that of her fictional character. She felt like her heart was going to explode. She just kept running and running.

She could feel the breeze picking up, stirred by the beating of the dragon's wings. It was almost upon her. She raced through the trees, too scared to look back.

I'm not supposed to run from dragons, she told herself. I'm supposed to slay them. This can't possibly be real, she convinced herself. I can't be hurt by a figment of my imagination, Emily concluded. She stopped in her tracks and looked around for a weapon of some kind but found none.

Emily turned to face the dragon.

"You can't hurt me!" she shouted at it. "You're not real!"

She stood firmly in place, refusing to budge one inch from the imaginary dragon. The dragon was immense and nearly on top of her when Emily was tackled to the ground, knocking the wind out of her. She heard the swishing sound as the dragon flew right over her and felt the rush of air against her body. Someone grabbed her hard and yanked her to her feet.

"That dragon would have swallowed you whole," he said with panic in his voice. "We must run before it comes back."

Emily was half dragged, half pushed along the dirt path and down into a gully.

"Move along! We haven't much time before the beastie returns."

She pulled herself free from the stranger's grasp.

"Let me go!" she demanded.

The stranger's clothes were torn and dirty, much like her own at the moment. He was much different in appearance than the medieval gentleman she had encountered earlier.

"Are you mad, child?"

"Yeah, I'm mad because you keep pulling me around like a doll," she snapped back.

"Are you trying to get yourself killed?" He glanced frantically over his shoulder.

The dragon was headed their way again.

"Look," she protested, "this is a dream, okay?"

"You were running pretty fast from a dream, child. We're almost at the cave. Hurry along now."

He continued to pull her along much to Emily's dislike. He gave her a hard shove and she fell forward into a small cave.

"Was that really necessary?" she asked.

He ignored her question and watched cautiously out of the cave opening for any signs of the dragon. Emily tapped him on the shoulder.

"Excuse me."

"Hush, child."

"I said, excuse me?"

The ground shook inside the cave. Emily lost her balance.

"What was that? An earthquake?" she asked.

He shot her a look and put his finger to his lips to silence her. Emily was about to protest when she looked past his shoulder and saw what appeared to be the wing tip of the immense dragon. It was sniffing the ground, hunting them.

The stranger pushed her further back into the cave. Emily pressed as hard as she could against the back wall, fascinated by what she was seeing. She still refused to believe that this was anything but a dream. She must have fallen asleep in the forest and was having the most vivid dream of her life. If this dream was going to continue, then she might as well enjoy it.

The dragon was large and menacing, a dark reddish color, beautiful despite its deadly desire to make a meal out of her. It was turning in circles near the mouth of the cave, sniffing the ground trying to pinpoint their location. Occasionally, a pointed tongue would dart from its mouth, tasting the ground. It was determined to find them. It flapped its mighty wings seemingly to bounce in the air from one spot to the next.

"Wow," Emily said in a hushed voice, "that is so awesome."

The stranger shushed her again. Emily frowned, watching the dragon intently. Moments later, it screeched loudly in protest, angry that it had lost its meal. Its movements became more frantic. It turned quickly, retracing its steps. It screeched once more and then lifted into the air. From within the cave, only the sound of his beating wings could be heard. Letting out a sigh of relief, the stranger turned to look at Emily in dismay.

"Not in all my days have I seen anything so reckless. Are you from the dark side?" he scolded.

"The dark side, as in… *Luke, I am your father?*" she said in her best Darth Vader impression and chuckled.

The stranger just stared at Emily.

Laughing, she asked, "Don't you understand?"

He shook his head no.

"How about this? Your mother is so hairy that the only language she can speak is Wookie," she laughed and then did an impression of Chewbacca within the small confines of the cave.

The stranger took a step back, fearing she was either mad or bewitched. She stopped her impression when she saw the look on the man's face.

"Haven't you ever seen *Star Wars*?"

He eyed her curiously. She looked at him in disbelief.

"What happened to your ears?" she gasped. The stranger's ears were pointed at the tips, barely noticeable beneath his shaggy brown unkept hair. He gently touched the tips of his ears.

"My ears are fine."

"Uh, yea, if you're a Vulcan. Or an elf…" A smile crossed Emily's face. She jumped up and down in excitement. "Is that what this is? I'm dreaming about middle-earth? I love *The Lord of the Rings*." She took a step back and looked at him closely. "You're too short to be an elf. Too tall to be a hobbit. No facial hair, so you're not a dwarf. I know my Tolkien pretty good."

"I am a white lighter…"

"A what?"

"A white lighter."

Emily stared at him with a blank expression.

"I have no idea what you're talking about."

He bowed slightly. "My name is Thalien. You are my charge. Mira sent me here to protect you. It's a good thing I found you when I did." He threw a cautious glance outside. "You could have been killed. We'll have no more of that nonsense, child."

Emily studied him momentarily. This was indeed a very elaborate dream she was having. "Who is Mira? And, what is a white lighter?" she asked sincerely.

"Mira is a powerful sorceress of the light side. White lighters – watch, heal and intervene when necessary to help those in our charge," he explained.

"Sorceress? I don't believe in witches. I'll wake up soon and this will all disappear, including you," she told him.

His eyes crinkled in amusement. "Will I now? You think this is a dream? And you don't believe in sorcery? You should. Come now. It's getting late. Stay close to the trees for protection."

"I know I'm dreaming because I don't recognize where I am. And, we don't have dragons in Glendale," she mused.

"Glendale? Is that where you are from?"

"Yes, Glendale."

"I am afraid I have never heard of such a place."

She looked around in frustration.

"You really have no idea where you are, do you?" he said sympathetically.

"No, and my head is starting to hurt. I just want to go home. Or wake up." She looked down, feeling a bit weary and defeated.

Thalien swept his arms in a circle, gesturing to their surroundings. "This is Aquila."

"Never heard of it," she admitted.

"I imagine not."

She touched her head again.

"Let me take a look at that," he offered,

She stepped back. "It's fine, really. Just a bad headache."

He frowned and closed the distance between them. "Stand still." He raised his hands and put them near her head wound. A bright white glow came from his palms.

She pushed his hands away, "Whoa, touch me and you die. Don't make me go all Buffy on you."

He lowered his voice and spoke to her, "Ssshhh. Calm down, child. I'm not going to harm you. Allow me…"

She reluctantly nodded. He raised his hands beside her head and closed his eyes. Emily's head tingling and she felt energy being generated from his hands. It only lasted a moment. He opened his eyes. Emily touched her head. The wound was gone.

"How did you do that?" she asked with wonder.

He smiled proudly. "Your head wound is healed, but we should get you to the clinic at once to have you examined."

"Okay, I guess. Let's get on with this dream."

Thalien let his eyes drop briefly to the necklace around Emily's neck. He was taken aback, but said nothing. He shifted his attention to the mouth of the cave and stepped out cautiously. With no dragon in sight, he motioned for Emily to follow.

"Stay on the path, close to the trees," he warned.

"Which way to the Stargate, my good man?" she asked.

"The what?"

"Nothing," she said. Her humor was useless on Thalien.

Forgive me, but I haven't asked your name?" he asked.

"You're supposed to protect me. Don't you know?"

"It doesn't work like that. It's a feeling. We sense our charges, drawn to them like a moth to a flame," he explained.

"Well, thank you for saving me from that dragon."

He bowed slightly and looked up at her. "Your name?"

"Emily. Emily Richardson."

"Nice to meet you, Emily. Emily Richardson of Glendale."

She looked around at her surroundings. "Aquila, huh?"

"Yes, Aquila."

"Will I meet this Mira you mentioned?"

"Soon, yes."

"Okie, dokie."

He followed the tree line with Emily close behind.

# Chapter Six

The thick jagged walls rose high into the dark sky. The vast fortress was built into a rocky mountain, cold and unforgiving. Within it a tower loomed, impenetrable, black as coal. The Keep, the most feared place in all the lands. Known for its cruelty, torture, lingering smell of death and the unmistakable sense of evil within its walls and deep within its bowels. Death was preferable than becoming one of its forgotten inhabitants. Plagued by disease, the lost souls kept within had no hope whatsoever of mercy. All mercy had forsaken this place. Here the banished and condemned lived out the remainder of their lives in doom and misery.

A black swirling mist churned overhead, like a gaping mouth waiting to swallow the world whole, blotting out the light. For thousands of years the Keep housed prisoners, innocent or guilty…it mattered not. Its walls welcomed death and misery. It was an ageless prison near the border of the light and dark sides. There was only one way in, and that was through a massive iron gate. And, only one way out for its occupants…death. Mass graves littered the bleak terrain, piles upon piles of rotted corpses.

Miranda held dominion over the Keep. She skulked along the passageways. Her heart as dark as her mind. Her features were long and drawn, and her skin a deathly gray ash color. Long black hair silhouetted her face. Dark, fierce eyes were her most prominent feature. When she looked at you, she looked through you and into you. Few were brave enough to hold her gaze. Her form hunched over beneath heavy black robes. In her younger days, she was quite beautiful, but beauty gave way to bitterness which corrupted her to the very core. There was nothing beautiful about Miranda any longer.

Her minions trailed close behind to do her every bidding. They were hideous, foul creatures of Aquila's underworld, feeding off the remains of those less fortunate. They snapped and nipped at each other, like rabid animals, shoving one another out of the way to get as close to Miranda as possible, always lingering to be in her favor.

She received word of yet another failure. She cared nothing for the loss of life in pursuit of her end game. However, she was annoyed at the complication the messy incident would cause. The terror that she was about to unleash was unstoppable. Miranda would do the unthinkable to win. She didn't need border patrols fumbling about, sticking their noses where they did not belong.

Her body shook as she coughed from the dampness in the air. It was a long, slow walk to the chamber she sought. She rarely ventured there, but it was necessary. She dared not bring the occupant to her. No, that was far too dangerous. Someone might see and she could not risk that. Secrecy was of the utmost importance, the continuation of a lie spun long ago. If she strayed but a little, the web she wove could unravel. She had come too far to make any careless mistakes. Cautiously, she made her way deeper within the confines of the Keep.

Her thoughts crept back to her session earlier that evening. Disturbing images had forced her to confront her special guest. She refused to let anything jeopardize her plan.

The girl again... Why always this girl? Not quite in focus, yet sharp enough to get an impression. Why did this girl matter?

Find me the traveler. Find me the girl. Eliminate the threat. Time and time again, she sent out her spies, ordering more seekers be brought in for one singular purpose.

Find the keystone. Find the girl. Deliver one. Destroy the other. Miranda required seekers for their visions. She used her black magic to harvest the thoughts right out of their minds, tapping into their special abilities, only to dispose of them when their life forces had been completely drained.

Guards lowered their heads and stepped aside to let Miranda pass. Moans and pleas for mercy rang out as she walked past the endless rows of cells. Torches lit the darkness offering little comfort to those trapped within. She removed a key from beneath her robe and opened the door leading down a passageway.

No one followed her beyond this point, not even her minions. Only one chamber occupied this wing. She pulled herself upright and unlocked the chamber door. The rusty hinges creaked in loud protest, breaking the silence of the inner chamber.

"You lied to me!" Miranda hissed the words as she stepped inside the chamber, the hatred behind her words spilling out.

A woman sat on a tattered couch across the room. She tilted her head slightly at Miranda's voice, but did not turn to face her. A fire blazed behind her from a stone fireplace. There were piles of wood beside it. The chamber was sparsely furnished, drab and depressing. Stacks of books were piled on a small wooden desk.

Miranda closed the door and crossed the room. The woman stiffened as Miranda approached.

"You lied to me!" she spat angrily. "She's alive. I know that face. It's your face. You lied to me! You told me she had died."

The woman put down her book, folded her hands neatly in her lap and lifted her head to look at Miranda.

Miranda struck the woman hard with the back of her hand, knocking the woman's hair loose, causing it to fall in front of her eyes. The woman flinched. Her cheek had a fiery imprint where Miranda's hand had struck. Yet, she did not shed a tear, nor make a single sound. Her expression was eloquent. This had been done to her many times before. She slowly tucked her hair back behind her ear, revealing no emotion whatsoever to the irate sorceress hovering over her. Miranda leaned in and got within inches of her face. Her foul breath made the woman's stomach churn.

"You lied! You told me that the threat had passed and that all I needed was the keystone, but the bloodline lives on!"

Only with these words did the woman betray a hint of emotion in her eyes.

"She is here on Aquila then? You have seen her?" the woman asked softly with renewed hope.

"I suspect she is here, making a nuisance of herself. But you already know that, do you not?" Miranda hissed at her. "I will murder every child on Aquila to find her and chase her across time if I have to, but she will die. I promise you that."

71

"How black is your heart that you would do such a thing to innocents?"

"No one is innocent. Not from their first squealing breath to their last. It matters nothing to me to rid the world of them."

"Because you have never known love," injected the woman.

"Choose your words carefully," Miranda warned her. "For it is you who took love from me."

"He was not yours to take... and never was."

Miranda let out a hideous laugh. "Many a night has he found comfort with me. You have been long forgotten," she boasted.

"You poison his mind. You delude yourself into thinking he could ever have true feelings for someone as wretched as you."

Miranda struck the woman again. This time drawing blood. The woman wiped the blood from the corner of her mouth.

"He still has free will within him," Miranda said angrily.

"I doubt that very much," the woman argued.

"You are right, of course. I have always felt that free will was highly overrated. Many wars have been waged in its defense. I plan to rid the world of that burden. One ruler, one vision."

"Your singular vision."

"Yes, that is the idea. There will finally be peace," Miranda rationalized.

"Peace? You call stripping us of our free will and domination a peaceful resolution?" she asked.

"Anything that maintains order," Miranda stated.

"You deny free will to obtain order. It is not your place to do so," the woman argued.

"Who's place is it? The gods? Men? They had their chance. No more. Now it is time for a new world order. I will unite the kingdom under one banner," Miranda spat angrily.

"A dictator and a tyrant," the woman added.

"They will bend to my will or die. I have assembled an army strong enough to defeat any foe. I've awakened an evil so great that I cannot be defeated. Once I find the keystone, I will be unstoppable," Miranda paced the room, feeling empowered.

"Awakened an evil...?" the woman asked.

Miranda was no longer listening.

"Miranda what have you done? And, what of Merrick?" the woman asked. "Answer me!"

Miranda ignored her. She was lost in her own thoughts of bloodlust. The woman let out a sigh.

"You will not succeed," the woman said.

This Miranda heard. She charged towards the woman and pulled out a dagger, sticking it right against the woman's throat.

"I should kill you now," Miranda fumed.

"You cannot kill me, Miranda." She looked up at the sorceress defiantly. "I am already dead."

She lowered the blade. "You look well enough to me."

"This shell you gave me? It is cold within. Kept here for your own entertainment. Why do you hate me so?"

Miranda turned away from the woman.

"You took what once belonged to me…"

"Merrick belongs to no one…If you do not let it go, you will never find peace in this world or the next one. Is that what you want?"

Miranda turned back to face the woman, anger showing in her worn and ragged face.

"You stole my life from me. For that, I have stolen yours."

"And, cursed me for all eternity."

"As you so rightly deserved!"

"Did I deserve exile and torment?" the woman asked.

Miranda dismissed her question. "Where is the girl? What is your plan?" she demanded to know.

"I know of no plan. How could I, trapped in here? I have been locked up for years. Isolated and alone."

Miranda struck the woman a third time. "Don't play coy with me! We both know the power you and your kind possess, how far your reach is even behind these thick walls," Miranda scoffed.

The woman touched her cheek where she had just been hit. It was starting to swell.

"My prison has become too comfortable for you. Perhaps you should spend more time reflecting on my hospitality?"

73

"May the heavens help you." the woman said softly, lowering her head.

"The heavens have forsaken me long ago. I make my own fate now," Miranda said with contempt. She pointed a boney finger at the woman and narrowed her gaze. "I will get to the bottom of this. I will find her. And, when I do? You will watch her bleed a slow and agonizing death."

Miranda stormed out. Slamming the heavy door shut and locking it once again. Cursing its inhabitant. Miranda had her pieces in place, poised to strike. They would be called upon when the time came, the enemy within. The sorceress chuckled to herself. They would never see it coming. An evil grin spread across her face. She would take it all. Revenge would be sweet indeed. Not just revenge on Merrick and his family, but on all mankind. And, anyone that dared to stand in her way.

Checkmate.

The appearance of the girl was worrisome. Something she failed to see? Unlikely, and yet… Miranda was determined to figure out how the child had escaped detection for so long. Who was clouding her visions? Who was protecting the child from her grasp? Who possibly had that much power? More so than her own? She wondered. There was only one she knew of that could come close to her own powers, but that was impossible.

Unthinkable. Surely, it could not be so.

Miranda paced outside the chamber, milling over the thoughts racing through her head. The realization came as suddenly as the question entered her mind. She stopped pacing and stood perfectly still. A new hatred filled her heart.

The betrayer… Mira.

Miranda's own sister…

# Chapter Seven

Thalien and Emily walked in silence for what seemed like miles. They reached the top of a slight rise and stepped out of the forest, giving Emily her first good glimpse of the valley below. She stopped to take it all in. The sky was a purplish color, but that wasn't what took her breath away. Two giant moons hung gracefully in the horizon, one white as snow and the other pale yellow with rings around it. It was beautiful. They seemed so close.

She raised her hand as if to touch them. They were clear as day, even in the harsh sunlight. She looked straight up and could make out a glorious canvas of stars in the sky, still present in the light of day. She prided herself on being a junior astronomer, but here? The constellations were all wrong. It puzzled her. She cast her gaze back across the valley before her.

As far as she could see, there was natural beauty. Snowy mountains rose above a vast lush canopy. Rivers and streams weaved their way through green valleys. The air was fresh and crisp. She inhaled deeply, amazed at what she was witnessing. There was not a factory or skyscraper in sight. No pollution billowing into the air. No freeways congested with cars. No crowded suburbs or cities. No deforestation. Wherever she was – Aquila – they clearly lived in harmony with their environment.

She marveled at the mountain peaks with the clouds hugging their tops. Some of the peaks were so incredibly massive that she could easily make out waterfalls spilling down their slopes and into the water's edge below. She could hear animals and birds all around her. None she was familiar with. Emily could also see large flying beasts – dragons – off in the distance, gliding majestically in and out of the clouds in this fairy tale setting.

She smiled. It was without a doubt the most beautiful place she had ever seen in all her young life.

"Wow," she said in awe.

Thalien smiled and nodded.

"I never grow tired of Aquila's beauty," he told her.

"Those moons," she pointed out.

"Yes?"

"How can that be? We've been walking a long time, but the sun has not changed its position."

Thalien did not answer. He continued down the path. "Come along, child. We are not far from the clinic."

She quickened her pace to stand beside him. "What's that over there – that cloud bank? It seems to go on forever."

"That is the mist wall," he told her. "It protects those on this side from those on the dark side. Before that wall, people could pass freely among all the lands."

"What do you mean by the dark side?"

"There is a light side and a dark side on Aquila," he explained. "We are obviously on the light side."

"This place is beautiful. What's the dark side like?" she asked.

He sighed deeply. "The dark side is some place you never want to go. It is a place of evil."

"Sounds charming," she said.

He stopped walking and turned to her. "This is no joking matter, Emily. It is evil. Stay away from that horrid place. I am here to keep you safe from what is behind that mist wall. I am afraid there is a limit to how much I can do to protect you. At the very least, you can stay out of harm's way."

"No need to be cryptic," she told him.

He shook his head in disapproval. They continued walking in silence. It wasn't long before Emily spotted a building ahead of them. If this was the clinic, it was not like any doctor's office she had ever seen before. It was out in the middle of nowhere. No parking lots. No cars. Nothing.

She marveled at the clinic as they got closer to it. It looked like fingers reaching into the sky with its shimmering towers gleaming in the sunlight. It was surrounded by several beautiful gardens, including a maze made from thick hedges. Several children played outside, running in and out of the maze. Their laughter could be heard in the air. A couple strolled casually beside a calm lake, smiling and holding hands. A rich blanket of flowers covered the pathway on either side leading up to a set of doors. It was all very serene.

"How long has this been here?" she asked.

"Thousands of years. It was built by our ancestors."

"It's beautiful, comforting," she admitted.

"It is better for the healing body and mind to be surrounded by beauty and tranquility. Do you not agree?"

"Totally," she replied.

Emily stopped to watch the children play. Then hurried to catch up to Thalien.

The clinic itself was made from smooth white stone, featuring tall spiral towers reaching high into the sky. The stone almost glistened, giving the exterior an angelic illumination of sorts that Emily found quite appealing. It was warm and inviting. There were tall glass windows that allowed natural light to filter into the building. Vegetation grew in and out of the clinic, hugging the tall spiral towers.

They walked towards an atrium full of plants and flowers, as well as benches for visitors to rest and meditate upon. The building branched out into many directions, like a pinwheel. For something so old, it was immaculate. Soft music from an instrument Emily believed to be a harp traveled through the air providing a calming force to those within. It seemed more like a sanctuary than a medical clinic, she surmised.

Once inside the clinic, Emily noticed the brightly tiled walls and high ceilings. The sunbeams overhead caught the stained glass and playfully bounced color off the walls like a giant kaleidoscope. The effect was mesmerizing. It was a busy place. An orderly pushed a food cart past her, reminding her that she had not eaten anything substantial since the apple earlier. Her stomach growled in protest.

Thalien approached a woman seated at a desk and spoke with her in hushed voices. Occasionally, they would glance over at

Emily and the woman would write something down on a notepad. Another woman, wearing a white nurse uniform of sorts, came over and joined the conversation. Thalien and the nurse spoke briefly and then approached Emily.

"Emily? Hello, my name is Claire. Please come with me so a doctor can examine you."

"Okay," she obliged. Thalien did not follow them. Emily turned back to him, "Aren't you coming along too? You said you were supposed to keep me safe?"

"You are perfectly safe here in the clinic, Emily. This is where my journey ends with you for the time being."

"What does that even mean? You said I was your charge. When will I see you again?" she asked feeling suddenly alone.

"Soon. Very soon, but for now you must remain here."

Emily was confused and didn't know what to think. This didn't feel like a dream anymore. Everything she was seeing, hearing and feeling defied all logic as she knew in her own life. And, yet...there it was. This new world. These people, the dragons... She was starting to believe that this was no dream at all. Emily realized that she needed to be extremely careful, for fear of the unknown. She was the definition of a stranger in a strange land.

The nurse led Emily to a vacant examining room. "Please, take a seat. The doctor will be with you shortly," she said kindly.

Emily looked around the room. She walked over to a small mirror on the wall to examine her appearance. She looked disheveled and muddy.

"How flattering," she said to herself. "No wonder Thalien thought I needed a doctor. I look like a feral child." She attempted to wipe some of the dried dirt from her face. She didn't have a brush, but she did her best to fix her hair in a more presentable fashion.

In another wing of the clinic, Thalien paced nervously inside Doctor Pernell's office. He didn't have to wait long before the doctor entered. Thalien began speaking before the doctor even had a chance to sit down.

"Did the nurse speak with you?"

"Nice to see you too, Thalien," the doctor said with a smile.

"We don't have time for pleasantries."

"There is always time for pleasantries," the doctor stated. "I am curious as to why you brought her here. There is nothing our medicine can do for her that you as a healer cannot do yourself. I do not understand," Doctor Pernell admitted.

"She's the one," Thalien blurted out.

Doctor Pernell looked back into the hallway. He closed the door behind him to protect their privacy. He leaned forward in his chair and spoke in a controlled tone, choosing his words carefully.

"And, you know this how?" he said in barely a whisper.

"Mira sent me to protect her."

"That does not prove that she is the one the prophecy speaks of," Doctor Pernell argued.

Thalien shook his head in earnest.

"She could simply be another traveler that has lost her way," Doctor Pernell continued. "We do get them here from time to time. You are aware of this anomaly. It is not unheard of."

Thalien paced nervously. Finally sitting down across from the doctor.

"She has it. I've seen it with my own eyes."

"She has what?" Doctor Pernell asked.

Thalien leaned in and whispered so quietly that Doctor Pernell could barely make out his words.

"The keystone."

Doctor Pernell was noticeably shocked by this revelation. The hair on his arms stood up and a chill ran down his spine. Thalien nodded knowingly at him. Doctor Pernell's expression spoke for itself. He let out a deep sigh and sat back in his chair, staring at Thalien. They were both silent as Thalien let this news sink in and the breadth of its meaning.

Finally, Doctor Pernell spoke. "Then you did right by bringing her here. She is in grave danger. Not even Mira's magic can protect her once Miranda learns the keystone has appeared and the girl with it. This is the beginning of the end," he said soberly.

Doctor Pernell stood and paced around his office, trying to process what was going on and what needed to be done. He stopped and turned back to face Thalien.

"Does the girl know what she has? Or who she really is?"

Thalien shook his head. "She knows nothing."

Doctor Pernell nodded. "Good. That will work in our favor. Her thoughts cannot betray her to Miranda or her seekers if she has no idea what she carries, nor the importance of who she truly is. If the girl does not understand its significance, then I strongly suggest we keep it that way for as long as possible."

Thalien stood to leave. "I will notify Mira of your thoughts."

Doctor Pernell put a hand on Thalien's shoulder. "Stay a day or two, Thalien. Mira will surely want to see the girl herself. Give me time to arrange a suitable escort for you both. It is a long journey and the way can be perilous," he urged.

"Why don't I just pop off to Mira?" Thalien asked.

"If she has no idea what is happening, then I don't think disappearing into thin air and reappearing elsewhere should be the first order of business. Let's not overwhelm her upon arrival. Traditional travel would be best for now," the doctor said.

"If you think that is best," Thalien responded.

"I do. Tell Claire that you will be staying overnight at my request. She will make suitable accommodations for you. I need to go meet this girl."

"There is the matter of her seeing a dragon," Thalien added.

"What? She saw a dragon?"

"She was nearly eaten by one actually," Thalien clarified.

"Oh dear," Doctor Pernell scratched his chin.

"She thinks she is dreaming," Thalien added.

"Interesting," the doctor replied. "Dragon or not, let's try to introduce her to her situation slowly, agreed?"

"Whatever you feel is best, doctor."

Doctor Pernell left his office and headed for the examining room where Emily waited.

He knocked gently on the door.

"Come in," Emily said.

Doctor Pernell stuck his head inside. "Emily, I presume?"

"Yes," she responded.

He came in and shook her hand gently. "It is a pleasure to meet you, Emily. My name is Doctor Pernell. I run this clinic."

"It's really nice," she told him.

"Thank you. We try to make our patients as comfortable as possible. I understand that Thalien healed a head wound for you. Let me take a look at it and clean some of that blood off."

He took out some swabs of cloth from a drawer and washed the dried blood from her head with warm soap and water.

"That must have been a nasty cut you had there. How did it happen?" he asked Emily.

"Well, I was late for school and took a short cut through the woods."

Doctor Pernell nodded, "I see."

"It started raining. I was running to get under the trees. I slipped and hit my head on a branch," she explained to him.

"Ouch!" Doctor Pernell said empathetically.

"It was nothing really. I didn't even know I got hurt until I saw blood on my hand. Anyway, I crawled under some bushes, looking for a dry spot to wait out the rain. I guess I got turned around somehow and ended up here. I have no idea where I really am. So, I'm either number one – lost. Number two – having a crazy dream. Number three – I've been abducted by aliens."

Doctor Pernell stifled a laugh. "Abducted by aliens?"

"Yea, and then this man almost ran me over with his horse!"

"Really? And what did this person look like?" he asked.

Emily wrinkled her nose and frowned. "Well, he was really tall and had blonde hair. He had a really bad temper too. He was dressed like he was going to a Renaissance festival. But come to think of it, everyone around here is dressed differently."

"I do not suppose you got his name?"

"No, he took off as soon as we heard the dragon…"

"Really?" Doctor Pernell said with intense interest.

81

"Yea, a dragon. This must be some whacky dream…"

"What makes you think this is a dream?" he asked.

"Well, the dragon for one."

"You do not have dragons where you come from? And, where did you say you were from?" he asked curiously.

"No, we don't have dragons in Glendale."

"Glendale?"

She nodded. "Yea, Glendale, California in the good ole U S of A. I broke my watch and my cell phone isn't working. My parents are going to freak when they find out I missed school."

He studied her curiously for a moment. Doctor Pernell patted her on the knee and stood up. "Say, that is an unusual necklace you are wearing."

Emily instinctively put her hand on it.

"My grandma gave it to me," she said.

"May I see it?" he asked.

Emily shrugged, "Sure."

She unclasped the chain and placed it into Doctor Pernell's hand. He held it up to the light. A mist swirled within the jewel and the doctor could feel its incredible power.

"Fascinating," he said quietly. He handed it back to Emily and she placed the necklace back around her neck.

"Do you think you would recognize the man on the horse if you saw him again?" he asked.

"Most definitely," she said. "I've never seen anyone with eyes that color. They were almost silver, a silver blue."

"Silver blue, you say?"

"Yes, I'm positive."

He moved towards the door.

"Would you excuse me for a moment? I will send someone in to finish your examination and then talk to you again shortly."

"Okay, thanks."

Pernell gave her a pleasant nod and stepped out of the room. He turned a corner to find Martin going over patient files, deep in thought.

"Excuse me, Doctor Stewart."

"Yes?" replied Martin, looking up from the stack of paperwork.

"There is a patient in Room 3 that I wish you to examine," he directed. "She had a head wound that was mended by a healer."

"Mended by a healer? Then why does she need to see me?" Martin asked.

"Just check her vitals. Routine things."

Martin was perplexed, "Alright, if you insist…"

"Oh, I insist…"

Martin put down the files and headed towards the examination room where Emily was waiting. He tapped lightly on the door and then entered. Emily was staring at her feet. Martin had an immediate reaction to her.

"You again!"

She looked up and had an equal reaction to seeing him also. She got off the examination table and stood in front of Martin.

"You! What are you doing here?" she asked.

"I happen to work here," he informed her.

"As what?" she scoffed.

"A doctor," he informed her.

"You? A doctor?" she laughed out loud. "In that costume? Do you always run over people with your horse for fun? Is that how you find your patients?" she said sarcastically.

He sighed in frustration. "You were standing in the middle of the road."

"You should have been watching where you were going!" she cut him off.

"You are insufferable," he said, walking around the room in annoyance.

"And, you can't drive a horse worth squat?"

He turned to face her. "Drive a horse? You mean ride of horse."

"Whatever, you know what I meant," she said angrily. "Oh, and while we're on the subject, thanks for leaving me behind to be eaten by a dragon!"

Martin looked her up and down. "You do not appear to have been eaten by a dragon. Although, I think it would have served Aquila well if you had actually been a dragon's dinner," he chided her, raising his voice slightly.

She stood up on her toes to try and match his height. "I ought to punch you in the snout."

Martin stepped back and laughed. "I would like to see you try!" he taunted her.

Emily kicked him in the shin. "That's for leaving me behind for the dragon!"

Martin hopped back.

"Why you little…"

The door opened and Doctor Pernell stepped back inside. He looked at Emily and then back at Martin and smirked. Emily had her fist curled up in a ball ready to strike Martin again. Martin was holding his shin wincing in pain.

"Ahhh, I see you two are getting reacquainted," he smiled widely. "Emily, please sit back on the examination table for a moment, if you are through conversing with Doctor Stewart."

Doctor Pernell was quite pleased with himself. He watched Emily sit back on the table and then walked around Martin, eying him with amusement.

"Doctor Stewart are you in need of medical assistance?" he asked light heartedly.

"She needs her head examined," Martin muttered angrily.

"Doctor Stewart, you truly have a way with people," Doctor Pernell said with amusement.

Martin pointed a finger at Emily. "She kicked me."

Emily rolled her eyes. "He had it coming."

"Indeed? I don't suppose her kicking you had anything to do with you leaving her behind to be eaten by a dragon?"

"Exactly!" Emily added.

Martin addressed Doctor Pernell. "Oh, she told you that?" With respect, clearly, she was not eaten by a dragon."

"Yea, but I could've been!" she argued with Martin.

"She did mention the dragon, yes. Honestly, Doctor Stewart, I will never understand how someone in our profession, such as yourself, can be so narrowminded. We took an oath to help people, not turn our backs on them," Doctor Pernell said to him.

Martin had no rebuttal for that and continued to rub his shin as if he had been mortally wounded.

"Well, if you are going to put it like that," he frowned.

"Let me properly introduce you – Emily this is Doctor Stewart. Doctor Stewart this is Emily," Doctor Pernell grinned.

Emily and Martin both glared at each other.

"I'm not calling you doctor anything," she said adamantly.

Doctor Pernell tried not to chuckle at the obvious posturing between the two. "Let's dispense with the formalities for the time being. Emily, you may call him Martin," he suggested.

Martin shot him a look and was about to protest, but Doctor Pernell raised a hand to silence him.

"Emily here has a very interesting necklace. Have you seen it?" Doctor Pernell motioned for Martin to step closer and look. Martin gave Doctor Pernell an odd glance but obliged his request.

"Watch those feet now," Martin warned her, as he moved closer to Emily.

He stepped in to get a better look at her necklace. His facial expression changed immediately. Martin looked back and forth between Emily and Doctor Pernell before fixing his eyes on the necklace she wore.

"Where did you get that from?" he asked Emily, visibly shaken.

"From my grandmother, why?"

Martin backed away and looked at Doctor Pernell.

"Emily, I'd like to keep you overnight for observation," Doctor Pernell informed her. "To be on the side of caution."

"Overnight?"

"That is correct," he confirmed.

"But I have to go home," she objected.

"You said you were from someplace called Glendale."

"Yes, Glendale, California."

Martin and Doctor Pernell glanced at each other.

"Emily," Doctor Pernell continued. "You also said you believed you were dreaming."

"Well, yes. But everything seems so real..."

Doctor Pernell smiled at her, "Then let us suppose that you are dreaming. I think it is best that you stay overnight."

Martin had a strange look on his face that did not escape Emily. His entire demeanor had changed.

"Is something wrong?" she asked Doctor Pernell, looking back and forth between the two men.

Doctor Pernell followed her glance, "No, everything is fine. No need to worry. I will have a nurse come take you to your room," he assured her. "We will talk more later. Once you have had a chance to rest and have a warm meal."

"Okay," Emily agreed reluctantly.

Doctor Pernell and Martin left the room to speak in private.

"You recognized it then," Doctor Pernell asked Martin.

"Of course, I did," Martin said emphatically. "It belonged to my mother."

"I thought as much..."

"How...how did she get it?" Martin asked.

"Questions with few answers right now. She may be the one the prophecy speaks of. Mira and Thalien believe it to be true," Doctor Pernell confided.

Martin looked sharply at Doctor Pernell. "Her?"

"Yes, her."

"Then may the heavens help us," Martin said in alarm.

"The heavens may have done just that. How else do you explain Emily having the necklace? She does not even realize where she is or how she came to be here," Doctor Pernell added.

"How did she come to be here?" Martin asked him.

Doctor Pernell motioned for Martin to walk with him. "She is wearing the keystone. It has power that transcends all worlds. If it brought her to this place, then Emily has purpose in all of the chaos that has threatened to destroy our world," he told Martin.

Doctor Pernell paused momentarily to make sure no one could overhear what he was about to say. "It is said that Miranda has gathered an army to do her bidding. It is also said that she has summoned the Hell Fire dragon to unleash its terror…"

Martin interrupted him, "That is not possible. Those are just stories. I heard the same tales when I was a child. The Hell Fire dragon is something elders made up to frighten children."

Doctor Pernell shook his head in disagreement. "Many a truth can be found in those tales, Doctor Stewart. And, there is something else I need to share with you that few know."

"What is it?" Martin asked intently.

"The mist wall is collapsing."

This revelation took Martin completely off guard. The mist wall was the only thing stopping the evil of the dark side from devouring all within the light. Martin stared hard at Doctor Pernell.

"How can that be?" Martin asked with concern. "If the mist wall collapses, there will be nothing to hold the darkness back."

"Some with knowledge on these matters believe it has something to do with Miranda's use of powerful black magic," he paused. "And, your father is involved too, I am sorry to say."

Martin recoiled at the news of his father. "My father? I can assure you that my father is neither a mystic nor capable of such a feat. He is too busy wallowing in his own self-pity to care about this world or the next," Martin said vehemently.

"Perhaps," Doctor Pernell said understandably.

"My father is nothing at all," Martin said bitterly.

"Again, perhaps. However, you must know that the sorceress manipulates his pain, feeds off it, and has built an empire around it, using your father as her pawn."

"Nonsense, I do not see how any of this has anything to do with me or that girl in there."

"It has everything to do with you both. It is said that this time would come. The end of days when a great evil would arise to swallow the light. It is said that one that remained hidden from an ancient bloodline would emerge to restore order and defeat the evil once and for all, uniting both the light and the dark," Doctor Pernell said passionately.

"More fairy tales," Martin said angrily.

"No, it is not a fairy tale. It is happening now. Right before our eyes. It is also said that another would return to serve as guardian, the shield. All would be called upon in this fight, even the Council of Dragons," Doctor Pernell concluded.

Martin stared at him in disbelief. "The Council of Dragons? They no longer answer to the call of men. If she is who you think she is? Then, she was brought back to fulfill some destiny. Do you know what you are saying? It is ludicrous. I have never believed in those old tales."

"Perhaps it is time that you start believing. The Council of Dragons may answer to the keystone, if not the will of men. I am not one to believe in coincidences either. Of all the outposts that you could have drawn, you end up back here, near your home. The very place you tried so hard to leave. And, this girl just happens to appear out of nowhere at the same time that you arrive. You don't find that striking?"

"No, I find it to be bad luck," Martin said dismissively.

Doctor Pernell frowned, "The keystone brought her here. You cannot deny she has it in her possession. It brought you both back here. There are forces at work that you and I are not privy to."

He took a long deep breath before continuing. "And, if the mist wall collapses? It would make the threat of civil war look like – child's play. It separates good and evil. If Miranda harnesses enough power to collapse the mist wall, that would mean she has the ability to punch a hole into any world she pleases and destroy it. The implications are devastating. For our world, Emily's world, countless worlds," Doctor Pernell said with grave concern. "If Miranda possesses the keystone, there will be no stopping her."

Martin looked troubled, "I did not come here to fight a war."

"War may have found you whether you like it or not."

Martin did not like what he was hearing.

"There are moments in life when you choose a path and it changes your life forever. You are on that path right now. Both of you are. Choose wisely. All our fates could very well rest in the choices you now make," Doctor Pernell pleaded.

"I turned from that path long ago," Martin admitted. "I am no hero."

"You are the son of kings," Doctor Pernell reminded him. "It is time that you remember that."

"A king with no kingdom," Martin said ironically. "My father saw to that…"

"Your father has paid dearly for his sins," Doctor Pernell pointed out.

"Have not we all?" Martin snapped.

"Indeed, we have. You have a chance to set things right. Put things back the way they are supposed to be. Restore the kingdom of old."

"You have the wrong man, Doctor," Martin told him, angrily. "My father got exactly what he deserved. Our family was destroyed. Our lands laid to waste."

"No, this is not the end of the story. Miranda had a hand in what unfolded. She too is to blame," Doctor Pernell argued.

"Again, you have got the wrong man," Martin insisted.

Doctor Pernell shook his head, "No, I have the right man. You have to believe in yourself once again."

"I believe in myself just fine. I am a doctor. I am not a knight, a soldier or the son of a king any longer," Martin argued.

"You cannot hide from your past forever. And what about that girl in there?"

"What about her?" Martin asked apathetically.

"We must protect her. She is innocent in this."

"I have a bruise on my shin that says otherwise," Martin said sarcastically.

"You know what I mean. Miranda will hunt her down. If we know who Emily is? Then, it will not be long before Miranda knows too. She has spies everywhere. That girl is in grave danger. Deny all you wish. Your apathy could be the death of her," Doctor Pernell said urgently.

Martin looked away.

Doctor Pernell placed his hand on Martin's shoulder and spoke softly to him, "And, haven't we both seen enough pain, enough death in this lifetime? Look what you've witnessed just since you arrived back at the clinic. A little girl's parents were murdered? Have you forgotten that already?"

"Of course not," Martin replied with annoyance.

"When does it end? Maybe, just maybe, Emily can put a stop to all of it. Isn't that worth fighting for?"

Martin looked back at Emily's room, weighing Doctor Pernell's words carefully. He sighed, troubled by what he was hearing. Conflicting emotions betrayed his thoughts.

"What are you asking of me?" he finally asked.

Doctor Pernell noticeably relaxed. He had finally broken through Martin's stubborn demeanor. For all that Martin had become, he was still a good man. He wasn't going to sit idly by and let Miranda murder Emily, whether he liked the girl or not. There was still hope and a sense of honor within Martin.

He left Martin with these words.

"We must protect her at all cost."

Doctor Pernell nodded and left Martin standing alone in the corridor. Martin closed his eyes for a moment.

"Protect her? Great," Martin sighed.

# Part II

## Fragmented

*There are moments that mark your life.*
*Moments when you realize that nothing will ever be the same.*
*Time is divided into two parts.*
*Before this. And, after this.*
*Sometimes you can feel such a moment coming.*
*Strong people keep moving forward.*
*No matter what they are going to find.*

~ Fallen

# Chapter Eight

Fear engulfed her. Everywhere she turned there were people running frantically. The girl could hear screaming and children crying out. Torches lit up the darkness. Through the flames she could see men being brought down swiftly, swords being driven into their bodies.

Riders on horseback, dressed in black, stampeded around the frightened villagers, pulling down crudely constructed wooden shacks and setting them ablaze. The ground shook beneath her feet. The sense of panic was overwhelming. The dirt clung to the sweat on her face.

A dark rider spotted her and turned his horse towards her, digging his heels into the poor beast's side demanding it charge faster. She turned and ran, weaving in and out of the flames, stumbling over fallen bodies and debris. She was running blindly and wildly, desperately trying to stay out of his reach.

He still pursued her despite her best efforts to elude him. She felt herself lifted into the air. She was violently thrown back to the ground, knocking the wind out of her. She struggled to stand up. The rider dismounted his horse and moved towards her. She stumbled to her knees and crawled forward, digging her nails into the ground, until she backed into a small wooden animal pen. She was cornered and had nowhere else to run.

Trembling, she curled up into a ball to protect herself, cowering in fear as he stood over her. The screams of agony from the other villagers served as a warning as to what fate awaited her. He pulled her roughly to her feet and struck her hard across the face. Her lip split and began to bleed. She tasted blood. She struggled to get free, but she was no match for him. His grip was like a vice. Tears welled up in her eyes. A sickening smile of pleasure crossed his face. He was enjoying her demise. He tightened his grip on her throat and lifted her higher until her eyes were level with his.

She struggled and gasped for air, digging at his fingers to no avail. She pounded on his arm, trying to free herself, feeling her lifeforce leaving her. The dark rider quickly ripped off her necklace and threw her aside. She landed hard against a pile of timber. Her limp form wracked with pain.

He held the necklace up to a nearby flame and watched the fire swim within it. He sneered at his prize. He had the keystone. His master would be pleased. This changed everything.

The girl tried to lift her head, stabbing pain prevented her from doing so. She stretched out a trembling hand, reaching for the necklace, hoping she could regain strength. Her hand fell back down to the ground. Darkness swept over her. She closed her eyes, drifting further and further away.

~~~~~~~~~~~~~~~~~~~~~~~~~~~~

Emily bolted upright in her bed and gasped. She hurt all over. Doctor Pernell stood at the foot of her bed, watching her.

"What was that?" she cried out.

He pulled a stool next to her bed and sat down.

"That was the other side of the mist wall. It divides this entire planet into two parts, one always in light and the other always in darkness," he explained, studying her intently.

"Yea, I saw it earlier. Thalien told me about it," she added.

Emily lifted her fingers to her lip. She could still taste blood from being struck by the dark rider. Her hand quickly dropped to where her necklace rested safely around her neck. She breathed deeply when she touched the familiar object.

"It seemed so real…"

Doctor Pernell stood and walked over to a table, returning with a small mirror, which he held up to Emily's face. She looked at it and saw that her lip was in fact bruised and swollen.

"Oh," Emily gasped. She didn't know what to make of it.

"I will have a nurse bring you some ice for that lip."

"It happened. It really happened? Why don't you even seem surprised?" she asked him.

"On Aquila, nothing surprises me."

"A rider dressed in black hit me across the face and tried to choke me to death. Then he took my necklace," she told him.

"The necklace is still in your possession," he pointed out.

"But look at my lip!"

"Indeed," Doctor Pernell said.

"Something very bad is going on here," she said.

"Yes, I know," he said sadly.

"I thought I was dreaming, but…" She looked back at the mirror and could see the hand imprint on her neck where she was being choked.

Doctor Pernell sighed. "We have a lot to talk about, young lady. You must get some rest. I will send Claire in to tend to that lip of yours."

"Thank you," she said sincerely. She felt drained mentally and physically from what she had just experienced.

He smiled gently and left the room. Emily leaned back against her pillow and closed her eyes. She was worried. How could something she dreamt about physically harm her?

She remembered hearing her mother talk to her father in hushed voices, about grandma believing she was clairvoyant. Her father never believed a word of it and quite often called her grandmother "crazy." Her dad used to say she needed to be locked up in the looney bin.

Emily had visions herself from time to time, things she couldn't explain. She never mentioned them to anyone. She certainly didn't think her grandmother was crazy. A colorful character, funny as all else, but crazy? No. Her grandma asked Emily one time if she had visions too. Emily said no, but that was a lie. Emily just didn't want anyone to know. She didn't want to be labeled crazy either.

When she first heard her mom and dad talk about it, she didn't understand what the word "clairvoyant" meant. She looked up the word in the school library the next day.

"Clairvoyance: perceiving things beyond the natural range of sense, foreseeing the future, second sight."

Her grandmother had since passed away and Emily regretted not being honest about her own visions. Emily regretted never discussing the peculiar gift they shared, especially considering her present circumstances. She was being drawn in by her own visions and they seemed real in startling ways.

This was beyond being clairvoyant. Emily's vision had attacked her and left traces of that attack behind. She felt her lip again, wondering what would happen if she died in her vision. Would she then die in this world too? What about her own world? Would she die there as well? She didn't want to find out the answer. The possibility was just too scary for her to comprehend.

Whatever was happening, Emily felt small and out of her depth. Spending her days sparring with imaginary foes never conjured up any real risks, aside from getting in trouble with her parents. This was different. This necklace was valuable to these people, worth killing for. That alarmed her a great deal. She didn't understand her place in all this, and most certainly didn't feel worthy of being the one trusted with this necklace. Why was it given to her?

As a matter of fact, she did not feel worthy at all. She felt a stirring within her that she could not understand. Something hidden deep, something she was supposed to know, but it was just beyond her grasp. Nothing had prepared her for this. Nothing. She came to the realization that this was not a dream at all, and she was in no way prepared. She was never more afraid of failure than at this very moment. She was scared, really scared for the first time since crawling out from under those bushes.

Be brave, Emily, she told herself. Be brave...

She instinctively pulled the covers around her, wanting nothing more than to be home safe and sound, sorely missing her mom's hugs, welcoming the scolding from her dad, and even missing the tattling from her baby sister. She had never felt so alone in all her life.

She spent so much time wishing she could be somewhere else other than the world she lived in... and now? All she could think about was getting back home. Dreaming of another world and living in it were two completely different things. The bruising around her neck was an unpleasant reminder of that fact.

He was so strong, the man from her vision. He could have easily snapped her neck. She fought with all her strength, but she still couldn't pry his fingers loose. She never wanted to feel that vulnerable again.

The nurse soon appeared with a cup of ice instructing Emily to hold a cube to her lip to reduce the swelling. Emily noticed that the nurse did not even bother to ask her how she hurt her lip in the confines of her room, as if it were an everyday occurrence. This did little to ease Emily's fears that she was in danger.

Emily fought to keep her eyes open. She was so incredibly tired, but she was afraid if she fell asleep that she would encounter the dark rider again. Maybe this time he would actually kill her. She had to stay awake...

When the nurse walked past Emily's room thirty minutes later, Emily was sound asleep. Claire removed the cup of ice before it fell out of Emily's hand and then pulled the curtains closed to keep the light out.

~~~~~~~~~~~~~~~~~~~~~~~~~~~

A gentle breeze blew through Emily's hair. The temperature was pleasant, not too warm. She could smell the lilac around her. The beauty of the forest was breathtaking. Evergreens and pines stretched to the sky. It reminded her of the Pacific Northwest, reminiscent of the days visiting her grandma, west of Seattle. She turned to look around, lifting her face to the warm sun.

She heard music and laughter nearby. She followed the sounds of merriment up a winding path as several children rushed past her. They giggled and played happily with not a care in the world. Emily smiled at them.

The path ahead opening into a large clearing where a magnificent castle stood proudly. The grounds were immaculate. Beautiful gardens and fountains dominated the courtyard, while birds resembling peacocks roamed the grounds freely.

The castle itself was constructed of white stone with four blue topped towers on each corner of its square shape. Banners flapped in the wind, woven of bright gold, green and burgundy colors, featuring a family crest. Outside the castle walls people in brightly colored clothing danced and laughed in good cheer. The feeling of good will was infectious. Emily was eager to join in. Young girls in beautiful gowns danced gracefully around a May pole, with ribbons streaming in their hair. A band of musicians playing renaissance music strummed their instruments to the cheers of onlookers.

It was a glorious day!

Emily walked unnoticed among the crowd, gazing up at the castle. It was the most magnificent thing she had ever seen. To live in a place like this, well, that was something she could only write about. Yet, here she was standing at the foot of this marvelous castle, like a fairy tale come true.

Emily spun around and danced happily, caught up in the mood of the moment. A young boy with short blonde hair ran through the crowd and nearly ran into her. He stopped and looked up at her in bewilderment. She smiled at him. He looked at her the way a child can do when they are trying to figure something out. He couldn't quite place her.

Those eyes, Emily thought, I know those eyes. The boy had the most brilliant silver blue eyes she had ever seen, with a piercing gaze. How could it be? Emily leaned forward and whispered to the little boy.

"Martin?" she asked in astonishment.

He tilted his head slightly and smiled at her. Then, he took off running into the crowd, looking back over his shoulder at her with a grin on his face, daring her to chase him. She started to follow him and thought she lost him in the crowd. It was then she noticed Martin clinging to the leg of a man.

Emily assumed the man was Martin's father. The family resemblance was undeniable. He was tall as a tree and looked as strong as one. Broad shoulders, blonde hair, steel clear blue eyes, beaming with authority. He could have easily been Emily's

98

version of a knight straight from one of her own stories. Even the other men standing by Martin's father paled in comparison to this formidable man. He looked regal, a born leader with a commanding air of authority. He was well respected, exuding confidence, dignity, honor and strength. He had a warm smile and a hearty laugh.

Emily was surprised to hear someone refer to him as king. Martin's father was a king? Royalty? Martin was a prince? This was a noble family. Even at Emily's age, she could appreciate his presence. And, when he laughed, it made Emily smile. Not too proud that he could not enjoy a good laugh or two. She liked the man immediately. Martin clearly idolized his father. The charismatic man placed his hand softly on Martin's head and whispered something into the little boy's ear. The boy laughed and ran off to play with the other children.

Emily studied the man as he fondly watched his son run off to play, the proud father. Picture perfect was the only way to describe this setting. The castle, the grounds, the people were all healthy and happy. Young Martin was happy. His father was content and without a doubt the most handsome man Emily had ever seen. Emily couldn't stop staring at him.

Martin's father returned his attention back to the group of men conversing with him until something caught his attention. He smiled and excused himself. Emily turned to see who he was being drawn to. She spotted her instantly. A remarkable woman, as elegant as Martin's father was debonair. She was strikingly beautiful. Long, flowing red hair with emerald green eyes, tall and graceful, wearing a cream-colored gown with gold trim. She was carrying a baby in her arms, whispering gently to it as she walked towards her husband. A smile beamed on her face. It was like looking into the face of love.

The woman wore a necklace around her neck, dragons with their arms embracing a purple stone. Emily's necklace. Emily gasped and put her hand to her own neck. Her necklace was gone. She was sure this woman was wearing the exact same necklace. She looked back over to the happy couple.

Martin's father embraced the woman and gave her a kiss on the cheek. He then leaned over and gently kissed the sleeping child bundled in her arms. They laughed at private words exchanged between them. Emily couldn't help but smile too. It was obvious how deeply in love they were. Everyone else seemed to melt away. This was definitely a happily ever after moment that Emily was witnessing. They were so happy, so much in love.

Emily was fascinated with the couple. The gentle way they touched one another. He would whisper in her ear and make her smile. It was so incredibly romantic. The warmth between them was quite magical. This was a very good place, concluded Emily. Everything was as it should be.

Someone tugged at Emily's pant leg. She looked down to see young Martin grinning at her before he darted away again. She smiled at him and laughed. He was such a joyful child. She was happy for him. She turned back to watch Martin's mother and father. They were walking away from Emily now, towards the river's edge, off to her right. He had his arm gently around his wife's waist as he talked softly to the baby.

A man approached Martin's father from behind and spoke to him briefly. Martin's father stopped and looked concerned. He excused himself from his wife's presence, kissing her gently on her cheek, and followed the man back to the castle.

Martin's father walked past Emily. "Good day to you, young lady," he said with a gracious smile and a polite nod. He had a smooth baritone voice, warm and inviting.

Emily wasn't expecting him to speak to her. Her mind went completely blank. Her mouth dropped open and she merely gawked at him. She felt her cheeks flush. The man grinned handsomely and kept walking by. He was used to ladies being smitten with him and thought nothing of Emily's reaction.

He did look back at Emily, however, eyeing her curiously, memorizing her face, noting the way she was dressed, no doubt. She appeared harmless enough but she seemed out of place.

Emily continued to stare at Martin's father like a wide-eyed doe. She was instantly infatuated with him. She immediately chastised herself for acting so silly. That wasn't like her, but wow! He was just so darn handsome and those eyes. Even his voice was mesmerizing. Holy moly, he was so much better than Legolas – her current crush. And, Martin's father was real! Not a character from a book. Poof! Sigh. Legolas, who? She willed herself to snap out of it and stop acting like such a goofball.

Emily saw Martin run after his mother towards the water, while his father was engaged in a rather heated discussion with someone. She moved closer in hopes of overhearing what they were saying. No one was paying any attention to her. The closer Emily tried to get to Martin's father the slower she seemed to be moving. It felt like she was walking in quicksand now. Time was slowing down. She could feel it, but just didn't understand why.

Suddenly, a scream tore out near the water, shattering the peace. Everyone stopped what they were doing and turned towards the sound. Martin's father immediately raced past her, while other men followed, swords drawn.

Emily tried to follow them but found that she could no longer move. Everything started spinning around her. Only the sound remained, and it was becoming distorted and unclear. She could hear women screaming and panicked voices, splashes of water and hurried cries for help slowly fading out.

Emily felt like she was floating through space and time. Weightless. Flashes of sounds and images filled her mind in no order, merely a stream of consciousness, with no beginning and no end. Darkness closed in on her, followed by silence.

When Emily opened her eyes, she was standing on the exact same path as she had previously stood, except thickets had overgrown the forest floor where heather once had dominated the ground. A cold empty silence greeted her. No children ran past. No music filled the air. She hesitated to journey further up the path for fear of what she might find.

Everything had changed drastically. The calmness and contentment she had previously felt had been replaced with a feeling of dread and unease. Something scurried under a bush, startling Emily. Even the trees had changed. Gone were the proud evergreens she had seen before. Only remnants of snarling, angry trees, with grotesque limbs reaching out for her remained.

Cautiously, she approached the clearing where the castle once stood. Her mouth dropped open. What was once the heart of Aquila was now deserted. Gone was the magnificent castle where guests danced and laughed. All that remained was an empty shell, abandoned to the elements, picked clean by scavengers. Neglected and forgotten.

This land had been cursed.

No one had lived here for a very long time by the looks of it. Emily heard more scurrying from behind her, followed by a low growl. She knew she was being watched. But, by what?

Emily frowned and slowly approached the castle. The drawbridge was down, and she debated whether to go inside or not. She turned to look behind her again and was alarmed to see darkness covering the path and slowly closing in on her. She shivered, feeling very ill at ease.

There was no turning back now. She quickened her pace and walked into the eerily silent hall. The only sounds within were that of her footsteps on the hard stone floor and the wind whistling outside, stirring up dead leaves and debris.

The remains of the torn banners, which once hung proudly, smacked against the cold walls, thrown about by the wind coming in through the castle windows. Cobwebs hung from the unlit torches on the walls and from the wood ceiling beams. The air was stale and putrid.

Beyond the great hall, she saw only darkness. She caught a glimpse of something moving fast to her left, but when she turned to see what it was, it had already disappeared into the darkness.

"Oh great," Emily sighed, "Now what?"

Something looked back at her from the darkness in front of her. She could just make out its glowing red eyes. It took a few steps closer to her and then scurried back into the dark. She only caught a quick glance. It was small, human in appearance, long hair and a beard, wielding some kind of a weapon. It couldn't have been more than two feet tall.

"Okie dokie, please go away," she said out loud.

She had nothing to protect herself with, and she didn't relish the thought of being attacked by a tribe of carnivorous garden gnomes. All the warmth had left this place a long time ago. Only darkness remained within its walls.

Emily noticed a painting hanging near a darkened staircase. She walked slowly across the hall to examine it more closely. The painting had been weathered with age and neglect. It was completely torn on one corner, exposing the wood frame beneath it. There was no mistaking its subject matter.

The beautiful young woman she had seen earlier was seated in a chair. She was wearing a rose-colored velvet gown, utterly content. She was breathtaking. Her husband stood beside her with his hand resting gently on her shoulder looking quite regal. He wore all black with just a hint of burgundy beneath his cape. A small dog rested at their feet. A fire blazed behind them and books adorned the shelves on either side of them. They looked perfectly happy. Emily wondered what they were thinking just at that moment in time. It was hauntingly beautiful. She stepped closer to the painting to read the artist signature.

"You again," came a voice from behind her.

She jumped. She had not heard anyone come in.

"Martin?" she said more to herself than to him.

"That's Doctor Stewart to you. What are you doing here?" he asked crossly.

She hesitated. "It was open. I was curious."

"You thought you could just come in?" Martin asked as he looked up at the painting.

"I have no idea what I'm doing here, actually," she explained. "I was at the clinic one minute and here the next."

He turned away from her and walked into a nearby room. Emily followed him. She felt much safer staying with him than out in the great hall with the creepy garden gnomes lurking about.

"Who are these people in the painting?" She already knew the answer, but she was trying to get him to open up about them.

"My mother and father," he said quietly.

"What happened to them?"

"They are gone," he said sharply, looking away.

She shuffled her feet uncomfortably. "I'm sorry."

He turned to look at her. She could see the pain and sadness in his eyes.

"Does that satisfy your curiosity now?" he said angrily, walking away from her and out of the room.

She called out into the darkness. "Doctor Stewart? Hello? Where did you go? Please don't leave me again. It's creepy in here…"

Her own voice echoed within the castle.

No other sounds could be heard.

Martin was gone, vanished as silently as he had appeared. She walked over to the painting once more. When she looked at it this time, she could hear the faint sounds of children laughing playfully from somewhere within the castle, as a scene from a childhood memory played out in her mind. A residual from days long past. This castle has a heart, she thought to herself, but that heart had been broken. She was overcome with sadness, a deep painful sadness.

The sounds faded from her mind, and Emily was alone again.

~~~~~~~~~~~~~~~~~~~~~~~~~

Noises from outside woke Martin up. He rolled over and stared at the ceiling. His dreams had left him uneasy, taking him to a place he did not want to return to. He was not at all happy with the way things were happening.

This internship was supposed to be routine. Yet, he had already been present at the aftermath of a brutal double murder, and had a visit from some ghoulish creature pretending to be his deceased mother. Then, he nearly trampled a young girl with his horse, and now, well, the dreams had started again.

"I should have never come back here," he muttered to himself, burying his head beneath his pillow.

# Chapter Nine

Emily awoke to the sounds of Thalien and Doctor Pernell talking in the corridor outside of her room. She felt drained from the visions that haunted her sleep. She yawned loudly and got out of bed slowly, still aching from the assault she endured. She walked across the room and pulled back the curtain slightly, allowing the bright sun to spill in.

"Wow, they weren't kidding. It's still daylight. That would totally suck if you were a vampire here," she mused.

She pulled the curtain closed again, not quite ready for the sunshine to consume her. Emily yawned again and walked over to the mirror. She winced when she saw herself. She had fallen asleep before getting cleaned up.

"Oh, geez," she groaned, frowning at her reflection. "I look downright frightening."

She touched her lip. The swelling had gone down, but the bruising remained on her neck from the assailant's grasp.

She looked around the room. A fresh set of clothes had been left for her, neatly folded on the nearby chair, as well as personal items for her to freshen up with. A water basin sat nearby with fragrant soaps, sponges and towels. She was grateful for the opportunity to wash up and feel human again.

With the water she had left in the basin, she washed her hair and towel dried it. She was happy to rid herself of any remaining muck from the previous day. She brushed her hair and tied it back with a hair band, letting her red bangs fall softly, framing her face. Emily inspected herself in the small mirror.

"I know you," she smirked, pleased that she looked presentable once again.

She examined her new wardrobe before dressing. Dark stirrup type leggings with a fitted burgundy tunic, warm woolen socks with knee high boots that laced up the front. She approved. It was nothing fancy, but it would allow her to fit in more with those around her. It was nothing she hadn't seen before at Celtic or Renaissance festivals.

The tunic was slightly large on her, but she hoped she could find a belt with perhaps a place for a dagger of some kind – just in case she encountered the black rider or the creepy garden gnomes again. Not that she had ever used a real weapon before, because she hadn't. She had certainly pretended with her real friends and imaginary ones. She was going to have to ask about getting something to defend herself with. She would need it, if they were going to journey through this beautiful, but dangerous land.

There was a large satchel sitting on the floor filled with extra clothes, additional personal items, a basic first aid kit and other supplies.

A tray of assorted breads, fruits and juice sat next to her bed on a stand. She didn't recognize any of the fruit, but she was ravished. She smelled the fruit, tasting it cautiously. She hungerly ate the food, washing it down with the tart flavored juice. Not knowing when she might get another meal, Emily wrapped the remaining food in a cloth and put them inside her backpack. Better to be prepared, she told herself. She then shoved the backpack into the satchel they had provided.

"Hello?" she called out to Thalien and Doctor Pernell.

Thalien stuck his head inside and entered the room.

"Good morning, Emily."

"Good morning," she replied.

"Don't you look pretty," Thalien said with a smile.

"Thank you," she responded back cheerfully.

Thalien asked Emily if she was able to get some rest. She told him about her troubling vision. She didn't mention seeing Martin as a young boy. There were some things she wasn't quite ready to share.

Doctor Pernell was talking with a nurse, but entered Emily's room as soon as he was finished, scribbling something on his notepad. He noticed the empty food plate.

"You have eaten. Good, I am glad."

"Yes, thank you," she responded.

Doctor Pernell looked up from his notepad and paused. He was astonished by her appearance. Few things surprised him anymore, but seeing her transformation took him by surprise.

With the filth from the previous day washed away, Emily's true physical beauty was revealed. His eyes lingered on her red hair and her face. He didn't mean to stare but she looked so familiar. Yes, he could see it now. The resemblance to the bloodline. Would Martin see it too, he wondered? How could he not?

Emily noticed the odd way the doctor was looking at her and started fidgeting.

"Is everything okay?" she asked self-consciously, smoothing down her hair and straightening her tunic. "I know I looked like a wild child yesterday, a complete mess," she admitted.

He smiled, finding her concern over her appearance to be endearing. She was at that age, he noted, becoming a young woman, still so young but no longer a child.

"Everything is fine. You look wonderful, quite lovely," Doctor Pernell replied sincerely.

"Thanks," she smiled brightly, appreciating the compliment. "I think I need a belt though. I could fit three of me in this," she laughed and held up her arms, showing how much larger the tunic was for her frame.

He laughed with her. "Yes, I will see that you get a belt or a smaller size. Are you feeling up to a trip today?" Doctor Pernell asked.

"To where?" Emily inquired.

"There is someone we would like you to meet," Thalien told her. "I mentioned her to you when we first met – Mira."

"Okay," Emily said a bit reluctantly.

"No need for concern. Mira is very wise. It is a two day journey from here," Thalien explained to her.

"And, it will not be an easy journey. I have arranged an escort for you and Thalien," Doctor Pernell added.

"When do we leave?" she asked apprehensively.

"After lunch, if you think you have room for more food. Thalien will be waiting in the courtyard for you. Join him when you are ready." Doctor Pernell gently touched her arm. "Good luck, Emily. May the heavens watch over you and keep you safe from harm."

She appreciated his genuine concern for her.

"Thank you," she said.

Doctor Pernell nodded as he and Thalien left her room.

Emily hoped she was being taken to someplace where she could finally get some answers. She felt alone and more than a little scared. She didn't like feeling this way. She always envisioned herself as a warrior at heart. She guessed she was about to find out what she was really made of. She hoped that she would do herself proud and not be a coward as she faced the unknown.

She missed home. Would she ever see her family again? She pushed those unsettling thoughts out of her mind. Just the day before, her greatest concern was getting back home before dinner and keeping up her grades at school. Her idea of stress was getting to the next levels of her *Resident Evil* or *Silent Hill* video games without using a strategy guide.

This... was life or death. She saw that firsthand from her visions. And, that dragon that tried to eat her? She couldn't hit the pause on the game controller for this one. She tended to be flippant about life, because academics and arts came so easily for her. Being a tomboy gave her a broad range of activities to choose from too.

She knew she couldn't be that way in this world. She had been thrown into this weird dream state, from which she could not awaken. She sensed that the worst was yet to come. The screams and cries of the villagers haunted her mind. She hoped that their escort could protect them from the dangers that awaited.

A nurse entered her room and handed Emily a woven belt to wrap around her waist. It helped her tunic fit properly instead of looking like she was wearing a tent. The nurse then directed her to the dining hall. Emily was still hungry even though she had eaten a great deal of the fruit plate. She took a seat at a table and was brought a warm meal that resembled oatmeal, eggs, breads and jams. She helped herself to generous portions.

Across the dining hall, she noticed a sad looking young girl sitting by herself. The girl was holding a fork in her hand, just staring at her plate.

Emily picked up her tray and walked over to join her.

"Can I sit here?" Emily asked.

The girl didn't answer.

Emily stood by the end of the table for a moment before sitting across from the girl.

"Hi," she said. "My name is Emily."

The girl continued to stare at her food. There were five coins on the table by the girl's hand.

"What's your name?" Emily asked. She pointed at the coins. "Are we supposed to pay for our meal?"

The little girl didn't respond but she covered her coins with her hand.

"Don't worry, I'm not going to take your money," Emily assured her. Emily sat in silence and continued to eat her meal. The girl peered up at her but did not speak.

"Are you okay?" Emily asked, seeing the girl's eyes were red and swollen from crying.

The girl finally spoke.

"I'm Rebecca. Were your parents killed too? Is that why you're here?" she asked.

Emily stopped eating and looked at the girl.

"What?" Emily asked, troubled by what the girl had said.

"My parents were killed. This is my home now," she told Emily, before staring back at her food.

Emily wasn't sure how to respond to that tragic news.

"Um, I'm really sorry about your parents," Emily said sincerely. "No, I don't live here and my parents are fine, as far as I know."

"Then why are you here?" the young girl asked.

"Just passing through," Emily told her.

"Why are you here?" a voice from behind Emily asked again.

She looked over her shoulder. A dark-haired boy was standing there, looking harshly at both of them.

"Who are you?" Emily wanted to know.

"I asked a question. Why are you here?" he pried.

"Not big on manners, huh?" she frowned at him, turning back to her food and ignoring his question.

Emily disliked him already.

"You're not from around here," he said.

"That's right. I'm not," Emily confirmed.

The boy kept staring at her.

"Where are you from? Why are you here?" he pressed further. "Answer me," he ordered.

Emily felt a weird tingling in her head, a strange sensation. It reminded her of a brain freeze from eating ice cream too fast. She put her fork down and looked back at the boy. His eyes bore down on her. Emily didn't appreciate his attempt to intimidate her.

"Do you mind? I'm trying to enjoy my food. And, quite frankly, you're being rude. Bye bye now," she shooed him away with her hand. Emily turned her attention back to her meal.

He didn't move.

He said nothing.

He just continued to stare at her.

"He stares at everybody," Rebecca chimed in.

The boy shot her a look. "Was I talking to you? Did anyone say you could speak?"

Emily frowned, put her fork down and stood up to face him. She was much taller than he was. She stared down at him, unphased by his cold stare.

"She can talk if she wants to," Emily corrected him.

"No, she can't," he snapped back.

"What's your problem? Leave us alone. I'm not answering your questions. And, I'm really not in the mood for whatever game you're playing," Emily told him.

She crossed her arms and looked down at him defiantly.

He stared coldly back at her.

Her head was beginning to throb.

The boy grinned wickedly at her.

"Answer my questions," he demanded again.

Emily chuckled. "Um, no," she refused.

"Go away," Rebecca told the boy, sounding somewhat fearful of him.

"Shut up," he snapped at Rebecca in a raised voice.

"Whoa," Emily held up a hand to silence him, suddenly feeling very protective of Rebecca.

"Back off," Emily warned. "What are you? Like seven?"

"His name is Donovan and he's eight," Rebecca told her.

"Donovan? And, you're eight?" Emily repeated. "Well, where I come from, it's not cool to be a bully."

He glared at Rebecca and then turned his full attention back to Emily. His glare turned to a menacing grin.

Emily sighed and rolled her eyes. "Does that work around here? That scary face you're making? Because it's not doing anything for me but making you look ridiculous. I can make faces too," she told him.

She squeezed her face tight with her hands and stuck out her tongue, like a frog, only aggravating Donovan further.

"This has been fun but I have to go," she said sarcastically. She turned back to Rebecca. "It was nice meeting you. And, I'm sorry about your parents. I really am." To Donovan she said, "Leave her alone."

She started to leave but Donovan stepped in front of her, blocking her way.

Emily gave him a surprised look and then laughed.

"Really? You're joking, right?"

He said nothing.

"You're like what? 4 feet tall at best? And, in case you didn't notice, I'm much taller than you, like giant size. You're the size of a hobbit," Emily laughed.

"What's a hobbit?" Rebecca asked.

Emily glanced back at her, "I'll explain some other time." She turned back to meet Donovan's gaze, giving as much attitude as she could muster. "Move," she said to him.

He didn't budge.

She leaned in towards him. "Look, I don't know what your problem is and no offense – I don't care. But get out of my way or I'll move you myself..."

Emily was many things, a tomboy being one of them. She wasn't about to let this boy bully her. She stared back at him.

A nurse called over. "Is everything alright over there?"

Emily waved at her. "Perfectly fine."

Emily stepped around Donovan, intentionally bumping into him as she walked past. He stumbled backwards. With that, she left the two young children alone. They watched her leave. Donovan's eyes never left Emily. She looked back over her shoulder and just shook her head disapprovingly at him.

~~~~~~~~~~~~~~~~~~~~~~~~~

Martin was pacing impatiently around Doctor Pernell's office. The doctor watched him with mild concern.

"Doctor Stewart, you are doing the right thing."

"I was not given much choice in the matter," Martin reminded him.

"You could have refused," Doctor Pernell pointed out.

"That was never an option and you are well aware of that fact," Martin said with annoyance. He put his hands on the doctor's desk and leaned forward. "I came here for my internship, not to babysit."

"I think babysitting is understating the seriousness of the situation, is it not? By the way, how is your shin this morning?" Doctor Pernell smirked.

"That is not funny," Martin protested.

"Actually, it is." Doctor Pernell smiled warmly up at him.

Martin paced around the room again. "Have you considered sending her back to where she came from?"

"We are beyond that now," Doctor Pernell reminded him. "The keystone brought her here. We have no choice but to see this through and protect her."

Martin frowned. "Certainly, there is someone more qualified than I to escort her to Mira. I am liable to kill her before we even get there. She...irks me so."

Doctor Pernell grinned. "You'll manage. There is no one more suitable than you. You know it is true and that annoys the hell out of you. I guess your past has come back and bit you in the rear, has it not?" Doctor Pernell said with amusement.

"You are enjoying this, are you not?"

"I enjoy seeing that young spitfire get under your skin, yes. I am delighted that you and Thalien will be watching over her. She could not be in better care. And, there is something quite special about her. It gives me great hope," Doctor Pernell admitted.

"Are we talking about the same girl?" Martin quipped.

Doctor Pernell smirked, "Yes. You'd see it too if you gave her half a chance."

"I pass," Martin scoffed.

Martin crossed his arms and looked down at the sword that now hung at his side. He sighed heavily.

"I cannot believe I am standing here with a sword at my side," Martin said, defeated.

Doctor Pernell smiled and stood up. "I have every confidence in you, Doctor Stewart." He stretched out his hand for Martin to shake. Martin frowned but accepted the gesture. "Travel safe," he added.

~~~~~~~~~~~~~~~~~~~~~~~~

Emily found Thalien outside of the clinic waiting for her. He was checking gear that had been gathered for them to take. He waved at her as she approached. She looked around but saw no one else.

"Where is our escort?" she asked.

"Here…" came a familiar voice.

Emily turned to see Martin walking towards them. He was dressed quite differently now. He was wearing a dark burgundy tunic over black trousers. A hunter green colored cloak was draped over his shoulder. He had a broadsword strapped to his side. Gone was the smug arrogance she had previously witnessed from him. His jaw was set and he looked miserably serious.

Emily grinned.

"You're our escort?" she asked light heartedly.

Martin gave her a look and ignored her question.

"Kill me now," she joked.

"Do not tempt me, child."

"Ah, ha. You're still in there. You looked so serious when you walked over that I thought for a second that Doctor Pernell gave you a personality transplant. Downright dismal."

Martin continued to ignore her. "We could arrange one for you, if you would like," Martin shot back.

"Touché," she smiled.

Thalien watched the exchange between the two with interest. He kept his mouth shut and let them spar.

"And, don't you look spiffy," Emily teased. She walked around him, eying his new attire. "Like a grown-up boy now."

Martin looked at her with contempt. She stepped closer to examine the intricate design of his wardrobe. She noticed that his clothing matched the colors of the banners she had seen flying at his family castle.

"Touch me and you die," he warned her, scowling.

Emily eyed him humorously and stretched out a finger and poked him. "I'm still here."

Martin looked at her with disbelief.

She poked him again.

"Stop poking me," he said angrily.

She poked him again and snickered. "Oh, you can't kill me. It's your job to protect me. Oh, this is going to be fun," she teased.

Martin huffed angrily, "You are insufferable!"

She poked him again.

Martin looked over his shoulder and saw Doctor Pernell watching them from the clinic doorway.

"She keeps poking me!" Martin shouted to him, clearly irritated.

Doctor Pernell smiled, trying not to laugh, waved back and said nothing.

"Please make her stop!" Martin shouted, exasperated. "She is driving me crazy!"

Emily continued to poke him. Martin shot another angry glance over at Doctor Pernell, who finally intervened.

"Emily, please stop poking Martin," Doctor Pernell piped in.

"Okay," Emily agreed.

Martin looked back and forth between the two.

"You stop when he tells you to? Not when I ask it of you?" Martin remarked, infuriated.

Emily shrugged. "He asked nicely."

Martin glared at her.

"Let us get something clear," he told her scathingly. "I do not like you. I do not want to be here but I have a job to do. My job is to get you from here to Mira safely. Stay the hell out of my way and let me do my job. Do not speak to me. Do not even look at me. Understand?"

She crossed her eyes and made a face at him, going out of her way to be obnoxious.

Martin's mouth dropped open. He was trying hard not to lose his temper. He clenched his fist and took a deep breath.

"So odd," he muttered under his breath.

Emily noticed his jaw tighten.

"See? Told you so. Anger issues," she spouted back.

Martin turned his back to her and began walking down the path.

"Seriously? We're walking?" she asked.

Martin ignored her and kept walking.

"Where's your horse? The one you almost ran me over with. What was his name? Thundercat? Rainbow kitty? Sea Biscuit?" she called after him.

115

Thalien looked back at Doctor Pernell and then back at Emily, unsure of what to make of this exchange.

"It will be fine," Doctor Pernell called out to Thalien, trying to convince himself as well.

Emily saw Martin's hand resting on the hilt of his sword as he walked angrily away.

"Do you even know how to use that sword? Or is it just for decoration?" she asked him sarcastically.

Without a word, Martin turned on his heel and walked angrily back to Emily.

In a flash, Martin drew his sword and swung it swiftly through the air in a wide circle, bringing it back in front of him in a stance that would give anyone pause. She jumped back, startled. He leveled the sword directly at her and held it perfectly still at eye level, daring her to utter one more word.

Emily's eyes widened.

She swallowed hard, afraid to move.

She was speechless and equally impressed.

In that moment, she was reminded of what she had witnessed in her vision. Martin was indeed his father's son. She saw the little boy with fiery determination now standing before her as a grown man.

It was best that she didn't forget that fact. And, perhaps – just perhaps – show him a wee bit of respect, she realized. Martin was still holding his sword in strike position, daring her to challenge him.

Their eyes were locked. His was the deadliest stare she had ever seen. He didn't move a muscle. His gaze was unwavering.

"Holy moly," she thought to herself.

Neither said a word.

Thalien and Doctor Pernell watched the entire exchange nervously.

Emily finally blinked and made the first move. She backed away gingerly and held up her hands in front of her, trying to diffuse the situation.

"Peace," she conceded.

Martin glared at her, a silent warning. He was tired of her childish games. He held firm for a few more seconds. Finally, he lowered his sword back into its sheath, never taking his eyes off Emily. He gave her a look of utter contempt before turning back around and continuing on the path before him.

Doctor Pernell let out a sigh of relief.

Emily watched Martin carefully.

She just stood toe to toe with a real knight and she was in awe. She couldn't even move. She stood there watching him walk away.

"Are you alright?" Thalien asked in a worried voice.

She didn't even respond.

"Emily?" Doctor Pernell called to her, equally concerned.

She slowly smiled, accepting her newfound respect for Martin. She wasn't too keen on letting him know that just yet. She felt safe with him. She knew now that he could take care of himself and her. She was suddenly glad that he had been chosen to escort them.

One thing was obvious, Martin was not to be messed with. He was serious, deadly serious. She had not really intended to make an enemy out of him, and they obviously got off on the wrong foot. Perhaps she should make the effort to mend that fence, for all their sakes, she realized. Martin was a good distance in front of them and he never looked back over his shoulder. He expected them to follow.

Emily looked back at Doctor Pernell. "I'm okay. But I don't think he likes me," she admitted.

"You'll be fine," he said, as he waved goodbye.

"We best catch up to him," Thalien insisted.

He and Emily began following Martin.

"You've made quite an impression on him," Thalien pointed out. "This is going to be an interesting journey."

Emily was about to speak, but Martin yelled back at them.

"Keep up," he bellowed.

They quickened their pace to close the distance between themselves and Martin. They walked for miles, stopping only briefly for food and water. Martin was clearly in charge and not interested in banter. He stood apart from them, leaning against a tree, always with his back to them. He had not spoken a word in hours. Martin's stony silence was making Emily uncomfortable.

"Is he always this…gloomy?" she asked absently, loud enough for Martin to overhear.

"Do not fret. Martin carries a heavy burden. But we are in good hands," he assured her, sensing her unease.

She continued to watch Martin from a distance for any signs that his anger had subsided. He continued their journey without so much as a word. His eyes were peeled to the terrain for signs of any danger. His instincts were on alert and his senses in tune with his surroundings. Thalien and Emily hurried to catch up to him but remained several paces behind.

Emily's eyes burned into Martin's back. She was studying everything about him – his walk, his mannerisms, his steely gaze. She could imagine him stepping right out of a historical fiction – the dashing knight, rushing in to save the day. Gone was the annoying man that nearly ran over her with a horse. She saw no trace of the doctor anymore either. Martin had taken on a completely different persona since they had left the clinic.

He was certainly not at a loss for words any other time she encountered him, but now, he barely spoke. He was taking his responsibility of assuring their safe passage very seriously. She had no doubt he could handle whatever danger they might encounter.

Emily was finally face to face with a genuine knight of the highest order and he couldn't stand her, she sulked, regretting her behavior. She could learn so much from him, if only he allowed her to do so.

Martin looked over his shoulder, seeming to sense he was being stared at. He didn't speak but gave her a look that forced her to shift her gaze elsewhere. She looked away. She slowed her step to walk beside Thalien and whispered to him.

"Can you tell me about Martin?" she asked.

Thalien had been waiting for her to ask.

"Martin is of noble birth, a descendant of kings. His family had long ruled these lands in peace and prosperity, until a tragedy tore their family apart..." Thalien went silent and lowered his head, sadly. "A horrible accident..."

Emily looked at Martin in front of them and then back at Thalien. "What happened?" she asked.

"His mother drowned on his 10th birthday," he told her. "His father never recovered from the loss and fell into despair. It was a most unfortunate situation. Martin left home as soon as he was old enough to do so."

Emily recalled her vision, the celebration and then the cries for help. She also recalled an earlier vision where she saw a woman being shoved from behind and into the water.

"An accident, you say?" Emily asked.

"Yes, an accident..."

Emily had to say something. She had to share what she saw in her vision.

She continued, "...because I had this vision of a woman, I swear it was Martin's mother, but it wasn't an accident. She was hit from behind and shoved into the water," Emily said urgently.

Thalien stopped in his tracks and turned towards Emily, whispering excitedly. "What is this you say? Are you a seeker?"

"A seeker?"

"Someone that can see things – past, present and future."

"Second sight," she said, knowingly.

Thalien's eyes widened, "You are very important indeed, Emily. To be a seeker and this vision of yours?" he looked back at Martin. "Martin's father blamed himself for this tragedy, but if what you saw is correct, then it was..."

"Murder," she finished the sentence for him.

Thalien stared at her in shock. "Martin's mother, Isabeau, was a protected seeker, to have knowledge of this could only come from the power of the keystone, which explains why no one else has seen this," he reasoned.

"The keystone?" she asked.

119

He pointed to her necklace. "The keystone," he whispered. "But you must not speak of this further, until you talk to Mira."

Martin shouted from in front of them. "Keep moving!"

They hurried to catch up to him and spoke no more on this topic. Emily had a lot of questions and much to think about. She touched the necklace dangling around her neck. It was warm to her touch and tingled as she held it within her fingers. She was trying to put the pieces of this puzzle together.

She closed her hand over the necklace. What had Thalien called it? The keystone. What did that mean? She knew from her vision that it was important enough to kill for...

Was she the only one that truly knew what happened on that fateful day with Isabeau? The implications were very clear. It's something entirely different to lose your beloved wife in an accident than to learn she had actually been murdered. Who was behind the murder? Who was hunting for the keystone?

She realized that Doctor Pernell sent Martin along as her personal escort for a reason. It wasn't just because he was a competent bodyguard. Martin was involved in this mystery as much as she was... Emily was wearing the necklace that once belonged to his mother. Doctor Pernell must have known she was in danger, without even knowing about the murder. This did little to ease her fears. But, danger from what and from whom? She looked around, scouring the area for any signs of peril. She instinctively moved closer to Martin, shortening the distance between them. She felt safer with him at arm's length.

Martin stopped abruptly and looked sharply to his right. Emily ran into the back of him. He didn't budge. His eyes were fixed on a point to the right of them. He placed himself between Emily and where his eyes were fixed. Martin's hand went immediately to his sword.

Emily and Thalien stood perfectly still. She strained to see or hear anything of alarm, staring in the same direction as Martin.

No one moved.

No one spoke.

Without so much as flinching a muscle, Martin drew his sword and spun around bringing the heavy weapon down hard on an assailant that dropped from a tree directly behind Emily.

She gasped and jumped in fright. She had neither seen nor heard the attacker, but Martin's keen senses obviously detected danger. Emily was totally surprised. It happened so quickly. Martin had pushed Emily out of the way and placed himself between her and the assailant. The assailant dropped like a stone, blood gushing from the mortal wound Martin had inflicted.

Another assailant dropped from the tree. Dressed in black from head to toe, wearing goggles. Martin quickly moved forward to place himself in harm's way, shielding and protecting Emily. Thalien grabbed Emily and pulled her back closer to him. She didn't even have time to react.

The assailant had a dagger in his hand and charged Martin, who easily defended the blow. Martin struck the assailant hard with the hilt of his sword, bringing the attacker to his knees. Martin pulled off the attacker's goggles. The man screamed in agony. He buried his head in his hands, shielding his eyes from the harsh sunlight. Martin brought his sword within an inch of the man's chest, preparing to run him through and deliver a fatal blow.

A third attacker charged from the tree line.

"Look out!" yelled Emily.

Martin had already sensed the movement and swung, shoving his sword deep into the man's chest with such force that it lifted the attacker off the ground. The man screamed in agony as his body slid down further on Martin's sword, impaling him. Martin pushed the attacker's body to the side. He pulled his sword from the dying man and wiped the blood off on the assailant's cape.

The other man that was blinded by the sunlight, stood and charged towards Emily and Thalien, swinging his dagger erratically towards any sound. Martin moved Emily aside with his arm and brought the assailant down with one swift motion of his sword. The man fell down, a bloody mess. His midsection had been sliced open by Martin's blade, spilling onto the grass.

The ground turned red from blood.

Martin examined the attackers, making certain no life remained in them.

Emily began shaking uncontrollably. She had never seen anyone killed before. It was gruesome. Martin looked back and saw that she was in a state of shock.

"Are you alright?" he asked.

The stream of blood from the dead bodies continued to spill onto the ground, slowly creeping towards Emily, nearly reaching her boots. She stared down at the carnage in horror.

"She is in shock," Martin spoke urgently to Thalien. "Take her over there, away from this spot, give her some water. I shall be there shortly."

Thalien nodded and put his arm around Emily's waist to guide her away from the gruesome scene. She didn't resist. She sat down against a nearby tree.

Martin went about the dreary tasks of disposing of the bodies, pulling them back under brush. He would notify the marshals once he returned to the clinic.

"Where did they come from?" Thalien asked Martin.

"They had been tracking us for about an hour and came ahead of us after we took our break," he told him. "It was not wise to alert you of their presence. You would have naturally begun to look over your shoulder. By not telling you, it allowed me the element of surprise," Martin explained.

Thalien looked back over at Emily and sighed. "That was far too much for our young companion, I'm afraid."

Martin glanced over at the girl.

"Indeed," Martin agreed.

Martin finished cleaning his blade and returned it to its sheath. He walked over to Emily and knelt beside her. She looked over at the blood on the ground and then back at Martin. Her stomach was doing flip flops.

"Are you alright?" he asked, genuinely concerned.

"I think I'm going to be sick," she confessed. She struggled to stand. Martin helped her up. Emily walked quickly behind some bushes. Martin stood alert, his eyes scanning the area. He was close enough to protect her, yet allowed her the privacy required. He could hear Emily vomiting.

Thalien walked towards her with some water. She held her stomach, feeling lightheaded.

"It's never easy," Thalien said, trying to comfort her.

Emily rinsed out her mouth and walked on wobbly legs back to where Martin stood.

"Can you continue?" Martin asked.

He examined her closely. The color had left her face and he could tell she was still very nauseous.

Emily did not immediately respond.

"Can you continue?" Martin asked again.

"I can walk," she told him weakly.

With that, Martin turned and rifled through one of their supply bags. He returned with a piece of ginger root in his hand.

"Eat this. It will help calm your stomach," he instructed. He placed the back of his hand against her forehead. She felt cold and clammy, a result of the shock. She did as he asked and took another sip of water.

"I'll be okay," she said in a faint voice.

He noticed her hands were still trembling.

"We must continue," he told her. "It is not safe to linger too long in these woods. There will certainly be others, like those," he told her, looking back over his shoulder.

She nodded.

Martin suspected they were looking for her, but kept his opinion to himself. News of the stranger would travel fast among these lands. They would be wise to quicken their pace.

Martin turned away, gathered their supplies and threw Emily's bag over his shoulder to carry it for her. He began walking down the path again.

Thalien patted her on the back and stayed glued to her side.

"I am truly sorry you had to see that, child," he told her sympathetically.

She nodded. Martin glanced back at her after a few minutes but said nothing.

Martin had just saved her life.

She let that sink in…

She wanted to thank him.

First, Thalien saved her from a dragon.

Now, Martin saved her from three attackers.

Emily felt ashamed for the way she had been treating Martin, given how much she desperately needed him now. She would be dead if it had not been for him. D.E.A.D. She understood she was doing a poor job of taking care of herself. When faced with the attacker, she froze. She did absolutely nothing to defend herself. She was utterly useless.

Meanwhile, Martin didn't hesitate.

He acted immediately.

He didn't falter.

All she managed to do was…vomit.

Wow, some hero I turned out to be, she chided herself. It was a very humbling experience for her. She didn't like feeling this vulnerable.

Maybe Martin could teach her how to defend herself? She doubted he'd be willing to teach her anything after how obnoxious she had been towards him. She was resigned to get on his better side…if he had one.

After a short while, Emily felt somewhat better. Whatever Martin had given her had certainly helped her stomach and her nerves.

Emily quickened her pace to catch up to Martin.

"Excuse me?" she said.

He looked over at her but said nothing.

"Look, I just wanted to say thank you for what you did back there. I've never seen anything like that. You saved my life…" She was looking up at him, trying to be as sincere as possible.

He looked forward and continued to walk in silence.

She sighed.

"And… I just wanted to say I'm sorry for how I treated you before. I know I can be a little obnoxious…"

Martin frowned at her but still said nothing.

"I'm trying to apologize. And, I was hoping maybe…we could start over. I was hoping maybe you could teach me how to defend myself too…so you know, I'm not so – useless," she suggested, pleading to him sincerely.

She stopped walking beside him and hung her head down in embarrassment, feeling utterly defeated and very small. Martin stopped, paused for a moment and then turned to face her.

"No one expects you to be able to defend yourself. That is why I am here," he reminded her. He looked at her thoughtfully for a moment and then spoke. "I accept your apology."

He started walking again, but then stopped and turned back to her. "I can teach you a few things. It probably would be best if you did know how to use a blade, even if it just gave you some comfort and confidence. I have no objection to that," he admitted.

Emily's face lit up. "Thank you, I mean it. Thank you so much!" she said enthusiastically.

Martin just looked at her and turned to walk again.

Thalien smiled.

A truce… finally.

He knew that Martin and Emily had more in common than either of them was aware of. He was pleased to see this gesture of goodwill between them.

Emily clapped happily at the thought of having a real knight teach her a thing or two and ran back to walk with Thalien. She smiled admiringly at Martin.

"Well, that sounds promising, yes?" Thalien concluded.

"Thalien," she asked. "How did he go from being a knight to a doctor? I mean, obviously, he's like the coolest knight ever!"

Thalien smiled at her enthusiasm, "I imagine Martin decided that he would rather heal people than to fight them."

"I can understand that," she admitted, especially after what had just happened.

She was determined to prove her worth and earn Martin's respect. Emily had written about female warriors often in her own stories. Now, she had a chance to show her own true quality. She would have to summon the courage to do what she believed in her heart she could do. She sighed heavily. She was determined not to let anyone down.

# Chapter Ten

Emily was exhausted. The hours blended into one another. The rest breaks were barely long enough for her to take a nap. The sun beating down on them was taking its toll on her. The endless daylight was not sitting well with her psyche. She resisted the urge to complain, instead she dug into her backpack, donned her aviator sunglasses and put on her blue Mount Rainier cap.

She sighed heavily.

"It burns us. It burns us," she moaned, mimicking Gollum from Tolkien's famed saga.

Martin cast a sideways glance at her but said nothing. He moved off the path and led them through the dense brush that surrounded the base of the snow-covered mountain range.

"Are we there yet?" she finally asked, her voice tinged with boredom.

No one answered her.

As they got closer to the mountains, the temperature dropped significantly. Thalien handed her a cloak to wear from one of the bags. She nodded her thanks and kept moving forward, following closely in Martin's footsteps.

She was growing far too weary of the journey and anxious to arrive at their destination. Too much daylight, she thought to herself, looking up at the rays of light cascading down upon the forest floor. It would have been nice to see a sunrise or sunset. Twilight would have been a welcoming change.

They traveled in silence. Thick clouds began to offer protection from the sun. The brush gave way to a clearing at the base of a mountain. Martin stopped walking.

"We are here," Thalien announced.

Emily stopped and looked around the clearing and then back at the woods they had just left. She saw nothing. No signs of a dwelling, no signs of this Mira. She was puzzled.

"So, Mira's just wondering aimlessly out here in the woods?" she asked, motioning to their surroundings in confusion.

Martin gave her an odd look. He shook his head no and pointed upwards. Emily stepped back and looked up towards the direction Martin was pointing.

There, on top of the mountain, a castle sat in a most unusual place, looking dangerously unstable. The mountain was wide at the bottom, but pencil thin at the top, surrounded by clouds, which is why she didn't notice it as they approached. She pressed against the base of the mountain and looked straight up. If you didn't know where to look, you would not have noticed it. The clouds provided coverage for the castle to anyone approaching.

"Gosh, that's interesting." She took off her sunglasses and cap, returning them to her bag. "How in the heck did they build that castle up there? Seriously," she asked.

No one answered her.

"When I talk, do you hear me?" she asked, tired of being ignored.

"Unfortunately, yes," Martin said sarcastically.

"Then why don't you answer me?" she asked, annoyed.

"There are so many reasons," he injected, yawning.

Emily frowned. Thalien nodded apologetically to her.

"My apologies, Emily. I am not trying to be rude. I tend to get lost in my own thoughts," Thalien told her honestly.

"It's okay," she told him. "I tend to say whatever is on my mind," she admitted.

"I never would have noticed that," Martin countered with sarcasm, taking a drink of water.

She ignored his jab and looked back up at the castle.

The castle itself looked like it was chiseled right into the mountain. It was teetering on the very top and seemed to defy gravity with an amazing balancing act. It looked like it had fallen out of the sky and haphazardly landed on the tip of a mountain.

Emily could not see a way up. It was great for keeping your enemies at bay, with your castle a mile up in the sky and hidden from view. Emily suspected that "hidden" was the operative word here.

"How do we get up there?" she asked.

"You shall see," Thalien told her casually. He pulled a horn from his weathered backpack and blew into it, making a soft whistling sound. Martin found some shade under a tree and made himself comfortable.

"What? You're just going to sit there?" she said to Martin. "We barely stopped to take a break since we left the clinic and now that we're finally here? You're napping?"

Martin completely ignored her.

She looked around nervously. From where she was standing all she could see were the smooth mountain walls without even so much as a foothold to climb upon.

Suddenly, Emily saw something dropping down on them incredibly fast. She stepped back and looked quickly at Martin, but he did not appear to be the least bit concerned.

Thalien steadied her, "It's quite alright, Emily."

She couldn't believe her eyes.

A giant winged creature, resembling a bat, landed softly nearby and eyed them curiously. It was dark in color, with large ears and wide eyes. It was much taller than Martin. It had a light covering of brown fur over its body. Emily would have run away from it had Thalien not been holding her arm, preventing her from doing so. She noticed that Martin was not interested in the creature at all.

"Hey," she called to him, "Want to give us a hand here?"

Martin raised his eyebrow, gave her a look, leaned his head back against the tree and closed his eyes.

"What the heck," Emily said with alarm.

She picked up a small rock and threw it at Martin to get his attention. Without even opening his eyes, Martin's hand shot up and caught the rock before it could hit him.

"Whoa," she said. "Nice reflexes. Now, how about getting off your butt and helping us out here. Hello? Big bat thing standing here." She looked from Martin to the creature.

Martin continued to ignore her. The creature, for its part, was standing perfectly still and posed no immediate threat. It occasionally blinked its huge eyes.

"Emily," Thalien assured her, "Do not be alarmed. He will not hurt you."

"Yeah, that's what they always say before they bite your head off. Sacrifice the little one. Is that how it goes?"

Thalien laughed, "He will not harm you."

She wasn't convinced and looked back over at Martin. "Aren't you supposed to be protecting me?"

Martin yawned and continued to ignore her.

"At least get me a large stick!" she said, backing away from the creature.

Finally, Martin responded. "Thalien, if we ask nicely, do you think he will bite her? Just to silence her?"

Thalien laughed, "No, Martin. He is not a meat eater."

"Tis a Pity," Martin said looking sternly at Emily. "Do you think he might make an exception?"

"Hey," Emily cut in, "stop talking about me in the third person like I'm not even here. Hello? I can HEAR you! Stop trying to get that thing to eat me."

"Wishful thinking on my part," he muttered under his breath and closed his eyes once again.

Emily picked up a stick from the ground and waved it frantically in front of her, "Back off, bat boy."

Thalien chuckled, "Emily, put the stick down. I can assure you, he's quite harmless. They are friendly."

The bat creature started making a cooing sound.

Emily stepped back again, frightened. "What's it doing?"

Without even opening his eyes, Martin responded.

"He's laughing at you."

Emily looked from Martin to the creature again and then back to Thalien. He nodded in agreement with Martin. The cooing continued and then stopped.

"Laughing at me?" she asked. "Fine, whatever."

Thalien raised his hands, palms upward towards the creature. He spoke in a language that Emily did not understand. The creature tilted its head slightly and fixed its gaze on Emily. Thalien said it was no danger to her, but it was really making Emily uneasy. She'd watched too many horror films in her day to casually stand there and not be reminded of giant bats carrying away villagers. Her impressionable young mind was working overtime.

The creature lowered its head and approached them. Without so much as a glance at her, it picked up Thalien and Emily in its claws and swept them upwards with incredible speed. Emily shut her eyes tightly and screamed out loud. Martin watched them disappear up the side of the mountain and then settled in for a long wait.

Emily was feeling queasy again and lightheaded due to the rapid change in altitude. She didn't open her eyes until she felt her feet resting on the ground. Her legs were a bit wobbly. Thalien put his hand out to steady her. They were set down inside of a large courtyard, Emily looked around in every direction, but all she could see were the clouds. The creature lifted back up into the air and disappeared within the cloud cover, without so much as a sound.

"There is nothing to fear here," Thalien told her.

"That's easy for you to say," Emily argued. "What was that thing?"

"Mylox. They are called mylox," he informed her, looking at her intently. "You do not have mylox in Glendale?"

"Uh no. Mostly just cats and dogs. Lots of animals, but nothing like that," she told him with relief.

He nodded at her.

"Although, my Aunt Carol had a bat in her attic one summer. I think that scarred us all for life. It was fluttering around, buzzing past us. I'll never forget the screams as we tried to get it out of her house," Emily shivered, waving her arms frantically in the air, recreating that fateful day.

Thalien grinned.

131

"It was terrifying," she told him dramatically. "I slept with a scarf around my neck for a whole month after that. You know? Bats? Vampires? Dracula. Mom wouldn't let me keep the garlic hung up in my bedroom. She said it was stinking up the entire house, but…"

Thalien raised his eyebrow in amusement.

"Yea, so I'm not a fan of bats."

"How large are the bats where you come from?" he asked, sincerely interested.

Emily held out her fingers about four inches apart and nodded her head quickly, eyes widened.

Thalien smirked. "That big?"

She realized how silly she must have sounded given the size of the creature that just brought them to the top of the mountain.

"Well, it was probably larger than that, but…"

"I see," he smiled.

Giant bats for transportation? Emily shivered as she thought of being held by the strange creature's claws. It was not something she was eager to repeat any time soon.

A mysterious hooded figure, dressed in a dark robe, appeared out of the white cloudy mist, motioning for Thalien and Emily to follow. Not a word was spoken. Emily's eyes widened.

"That's not spooky at all," she remarked, apprehensively.

"Mira awaits us," spoke Thalien ominously.

Emily gave him a weird look.

"I'm just waiting for the massive pipe organ to start playing the Phantom of the Opera theme," she added. Her eyes darted all around, searching for some fiendish ghoul.

Thalien didn't comment.

They were led down a narrow passageway. Torches lined both sides of the walls and were flickering slightly. Their guide stopped outside of two large wooden doors and stepped aside.

"Select," Thalien instructed.

"Excuse me?"

"You must select a door."

"Uh, I don't have a clue which one to pick. You pick it," she told him.

"It is not for me to decide."

"How about I just go back down to the bottom and forget about talking to Mira? This is all too spooky for me," she confessed.

Thalien sighed. "I am afraid that is impossible. This is the only way out."

Emily turned around and saw that the passageway they had just passed through was conveniently gone. Only a solid wall stood behind them now. She was standing between the wall and two massive doors. She reached out to touch the wall in case her eyes were playing tricks on her. It was definitely solid rock. When she turned back to face the doors, their guide was gone. Thalien was right. She had no choice.

"Cute," she said sarcastically.

She stepped forward to examine the doors more closely. She turned back to ask Thalien a question, but he too was gone. Emily inhaled sharply.

She was alone.

The first thing she noticed was the silence. No howling wind, no creaking wood, no sound whatsoever. She was inside an air tight and sound proof chamber.

If she screamed, no one would hear her. She looked up and saw a small opening reaching high into the sky, impossible to reach. It was the only source of light within the chamber.

She sighed deeply, trying not to panic. Her hand went up to touch the necklace around her neck. She was feeling a bit claustrophobic. Her anxiety level was rising. She closed her eyes quickly, slowed her breath, trying to steady her nerves.

"This is so not cool," she said to herself.

She faced the doors, not knowing which one to select. Above the doors was a stone tablet with a message carved into it. She stepped forward to get a better look, standing on her tippy toes, straining to see it clearly.

There were instructions of some kind.

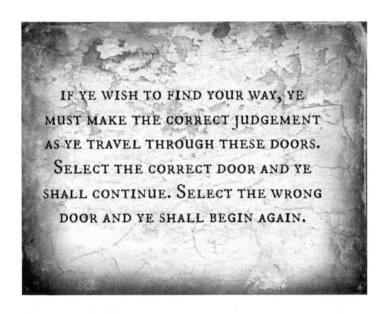

IF YE WISH TO FIND YOUR WAY, YE
MUST MAKE THE CORRECT JUDGEMENT
AS YE TRAVEL THROUGH THESE DOORS.
SELECT THE CORRECT DOOR AND YE
SHALL CONTINUE. SELECT THE WRONG
DOOR AND YE SHALL BEGIN AGAIN.

Underneath the larger tablet a smaller one said:

BE WARNED:
SIGNS MAY BE TRUE OR FALSE.

Emily frowned and read the messages again carefully. With some effort, she opened the heavy door on the left and nearly fell through it. She caught herself just in time. There was nothing on the other side of the door, except howling wind and an imaginary express elevator to the ground. Splat! There was not even a ledge to stand on. She couldn't even see the ground below.

"Holy moly," she said softly. She stepped back and closed the door tightly. With no other choice, she pulled the other door with both hands. It creaked loudly in protest. It opened into another chamber, almost identical to the one she had just been standing in. She faced two doors again.

I don't like this one bit, she thought to herself.

Unsure of what to expect, she carefully approached the next set of doors, looking for the clue. She read the stone tablet and it dawned on her that she was familiar with the pattern of questions.

"I know this," she grinned. "This is Mordin's Maze. I can do this." She smiled to herself, remembering the series of logic equations her mother had taught her a long time ago. She relaxed a bit. Mordin's Maze was a series of logic puzzles used to teach deductive and inductive reasoning skills. She concentrated to recall the details. Questions were meant to be deceiving. With this in mind, she examined the next set of clues.

"Think, think, think," Emily said out loud.

A. ONLY ONE OF THESE SIGNS IS FALSE.
B. THIS IS THE DOOR YOU MUST GO THROUGH.

Which door should she go through? Mira must like challenging her guests. Think, Emily urged herself. There was no way to prove that the first statement was not correct, so the second statement had to be false. She decided that door "A" was the correct choice. She slowly opened the door to find two more doors. Emily sighed with relief. She had made the right choice. She walked up to the next set of doors and studied the sign carefully.

A. THESE SIGNS ARE BOTH FALSE.
B. THIS IS THE WAY TO GO.

Mordin's Maze. Emily sighed. Statement "A" must be false. For it to be true, it would be contradicting itself. Statement "B" must be true. Emily turned the door handle and heard a loud creaking noise as she slowly pushed it open.

She must have made the correct choice because she stepped into another chamber. This time the room contained three doors and three statements. She studied them carefully.

A. EXACTLY TWO OF THESE STATEMENTS ARE FALSE.
B. THIS IS THE DOOR TO GO THROUGH.
C. ENTER THE NEXT ROOM THROUGH THIS DOOR.

Emily considered the sign for a moment, trying to recall the logic sequence required to successfully navigate through Mordin's Maze. She paced around the small space trying to figure out the answer.

If statement "B" was correct and statement "C" was false, then this would mean that statement "A" is also false, which is a contradiction.

If statement "C" is correct, then statement "B" is false. Again, meaning that statement "A" is a contradiction. She reasoned that statement "A" must be the correct choice.

Emily opened the door with the letter "A" above it. She entered another chamber. This time with four doors inside of it. Four doors...another riddle.

A. EXACTLY TWO OF THESE STATEMENTS ARE TRUE.
B. GO THIS WAY.
C. THIS IS NOT THE DOOR TO GO THROUGH.
D. DOOR B IS NOT THE WAY TO GO.

Emily spoke out loud.

"Okay. I assume statement "A" is true. If so, statements "B" and "D" disagree with one another. Statement "C" must also be false. That would make statement "D" true…"

She circled the room weighing all her options. She stood in front of the signs again, sighed heavily and concentrated.

"But, if I assume statement "A" is false, statements "B" and "D" disagree and if "A" is false that would mean that there is another false statement. "C" would be false too. That would make statement "D" true. Either way that makes statement "C" false. If statement "C" is false then that's the door I need to go through," she deduced.

With a slight pull, door "C" opened into a large expansive chamber, sparsely furnished. An elderly woman with unkept hair sat in a large chair with a high back. She was holding a large clear goblet filled with a light pink substance and smiled at Emily with great amusement. Thalien stood beside the woman. Emily stood in the doorway and hesitated.

"Come in, child," the woman said cheerfully. "Let me take a look at you."

Emily stepped into the chamber, closed the door quietly behind her and walked across the room. Her footsteps echoed within the large room. Emily looked at Thalien and he smiled approvingly at her.

"Did you enjoy my little game?" the woman asked.

"Yes, it kind of gave me a headache but yes," Emily admitted.

The woman laughed loudly and slapped her hand on her thigh. "You did remarkably well for one so young. Most impressive. Glad we did not have to scrape you off the ground!" she chuckled. She studied Emily up and down, scrutinizing her carefully. Finally, the woman nodded in approval. "Lovely, quite lovely," she concluded.

"Are you Mira?" Emily asked.

"I am. Pleasure to meet you. I've been expecting you."

Mira stretched out a thin hand, which Emily took gently.

Mira had kind, gentle eyes. She smiled warmly, patting the back of Emily's hand. Mira held Emily's gaze, looking deeply into her eyes. She seemed to be reading Emily's every thought and emotion. It made Emily somewhat uneasy. She felt a weird sensation pass through her body, a powerful energy, but not threatening in anyway.

Mira continued to hold Emily's hand and lowered her head. She appeared to be meditating. Emily started to feel faint from the powerful energy coursing through her body. Mira suddenly let go of her hand and touched Emily's necklace. She turned it over to examine both sides and stared at it for the longest time before finally letting go. Mira sank back in her chair.

"I have not seen this necklace for a very long time," Mira sighed heavily. "Please sit down, child."

Emily looked around, but there was only one chair in the entire room and Mira was sitting in it. Emily shrugged and sat down on the floor in front of Mira. Thalien smirked. She was anxious to learn from Mira and hoped she would finally find out what was going on. Mira made Emily feel completely at ease.

"We have a lot to discuss, do we not?" Mira told her.

"Yes," Emily agreed.

"Let us get started then. Ask anything you wish, and I will do my best to answer," she said. Mira waved her hand slightly to the side and a dark robed figure stepped towards Emily carrying a tray of fruit and refreshments. It startled Emily momentarily because there was no robed figure in the room two seconds ago.

"Do things have a habit of just popping in and out around here?" she asked curiously.

"Indeed, they do," Mira grinned and pointed in the direction of the door Emily had recently stepped through. Emily looked over her shoulder and saw that the door was no longer there.

"Sweet," Emily said. "Maybe you can teach me how to do that one day."

Mira laughed warmly and motioned to the tray seated next to Emily. "Please help yourself, dear. You have had a long journey. Longer than you realize…"

Emily picked up the stone cup and sipped. It was fruit juice, she concluded, and drank it down easily.

"Thank you," she told Mira.

"You are most welcome," Mira said, studying Emily. She grinned occasionally, exchanging a knowing glance with Thalien that only the two of them understood.

"You may begin," Mira said casually.

"Where am I?" Emily asked first.

"Aquila. Presently at my castle…"

"I know that, I mean…" Emily put her head in her hands in frustration.

Mira smiled again, "It is not so much where…as when."

Emily lifted her head. "What does that mean?"

"What year is it in…" Mira looked up at Thalien.

He leaned in and whispered to her softly, "Glendale."

"Glendale?" Mira repeated.

Emily looked at them both curiously, "It's 2008."

Mira nodded. "The 21$^{st}$ century, interesting time. Here on Aquila, it is the year 3059, my dear."

Emily's mouth dropped open. She was taken aback by this revelation. She didn't even know how to respond. She stared at them both, allowing herself time to gather her thoughts.

"How is that even possible?" she asked, stunned.

Mira thought carefully. "I will tell you all I know and hopefully we can sort out the answers together. I believe we have a lot to learn from each other. Does that satisfy you?" she asked.

"Yes," Emily agreed.

Mira took a long breath, choosing her words carefully.

"Merrick and Isabeau is where your story begins, my dear. Who gave you that necklace?" she asked.

"It was passed down to me from my grandmother."

"What did your grandmother look like in her youth?" Mira asked.

"Well, I've seen pictures of her when she was younger. She looked a lot like me, I suppose. Tall, thin, reddish blonde hair and green eyes…Why?"

139

Mira nodded. "Isabeau was lost to us in a terrible accident, a drowning. When Merrick lost her, he was overcome with grief. He no longer attended to the affairs of his kingdom. He lost interest in life itself. He completely succumbed to his despair. He neglected his rule, neglected his family. Self-pity and malice replaced his once noble demeanor. Merrick wallowed in hatred and bitterness. With Isabeau gone, he gave up all hope."

Emily lowered her head. She had seen how much they loved one another. It was heartbreaking to hear what had become of them. "I had a vision of that day," she told Mira.

"Tell me what you saw," Mira urged.

"I was there at the castle," she told Mira, "I saw Martin as a young boy. It was a celebration. Merrick and Isabeau were there. They were very much in love," Emily shared, reflecting on what she witnessed. "I saw them walking together with their little baby." Emily looked up at Thalien and then back to Mira. She tried to remember every detail.

"What is it, dear?"

"What happened to that little baby?" Emily asked urgently.

Mira and Thalien looked at one another. Mira stood and slowly walked around the room. She stopped and opened a small wooden chest, removing a large oval crystal.

"What happened to the baby?" Emily asked again.

Mira came to where Emily was seated.

"This is where the story becomes even more tragic," Mira said gravely. "Merrick was so consumed by his grief that he rejected the infant, wanting nothing further to do with her. To him, the baby was a constant reminder of what he had lost. His baby daughter, with the delicate features of his beloved wife. Martin's little sister…"

Mira gave Emily a moment to process this information before continuing. Emily thought of young Martin and his family, how happy they seemed in that moment. Her heart sank.

"Martin did not fare much better. His father's affections turned cold, distant and even violent. The once happy little boy became sullen, withdrawn and angry. His hatred for his own

140

father sustained him. Isabeau was not the only one that died that afternoon. With her passing, the entire family was lost. Merrick's inability to cope with her death cost him everything. He lost his wife and turned away from his children. His children lost their parents and each other, as well as the stability and security of their home," Mira said sadly, as she turned away from Emily.

"The baby?" Emily asked again.

Mira turned back to face Emily, raised the crystal in the air and waved her hand over it, causing it to glow a brilliant blue.

"You want to know what happened to the baby girl?"

"Yes, please," Emily responded.

"I will show you. Take my hand…"

Emily stood and took Mira's hand. The crystal filled the entire room with a brilliant pale blue light. Emily had the sensation that she was floating. The room melted around them. Flashes of images raced by, sounds that were barely audible screamed past. The effect was maddening. She could no longer feel the floor beneath her feet. Emily lost consciousness and awoke to find herself standing within Merrick's castle once again.

Merrick was hunched over a wooden table. The room was lit by a single candle casting an eerie shadow over his large frame. Heavy draperies covered the windows. Every single window within the castle had been boarded up, per Merrick's specific instructions. He would not allow even a sliver of sunlight to penetrate the castle since Isabeau's death, casting every inch of space into darkness.

Merrick had turned the entire castle into a crypt.

Young Martin stood in the doorway holding the hand of a small girl with flaming red hair and chubby cheeks, tears quietly streaming down her face. She was hiding shyly behind her brother. Their father was oblivious to their presence. Martin turned and left the doorway with his baby sister in tow.

Emily watched for several minutes. The scene faded and was replaced by two hooded figures in dark robes, slowly making their way through the dimly lit corridors.

She followed them up a long staircase. One stopped momentarily and looked over his shoulder directly at Emily. They did not see her. They only sensed a presence. She was being protected by Mira's magic.

They entered a bed chamber where the little girl was sleeping. They picked up Merrick's baby daughter, covering her mouth to muffle her cries. They were not aware that young Martin slept on the chaise lounge near his sister's bed, keeping watch over her. His sister's muffled cries woke him instantly. He leapt to his feet, rushing to help his sister.

His sister's tiny arms reached out for Martin to no avail. The intruder rushed the small child out of the room, disappearing down the staircase. Martin tried desperately to fight off the second intruder and reach his sister. He kicked and clawed with every ounce of strength he could muster.

Martin cried out for help, but none came. The attacker struck the boy hard across the face and threw him violently across the room. Martin crashed against a woodpile and moaned in pain, but immediately got back to his feet, racing for the door. The intruder slammed the chamber door shut quickly, locking Martin inside.

Emily watched in horror as Martin ran to the window and threw open the drapery, leaning out, screaming for help. The room was several stories high and there was no way out. Martin watched helplessly as the intruders below shoved his sister into a carriage, kicking up dust behind their horses as they raced away.

He searched the room for something to free himself with and grabbed the iron fire poker, hitting the door repeatedly. He beat on the door for hours until his hands were a bloody mess. A servant finally unlocked the door after Martin's wailing had subsided. Martin immediately ran to his father's bed chamber, demanding they search for the little girl. He pulled at his father, begging and pleading for some response. Merrick merely pushed the boy away and turned his back further to his young son.

"Leave me alone," Merrick ordered in an angry voice.

Martin pounded his bloody fists on his father's back and screamed, with tears streaking his face.

"I hate you! I hate you!" he cried, over and over again.

Merrick shoved the boy away, knocking Martin to the floor, He was emotionless, unmoved by his son's anguish. Merrick's heart was a deep void where once love existed.

Emily felt tears on her own face. She was crying too. What she had witnessed was absolutely heartbreaking. She understood Martin's pain and anguish. Martin lost his mother to treachery. He lost his father to despair. He lost his baby sister to abduction right before his very eyes, despite his best efforts to save her.

What fate awaited the little girl? Emily wiped tears from her eyes. She was suddenly afraid to find out. The room filled with brilliant blue light again and Mira was standing next to her once more. They were instantly back in Mira's room at the castle on top of the mountain. Emily sniffled and wiped more tears from her eyes.

"Did Martin ever find the little girl?" she asked tearfully.

Mira lowered her head sadly. "No, he did not. He searched for years, until he lost all hope of ever finding her. Then, he simply gave up. Martin has always blamed himself for what happened to the little girl. He believed that if only he had been stronger, he could have fought off her abductors and saved her..."

"But, that's not true...He was such a young boy and he tried so hard. It's not his fault at all," Emily injected. "There was nothing he could do," she added sadly.

Mira sighed. "Try convincing him of that. He has punished himself his entire life for not being able to protect his baby sister. With her disappearance, Martin was truly alone. He never forgave himself for being unable to find her. I am sure the task to protect you has struck a little too close to the heart with him..."

Emily hadn't thought of that, but she agreed.

"Why did they take her?" she asked.

"Merrick could no longer stand the site of her..."

"What did he do with the baby girl?" Emily asked mortified.

"Merrick only saw Isabeau when he cast his gaze upon his daughter. It was unbearable. She was a constant reminder of what

143

he had lost. An evil sorceress from the dark side fed upon his grief and offered to ease Merrick's pain, in exchange for the girl."

"Why would she want the little girl?"

"Because she herself was barren. She hated the love Merrick had for Isabeau. Jealousy. Resentment. What better way to extract revenge on one you hate than to stab at their child, born from love? Rip out the very heart of the family. Having the child was her prize. Merrick made a deal that would ease his suffering, or so he thought..." Mira explained.

"What deal?" Emily wanted to know.

"She cast a spell on him – one to make him forget. That is what he asked of the sorceress," Mira told her, as the sadness welled up in her eyes. "A spell to forget Isabeau, Martin and his daughter. Forget everything about who he was...All the love he once had in his heart was lost..."

Emily didn't know what to say. She had seen the love he had for his family. Merrick was eaten away by grief and allowed the sorceress to erase his memories. He abandoned his children in every possible way, as if they never existed at all. He turned his back on everything he was loved.

It was unthinkable and unimaginable.

The deep sense of betrayal Martin must have felt, to go from being loved to being unwanted. She couldn't even fathom that level of pain. She felt terrible for giving him such a hard time, after what he'd been through in his life. Seeing his bloody fists pounding on the heavy door for hours, trying to save his baby sister? Gut wrenching. She had completely misjudged Martin. She finally turned to face Mira again.

"What happened to the baby girl?" she asked sadly, deeply troubled by what she had just learned.

Mira looked away. "This will not be pleasant. Prepare yourself. You must see this to fully understand..."

Emily swallowed hard, summoning her courage.

"Show me," Emily said urgently, and with those words the world melted into nothingness once more.

# Chapter Eleven

The stench of excrement and vomit filled the air. Emily gagged and covered her mouth. She appeared to be in a series of underground caves, full of metal cages, dark and dingy. The cages were full of children, filthy and starving. Emily's stomach heaved from the deplorable living conditions the children were subjected to.

Stalactites and stalagmites dominated the interior. Fire pits were scattered throughout the winding passageways. Water dripped from the cave ceiling. Children had their mouths open, desperately trying to catch a few drops of moisture. Emily's stomach was churning. The cages were all bound together to form a star, a pentagram, part of some ritualistic nightmare in a world gone mad.

Time was running out for these children. Hundreds of voices called her name. She turned in circles, looking everywhere, but could not figure out where the voices were coming from. She walked up and down the rows of cages filled with children. Their cries and moans tore at her heart. Several of the children in the cages were either passed out from dehydration or already dead. It was a sickening sight.

In the glow of the darkness, the sounds around her were chilling. The large cavern was joined by smaller caves. In one close to her, Emily saw corpses stacked high. Her stomach heaved at the horrific sight. She threw her hand over her mouth to prevent herself from vomiting again.

Who would do such a thing? It was pointless violence, a silent tomb. There was a red river of blood flowing through the cave. A deep low growl came from within the dark cavern. It terrified Emily but she came here for answers. What could make such an awful noise? Emily peered into the darkness, letting her eyes adjust. She slowly crept inside. Her back hugged the wall for protection.

She felt somewhat secure that whatever was inside could not see her. She heard heavy jaws crunching on what she feared were human remains. Dark red piercing eyes from far back in the cave looked straight at her, but she couldn't make out the creature's form. Whatever it was? It was massive. It was feeding off the flesh of the dead. Someone had summoned this hideous beast.

It stopped crunching for a moment and shifted its position, spitting out morsels of food. Embers from a nearby firepit erupted. The flames illuminated the beast within the cavern. It sniffed twice in the air. Emily gasped. It was a monstrous creature. It resembled a dragon but it was much larger than the one she had encountered on the road earlier.

It was hideous. It had a long neck, like a serpent. Its body was covered with deadly spikes. Spiral horns protruded from the top of its head. The only vulnerable spots Emily could see were its underbelly and throat. From her vantage point, it looked like the creature had two sets of jaws – an inner jaw, set further back with razor sharp teeth to pull its prey deep into its throat, and an outer jaw to close on its prey, much like that of a moray eel.

This was not a dragon from a delightful childhood fairytale. No, this was a beast from your worst nightmare – a planet killer, devouring all in its path. It was ferocious, deadly and the embodiment of evil. Emily had seen nothing thus far in her travels on Aquila that could even remotely defeat this creature.

It snapped its jaws and looked directly at her. It reeked of rotted flesh and death. She cringed when it moved its head slowly toward her. Did it know she was there? It must have sensed her presence because it seemed to be tracking her movements within the dark cave.

Frightened, she stepped quickly back into the larger cavern where the children were imprisoned. They were terrified beyond measure. Some were praying softly for the nightmare to end. Others stared with vacant eyes resigned to their fate. A few held on to each other, seeking comfort.

Was Martin's sister in this horrific place? Emily began searching frantically from cage to cage. The children were covered in filth, barely recognizable. Emily checked each cage, trying to pull on the locks to free the children, but her hands passed right through the bars. She had no true physical form in this vision.

Finally, she came upon a cage filled with eight children crammed inside. A little girl was curled up in a ball, staring out. She had matted red hair, sad green eyes, and blood smeared on her face. Emily was drawn to her immediately. She was sure it was Martin's sister.

The little girl was shivering uncontrollably from cold and fear. Emily reached into the cage to touch the little girl, but she could not.

She put her face close to Martin's little sister and said, "I'm going to get you out of here. All of you. I don't know how, but I will. I swear," Emily said with conviction.

Tears ran down Emily's face. She felt rage building deep within herself.

In that moment, the little girl lifted her head and looked directly at Emily. Their eyes locked. Emily was shocked. She hadn't noticed how much she and the little girl looked alike, until now.

"Can you hear me? Can you see me?" she asked the little girl. The small child did not respond. She only kept looking right into Emily's eyes. The sadness in those green eyes was more than Emily could stand.

"I'm so sorry," Emily cried.

The child continued to look into Emily's eyes, connecting to her on some subconscious level. Emily began to tremble. The sounds, the smells and the sights were horrific. The sense of helplessness she felt in that moment was overwhelming. Emily had never felt this kind of anger before. The pain and cruelty being inflicted on these children was depraved…and for what?

The empowerment of an evil sorceress? What had Mira said? Jealousy? Revenge? Emily knew she wanted to help defeat the evil witch that was behind all this unspeakable horror.

A flood of thoughts and emotions raced through her mind. This was going to stop. The sorceress was already hunting her. That much she gathered from the attack in her vision and the attack in the woods with Martin.

Well, then maybe, Emily should take the fight to her.

End it all now. Strike first. She wouldn't expect that, right?

Emily couldn't take her eyes off the little girl. Slowly, the child pointed, as if it hurt to even move her hand.

"What is it? Can you see me?" Emily was excited. "What are you pointing at?"

The child said nothing but continued to point. Emily looked down. The necklace! The child was staring at the necklace. She could see it! She recognized it! It belonged to her mother. She was a baby when her mother died, but she was clearly pointing at the necklace. Was her bond so strong to it that she could see it, sense it, feel it – even here in this place? Emily was stunned.

The little girl closed her hand again and curled back into a ball. There were so many suffering children. So many dead, so many more awaiting their hopeless fate.

"I'm going to stop all of this. I promise you," she said. Emily reached into the cage to try and wipe the grime off the little girl's face, but her hand only passed through. This madness had to end.

Emily felt herself floating again. She returned to the room full of brilliant blue light. She fell to her knees, buried her head in her hands and started crying, overcome by the horror of it all. Mira and Thalien watched her somberly in silence.

"Who could do such a thing?" Emily asked through tears.

Mira sighed deeply.

"The sorceress, Miranda…my sister."

Emily lifted her head, looking at Mira in disbelief. "Your sister?"

Mira nodded sadly. Emily wiped tears from her face. She stood up with determination.

"I'm going to stop her," she said defiantly.

Mira nodded knowingly at Emily. "Indeed, you just might. When the elders of Aquila and I learned of the child's abduction, we searched all over for her, as did Martin. She was of noble birth and more than that, she was the bloodline that guards the keystone, as was her mother."

"Martin guards the keystone then too?" Emily asked.

"No," Mira corrected. "This is an honor reserved only for females of the bloodline. Men have proven their unworthiness of this task. They are too quick to anger and take too long to forgive. The keystone is an instrument of peace – in the right hands. Or an instrument of destruction in the wrong ones. The keystone has been passed down through Isabeau's bloodline since the beginning of recorded knowledge. Miranda knew this when she took the child. It was a deliberate attempt to end the bloodline."

"…and murder Isabeau," Emily injected.

"Murder? What is this you say?"

"I can't be sure if it was Miranda, but I saw someone hit Isabeau on the back of the head and push her into the water. It wasn't an accident," Emily said with absolute certainty.

A look of profound sorrow crossed Mira's face. Her hands began to tremble. "Then this is even more sinister than we imagined. Murder? Miranda was surely behind it. She is the only one who stood to gain from this tragic plot."

"What was that thing I saw in the cave? It was different from the other one I saw," Emily asked.

"The worst one imaginable, summoned by black magic. Larger than all others and lives for one purpose only – to devour all. Miranda resurrected the hideous beast to use in her campaign to rule the world and she is its master," Mira said with disgust.

"What about the other dragons on Aquila? Could they fight it?" Emily asked.

"It would take a force of dragons the likes of which Aquila has not seen for several lifetimes," she explained to Emily.

"I saw this monster…eating…children. I mean, I heard him crunching on bones. I saw a cave full of bodies and a river of blood. It was…" she searched for the right words, "I can't even describe how horrific it was. It needs to be stopped. Someone

149

has to ask the other dragons to help," she looked at Thalien. "You told me that some of them lived in peace with men, so ask them."

Mira and Thalien looked at one another solemnly.

"That is exactly what you must do, Emily," Mira told her.

"Wait, me?"

"You will have to summon the Council of Dragons and seek their aid," Mira explained.

"Um…why me?"

Mira pointed to the necklace resting around Emily's neck. "They will listen to you. You have the keystone. They will know you are of the bloodline."

Mira let her words sink in. Emily paced around the room.

"Well, there's been a mistake. I'm not from here. I already told you that," she reminded them.

Mira interrupted her. "The keystone brought you here. It was time. You cannot deny your place in all of this or your destiny, Emily. Whether or not you believe it, the keystone knows exactly who you are and the Council of Dragons will know as well."

Emily shook her head no. Her destiny was to go back home, finish her homework, take out the trash…

"I'm all for stopping the sorceress and that monster she keeps as a pet, but…," she told them. Her thoughts raced.

Mira sighed.

"My Grandma always said, '*Do something. Lead, follow or get out of the way.*' I'm a get out of the way kinda girl. I will help, I will cheer, I will do everything I possibly can, but I'm not that person. I'm not a hero," Emily added. She was talking more to herself than to Mira and Thalien.

"Didn't you promise the little girl you would stop all of this?" Mira reminded her.

Emily blinked hard. "Yea, but I was in the moment. I don't have a clue how to stop any of this! I read books. I play video games. I fight imaginary dragons in the woods behind my house, not real ones. That's who I am…" Her voice trailed off and she looked away.

The burden of responsibility was rearing its ugly head and Emily was trying to grapple with it. Self-doubt was her new best friend and she hated herself for it. It made her feel…cowardly. Emily looked from Mira to Thalien. She pleaded with him.

"Tell her, Thalien. I totally freaked out at that bat thing and was almost eaten by a dragon. And, Martin had to kill people. I threw up at the sight of blood. All those children in the caves? It's not like movies or books. I can't do this. It's not my destiny."

Mira interrupted her again. "Oh, but it is, and you must."

"I'm twelve!" Emily said defensively.

Thalien corrected her, "Almost thirteen."

She shot him a look, "That's not helping, Thalien."

Mira sighed, "Argue for your limitations and they become yours. It is too late to turn back now. Their search will lead them directly to your own front door, I am afraid. See for yourself, my dear."

Mira waved her hand over the crystal again and the room turned bright blue and melted away before Emily's eyes.

~~~~~~~~~~~~~~~~~~~~~~~

She looked around and gasped.

Emily was back home. Her sister's bike was leaning against the garage door. The neighbor's kids were playing outside. Dogs were barking. The ice cream truck drove past with its annoying "Pop Goes the Weasel" music churning out like a mechanical Jack in the Box. Teenagers were playing basketball across the street. Emily could hear a lawnmower nearby.

Everything seemed normal.

She walked to the front of her house, but stopped immediately when she saw three figures, fully dressed in black, emerging from the shadows. They snuck up the front porch steps and forced open the lock. They entered Emily's house, waiting to ambush her family. Emily saw her family minivan coming down the street and pull into the driveway. She ran to the front of the house and yelled out, warning her family, but no one could see or hear her.

Emily saw her little sister run up to the front porch, grab the doorknob and opened the door. Her mother commented to her father that she must have left the front door unlocked. Emily waved her arms frantically, screaming at her sister to close the door. Her sister heard no such warning. Sarah walked straight into the house, followed by her parents. The intruders were waiting. They pushed the front door closed behind them. Emily could hear furniture crashing and people yelling. One of the neighbors looked over, heard the screaming, and ran back into their house presumably to call 911, but it would be over before the police arrived.

Emily ran to the front windows to look inside. She saw her mother struggling to free herself from an intruder, defensive wounds on her hand. Her mother managed to pull off her assailant's hood and Emily got a good look. It was a female, much to her surprise, with long dark hair and a scar running up the side of her cheek. Emily watched in horror, committing the female assailant's face to memory.

Her younger sister, Sarah, was lifeless on the kitchen floor. Emily screamed helplessly. The other two intruders fought with her father. It was not long before they overpowered him. It was quick and brutal. Emily watched helplessly as her family was slaughtered by Miranda's raiders.

Once they finished off her family, the intruders searched frantically within the house. They were looking for her. They had chased across time to find her. They thought nothing of killing her family in the process.

Emily collapsed to the ground on her front lawn. There was a flurry of activity as the police arrived at her home. No intruders were found. They had already returned to where they came from. Only the bodies of her family were found, along with a ransacked house. They had been looking for the keystone and for Emily.

Emily saw the scene dissolve in front of her eyes. She once again found herself sitting on the floor in front of Mira and

Thalien. This time she did not speak to them at all. Emily just stared at the floor, trembling.

Mira waited a few moments and then spoke. "This is one possible outcome, Emily. Miranda will not quit, even if you do. She will not let you walk away from this now. If we know you are here, it will not be long before she does as well. She may already be alerted to your arrival. She has spies everywhere. She will stop at nothing to obtain the keystone and kill anyone that gets in her way," Mira said softly.

Emily sniffled and wiped her eyes. She'd been on an emotional rollercoaster since she crawled out from under the brush and first encountered Martin on the path. She lifted her head and looked at Mira. Emily's face was full of concern and her eyes were swelling with tears. She was unsure and scared.

"So, if I do this – stop her and that thing – then my family will be safe?" she asked, frightened.

"I hope so," Mira said honestly.

Emily lowered her head. "I feel sick."

Thalien stepped forward to comfort the young girl, but Mira put up a hand to stop him. Emily needed to come to this realization on her own, as difficult as it may be. It was no time to coddle her. This was a choice that only Emily could make. Mira understood this and cast a motherly glance at Thalien. He nodded, backing away.

"I warned you that it would be unpleasant," Mira added.

Emily sighed deeply, "So the little girl died?"

"No, she did not."

"Then, what?" Emily asked with renewed hope.

"We have our own spies in Miranda's inner sanctum. We began to hear rumors of her intent and of the beast she had awakened. When we received word of the children being held captive, we sent several of our bravest knights into the caves to find the girl and rescue the other children. We had cargo vessels in the river nearby to ferry them to safety. The knights had to fight their way in. For the most part, we were successful. We

153

saved many children that day. I am sorry to say that we could not save them all," she said sadly, mourning the loss of young lives.

"Martin's sister?"

Mira continued, "Victoria – her name was Victoria Rose. Does that name sound familiar?"

Emily's eyes widened and she sat up straight.

"Yes, my grandma's name was Victoria Rose."

"It became obvious that Miranda planned on ending the bloodline of the keystone. The little girl was no longer safe on Aquila, nor was the keystone. With it, Miranda could punch a hole in any world, causing one to spill onto another. She has already been using her black magic to weaken the mist wall that separates the light from dark," Thalien added.

Mira nodded. "It was agreed upon that the child would have to be sent away. No one was to know of this, not even Martin. Miranda uses her powers to corrupt the minds of men. She could have easily learned of our plans. A young seeker was chosen to care for her. Alexsiar, one of our most trusted dragons, took the child and the seeker deep into the protection of the mountains, where they awaited word from us."

Mira sighed, considering her words. "It had never been done before. But with the help of the keystone, we were able to send them back in time and far away from here. The keystone went with her to be protected by the young girl and her offspring. Only when called upon would the girl be told her true identity. A spell was cast upon the child to make her forget the horror she had known here. The only memory to remain was the knowledge that the necklace was of utmost importance and that she was to pass it down from mother to daughter in her bloodline."

"Never been done before? Then how do they plan on going back to kill my family?"

"To travel through time is strictly forbidden – to alter a timeline – well, the ripples alone could have devastating consequences. We only did so as a last resort. Miranda does not feel the need to follow any rules. It is of no consequence to her what damage she may cause," Mira admitted.

"So, you sent the little girl away and Martin didn't even know she was still alive?" she asked.

"Yes, we had no other choice. We had to protect the keystone and the child. The keystone was recovered from the river by one of our water horses and kept hidden until it was sent back with the girl, far from the grasp of Miranda."

After what she had experienced in the cave, she understood the necessity for such drastic measures. Emily knew in her heart that they had made the right decision, even though she felt sorry for Martin and the girl for what had become of their family.

"So, you're saying that my grandmother was Isabeau and Merrick's daughter? Right? That same sad little girl in the cage? That was my grandma?" she asked in disbelief.

"That is exactly what I am saying," Mira confirmed.

Emily's eyes welled up with tears. She always had these vivid dreams but could not see what was right in front of her.

"But wait – how can that be? Martin is the older brother – Victoria was my grandma. The age…"

Mira interrupted her. "Time passes much slower on Aquila than on your world. Doctor Pernell, whom you have met, is nearly three hundred of your earth years old."

Emily was surprised.

"I myself have lived for over a thousand of your earth years," Mira admitted.

"Wow… you look good for someone that is over a thousand years old," Emily pointed out.

"It was prophesized that Isabeau's bloodline would return to Aquila when called upon by the keystone. Miranda is close to harnessing enough power to bring down the mist wall. She would then be free to spread her terror beyond our world," Mira said.

"I don't understand," Emily admitted.

"Emily, the keystone sees and knows all. All the wisdom, knowledge, foresight and power were placed in the creation of that jewel around your neck. Its energy connects all worlds and all times. It was thought to be lost for a very long time, but it was merely hidden."

Emily touched her necklace. She was profoundly aware of its importance. She now knew that it wielded power that could change the course of this world and others.

"Can Miranda be stopped?" she asked, listening intently.

"Miranda is powerful, more powerful than I. She is so close to breaking through the binding spell that contains her. When that happens, she and her evil will creep across Aquila, blackening the land and darkening the skies. All in her path will fall prey to her hatred and cruelty," Mira revealed.

Emily didn't like the sound of that one bit.

"Miranda craves mayhem and discord. She takes great pleasure in inflicting pain, especially on men and children. It will take all of our combined efforts to defeat her. Merrick serves her now and he is a brilliant military strategist. Miranda uses many seekers to hunt down and eliminate anyone that she deems as a threat. She slaughters anyone she thinks could be remotely linked to Isabeau. Many innocent lives have been lost. You have seen the atrocities yourself," said Mira sadly.

Emily nodded.

The cages.

The children.

The bodies.

The blood.

The monster.

She would have those images forever seared into her memory. She also remembered the face of the woman that would murder her mother, the one with the scar.

"The keystone brought you here to stop this," Mira continued passionately. "You must defeat her before she destroys all of us – before all hope is lost. Stop her before we are swallowed by her world of darkness."

Emily listened carefully to every word Mira spoke. She had seen so much already. Her necklace was the keystone. She had always felt it was special and magical, ever since it was given to her by her grandmother. It was her most prized possession.

Mira explained its significance to Emily. The bearer could use the keystone to move back and forth in time and place. Mira also told Emily of the necklace's ability to bend creatures to its will or to set them free.

"If Isabeau is my great grandmother? And, if my grandma is Martin's sister? That means Martin and I are actually related," Emily stated more to herself than to the others.

"You most certainly are," Mira confirmed.

"Does he know this?" Emily asked.

"Not exactly, no."

"Oh boy, he's not going to like this one bit," Emily grinned.

Thalien smirked. He understood all too well the animosity that existed between Martin and Emily. They were both stubborn and strong willed, from very different worlds, clashing together.

To Thalien – Martin and Emily were two sides of the same coin. Discovering that Martin and Emily were in fact related made perfect sense. He had every confidence in her. Emily was different than anyone he had ever met. He believed she would breathe new life into Aquila. That notion was immensely refreshing to Thalien. He was honored that she was his charge.

"I believe that during your time with me that you have come to understand Martin a great deal, am I correct?" Mira asked.

"Yes," Emily nodded in agreement.

"Good," Mira nodded.

"But," Emily's voice trailed off.

"But what, dear?" Mira asked.

"What if I fail?" Emily turned her eyes up to both of them.

"You won't," Mira said confidently.

"I can't do this alone," Emily said softly, feeling unsure.

"You won't be alone," Mira assured her.

Emily looked down.

"Martin hates me," she admitted.

"He doesn't hate you," Thalien disagreed.

Emily looked at Thalien. "You were there. I kept poking him. He must think I'm a total brat. Oh, he definitely hates me. I made sure of that."

"He doesn't understand you. There is a difference," Thalien pointed out.

She frowned at him.

"Emily, listen to me," Mira said. She took Emily's hands within her own and looked deeply into her eyes.

"Yes?" Emily asked.

"Find a way to his heart and he will always follow you," Mira spoke softly with such tenderness and warmth that Emily felt a calmness sweep over her.

Emily met her gaze and held it.

"How?" she asked, with such innocence that both Mira and Thalien smiled.

"I believe the way will reveal itself to you," Mira replied.

Emily nodded thoughtfully.

"You are the protector of the keystone and with that comes great responsibility. You must summon the Council of Dragons to do your bidding. You must prevent the mist wall from collapsing. You must stop Miranda…" Mira's voice echoed within the chamber.

"Oh, is that all?" Emily said.

Thalien winked at her.

# Part III

## Defy Not the Heart

*Nothing is more dear to men than their own suffering...*
*They are afraid they will lose it.*
*They feel it like a whip cracking over their heads,*
*Striking them, yet befriending them;*
*It wounds them, but also reassures them.*
                                        ~Ugo Betti (1936)


*Courage is like love;*
*It needs hope for nourishment.*
                                        ~Napoleon I (1804)

# Chapter Twelve

The funeral procession was unprecedented. Children threw flower petals in front of the horse drawn carriage, blanketing the ground. Musicians played a single sustaining tone, signifying Isabeau's transition from this world to the next. It resonated within the forest, filling the air with the sound of sorrow and immeasurable, overflowing emptiness.

Young girls in white flowing gowns stood shoulder to shoulder, softly singing a melancholy tale of mourning, a haunting display of grief. Their braided hair adorned with laurel and perfumed flowers. As the casket passed by, onlookers wept, lowering their heads in respect and sorrow.

A little boy and girl walked directly in front of the casket, each carrying a single rose and lit candle – a symbol of the undying love between Isabeau and Merrick, two souls joined for all eternity.

The procession made its way through the town center before arriving at the family burial grounds, nestled deep within the woods near the castle.

Even the sun seemed to be mourning, as it dipped behind the clouds, leaving behind a light mist and a chill in the air. The trees bent gently in the breeze, seemingly bowing before her.

Aquila itself was mourning the loss of its queen.

As they approached Isabeau's final resting place, the boy stepped aside, allowing the girl to continue on her own. For in that moment, Isabeau would complete her journey alone, taking her place among the stars.

Isabeau – a shining light, loved by so many, had been taken far too soon. Her generosity and kindness would be dearly missed. Her love and affection for her family were irreplaceable. Her beauty would not soon be forgotten. Her spirit belonged to the heavens now but she would remain forever in their hearts.

Merrick, devastated beyond words, rode in a private carriage behind the casket, with the curtains drawn closed, away from curious eyes.

"We will meet again, my love," he whispered softly. "Wait for me and I will find you."

He wept quietly. His body wracked from grief. The pain he felt was crushing and unbearable. For all the strength he possessed, he did not have the power to bring her back.

In one hand, he clutched a chess piece – the bishop, a reminder of her resilience, courage, wit and humility.

In his other hand, he held the first white rose he had ever given Isabeau, when he pledged his love and life to her. She had preserved it all these years. Merrick stared blankly at it, finally crushing it within his grasp, letting the remnants of the dried petals fall slowly to the carriage floor, like the tattered remains of his heart.

Martin followed in a separate carriage behind his father. The infant girl remained in the castle, cared for by nursemaids.

Merrick had barely spoken since Isabeau's body was recovered from the river. Her death had been ruled an accidental drowning by the family physician. Everyone of any importance attended her funeral and commoners from all provinces traveled long distances to pay their respect.

Miranda lurked in the shadows, moving from behind one tree to another, trailing the procession, keeping Merrick within her sight. The son was of no consequence to her, but the infant daughter would have to be dealt with, she knew that. Patience was necessary. This was a delicate situation. Act too quickly and it would bring suspicion upon herself. Murdering Isabeau was a bold and strategic move on her part, and so far, all had gone exactly as planned in that regard.

Isabeau got what she deserved. Miranda grinned wickedly. All those years ago, Merrick had fancied her, she recalled, if only briefly. Many thought they would wed, until Isabeau showed up that evening at the Governor's dinner party and all eyes fell upon her, especially Merrick's.

Isabeau was the fair maiden from Lothian, a northeastern province of Aquila. She was well read, educated, witty and charming. She was rumored to be the most enchanting and beautiful young woman in all the lands. She was tall, slender, with reddish hair and striking green eyes, known for her kindness and grace. Miranda scoffed. Isabeau's beauty didn't save her from the bottom of the river.

Miranda had stumbled upon Merrick and Isabeau that next afternoon in the castle tower. She heard their laughter spill out into the corridor as she approached the library. She stopped in the doorway to observe them before making her presence known.

Merrick and Isabeau sat on opposite sides of a chess table making light conversation over a friendly game, laughing freely at something the other would say. Isabeau picked up the queen and moved it into position, glancing playfully at Merrick.

"Checkmate," she said, a smile of victory crossing her face. She picked up the bishop in her hand and smiled flirtatiously at Merrick. "Never take your eyes off the bishop," she teased.

Merrick leaned in towards Isabeau. He stared at the chess board, retracing his moves, straining to figure out where he had made his mistake. He looked at Isabeau and grinned. They locked eyes and let their gaze linger. The chemistry between them was evident. Merrick took the chess piece from her and let his finger brush over the top of her hand. She blushed slightly.

"Here you are, my darling," Miranda said as she entered the room. She spoke to Merrick but never took her cold eyes off Isabeau.

Merrick straightened up and broke his mesmerizing gaze from Isabeau. He stood and walked over to Miranda, kissing her lightly on the cheek. Isabeau rose and nodded to Miranda politely.

"A lady playing chess?" Miranda said in disdain. "How quaint," she added.

"You do not play chess?" Isabeau asked.

"I prefer other nocturnal games, my dear," she practically growled as she rubbed up against Merrick, who suddenly looked terribly uncomfortable. Isabeau looked away momentarily at the awkward display of affection and then watched their interaction curiously. Miranda leaned into Merrick and cooed softly, rubbing her hands across his chest.

Merrick, embarrassed by the inappropriate behavior, pulled awkwardly away from Miranda, and pushed her hands away, a move that did not escape either woman. He gave Miranda a harsh look of disapproval and turned towards Isabeau.

"I enjoyed our game. Perhaps another time?" he smiled curtly.

Isabeau nodded at Merrick, "Of course, I would like that. Thank you for your hospitality."

With that, Merrick left the room. Miranda's eyes bore into Isabeau, making her uncomfortable.

"It was nice meeting you, Lady Miranda," Isabeau excused herself and left the library in a hurry.

Miranda was not about to let this woman steal Merrick from her. She planned to rule beside him and would not step aside for this newcomer. Over my dead body, she thought to herself. Miranda laughed out loud. No, over *her* dead body...

Over the coming weeks, Miranda noticed Merrick spending more time with Isabeau. He was smitten with her, and she with him. Miranda found herself following them as they walked through the gardens. She saw Merrick gently kiss Isabeau's hand as they stood by the waterfall. He gently stroked her hair. Miranda was seething with jealousy. She did not recall Merrick ever acting so tenderly with her.

It was in that moment that she devised a plan to force Merrick's hand. She intended to entrap him. It took all restraint she could muster not to run over and scratch Isabeau's eyes out. Merrick was a man of honor. She would use that in her favor. She delved deeper in black magic to find a spell that would cloud Merrick's mind and judgment.

Miranda planned to visit Merrick in the night, seduce him and impregnate herself with his child. "Checkmate, indeed," she surmised.

She knew that Merrick believed strongly in the vows of marriage and the responsibilities of bringing a child into the world. He would never be so careless willingly, therefore she would have to trick him. She called upon the assistance of her sister, Mira, to help create the potion, without telling her sister the true reason behind her request. She deceived Mira, just as she intended to deceive Merrick.

Merrick woke the next morning with Miranda by his side. Their bodies entwined. Merrick immediately pushed Miranda off him, with no memory of how she happened to end up in his bed. He dressed hastily and demanded that she leave. Miranda did as she was ordered. The deed had been done. She had him exactly where she wanted him. Soon life would grow within her and Merrick would belong to her forever.

Weeks passed and Merrick avoided Miranda, choosing to spend his time with Isabeau. He had fallen in love with her. He couldn't stop thinking of her and planned to ask her hand in marriage soon. He wanted to spend the rest of his days at her side, gazing into her thoughtful eyes and raising a family together. He had never wanted anything so much in his life. She was the one for him. He felt a happiness with her that he never thought possible. He was prepared to pledge his life and his kingdom to Isabeau.

Meanwhile, Miranda's belly grew. She confided in her sister, Mira, that she was carrying Merrick's child. Mira knew immediately that she had been used for ill-gotten gain. Mira made a decision that would destroy her own relationship with her sister forever. She refused to be a part of Miranda's ploy to trap Merrick into marriage with a child, conceived with black magic. The fate of the kingdoms rested in Merrick's hands. It was not for Miranda to force his hand and dictate his fate. Mira decided to tell Merrick of Miranda's deceit and treachery.

Mira immediately requested private counsel with Merrick at the castle and revealed all that she knew. She told Merrick of the child conceived from deceit, unbeknownst to him. Merrick was furious beyond measure. He ordered Mira to keep quiet on this matter. He wanted Miranda to come to him. Merrick wanted to beat her at her own tricks. He would not stand for this, not now, not ever. He carried on as normal, not letting Miranda know that he knew about her little game.

The time came when Miranda's belly was growing too large to conceal. It was time, she realized. She approached Merrick in private and revealed to him that she was carrying his child. She expected Merrick to be surprised, but then delighted and of course, do the honorable thing and propose that they wed to give the child its rightful place of nobility.

Instead, Merrick's eyes narrowed into her with such hatred that she took a step back. His reaction was unexpected.

"I want nothing to do with you or that child spawned from trickery," he spat angrily at her. "I know what you did. Do you think me a fool?"

"But, Merrick…," she injected, alarmed, trying to place his hand on her belly. "Our child grows within me."

He yanked his hand away. "That is your doing. Not of mine. Make no mistake, I intend to wed Isabeau. You mean nothing to me, do you understand? You will pay for this."

He confronted her about the spell she cast upon him. Her shock was matched by his anger. Merrick stormed off furiously.

Miranda was stunned and outraged. She was certain Merrick would do the honorable thing and marry her. To use magic in such a manner was forbidden on Aquila.

Miranda lost her senses and ran after Merrick, begging for forgiveness, pleading with him to give her another chance. She begged Merrick to be lenient with her. He turned from her and called upon the castle guards.

From that moment forward, Merrick cast her out.

He banished her and her unborn child to the dark side. Miranda was forcibly removed. She cried hysterically, pleading for forgiveness. She struggled to free herself from the guard's grasp.

On Merrick's order, and without so much as a word, Miranda was pushed through the mist wall into the dark side. Mira placed a binding spell upon Miranda, to ensure that she was held there for the remainder of her days, never again to walk among the light.

Alone, Miranda fought to survive the harsh conditions of life in the darkness. Not long after her banishment, she lost her child, stillborn. That was the last time that Miranda ever shed a tear. With no one to love and no one that loved her, every shred of humanity that Miranda had faded away. It blackened her heart completely. She vowed to avenge the death of her child and the life that she lost on the light side. She made it her sole purpose to destroy Merrick by making him feel the pain that she now felt. She vowed to take Isabeau from him and lay all his lands to waste.

Miranda crawled barren into a cave. She was found by witches who could sense her intense hatred for mankind. They cultivated her, took care of her and molded her into a mistress of the dark arts. Miranda excelled in it. She became a powerful sorceress. Her dangerous power grew as her hatred deepened. She soon had minions at her beckoning and gathered those that embraced evil to do her bidding. She sent spies out into the light side, to gather information and others to wait for commands. They brought Miranda ancient teachings and scrolls that were believed to be long forgotten, giving her the spells necessary to bring forth the ancient evil – a monstrous beast, a dragon the likes of which Aquila had not seen in ages. She was driven by that purpose – to take back what was stolen from her.

Miranda's ambition did not stop there.

Merrick went about his life on the light side, with no further regard to Miranda. He married his true love, Isabeau, and she bore him two children. They lived happily in a glorious castle. That was my life, Miranda seethed. It should have been me, not her. Merrick was mine, she believed. He belonged to me!

Miranda watched from the darkness, lurking in the shadows. She had eyes everywhere, watching Merrick and his family, counting the days when she could strike back, knowing full well that she would dictate the final chapter of this story. She would watch through the eyes of those she enlisted – see what they could see, hear what they could here, smell what they could smell. It was a powerful black magic. It was so powerful that she often forgot that she was not physically there, only a bystander in someone else's mind.

Now, with the help of one of her loyal followers, Miranda stood hidden in the shadows again. This time watching Merrick, a broken shell of a man, hunched over, mourning the loss of his dear wife Isabeau. She stifled a laugh and knew this was only the beginning of his torment.

"How dare you cast me aside like an insect, Merrick," she screamed in her mind.

How dare you!

"You will remember me, I can assure you," she grinned wickedly. "You took a child from me, Merrick. Allow me to do the same to you," she said to herself.

She waited for hours until at last the casket was placed into the family crypt and sealed. Merrick placed flowers at the base of the marble entrance and walked slowly back to his carriage, straight past his son without so much as a comforting glance. The boy's eyes were red from tears. Miranda smiled. Good, she thought. Feel that pain, seething through you? Perfect.

When all had finally left the burial ground, she summoned her henchmen – the grave robbers.

The spell she cast on Isabeau kept her in a death status, even the most skilled medical doctor would be fooled by. Isabeau appeared to be dead, but in fact she was in a deep trance where her heart and pulse all but stopped.

The grave robbers carefully broke the seal of the crypt, opened the casket and removed the body, wrapped in a shroud. They resealed the crypt and placed the body beneath hay in a wagon. They then made the perilous journey back to the fortress in the dark side, where Miranda was eagerly awaiting Isabeau's arrival.

Miranda was quite pleased with herself. No one suspected a thing. Such a terrible tragedy. Tsk, tsk. She laughed hysterically when she saw Isabeau's lifeless body before her.

The only thing that had not gone as planned was the chain breaking and the necklace falling off Isabeau's neck into the water. That was an aspect she had not anticipated, but one that could be rectified. The riverbed was being search painstakingly, but the keystone had not been recovered yet. She did not know that Mira had already recovered the necklace. Miranda never stopped looking for the keystone, knowing that with it she would be invincible and denied nothing.

Isabeau's body was taken deep within the Keep where Miranda breathed life into it once again, imprisoning her for all eternity. She made sure that hers was the first face Isabeau saw when she opened her eyes. Alive, but believed to be dead. Only in dreams and visions could Isabeau reach out now, but Miranda's powers were so great. She made sure that Isabeau was nothing more than a mere ghost to the rest of the world.

As for Merrick, Miranda waited patiently until his grief had completely taken over, consuming him. Then, she slithered back into his life, by means of visions and dreams, pretending to care for his pain and suffering, clouding his judgment, offering a way out of the torment. She enjoyed toying with him, playing on his emotions, and she would continue to manipulate and punish Merrick as long as life remained in him. He started to hallucinate, believing Miranda was standing in front of him, gaining his trust again through her compassion, offering to ease his pain.

She offered a way for him to be released from his agony, released from his past, making him her pawn, offering him a new life on the dark side. A new life far away from the memories of love lost and the family that haunted his every waking moment. She ensnared him and rejoiced in her triumph. She had come full circle and now he was at her mercy, finally.

Mira advised Emily to rest for a while. The events of the day were overwhelming. Mira thought it best to resume their talks the following day. Emily was taken to a room in a tower where she found food, water, fresh clothing and a cot to rest upon.

The woman that brought Emily to her quarters turned to leave. Emily examined a milky substance in a ceramic jar sitting next to a wooden handled brush. She couldn't identify its aroma, but it was pleasant.

"Excuse me?" she called back to the woman.

She stopped and walked back to Emily, with her hands folded together in front of her.

"What is that? Am I supposed to drink this?" Emily asked, pointing to the jar.

The woman leaned in and spoke softly. "You stink of mylox, my dear. That is for washing your hair."

Emily wasn't quite sure how to respond to that. She held the front of her shirt to her nose, smelling the strange odor.

"Good evening to you," the woman nodded politely, closing the door to Emily's room as she exited.

"I stink of mylox?" Emily frowned.

Emily took another quick look around the small room. Dried flowers were hung on the walls giving the space a pleasant scent. A water basin and pitcher sat beside her cot, allowing her to freshen up. She picked up the square bar of soap and sniffed it. It smelled like wildflowers. She washed her long hair and donned a fresh set of clothing.

Emily chuckled to herself, imagining her mom scolding her because she "stank of mylox." Yea, not quite the same as a torn pair of jeans.

She stared out the tower window, into nothingness, as she ate some food. Her view was a cloud bank. She couldn't even see the ground below. Emily ran her hand across the cold stone wall. She sat down on the cot, letting her thoughts drift back to her family and the threat they unknowingly faced because of her. If Mira was attempting to motivate Emily, she had succeeded.

She was comforted, however, by the fact that Martin would be with her.

Yawning, the fatigue overtook her. She lied back on the cot, wrapped herself in the warm blanket and closed her eyes. Welcoming the chance to rest.

Emily dozed off, drifting further and further away in her mind, until she was floating. She found herself soaring above the valleys and forest below, dipping in and out of the clouds, following the winding river.

Emily looked down at her hands. She was holding onto a harness wrapped around the neck of a large bluish-green dragon. Its delicate wings beat rhythmically as the wind carried it over the mountains effortlessly.

She sensed a oneness with the creature and lowered her body to hug it instinctively. It responded to her touch and glided gently to the right, almost touching the tips of the evergreens. Then, without warning, it dipped down so low that the tips of its wings lightly splashed the water beneath them and caused ripples. Mist from the water drizzled over Emily's face before the dragon soared high into the air again.

Emily laughed out loud. She heard the dragon laugh too in her mind. She could sense its thoughts and feelings. She felt a deep bond between them that was heartfelt.

On the wings of a dragon, Emily traveled for miles, flying peacefully through the sky. She felt humbled by the vastness of space, with its swirling colors and twinkling starlight visible above her. Never in all her life had she felt such joy and exhilaration.

She didn't know where her dragon friend was taking her, nor did she care. They soared together through the clouds. She had been transported to this magical place and, in that moment, Emily felt like she was exactly where she belonged.

She no longer felt like a stranger in a strange land. She felt like she was home, as if something she had been waiting a very long time for had finally arrived. She realized the truth in Mira's words. She was a part of this world – connected to it. Yes, Emily could feel it.

Without realizing it, she whispered to the dragon.

"Take me home."

The dragon immediately banked left and increased its speed. It began to make another descent. Emily could see the outline of the magnificent snowy mountains. She spotted Isabeau and Merrick's castle in the distance. The dragon circled overhead. Beneath her, the ruins of the once beautiful castle rested sadly.

The dragon spoke directly to her mind.

*Home...*

That single first word moved Emily so deeply, given its meaning, that she felt tears swell up in her eyes.

Here on Aquila, this castle, with all its fallen glory, was indeed 'once upon a time' her family's home.

"Yes, that is our home," she agreed warmly.

Emily hugged the dragon tightly, letting the tears roll down her cheeks, never taking her eyes off the desolate castle below.

The dragon turned away from the castle and headed towards the mist wall. Alarmed, Emily sat upright, clinging tightly to the dragon's harness. The light disappeared and she was greeted by night.

Emily was on the dark side of Aquila. She shivered from the unknown, as the bitter cold smacked against her body. All warmth had forsaken this place.

She could make out a fortress in front of them, the light from the twin moons outlining its shape. It looked like a giant prison to her. Confused, she asked the dragon why it had brought her here.

*Annadune adelth mirash toongoden...*

"Yes, I know. I must protect the keystone."

"Within these walls, you must see...," the dragon spoke to her mind.

"See what?" she asked.

"You must see," the dragon repeated.

Suddenly, Emily was standing in front of a heavy wooden door, securely locked. Two armed guards stood at the end of a long corridor, oblivious to her presence. She passed through the door unnoticed and found herself within a large dark chamber.

Her dragon friend was gone.

Emily heard the crackling sounds of embers exploding in the hearth to her right. She slowly moved further into the room. It was musty and sparsely furnished. Emily noted that someone had tried their best to make it more suitable, with an abundance of old books, blankets and pillows being the only visible comfort items within.

A slender female sat alone on a tattered couch, reminiscent of the French provincial style furniture Emily had seen in art museums. Emily approached cautiously from behind. When she got within a few feet, the woman lifted her head and turned towards her. Emily recognized her immediately. This is what the dragon had wanted her to see.

Isabeau…

Emily gasped. The woman had aged, but there was no mistaking that face! She had found Martin's mother, imprisoned here in this dreadful place.

Isabeau was alive!

# Chapter Thirteen

Merrick had grown to hate everything the light side represented. He could not even recall the last time his life had meaning. He cared not for the betterment of men any longer. This was a war of conquest. All the light had been snuffed out of his existence and he was determined to do the same to everyone else.

He and Miranda had that in common. They both wanted to cover Aquila in darkness. Merrick's mind had been overthrown. His emotions had been poisoned. The passage of time had not made Merrick less intimidating. Anger gave him great power, without the messiness of remorse. He embraced the darkness.

To see Miranda's plans come to fruition was gratifying to Merrick. It appeared that the prophecies were coming true. He would see to it that the outcome would be in his favor.

It would be his final battle and he had no intention of losing. Once protector of the kingdoms, Merrick had now become an instrument in their destruction. He was tired of waiting. He just wanted the light to be gone. As long as it existed, a flicker of that pain from his past remained.

They called Merrick "The Dark Knight," mighty and powerful, the heavy hand that ruled Miranda's sinister army. She had her raiders, seekers and spies under her immediate supervision, but it was Merrick that commanded the massive army she had assembled to overthrow the lands. After Merrick turned his back on his own people, the only defense the light side had were the Marshals, and they were no match for Miranda's forces.

The dark towering figure paced around a dimly lit chamber with high vaulted ceilings. He glanced impatiently at the door and poured himself another tankard of mead. It was damp and cold within his quarters, despite his heavy cloak. No warmth came from the stone fireplace, despite its raging fire.

It was just the way of the dark side. Nothing quite penetrated the cold and harsh elements. The chamber door opened and a frail, shabbily dressed man entered. Merrick stopped pacing to face him.

"What is it?"

"I'm afraid the rumors are true, my Lord. It appears they have succeeded in recruiting assistance from the outside," the messenger told him nervously.

Merrick threw his tankard against the wall and grabbed the man by the front of his tunic.

"Who would dare challenge us?" he demanded to know. "Who is behind this?"

The man shifted uneasily, fearing retribution. He hesitated before answering.

"Mira, the elders, and...your son, my Lord."

Merrick's back stiffened and his eyes narrowed. His face contorted with anger. A chill ran down the messenger's spine. Merrick lifted the man off of his feet and tossed him across the room like a rag doll. He landed on a woodpile stacked in the corner and moaned in pain.

"I have no son, you fool," he scowled, voice dripping with contempt.

"Of course not, my Lord," the man corrected himself. He did not move until his master gave him permission to do so.

Merrick stormed around the room, seething with anger.

Had they overlooked something?

"What assistance from the outside?" he asked furiously, standing over the man with his fist clenched, ready to strike.

"It is believed to be a young girl, sir. The seekers have had many visions, but Miranda's raiders have been unsuccessful in locating her," the messenger answered, reluctantly.

"Why was I not informed of this sooner?" Merrick demanded to know.

"I am sure I do not know the answer to that question, my Lord."

Merrick mulled over what he had been told.

"A young girl? Absurd! How could a girl possibly hurt us?" Merrick shouted angrily.

"I am sure I do not know," the man replied again, fearing retribution.

Merrick continued pacing around the room, speaking loudly. "It must be a ploy of some kind, one of Mira's tricks. A desperate move on their part. Perhaps, some kind of diversion," Merrick frowned, concentrating deeply.

The messenger nodded cautiously.

"What are they up to?" Merrick wondered. He walked over to the chamber window and stared out into the darkness, deep in thought. Finally, he turned and pounded his fist upon the table, causing it to topple over. The messenger hurried to his feet to extinguish the flame from the candle before it set fire to the rug beneath it.

Merrick rushed out of the room, searching for Miranda without so much as a backward glance at the man, who was relieved that his master's wrath had not been more severe. Merrick made his way through the dark corridors and down the narrow spiral staircase where Miranda and her seekers spent most of the days amidst their spells and potions.

Flickering torches cast an eerie light upon the walls. The clanking of metal armor upon the stone floors from soldiers he passed, shattered the silence of the castle. They moved quickly aside to clear his way.

Merrick burst through the door of Miranda's meditation chamber to find her sitting on the floor with three other witches, all deep in a trance. He had no patience for this now and shouted to get their attention.

"Miranda!" he bellowed.

She and her witches opened their eyes and looked at him. Annoyance crossed Miranda's face. Merrick looked at the others in the room.

"Leave us," he ordered.

The witches scurried out of the room, without protest.

Miranda watched them leave and turned her attention towards Merrick. "How dare you interrupt me while I am meditating," she fumed.

He held up a hand to cut her off.

"Silence! What is the truth behind this new threat?" he shouted, trying to control his anger.

Miranda sighed and closed her eyes. After a moment, she opened them and looked at Merrick. She knew this time would come. She had kept it from him long enough. The last raid had drawn too much attention to her efforts. She could no longer hunt down the girl in secret. She studied Merrick carefully.

Merrick could be difficult to manage, but manage him she would, not the other way around. She excused his insolence for the moment because he had just learned that a credible threat was upon them. He was concerned and she understood that. The child had to be dealt with. She would have to appease Merrick for the time being. She did not need his unruliness when there was so much at stake.

"Calm thyself, Merrick," she advised strongly.

He stood unwavering, waiting for an answer to his question.

"I asked you a question," he demanded.

Miranda met his stern gaze. "You were warned of the prophecies, Merrick. Why act surprised?" she snapped back.

"I was not aware that they were coming true!"

"Truth is a relative term, my dear," she reminded him.

"Do not patronize me, Miranda," he warned sternly. "I am not one of your clueless minions."

"Merrick, you knew that once the mist wall began to weaken, forces outside our borders would do all within their power to prevent that from happening. And, we did bring forth the ancient evil. It requires many children to sustain it… It needs the so-called innocents, you knew this. Did you think the light dwellers would continue to look the other way indefinitely?" she asked.

He didn't answer right away.

"Well?" she sighed with annoyance.

"Of course not," he snapped. "However, I was not aware of any real threat upon us. You knew of it and kept it hidden from me."

"You had other concerns, mounting our army, preparing for battle. These other things would only distract you from your task. Truly, no concern of yours," she assured him.

"They concern me when my own flesh and blood are involved," he spat angrily, referring to his son, Martin.

Miranda sighed deeply. Someone had been wagging their tongue too much and she would deal with them later. Merrick was furious. He now knew that his son was involved in efforts to stop them, however futile those measures might be.

She rose slowly, circling Merrick. She ran her hands across his back and looked playfully in his eyes.

He recoiled from her touch and turned his back to her.

"Merrick," she appealed to him, "This is a chance for you to become ruler of worlds even greater than our own. Calm yourself and keep your thoughts clear. Do not become your own worst enemy. Your son's involvement only makes the game more interesting. There is no need for you to be overly concerned. He is of no consequence. Allow me to tend to such matters."

Merrick turned to face her.

"I will not be blindsided, Miranda."

"Understood," she told him. "I will try to keep you better informed. Would this please you?" she cooed, trying to deflect his anger.

"And, what of this girl?" he asked in a threatening tone.

Miranda stiffened. "She matters not. She is just another fly in our web. A weak attempt to undermine our efforts, nothing more," she assured him.

Merrick did not believe her. "Sending a young girl to undermine our efforts? There is something more you are not telling me," he replied heatedly.

The last thing Miranda wanted was to expose potential weakness to Merrick. She needed him focused and unwavering, not questioning her ability to succeed in her plan – the domination over all things, enslaving mankind, including him. Her army would follow him into battle, doing her bidding.

Merrick was too blind to see he was merely her pawn. He was a constant reminder that she shattered his cozy existence with Isabeau and this pleased her to no end. Merrick knew what she allowed him to know, and she intended to keep it that way.

She dismissed his defiance as an isolated incident but grew weary of their conversation. She did not feel the need to explain herself further, nor reveal the importance of the girl. This was a mere thorn in her side, which would be remedied.

"You have nothing to fear," she reassured him. "I will deal with Mira and her trappings. Do you think Mira is more powerful than I?" she asked.

Merrick did not answer. He knew Miranda was powerful. She didn't need to tell him that. She sensed that he was backing down. Miranda's seekers were invaluable. Certainly, they would foretell of any imminent threat. He was being an alarmist, he realized. He was caught off guard by the mention of his son and the insinuation that a young girl could pose a threat.

"You are certain the girl is harmless?"

"Not even worth mentioning," she lied, humoring him.

He shot her a cold stare.

Miranda smiled to herself. Think what you want, Merrick. She circled him again, massaging his back. He pulled away from her and stormed out of the room, slamming the door behind him. His heavy footsteps thundered in the empty corridor. She sighed deeply, retreating to the darkness once again. She would have to increase her efforts to find the girl – and if Merrick's son was in fact opposing them, then he too would pay for it with his life.

Miranda had Merrick. Isabeau could rot in her prison cell for all she cared. She closed her eyes and resumed her meditations.

~~~~~~~~~~~~~~~~~~~~~~~~~

The beast hidden deep within Miranda's hellish caves roared with hunger, waiting to be fed. It scraped its claws along the cavern floor impatiently, pulling on its heavy chains angrily, attempting to free itself.

One of its handlers smoked a pipe nearby, ignoring the hungry growls. He waved a lit torch in the direction of the beast to illuminate its massive form and shook his head.

"Stop the noise or I won't feed ye none," he yelled at the dragon. It snapped its jaws angrily in the air, narrowing its focus on the man. "I ain't afraid of ye," the man spat back, showing contempt. He took a few quick puffs, letting the smoke rise in a gentle cloud. "Not wasting a good smoke on a filthy beast," he mumbled.

The beast sniffed the air and roared in protest. The sound echoed throughout the cave. The handler chuckled and blew several puffs of smoke towards the creature, before turning his back to the beast. It snarled and then pretended to settle down, luring the handler into a false sense of security.

It appeared to drift off to sleep, lying motionless and breathing deeply. The handler finished smoking his pipe and walked past the sleeping giant, straying carelessly too close. The beast waited until just the right moment and then quickly snatched the handler off the ground, tearing him to shreds, devouring the man before he had a chance to scream. It roared triumphantly.

Unbeknownst to Miranda, while her terrifying beast thirsted for blood, another presence stirred.

Far away in the snowcapped mountains, amidst the icy glaciers and frozen tundra, the Council of Dragons – Aquila's celestial guardians – had awoken from their long slumber to see the light of day.

Preferring the isolation of the caves hidden deep within the mountains, they were the oldest lifeforms on Aquila, wise and tranquil beings. They could see beyond forever, into this world and the next, in harmony with countless star systems. They had chosen peace long ago. There was no higher authority on Aquila than the Council of Dragons. Entrusted with the protection of all creatures, the embodiment of enlightenment, they had been serving Aquila since its inception, existing for a greater good.

They answered to the keystone and no other. They had been summoned by it – called upon to aid mankind, to protect the mist wall and help stop the spread of evil across the land.

Some would be chosen to go out among the skies and fight the beast. The mightiest dragons would be chosen for this dangerous task, knowing it could lead to their demise. They did not fear death in the physical sense and accepted this responsibility willingly.

The Council of Dragons had defeated the beast once before, thousands of years ago, and drove it back to the fiery ash. That battle had nearly caused their extinction. They were prepared to make such a sacrifice again. Bound by duty, an alliance of men and dragons had been forged long ago. The Council of Dragons intended to honor that allegiance, pushing back against the darkness that threatened to devour all of Aquila.

The bearer of the keystone had returned. The Council of Dragons prepared for her arrival. Their minds had always been joined to the bearer, a mere whisper in her mind, watching over her, gently guiding her. She was near now. They could sense it. She had come such a long way, over the edge of time. So young, this one. They had much to learn from one another.

~~~~~~~~~~~~~~~~~~~~~~~~~~~~~~~~

The wind howled fiercely from the north, bringing with it the frigid cold. Martin pulled his cloak closer around him and kept watch over the base of the mountain.

Suddenly, he heard a woman singing nearby. He strained to listen. Martin recognized the voice. It was his mother. The song was so familiar. It was one of the lullabies she used to sing to his baby sister, Victoria. He remembered it well.

Martin stood, following the direction of the voice. He moved cautiously through the forest, finally spotting his mother. He saw her strolling through the nearby glens, holding the infant child closely, singing the lullaby. Her voice was soothing, almost hypnotic.

Martin called out to her. His mother looked over her shoulder and smiled at him. She kept walking along the river's edge and disappeared behind the bushes. He could still hear her singing. He needed to be near her.

Martin quickened his pace to find her. When he reached the flowing river, the singing stopped abruptly. Martin searched the immediate area but found no sign of his mother.

"Mother? Where are you?" he asked anxiously.

Nothing. He heard nothing. Even the birds had stopped chirping and the insects had gone silent.

He quickly returned to the water's edge. Martin heard his name being called repeatedly in a faint voice, gradually growing louder. It was his mother again. Her voice seemed to be coming from the water directly in front of him. He saw fabric from his mother's gown float to the surface. He bent down to retrieve it.

As his fingers dipped into the water, a hand shot up from beneath the surface, covered in rotted flesh. It grabbed his wrist tightly and began to pull Martin into the river. His mother's face emerged from below the water, calling his name, gurgling as she spoke. Her face was swollen, bloated and decayed. Her eyes were missing, only vacant sockets remained.

Martin struggled to free himself, pulling chunks of slippery flesh off her hand as he did so. She tightened her grasp, pulling him further into the water. He dug in his boot heels but she continued to drag him into the murky water.

"Martin," she whispered in a ghostly voice, "Join me…Why did you leave me all alone…? You should not have left me…"

She kept repeating the same sentences, pulling Martin deeper into the water until he was fully submerged. He kicked and fought to escape her grasp, to no avail. He struggled desperately for air, but his lungs began to fill with water.

Martin was drowning.

"Stay with me forever…," she said to him as he felt life leaving his body.

He looked back at the surface as his mother pulled his lifeless body down into the murky depths. He watched the sunlight slowly fade as he was dragged further downward. His eyes remained open as life completely left his body, joining his mother to die in their watery grave, swallowed by darkness.

~~~~~~~~~~~~~~~~~~~~~~~~~~

Startled, Martin bolted upright. He realized it was just a nightmare. He wiped moisture from his eyes and was thankful for the air that filled his lungs. For a moment before he awoke, Martin could swear he heard a young boy laughing.

Back at the clinic, Donovan smiled to himself. The weak minded were always a source of amusement to him. Then again, Donovan thought everyone was weak and easily toyed with. Their minds hid so many dirty secrets, so many evil deeds, so much deception, so much pain and suffering. People were like open books to him, revealing their inner most fears and desires.

He had killed a man once in his dreams, just for fun. The man had scolded Donovan, chastised him. That night, Donovan drifted into the man's dreams and had him walk off a cliff, falling to his death on the rocks below. The man's body lay bloodied and broken. He died a slow agonizing death.

It was so easy. Donovan let him die in his dream and prevented him from waking. The next morning, they found the man dead in his bed of no apparent cause. His face was contorted in pain. His eyes open in horror. His mouth was frozen in a silent scream.

Donovan believed he was special. Having so much control over another person's mind was exhilarating to him. He could just kill them at will in their dreams and that power corrupted him. He could have left Martin to drown in his dream. He could have shut down his mind and not allowed the air to return to his lungs. He could have made Martin's mind think that he did in fact drown.

However, Miranda would not have been pleased. For now, she decided who lived and died. One day that honor would be his. She alone appreciated his gift but advised him to keep his talents hidden. They wouldn't understand, she told him. They would see him as a danger, she explained. Fear him as a monster, she warned. They would lock him up and maybe even kill him, she advised.

His adopted mother thought he was a curse, a burden, a stain on their good name. She cast him out, ridding herself of the stigma of having him as her child. Others had tried to control and conform him, ultimately failing. Not Miranda. She encouraged him to use his abilities and cultivate his gift.

Donovan believed if his fake mother and Doctor Pernell knew how far reaching his powers were, they would indeed do away with him. No one knew what he was capable of, except Miranda. She protected him. He was her eyes and ears on the light side, waiting to do whatever task she asked of him.

Donovan had tried to read the new girl at the clinic – Emily. She knew nothing of any importance. Her mind was a cluttered mess, full of things he did not understand. He sensed great confusion within her. She was utterly useless to him. He didn't like her. She hadn't yielded to his will and that angered him. She openly challenged him in the dining hall and he hated her for that. He rubbed his shoulder absently, remembering how she forcibly bumped into him.

Doctor Pernell was also unreadable, unreachable. This too frustrated Donovan. He was confident that one day he could penetrate the doctor's mind, perhaps make him dance in the fountain. Donovan giggled at the thought. The doctor was a cleric and trained to fend off invasions of the mind. He was also protected by Mira herself.

Doctor Stewart was easier to read, but he didn't seem to know anything that was useful. Donovan found him especially interesting. His connection to Merrick and the woman locked away in the fortress did not escape Donovan. He was a person of importance, which was why Miranda had ordered him to be left

185

alone. Well, she didn't say Donovan couldn't torment him a bit. She merely said he was not to be harmed.

Donovan laughed. Martin carried so much pain within him about his family, his failed relationship with his father, the sense of betrayal, the loss of his mother and sister that Donovan could spend years playing mind games with him.

He enjoyed hurting people. He did his best to play innocent, but he was a wolf in sheep's clothing, preying on those around him. He was tired of people telling him what to do. He looked forward to the day when Miranda was the one true ruler of Aquila. Donovan would no longer have to hide his gift when that time came. She had promised him an unlimited supply of minds to torture and exploit. He anxiously awaited that day. Until then, he would play in the shadows of their minds, being careful not to get caught.

Doctor Pernell walked past him and gave a friendly wave. Play along, Miranda told him, and Donovan did exactly that. Doctor Pernell had no idea that Donovan had nearly killed Doctor Stewart in his sleep, moments ago. Donovan grinned wickedly as Doctor Pernell disappeared into his office.

Rebecca watched the entire exchange from her secret hiding nook in the garden where she would retreat to read her books. She went there often to think about her parents. Earlier, she saw Donovan leave the clinic and hide behind the trees, close his eyes and concentrate hard. His body went rigid and his head tilted back.

She was about to run for help when he suddenly opened his eyes, a frightening grin crept across his face. It chilled Rebecca to her core. What had she just witnessed? She was disturbed by the look on his face. It was quite sinister. She didn't like to tattle, but Donovan was up to no good. She was sure of it. She didn't trust him at all. She sensed that he only pretended to be nice. She decided to keep a close eye on him and to talk to Doctor Pernell about her concerns.

# Chapter Fourteen

Emily opened her eyes to see Mira sitting in the chair opposite the cot, smiling at her. She sat up in bed and stretched.

"Good morning, dear. Have a nice rest?" she asked.

Emily smirked gleefully. "Actually, it was amazing!"

"Really? And, why is that?"

Emily smiled widely and leaned forward, barely containing her enthusiasm. "I got to ride on a dragon across Aquila!"

Emily jumped to her feet, extended her arms and spun around in a circle. When she stopped, Mira laughed and clapped her hands, delighted at the girl's unabashed joy.

"Did you now?" Mira asked.

Emily sat back on the bed and proceeded to tell Mira all about her adventures with the dragon.

Mira listened enthusiastically, laughing heartily at Emily's sheer delight in retelling the story. Emily's face grew serious when she recalled where the dragon had eventually taken her, but she knew she had to be honest with Mira about what she witnessed. Mira sensed her concern.

"You can tell me anything, Emily," she assured her.

She told Mira of the fortress deep in the darkness, the one built into the stone, and of the inner chamber where the lonely woman was imprisoned. She paused before telling Mira the identity of the woman.

When she did so, Mira was visibly shaken and didn't speak for several moments. Emily sat silently on her cot giving Mira time to absorb what she had just learned. Mira looked away and stared blankly out the castle window. Finally, Mira looked at Emily with great sadness in her eyes.

"Even I could not have foreseen this treachery. All of this death and anguish brought about by one woman's jealousy and selfishness. It is difficult to comprehend," she admitted sadly.

Mira was talking to herself more than to the girl. Emily knew nothing of the prior relationship between Miranda and Merrick, but she listened intently with great interest. Mira lowered her head, quiet sobs followed. Emily stood and gently placed her arm around Mira's shoulder.

"How did it come to this?" Mira cried softly.

"I'm sorry," Emily told her.

"All the lives that have been destroyed. And, what is yet to come?"

"Well, maybe together, we can set things right," Emily said hopefully. "Isn't that why the keystone brought me here – to help fix things, to make things right? To stop what's going on before it gets worse? Before Miranda destroys everything?"

Mira wiped away her tears and looked up into Emily's young face. "Yes, we must not give up hope. You are correct, of course."

The knowledge that Isabeau's death had been staged and orchestrated by Miranda came as quite a blow to Mira. An entire family had been torn apart and countless others lost their lives in Miranda's heartless pursuit for power and revenge. This tragic incident had sent Aquila spiraling towards an uncertain future.

"We need to free Isabeau as soon as possible," Emily told Mira.

"Of course," Mira agreed. "We have to proceed with utmost caution. Many lives hang in the balance. However, we cannot risk everything for one life either."

Emily knew she was right.

"The needs of the many outweigh the needs of the few, or the one," Emily said quietly, quoting the infamous line by Spock, spoken before his death in *Star Trek II: The Wrath of Khan*.

Mira nodded her head, "Yes, indeed."

"Should we tell Martin about his mother?" Emily asked.

"Not yet. I do not think that would be wise. It would enrage him, causing him to turn a blind eye to all else, seeking only revenge. Right now, we need Martin clear headed, calm and focused on the task that lies before us, which is getting you to the

Council of Dragons, killing the beast, defeating Miranda's army, restoring order...," Mira said, like she was checking off items on a grocery list.

Emily frowned.

Mira continued, "The time for him to confront his past will come soon enough, and then the truth will be known."

"Okay," Emily agreed. "What about the other stuff...about us being related, I mean? About his sister?"

Mira sighed heavily. "I will leave that up to you. You will know when the time is right. He already suspects some connection, no doubt. After all, you are wearing his mother's necklace."

Mira sighed deeply, embracing Emily.

"It is time for you to go." She looked gently into Emily's eyes before continuing. "Be careful who you trust, young one. Here on Aquila, things are not always as they appear. Dark arts are used by many to deceive the unsuspecting. Trust your instincts. Trust your heart when your eyes fail you. Your quest will be full of peril, but I have faith that you will prevail."

Emily listened to every single word Mira said.

"There is much to do and no time to waste. Martin will take you to meet the dragons and from there a guide will give you safe passage through the dark side," Mira continued.

Emily interrupted her.

"What guide?" Her eyes widened, envisioning the ferryman transporting her across the River Styx to the Fifth Circle of Hell, from Dante's *Inferno*.

"This will be revealed to you soon."

Emily frowned and sighed. "You never said anything about me going through the mist wall to the dark side. Thalien told me never to go there. We should really follow his advice," Emily sounded alarmed.

Mira tilted her head slightly and smiled at Emily's attempt to shift the narrative away from what was inevitable.

"Well, we could wait for Miranda to come to you, but it is better if we have the element of surprise on our side, do you not agree? And, did you not say it was best to strike first?" Mira pointed out.

"Did I say that?" Emily asked, trying to recall her exact words from the previous day. "Because that doesn't sound like something I would say," she protested, self-doubt written all over her face.

Mira took Emily's hands in her own.

"Do not fret, child. You will find the courage you seek," she smiled warmly.

"Or die trying," Emily replied grimly.

"Let us hope not," Mira added.

Emily looked even more alarmed. "Isn't this the part of the story where you're supposed to say that I'll be safe, no matter what?"

Mira gave her a motherly smile, full of understanding. "I cannot tell you something that I am not sure of, Emily."

"Well, that's not comforting at all. We were attacked on our way here," she reminded Mira.

"Yes, it is quite a frequent occurrence unfortunately. Raiders looking for resources, robbing, killing, doing anything to cause havoc. Others are searching for – well, I believe they are searching for that very necklace you are wearing."

Emily found no comfort in this knowledge.

~~~~~~~~~~~~~~~~~~~~~~~~~~~~

Mira had delivered horses to Martin at the base of the mountain to assist on their journey. He and Emily would continue alone. Thalien would remain behind to be called upon if needed, as was his charge.

Martin saw no point in protesting when Thalien informed him that he and Emily would be traveling further into the mountains. Doctor Pernell made it perfectly clear that this was Martin's responsibility. The girl wore his mother's necklace, and that alone kept Martin invested in this task. He wanted answers.

He sighed deeply, recalling the nightmare from only hours before. The ugliness that lurked within Aquila held little comfort to what the days ahead would bring. He hoped the girl had the stomach for it.

Emily was brought back down to the surface by the mylox. Her previous fears seemed to have subsided. She laughed when her feet hit the ground.

"That was fun. Can we do that again?" she asked.

Martin looked at her and shook his head no. The mylox made its strange cooing noise and returned to the castle above. Emily walked over to Martin, determined to get on his nerves as little as possible.

"Hello, Martin," she said cheerfully.

He gave her a sideways glance.

"I trust your time with Mira went well?" he stated.

Emily tapped her chin with her finger, searching for the right words, before saying, "Yes, it was illuminating."

Martin rolled his eyes.

"What's with the horses?" she asked.

"We have quite a long journey through the mountains. The horses are our transport," he informed her.

She walked around to the front of the horses, one light brown and the other jet black. She gently patted each of the horses on their head and touched their long manes. The horses neighed softly and rubbed their heads on Emily.

"They like me," she said.

"No accounting for taste," Martin said under his breath.

"I've never ridden a horse before. Is that going to be a problem?" she asked, continuing to pet the horses.

"Not for me," Martin said absently.

"Actually, I've never even sat on a horse before, except for the merry-go-round," she admitted.

He stopped what he was doing and turned to face her, curiosity getting the better of him.

"Merry-go-round?" he asked.

"A carousel of horses."

He had no idea what she was talking about.

"A merry-go-round," she repeated. "You sit on a horse and it goes around and around, up and down, in a circle while music plays."

He looked puzzled. "Why would you sit on a horse and ride it repeatedly in circles? Hardly seems productive or an effective means of reaching any destination."

"It's for fun," she explained.

"You are very strange."

He turned back to the saddlebags and took out an object wrapped in fabric.

"Do you know what fun is?" she asked with sarcasm.

"I have something for you," he said, ignoring her remark.

He handed it to her.

Emily smiled and unwrapped it. Her eyes lit up when she saw what it was. It was a dagger, about twelve inches long, slim and tapered to the point, with burgundy leather straps wrapped around the hilt. There was a decorative engraving, featuring a dragon with a long tail, running down the length of the blade. It was quite beautiful.

"Wow…thanks," she said sincerely, admiring it closely.

"You are welcome."

There was some kind of writing on the other side of the blade, in a language she was not familiar with.

"What does this say?" she asked Martin.

He leaned over and looked at the dagger.

"May the heavens guide you," he told her. "That is the ancient language of our elders."

"Cool," she smiled. She stepped back and began waving the dagger frantically in the air at some invisible assailant. "This could do some serious damage," she said approvingly.

Martin turned to face her. With his hand, he slowly lowered the dagger that Emily was waving around. He motioned for her to raise her arms so he could put a belt around her waist and asked for her to tie the sheath strap to her inner thigh.

"Let us be careful with that, shall we?"

Emily grinned and raised her dagger in the air, pulling off an imaginary helmet.

"I am no man!" she shouted dramatically and lunged at the air, thrusting her dagger forward while letting out a battle cry. "That was Eowyn killing the witch king of Angmar from *Return of the King*."

Martin stared at her.

"It's a book."

He had no reaction.

"You know what a book is, right?" she said sarcastically.

"Of course, I know what books are, heavens. I am a doctor, need I remind you," he frowned.

"Well, you didn't know what a merry-go-round was either, just saying," she countered.

"I have a real horse. I do not need to pretend that I own a horse, then merely sit upon it while traveling in circles, going absolutely nowhere," he snapped.

"Yea, I know. Thundercat, right?" she smirked.

Martin raised his voice. "Thunderbolt. My horse's name is Thunderbolt! Dear heavens, why am I arguing with you?" he asked, looking up at the sky. He took a deep breath, rubbed his temple and looked back at her.

Emily noticed.

"Are you okay?"

"I believe you are giving me a headache," he said seriously.

"Yea, I get that a lot," she said dismissively, turning her attention back to the dagger, continuing to swipe at the air.

"Do I need to take that back?" he asked, pointing at the dagger.

She frowned and put the weapon in its sheath. "Dream squasher," she muttered.

"What was that you said?" Martin asked annoyed.

"Nothing," she replied, fiddling with the dagger strapped at her side.

"May the heavens help us. Now she is armed," he grumbled.

The weather was turning foul. The trees bent from the strain of the wind. Martin looked up at the storm clouds approaching.

"We must hurry," he told her.

Emily moved around the horses, examining other weapons Martin was bringing with them. She ran her hand over the two broadswords and a crossbow, admiring their craftsmanship.

"And, when do I get to learn how to use a sword?" she asked innocently.

"Not in my lifetime," he muttered.

He scooted her away from the weapons and checked to make sure they were securely fastened. He then attached blankets, miscellaneous supplies and their gear.

When Martin was distracted, Emily untied his crossbow and looked at it carefully. She had always wanted to learn how to use one. His was particularly unique. It was a double crossbow. Martin turned his back to Emily and filled another bag with food that Mira had provided.

"Lucy! You got some splainin to do!" she teased, holding the crossbow in the air.

Martin ignored her. He refused to engage and ask why she had just called him "Lucy."

He did not see Emily pull out an arrow, place it on the crossbow, pull back on the string and release the trigger. However, he did hear it whizzing. Martin instinctively ducked, as the arrow flew past his right ear and planted itself in a tree next to him. The wind caused it to veer right, narrowly missing him.

"Whoopsie!" she said immediately and winced.

Martin cursed under his breath, walked around the horse and yanked the crossbow out of her hands. She shrugged and grinned sheepishly at him. He gave her a dirty look.

"Are you trying to kill me?" he scolded her.

"I've got to get one of those," she said enthusiastically.

"Kindly stop touching everything," he complained. "My heavens, you are worse than a toddler."

Just as Martin finished his sentence a roar came from the woods behind them. They both turned towards the sound. Several heavily armed raiders charged into the clearing with swords raised. Martin immediately drew his sword and pushed Emily to the ground. He slung the crossbow over his shoulder and grabbed several arrows.

"Get down and stay down," he yelled as he charged forward to meet the attackers head on.

With his sword held high, Martin slid to one knee and took down the two men directly in front, quickly and swiftly with one swipe of his weapon, slicing across their midsections. They fell to the ground, grabbing their stomachs, screaming in agony. Martin was instantly back on his feet.

Emily watched. Martin was quick, so quick. The raiders were clumsy and sluggish. Martin was a stark contrast. He moved effortlessly. His strategy was orchestrated and deliberate. As he swung his sword at the third raider, Martin brought his crossbow to the front, loaded it and managed to shoot multiple arrows at two assailants approaching from his right. Then, he immediately dropped to one knee and thrust his sword upward just as another assailant charged him. Blood gushed out of the man's mouth. Martin pushed the man's body off his sword and instantly went back into attack mode for the remaining raiders.

Martin tossed his crossbow to the ground and ducked as another raider swung a mace at his head, barely missing him. With the mace in one hand and a sword in the other, this attacker was more skilled than the others. He parred with Martin and they exchanged several blows. The clanging sound of metal hitting metal cut through the air. Their swords locked briefly. Martin pulled the assailant closer and punched him several times in the head, knocking the assailant to the ground.

Emily looked at the crossbow near her and scooted on the ground trying to reach it. Martin caught the movement in the corner of his eye, as he continued fighting with the raider. He held the raider at bay with his sword in one hand. He pointed at Emily, apparently reading her thoughts.

"Stay!" he shouted.

She frowned but did as she was told.

The remaining raiders joined forces and circled Martin. They had surmised his skills and recalculated their strategy, coordinating their attack against a far worthy opponent. Martin spun in a circle, keeping his sword in front of him, switching between his left and right hand. He could fight equally well with both. He was surrounded. One of the raiders broke ranks and charged at him from behind.

"Martin, look out!" Emily yelled.

He spun around, stepped to the side and swung his sword high, instantly decapitating the man. Emily felt her stomach churn when the severed head rolled towards her. She kicked it away with her foot.

Another attacker rushed forward and swung his sword. Martin deflected the blow and grabbed the man by his clothing, throwing him to the ground. He then plunged his sword deep into the man's back, ending his life. Despite being outnumbered, the raiders were no match for Martin's superior fighting skills.

Another raider lunged at Martin, only to be lifted off the ground. Both Martin and Emily looked up. A mylox had grabbed the attacker with its claws and carried him off, high above the trees, and then dropped him. The man screamed in terror as he plummeted to his death. The remaining raiders took this as their cue to fall back. They turned and ran, looking up at the skies, scared of more aerial attacks. Martin chased after them, knocking one of them down, tackling him from behind.

Martin lifted him to his feet and spun him around, as he did so the attacker stabbed Martin's shoulder with a dagger. Martin winced in pain before punching the man. The man was dazed. He took the raider's dagger and held it to his throat.

"You have no place here. Go back and tell my father to stay where he belongs or he will answer to me. Do you understand?" Martin fumed. The man was barely conscious but shook his head yes. "Go! Now!" he ordered.

The man staggered and ran into the woods. While Martin's attention was focused elsewhere, another assailant used this advantage to sneak up behind Emily. He covered her mouth with his gloved hand and grabbed her from behind. She bit down hard on his hand to free herself. He yanked his hand away and knocked her to the ground. She pulled out her dagger and held it in front of her with both hands. The attacker laughed at her, showing rotted teeth. He quickly snatched it out of her hand. He grabbed Emily by her hair and dragged her into the woods, kicking and screaming.

"Now I have you," he hissed.

As he spoke those words, two arrows pierced his body. One in the shoulder and the other in his back. He fell to his knees. Emily immediately started backing away from her attacker. He grabbed her foot and wouldn't let go.

In a flurry of motion, Martin tackled the raider, forcing him to release his hold on Emily. Martin picked him up, throwing him several feet away. He landed with a hard thud. Martin grabbed the assailant and drove the arrows deeper into the man's flesh, finishing him off with a knife to the gut.

Only then did Martin grab his shoulder, acknowledging the searing pain he felt. He cleaned his weapons and pulled the arrows from the deceased men. He looked down at his shoulder. It was a deep wound. Suddenly, Emily grabbed him from behind. He flinched from pain. She hugged him tightly. Martin gently pried her arms off and turned to face her.

"Do you intend to squeeze me to death?" he asked, slightly amused.

"Sorry," she said, embarrassed. She hugged him again.

He winced in pain, pulled himself free and laughed.

"Enough," he grinned.

"You saved my life," she looked up at him.

"Again," he corrected.

"Yeah, again," she agreed.

"You made a good accounting of yourself. Many would have fled. Did he harm you?"

"I'm okay. There were so many of them," she pointed out.

"I did have some help from the mylox," he reminded her, looking towards the clouds.

"Thank you," she said genuinely sincere.

He studied her face for any trace of sarcasm but found none. He accepted her heartfelt thanks.

"You are most welcome," he bowed graciously.

She suddenly smiled at him and her eyes twinkled. Martin took a step back and held up his hands.

"You are not going to embrace me again, are you?" he asked.

"Naaaa, but that was just cool, watching you fight like that," she said admiringly.

He rubbed his shoulder again. "It has been quite a while, and I am a bit rusty," he admitted.

"You'd never know it."

He grinned. "Numbers matter not if you are clumsy with a blade. A knight must use his mind, just as much as his might – to anticipate his opponents moves, to see what they cannot see and strike accordingly."

"In other words, you kicked their butts," she grinned.

He pulled open his cloak and looked down at his shoulder.

"Not before one of them took a piece out of me."

Emily saw the blood seeping heavily through his tunic.

"You've been hurt," her eyes widened in alarm.

"There are bandages in the saddlebag. Fetch them and fresh water, please, so I can tend to this wound."

She did as he asked and returned with strips of cloth and a water bag. "Here, let me help you," she offered.

He waved her off. "I do not wish to be your pin cushion. I can manage," he stated.

"Stop being stubborn. I can do it. I took a first aid class at the Y," she told him.

"At the why? Why what?" he asked.

"Not, the W H Y... The Y," she corrected.

"I literally said the exact same thing – the why?" he argued.

"No, not why... I mean the letter Y...as in YMCA," she tried to explain, while spelling the letters with her arms.

"What in heavens are you doing? Why are you forming the shapes of letters with your arms?" he asked, confused.

She poured water onto the cloth strips.

"Never mind. Stop squirming. Let me help you, geez."

"I am quite capable of tending to my own wound," he argued, trying to pull the cloth away from her hand.

She pointed to a tree stump.

"Sit and shush," she argued back.

Martin frowned, but unclasped his cloak and set it aside. He removed his bloody tunic, folded it neatly and pressed it against his shoulder to help slow down the bleeding, before sitting down.

Emily stepped back and looked at him.

"Geez, do you work out like every day?" she asked curiously, commenting on his muscular build.

"What?" he asked, surprised by her candor.

"I mean, you're like Superman buff," she pointed out.

"I beg your pardon?" he asked perplexed.

"Yea, I worked out – once," she admitted. "My parents got this trial membership. Yawn. My mom was on this total health kick at the time, so we tried it. But then, they built this donut shop down the road – Daisy's Donuts. It was kind of pointless, you know? To spend an hour at the gym, bored out of my mind, only to grab a chocolate glazed donut on the way home. So, to make a long story short – the donuts won," she laughed, pretending to punch Martin on his good shoulder.

"Daisy's Donuts?" Martin shrugged, shaking his head in confusion.

"Yea, I like the ones with rainbow sprinkles on them, but you don't strike me as a sprinkles kind of guy," she grinned.

He began rubbing his temple again.

"Oh wow, are you getting another headache?" she asked.

He didn't answer her question. "Please, my shoulder?"

"Sure, sorry."

She leaned in to get a closer look and inhaled sharply. It was a nasty wound. The dagger had passed straight through.

"That's got to hurt," she said with concern.

"I have had worse," he said, looking away.

She poured fresh water on his injury and pressed a clean cloth against it. "Hold this and apply pressure," she instructed.

"I am aware of the procedure," he retorted. He held the cloth bandage tightly against his shoulder, grimacing from the pain.

Emily walked behind Martin to clean the exit wound. She glanced down at his back and instantly froze. Her mouth dropped open. What she saw took her breath away.

Martin wasn't exaggerating. He had in fact been hurt far worse before. Numerous scars covered his back, several of them were very long and could have only been made by a sword. Other scar tissue appeared to have been made by some type of strap or belt, tearing into his flesh. It looked to Emily as if he had been severely beaten, repeatedly. She reached out to touch his back, but quickly put her hand down.

She shrank back a little and lowered her head, feeling quite silly for talking about rainbow sprinkles, given everything Martin had endured in his life.

He was so brave and she was…not.

She shut her eyes tightly. It made her sad. Her mind raced back to the children she saw in those horrible cages. So much blood. So much pain. She felt oddly empty inside.

Martin looked over his shoulder and cleared his throat. She jumped slightly, opening her eyes. He was staring at her.

Emily looked away, uncomfortably.

"Sorry. I'm really sorry. I wasn't trying to be rude."

She continued cleaning his wound in silence, doing her best to wrap clean strips of cloth over it, applying pressure to stop the bleeding.

Martin looked back at her a few times, but said nothing. He saw that her hands were trembling. Her mood had become quite somber. She was not accustomed to this kind of violence. He reminded himself that she was still quite young, despite her sharp wit. The last few days had surely been difficult for her. She was frightened, understandably. He chastised himself for not being more sensitive to that fact. He sighed heavily.

"I was tired of fighting, tired of bloodshed," he explained, choosing his words carefully.

Even the forest grew quiet as he spoke. Emily said nothing but continued to treat his wound.

"I thought becoming a doctor would be – safe. Apparently, I was wrong. I believed that saving lives would protect me from the darkness. However, no matter where I went? No matter what I did? It always seemed to follow me," he shared quietly, a tinge of pain and regret surfaced in his voice.

Emily felt the sorrow in his words. She looked back down at the scars left behind, the ones she suspected were at the hands of his father, Merrick, after the death of his mother. It was a pain that did not go away once the wounds had healed. Martin had carried that anguish his entire life.

She finished bandaging his shoulder. It wasn't pretty, but it would protect the wound and allow him to use his shoulder.

"I hope that's okay," she told him, unsure of herself.

He looked at his shoulder. "The wound looks worse than what it actually is. I am still a doctor," he assured her.

"Not like any doctor I've ever seen," she said softly.

He tightened the bandage and secured it underneath his arm, satisfied that it was adequately treated. He moved his shoulder in a circular motion. It was painful but not unbearable.

"Well done," he thanked her. He stood, gathered his cloak and walked over to their horses to retrieve a fresh tunic.

Emily stood there watching him for a moment longer, grateful that she was not alone. Things had been happening so quickly around her. She was scared. Too many people were depending on her. She felt vulnerable and overwhelmed. She stopped looking at Martin and stared at the ground. She retreated into herself, believing if she didn't move a muscle? Then, perhaps all of this would simply go away and she'd be home again.

Martin readied their horses and looked back. Emily hadn't moved. She was still standing by the tree with the bloody cloth in her hand. He turned back to his horse and sighed.

"Damn," he muttered softly under his breath.

He couldn't do this for her. It was her or no one. And, that was an incredibly heavy burden. He didn't know her well enough to make judgments. But he did know that the keystone brought her to Aquila. It would not have done so if it did not believe she was worthy and capable, of that he was certain, even if it was against all odds.

He knew her situation was going to get far worse from here forward. But to look at Emily now? Courage was not something he could teach her. Courage was something she would have to find within herself. This wasn't her world. What right did any of them have to ask this of her, a sacrifice that could very well claim her life? He wondered if she realized how much danger she was truly in. He lowered his head, searching for some words of wisdom to share with her. He looked back at her again. She looked lost, too frightened to take one more step.

"Emily?"

She blinked, jerking her head towards Martin. It was the very first time Martin had ever called her by her name. Her eyes met his. She tried to steady her nerves.

"Come now. We need to keep moving. We have lingered here far too long," he urged gently.

"Okay."

She slowly walked over to him, without so much as a word, looking defeated. Martin helped Emily onto her horse. She stared straight ahead. He glanced back at her after he mounted his horse. Emily was sitting stoically, touching her necklace. He lightly nudged his horse and circled back to Emily.

"May I ask a question of you?"

"Sure," she said, eyes fixed ahead.

He leaned in towards her, as if he didn't want anyone else to hear. She glanced at him, before staring shyly back at her hands.

"What exactly is this Thundercat you speak of?" he grinned.

Emily turned her head slowly towards him. She saw the huge grin on his face and the kindness behind his eyes.

She smiled back at him, appreciating the gesture.

He nodded politely at her before nudging his horse onward. With Martin in the lead, Emily's horse followed dutifully.

~~~~~~~~~~~~~~~~~~~~~~~~~~~~~~~~~~

They ventured deeper into the snowy mountains. Rain mixed with snow fell down upon them. She wrapped her cloak around herself and pulled the hood over her head to ward off the chill. She held on to the reins tightly. Riding the horse took little effort. Hers simply followed the other.

Neither Martin or Emily spoke. They traveled for hours in frigid conditions, occasionally the clouds would break, allowing the sun to slightly penetrate the cold, under the purple sky. It seemed like such a beautiful tranquil place but Emily knew better.

Martin stayed alert at all times, while Emily yawned, fighting sleep. Her backside was sore from sitting on the horse for so long. She considered complaining to Martin, but then thought better of it. There seemed no end to their journey. Emily started to drift off to sleep and nearly fell off her horse. The horse whinnied to alert Martin. He looked back at her but said nothing.

Her thoughts drifted back to her family. They'd never believe this, she realized. They would think she made the entire thing up. That's what I get for making up so many stories in the past, she said to herself. She touched the necklace dangling around her neck, remembering the face of her grandmother and the woman imprisoned in the fortress.

Martin finally came to a halt near a creek.

"We'll stop here. The horses need rest."

"So do I," she said.

Emily half climbed and half fell off her horse.

Martin pretended not to notice.

"That was graceful," he muttered.

He found a dry patch under some tall pine trees and rolled out the blankets on the ground for them to sleep on, using the pine needles as cushion. He excused himself to gather firewood nearby and let the horses drink water. He remained where he could see her. With every step he took, he always had her in his sight. When Martin returned, he started a fire by using his steel blade to strike a piece of hard quartz, igniting a spark. He rubbed his hands near the fire.

"Come," he ordered Emily. "Sit closer to the fire and stay warm."

She scooted over closer to the flames and sat across from Martin. She was so tired. She could barely keep her eyes open. Emily shivered and looked at the flurries coming down.

He handed her bread, cheese and fruit, wrapped in a cloth.

"You must eat," he told her.

"I'm not hungry," she yawned.

"It matters not. Eat, keep up your strength," he ordered.

She frowned but accepted the food he gave her. A loud blood curdling screech came from somewhere deep in the woods. They both looked towards the direction of the sound.

"What was that?" she asked.

"Nothing to worry about," he assured her.

"It sure sounded like something to worry about," she replied.

When she was finished eating, she curled up in her blanket and stayed as close to the fire as possible. Martin checked the perimeter, keeping a close eye on their surroundings. His eyes darted around like a hawk looking for prey.

Emily studied him through the flames.

"Aren't you going to sleep?" she asked.

He shook his head no. "I will keep watch over you. Rest now."

A sound from the woods caught his attention. He stood up for a better look, listening intently, hand on his sword. Emily fought to keep her eyes open, but within moments she fell asleep. She was safe in Martin's care.

Soon, Emily began thrashing in her sleep. Martin watched her closely. He knew her dreams were taking her someplace that he could not follow.

# Chapter Fifteen

She searched frantically for a way out of the village. The horseman was still chasing her. She had been running too long. Her legs were getting wobbly and she could feel herself slowing down. She couldn't keep up this pace for much longer. She stumbled to the ground, skinned her knees and struggled to get up.

A strong hand, like a vice, grabbed her from behind, swept her off her feet and onto the back of the horse. She was being held so tightly that she could barely breathe. He was crushing her. She tried to free her arms, but he had her completely pinned down. She tried biting him to gain some leverage.

He struck her hard on the back of her head. "Try that again and I will snap your neck like a twig!" he shouted.

He rode off into the night, towards the dark fortress. She could make out the occasional lit torch. The sounds of screaming eventually faded away. The horse slowed down. The sounds of hooves landing on stone replaced the thudding on the dirt path.

She turned her head to look at the sinister castle. He stopped, dismounted and pulled her roughly off the horse. Without a word, he dragged her into the castle. A massive wooden door was opened, and she was forcibly shoved inside. She shivered from the cold and dared not move.

Across the room a man stood with his back to her. He was dressed entirely in black, with a heavy cloak draped over his shoulders. She noted how tall he was and how broad his shoulders were. He was a giant among men, strong and powerful. What did he want with her? She wondered. She could not see his face until he turned and stepped into the light cast by the fireplace.

It was Merrick.

However, it was not the Merrick she had previously seen at their family castle. This Merrick's eyes were cold and dead. He'd spent years in the darkness and there was no trace of humanity left in those eyes. He walked across the room and slapped her hard across the face, knocking her to the ground. Searing pain shot across her cheek and she tasted blood in her mouth.

She was lying on the cold stone, stunned and unable to move from the sheer force of the blow. She turned her head to face Merrick, who said nothing. Not one word. He asked no questions. He made no comment. He kicked her hard in the stomach. She felt something crack inside of her, perhaps a rib. She cried out in pain, moaning on the floor, tasting more blood in her mouth. The wind was knocked out of her and she struggled to breathe.

She could see past Merrick. Standing behind him, near the fire, almost hidden in the shadows, was the boy from the clinic. She couldn't recall his name. Their eyes met, but he didn't try to help her. He just stood there watching Merrick hit her over and over again. The boy looked at her with amusement.

She cried out from another blow to the head, pleading for Merrick to stop, tears mixed with blood, streaming down her face. The pain was intense. Her head was throbbing and every part of her body hurt. She felt herself going in and out of consciousness.

Merrick was beating her to death.

The boy grinned. He was enjoying her demise. She was gasping for air, raising her arm in an effort to deflect Merrick's blows. His foot connected with her stomach again and this time she coughed up blood. She finally passed out.

~~~~~~~~~~~~~~~~~~~~~~~~~~

Martin ran over and held Emily tight. She was thrashing wildly in her sleep. She opened her eyes suddenly, rolled over and spat out blood. She gagged and struggled for air. Martin sat her upright, trying to help her breathe.

"Emily? What is wrong?"

She couldn't speak. Her body went limp. She rolled onto her back and stared into his eyes. He quickly examined her but found no signs of external injuries. Emily's pulse was racing. Martin noticed a deep red handprint across her face where she had been struck. Someone had been beating her, he realized. He felt anger within. There was nothing he could do for her. She needed a different kind of healer.

Martin called out for Thalien.

Emily pulled herself away from Martin and crawled into a ball, moaning in pain. Her body hurt all over. He moved beside her again and held her close, despite her protest. Martin pulled the blanket around Emily to protect her from the cold and carried her closer to the fire. He could do nothing but try to calm her.

"You are safe now...breathe slowly. You are safe," he repeated.

After several minutes, she noticeably relaxed in his arms and her breathing calmed. She opened her eyes and tried to speak.

"The boy..."

Martin leaned in closer to try and understand her words.

"What is it?"

"The boy...from the clinic," she repeated weakly. Her voice trailed off. She coughed up more blood and her body began to shake. Martin wiped the blood off her mouth. Emily closed her eyes again.

He held her closely, trying to comfort her. He wished he could protect her from whatever was harming her in her dreams. He knew all too well how horrible they could be. He was worried for her. Aquila's ugliness would not even allow her to sleep peacefully. Martin took a deep breath, lowering his head, frustrated that there was not more that he could do.

~~~~~~~~~~~~~~~~~~~~~~~

Rebecca was told that Doctor Pernell was away for the rest of the day. Speaking to him about Donovan would have to wait. She thought it was best to keep a close eye on him until the doctor returned. She followed Donovan the rest of the day, staying safely out of sight. She saw nothing unusual and was beginning to think that maybe this was all a figment of her imagination.

After dinner, she followed Donovan outside the clinic and back into the forest. She stayed far enough away to avoid detection. He went into a section of the woods that they had been told not to enter. It was rumored that this part of the woods was haunted.

Rebecca reluctantly followed. She didn't trust him and was determined to find out what he was up to. She slowly shadowed him through the forest, taking care to use the trees to hide herself.

She didn't like being this far from the clinic and knew they would both get into trouble if Doctor Pernell discovered they had wandered off like this. Donovan walked deep into the woods before stopping. She moved closer to him and watched him do the same thing he did before. He went into a trance like state and then a sinister grin crossed his face when he was finished.

Maybe her eyes were playing tricks on her, but she noticed a distortion among the trees, slight variations in the shadows moving closer and closer to Donovan. It stopped directly in front of him. Suddenly, the shape took form. Standing before Donovan was a dark-haired woman, wearing a black hooded cloak.

Rebecca could see her clearly now. The woman had stark haggard features. She kept fading in and out, using shadows to conceal herself. She and Donovan spoke for quite some time. Her appearance startled Rebecca.

The little girl had seen enough and lost her nerve. She turned to go back to the clinic, stepping on a twig. It snapped loudly. Both Donovan and the strange woman turned towards the sound. Rebecca ducked behind a tree, hoping she had not been seen.

She waited a few moments and then carefully peered around the tree. Donovan and the woman were both gone. She ducked behind the tree again and looked around frantically. Spooked, she took off running, back towards the clinic. She didn't even stop to look behind her.

Once inside the clinic, she slowed down her breathing. She was scared. She looked out the nearby doors and windows but saw nothing. She saw Doctor Pernell walk across the courtyard. Rebecca ran outside to catch him.

"Doctor Pernell!" she called.

He stopped and turned. "Good evening, Rebecca. What are you up to?"

She ran up to him.

"I have to talk to you right away," she said.

"Let's go to my office. I have some free time."

He walked her to his office and closed the door behind them to speak with Rebecca in private.

"Have a seat, Rebecca," he instructed. "Now suppose you tell me what has you so worked up this evening."

She sat in a chair across from him. He poured a glass of water and slid it across the desk to her. She drank it down quickly.

"It's about Donovan."

Doctor Pernell looked extremely interested. "What about him?"

"This might sound strange, but I think he's doing something wrong," she said nervously.

"What kind of things?"

"I don't know for sure, but twice now I saw him go off by himself and get in some kind of a trance. It was so weird. Then, he opened his eyes and well, he didn't look right. He looked mean, scary. His appearance had changed. The kind of face bullies have after they hurt you, you know what I mean? I get picked on at school sometimes and I know that face."

Doctor Pernell nodded. "I see. Aside from looking scary, do you have any other reason to suspect Donovan is up to something?"

"Yes, sir," she said sheepishly. "After dinner, I followed him into the woods beyond the west grove."

"Rebecca – you have been warned not to go there," Doctor Pernell said sternly.

"Yes, I know, but wait till I tell you what I saw."

"Continue," Doctor Pernell said calmly.

"After he did his trance thing, some strange woman appeared right out of the shadows. It was almost like she was a ghost. They were talking in the forest for a long time. She was scary looking. Something wasn't right with her," she said, talking quickly to get her story out.

Doctor Pernell rubbed his chin. "Anything else?" he asked.

"No, then I ran back here as fast as I could."

"I see," said Doctor Pernell. He stood and walked around the office.

"I think he's up to no good," she told him.

"Well, it does not look like you have any evidence to back up your claims. It sounds like nothing more than an active imagination on your part," he scolded her, returning to his seat.

Rebecca leaned back in her chair. She was disappointed. She was trying to do the right thing and expected Doctor Pernell to react differently. He didn't seem upset at all. Or even mildly concerned. Even Rebecca knew that all visitors were supposed to be approved by the clinic. Doctor Pernell didn't even seem to care that Donovan was talking to a stranger in the forest or that he was sneaking around. He was usually very strict about following the rules.

"But, Doctor Pernell," she injected.

"As a matter of fact, the only one here that seems to have done anything wrong is you, Rebecca," he looked at her sternly.

"I don't understand," she said.

"Spying on Donovan? Following him into the woods? Accusing him of things? Do I need to continue?" he asked.

She shook her head no, confused.

"No one likes a snoop or a tattle tale. As a matter of fact," he added, "the only one that is really guilty of anything is – you."

"What?" she said meekly.

"You are the reason your parents were killed."

Rebecca could not believe her ears. A look of shock crossed her face. "That's not true," she said.

"It's all your fault. After all, the raiders were looking for you," he reminded her coldly.

"No," she said in a shaky voice, fighting back tears.

"Oh, but it's true." He opened his desk drawer and pulled out a file. He rifled through a few pages. "See? It says right here. The Marshals reported that the raiders were looking for you and killed your parents as a result of that search. All your fault. Clearly says so in the report."

She looked at the papers in his hand.

"No," she whispered through tears.

"They were killed because of you. And, everyone knows this," he persisted.

"What...what?" she said through tears, slightly stammering.

"What...what?" he mocked. "You should not be casting stones. You're the one with all the blood on your hands," he said with distain.

She looked at him, eyes full of pain. Doctor Pernell was supposed to be her friend. He was supposed to care about her. She had lost her parents. She lowered her head in disbelief.

"I don't understand," she whispered.

"How does it feel to know they died because of you?" he asked, showing no mercy.

"I'm sorry," she said softly.

"I would not go pointing that little finger at Donovan, do you understand? Mind your own business," he scolded.

"Why are you doing this to me?" she asked tearfully.

"Is it not obvious? No one likes you here. You have been living off our generosity long enough? You are a parasite," he hissed, practically spitting the words out.

She shook her head no. She was trembling. Tears streamed down her face.

"I thought this was my home now?" Rebecca pleaded.

"No one wants you here," the doctor stated. He stood up abruptly and opened the door. "Get out of my office. Do not bother me again. Do us all a favor – leave."

She stood, wiped tears away, and rushed out of the room.

The doctor smiled and closed the door behind him. Once Rebecca was well out of range, Doctor Pernell disappeared and

211

only the boy remained. Donovan sat back down in the chair and laughed out loud.

"That ought to shut you up," he smirked.

Donovan was very pleased with himself. It had been a grand day indeed. He had almost drowned Martin in his dream and he saw the most unusual thing – the new girl, Emily, was with Merrick in one of his visions. Had they shared the same vision? They must have. They locked eyes. Why was Merrick beating her? It was worth mentioning to Miranda.

In the forest, he told Miranda what he saw. Miranda was extremely excited. She said it was the missing piece she had been searching for. She now had the girl's name and face. Donovan told her that Emily had left the clinic with Doctor Stewart. Miranda now knew that Martin himself was the girl's guardian.

The irony of this situation did not escape her. She instructed Donovan to keep a close eye on the doctor's whereabouts and suggested that he continue to visit Martin in his dreams, perhaps drive him a bit mad, she suggested

"Always keep your enemies close," she told him.

It would only be a matter of time before they captured the girl and obtained the object Miranda sought, Donovan realized.

Donovan didn't understand it all but he was happy to be a part of it. Seeing Rebecca in the woods gave him an excuse to get rid of her. How dare she spy on him! She didn't know who she was messing with, and she was foolish to think someone as insignificant as her could get in his way. He sure showed her. He laughed again.

"Sleep well, Rebecca. I know you won't," Donovan grinned smugly.

Back in her room, Rebecca took out what few possessions she had and stuffed them into a canvas bag, along with a few pieces of fruit. She grabbed her five coins and headed straight out the front door, putting as much distance as possible between herself and the clinic. She disappeared into the edge of the forest just as Doctor Pernell rode up to the stables behind the clinic.

He looked up at the building and saw Donovan watching from a second-floor window. He waved at the boy. The doctor dismounted his horse and walked the animal back into the stable. He headed back to the clinic, stopping by the nurse's station on the way in.

"Justeen – would you mind having someone run this up to Rebecca's room?" he asked, pulling out a children's book from his travel bag. "She asked me to pick up a new book for her and I want to make sure she gets it as soon as possible."

"Of course," said the nurse, placing the book on the table beside her.

"Thank you."

Doctor Pernell walked towards his office and noticed Donovan was now watching him from the doorway of the dining hall. He stopped and spoke to the boy.

"Is there something you wanted to see me about?" The boy shook his head no. "Then go back to your room. It's late and you are not supposed to be wandering around after hours like this," he instructed.

The boy said nothing and walked around the corner towards his room. The doctor watched for a few seconds, then continued to his office when he was satisfied the boy had done as he was told. When he entered his office, he found Rebecca's folder opened on his desk. He put down his bag and picked up the folder.

"This is strange," he muttered. He stuck his head out of the door and called down to the nurse. "Who has been in my office?"

"No one that I am aware of," she told him.

"How odd…" He put it back into his desk drawer.

Another nurse came to his door. "Doctor Pernell?"

"Yes?" he answered while pouring himself a drink.

"We seem to have a slight problem."

Doctor Pernell put down his cup. "What is it?"

"Rebecca, sir."

Doctor Pernell was immediately concerned. She was such an emotionally fragile child. "What is it?"

"She appears to have run away. We sent the book to her room and she was gone, so were her belongings."

"Oh no. Send all available personnel out to search the grounds for her," he ordered urgently.

"Yes, sir." She rushed down the hallway to organize the search.

Doctor Pernell looked back at his desk, wondering about the folder he found on it. He looked up and saw Donovan standing in the doorway, staring at him. "Did I not tell you to return to your room, young man?"

Donovan shrugged, "I guess so."

The doctor was in no mood for Donovan's peculiar games.

"What do you know about Rebecca's disappearance?"

A slight grin appeared on his face. He masked it quickly, but not quickly enough. Doctor Pernell caught it. Donovan looked at the ground and shuffled his feet.

"I don't know anything," he said slyly.

Doctor Pernell frowned, sensing that something was off with the boy. He removed his glasses and looked at Donovan. He suddenly felt uneasy, but he didn't betray his emotions to the boy. That was exactly what Donovan would want him to do. He knew Donovan had a habit of mentally spying on people. The doctor closed off Donovan to his mind. He didn't want the boy to know that he suspected his involvement. He addressed Donovan again.

"Well, I am sure it is nothing to be concerned about," he told Donovan. "Run along to your room now," he ordered.

"Sure, Doctor Pernell," he grinned.

Doctor Pernell watched him leave. There was more going on with the boy than shifting. He would have to pay closer attention to him. There was something deeply disturbing about him. He hoped that Rebecca was safe. He suspected that the boy was involved by the sly look in the boy's eyes and complete lack of empathy. Doctor Pernell knew he needed to be careful, not knowing the full extent of the boy's abilities.

Martin paced around the campfire, watching Thalien closely. He had come to heal Emily. Martin knew that her injuries were internal from the blood she spat up. They were a good three days ride from the clinic now and Martin did not think she could survive the journey. Thalien huddled over Emily, deep in concentration, his hands moving above her. Finally, he stopped and walked over to Martin and sighed deeply. Martin looked past Thalien. Emily was lying on the blanket with her eyes shut tightly.

"Is she going to be alright?" he asked.

Thalien followed his gaze and looked back at Emily.

"Yes, she will be fine, physically anyway. These visions are taking an emotional toll on her. Seekers with her ability are trained at a very young age. I am afraid Emily has been given no time to adjust or prepare for her gift. It is completely draining her emotionally."

Martin's eyes never left Emily. "My mother used to have bad visions too sometimes. She would have unexplained bruises. When I was a little boy, I thought my father had struck her. I asked her about it a few days before my 10th birthday…a few days before her…death," he said sadly. "I did not understand," he admitted, "and I am not sure I understand now either. I do know that the visions are very real."

"Indeed," Thalien agreed. "It must have been hard for you to understand. Much as it is difficult for Emily to understand what is happening to her. She is scared and confused, but doesn't want to admit it, especially to you."

Martin looked at him, "What do you mean?"

"She wants very much to earn your respect," he confided.

Martin looked back at Emily. "She said something just as she woke…"

"What?"

"She said 'the boy from the clinic' – now the only boy I saw at the clinic that struck me as peculiar was Donovan, a shifter. Do you have any idea why she would mention him, assuming he is the boy she was referring to?" Martin asked him.

"None whatsoever, but I will inquire with Doctor Pernell at once on this matter. We cannot take any chances."

Martin nodded in agreement. "Good – because we do not know if she was trying to tell us the boy was in trouble…" He looked back to Thalien, "Or whether she was warning us about him."

Thalien patted Martin on the shoulder. Martin winced.

"You were injured?" Thalien asked.

"Yes, a skirmish. Raiders attacked us again, but Emily tended to my wound."

Thalien smiled and looked back at the girl. "Did she?"

"Yes, she did an adequate job too."

Thalien nodded in approval. "I must see Doctor Pernell at once. When she wakes up, perhaps she can remember more. Do not press her too hard. She took quite a beating from someone. If you learn anything, please let me know."

"I shall," Martin responded.

Thalien placed his hand back on Martin's shoulder and held it there for a moment. Martin felt a strange sensation and moved his shoulder.

"Your shoulder is healed now," he smiled.

Martin reached up and looked at his wound beneath the bandage. It was completely healed. Martin pulled the cloth bandages off and discarded them.

"Thank you," he said with gratitude.

With that, Thalien disappeared right before Martin's eyes, leaving him alone with Emily, who was sleeping soundly by the fire. Martin took out a skillet from the travel bag along with broth and vegetables. He prepared a stew.

His thoughts drifted to Donovan. Martin wondered what the boy was fully capable of doing. They would have to find out what danger the boy posed, if any.

# Chapter Sixteen

Sacrifice. Rayven knew the meaning of this word all too well. Growing up on the dark side was a harsh, brutal life. Most of her life was spent living with her parents and baby brother in a small room above a tavern. Her mother used to be a servant in Miranda's fortress and her father was a known criminal. He was eventually banished to the Keep when she was only a young girl, leaving them to fend for themselves.

Being banished to the Keep for a crime was a contradiction in itself since Miranda encouraged raids on the light side. The catch was that she sanctioned the raids. If he had robbed someone on the light side, he would not have been imprisoned, but he stole from others on the dark side to buy mead and was sent to the Keep.

Rayven hated the man. She watched her father destroy their family, piece by piece, beating her mother into submission. He had no love for his children, and they had none for him. She remembered curling up on the small mattress with her mother, talking of the day when the three of them could escape to the light side and begin a new life, far away from her abusive father and the ugliness of the dark side.

These dreams sustained them. Her mother held on to this hope, before her father robbed her of this too. Over time, the abuse began to erode her mother's life. She developed a fatal resolve that one day she would be murdered by her husband and that fear emotionally crippled her.

The continued onslaught of abuse stripped her mother of her self-worth and dignity. His history of violence had a profound impact on Rayven's life. She was glad when he was finally caught and sentenced to life in the dungeons for stealing. His banishment came far too late for her mother, however, who was now an empty shell. Her spirit had been broken and dreams for a better life had been long abandoned. It was agonizing watching her mother suffer so much at the hands of her father. She was a loving mother but could not overcome the years of abuse.

Her baby brother, Philip, was small for his age and sickly. Her mother always fretted over Philip, worried that he would not survive the frigid temperatures. He was so frail. Her father was particularly harsh on the boy, calling him a waste. Rayven did her best to protect both Philip and her mother. She volunteered for fight training at an early age, mostly with other boys, hoping that one day she would be able to defend her mother against her father's vicious attacks.

His thieving caught up with him before she had a chance to slit his throat and watch him die. Her training was not a complete loss, however. She had become quite proficient with a sword. Her speed and accuracy were as good as many of Miranda's skilled soldiers.

Rayven was certain that her inner rage and hatred towards her father only enhanced her skill set. Rayven's abilities were good enough to attract the attention of the high guards and she eventually became one of Miranda's handpicked raiders. In her late teens, she started having visions and was identified as a seeker, a valuable asset to Miranda.

Her brother, Philip, grew up to follow a different path and had no desire or interest in serving Miranda. He abhorred violence and aggression of any kind, refusing to even carry a weapon. He was a thief himself, much more adept than his father. Philip was cunning and had the ability to get in and out without being detected. He excelled at it. Philip would regularly steal food to put on their table, a crime also punishable by imprisonment.

Rayven constantly fought with her brother. Philip lived by his own rules, not Miranda's. Rayven thought he was careless and foolish. The only thing Philip seemed interested in was magic. He thought it was more honorable to learn magic tricks, slight of hand, and steal for food than to take up a sword and fight.

He avoided black magic. He wasn't interested in the sinister side of spells that could manipulate or corrupt minds. He had too much of his mother's gentle soul in him for that kind of nonsense. She was an honorable woman and did not subscribe to trickery or black arts. She instilled in him the need to do good. Rayven would argue that stealing was not doing good, but Philip was providing food, clothing and necessary items for his family. He saw that as a noble endeavor.

Miranda had risen to power with Merrick at her side. He was a puppet, nothing more. Philip could not stomach their methods. He frequently clashed with his sister over her decision to serve Miranda in her brutal quest for dominance.

In one particularly heated exchange, Rayven accused her brother of being as weak minded as he was frail in body. She never saw him again after that. Occasionally, food would be left outside their door. She knew it was from Philip. If he came to visit their mother, he did so when Rayven was out.

Rayven didn't like Miranda anymore than Philip did, but she saw an opportunity for advancement in her life and she took it. She was now a trained killer and assassin. Her position allowed them to keep their tiny room above the tavern. Most others were not so fortunate, forced to live in whatever shelter they could find, fighting over what little food there was, working the mines for scraps till they took their last breath. It was a stark contrast to the riches and lush life the inhabitants on the light side of the mist wall led. They seemed to have an abundance of everything. She hoped that Miranda was successful so that they could all partake in the wealth. Rayven had a sense of purpose.

Philip preferred to gravel in the dirt, stealing to survive, rather than bend to Miranda's will. He was not Rayven's problem anymore. Philip was as dead to her as her father. You were either with Miranda or against her. There was no gray area.

There was always a nagging in the back of Rayven's mind that this was not the life for her. The darkness took everything from everyone, and her father robbed them of a loving family. Even to this day, before Rayven closed her eyes at night, she drifted back to those moments of peace with her mother that she treasured so much.

She recalled the warmth of the fire, the embrace of her mother's arms, listening to the stories of beauty and wonder on the light side, and how she yearned to be there. Hearing the tales of lovely ladies in elegant gowns appealed to her mother. There was no room for such foolish indulgences when you were trapped on the dark side. No warmth or beauty whatsoever to be found here.

Her mother had given up hope long ago. She no longer talked about starting a new life on the light side. Her mother barely spoke at all anymore. Rayven wanted to escape, but she couldn't just leave her mother behind to waste away and die alone. Her mother lived on the brink of madness now. Her mind was locked in the past. She often talked to Rayven as if she were still a little girl. Taking care of her children was the one place she still felt safe and comfortable. Her mind retreated to that time and stayed there.

Her mother would not even leave their home anymore. Rayven would try to get her outside, but her mother would wail and cry. She didn't have the heart to leave without her. Who would take care of her mother if she fled? Her mother had taken care of them all those years and deserved better. She deserved to feel the warmth upon her face and deserved to walk barefoot among the flowers. She deserved to sit peacefully beside the water's edge and listen to the birds sing in the trees. Her mother's only purpose in life had been to care for her children and scrub the floors of the fortress, day after day.

Rayven didn't resent her mother. She was a broken woman. Rayven understood this and blamed herself somewhat. If only she had been stronger when she was younger, perhaps she could have stopped her father's cruelty. Perhaps, the three of them could have left together and found a better life. Her mother had lost her courage and the will to live. She had worked hard and sacrificed for them. Rayven would remain by her mother's side. It was a sacrifice that she was willing to make.

Rayven had been to the light side many times on raids. She still held on to hope. If Miranda was successful, perhaps the riches of the light side would be available to all, and not just to a privileged few. Then, Rayven would get her mother a thatched roof cottage with a little garden that she had always dreamed of. She was sure that once her mother saw the beauty of the mountains and felt the warmth of the sun that she would awaken from her self-imposed prison and live again... Finally, have a chance to be happy. Rayven served Miranda to give her mother that chance.

Rayven looked around at their cramped dark living space. The wind whistled through the shutters and she heard rats scurrying in the rafters overhead. The straw mattress occupied one side of the room. She had seen how the other side lived and she wanted it for herself. She stirred the soup in the pot and glanced back at her mother. Her mother sat quietly in the only chair in the room, rocking back and forth, staring blankly into space. Then her mother started muttering to herself, engaged in an imaginary conversation with her son, Philip.

Rayven didn't entertain the thought of love or a family of her own. Those notions were ludicrous. To raise a family in this dreadful place? And, love? Never. She didn't believe in it and saw nothing here to convince her otherwise.

All she saw was the light dim from her mother's eyes as love vanquished, replaced by acceptance of her fate. She saw the painful sadness that followed. Rayven could not recall ever experiencing love for another, outside of her mother and brother. It was something silly girls clung too. Rayven's reality was cold and lonely. There was no love to be found here. It seemed to have been snuffed out by the darkness. There was more than an abundance of pain, torment and heartache...

Where the years of abuse destroyed her mother, they only made Rayven stronger, strengthening her resolve. She was determined to never let a man control and degrade her the way her father did to their mother. Rayven didn't need a man to make her feel better. She was a killing machine and a seeker, nothing more. The only tenderness she displayed was towards her mother.

Rayven wore the scars from many scrapes over the years. The scar that ran up her face did not diminish her beauty but served as a constant reminder that life was to be fought and not enjoyed. Complacency led to death. It was survival here. She was tough and had no place for foolish sentiment among men. Her emotional scars were far deeper than any scar a weapon could ever make, and her inner wounds had yet to heal.

Only in those fleeting moments of silence and darkness before sleep overtook her did she allow herself to think…what if…what could have been…if only. She only half believed the stories her mother used to tell of the light side, until she finally saw it for herself.

The abundance of life on the light side was intoxicating. The sights and smells were invigorating. The happiness displayed on the faces of the children as they played were so carefree. She could not relate to it but craved it on some primal level. The beauty of the mountains almost brought tears to her eyes the first time she saw them.

The dark side was nothing but a barren wasteland, rugged cliffs and caves, dead soil, thorny thickets and twisted dead trees. Nothing bore fruit or life. The fortress itself was surrounded by destitute villages and towns. They paled in comparison to the castles and grand manors that scattered the landscape on the light side. Even the humble cottages and farmhouses appealed to her. The towns were full of merchants and shops selling goods. While the dark side was full of thieves, beggars and merchants selling magic. There were more than enough taverns on the dark side. It was far easier to drown one's sorrows in drink than face the harsh reality. Every day was a fight to survive.

Rayven had never owned a dress or danced to the merriment of music. She was careful not to let her thoughts betray her. Fleeting thoughts of life on the other side were treasonous and punishable by death.

It was said that the mist wall separated good from evil, and that those on the dark side could not pass over. Those that tried never returned, but then again, why would they? Who would willingly live in darkness when you could walk among trees in the daylight?

What Rayven did not know was that the ruler of the dark side was not truthful. The proclamation that no one could crossover was a lie. Miranda neglected to tell the inhabitants that it was possible for some to crossover, but only if they were pure of heart. Only then could you pass through the barrier. Those who tried to pass through whose hearts were full of hatred, malice and ill will were absorbed by the wall, never to be seen from again.

Most inhabitants of the dark side belonged exactly where they were. Others came here willingly, such as Merrick, to hide from his former life. Although in the case of Merrick, Miranda played a large part in poisoning his mind. Others were exiled here. Many were born on the dark side, but did not belong here, not realizing they had a chance of escaping and leaving this hellish place behind.

The great lie…

To control was to deny all hope.

To enter the mist wall was not something to be taken lightly. It took Miranda's powerful magic to protect her raiders from the mist wall, allowing them to pass through unharmed. If she managed to bring down the mist wall, evil would spill out over all the lands.

Rayven looked at her mother's sad eyes and tried to give her a small spoonful of soup. She took a rag and wiped away the warm liquid dripping down her mother's chin. Her mother's name was Grace, and sometimes calling her name was the only way to get her attention.

"Come now, Grace," she said to her mother gently. "Please eat some soup. After dinner, maybe we can play a game of cards. Would you like that?"

Her mother just stared back at her and did not respond.

Rayven lifted the spoon again. Her mother did not open her mouth.

"Grace, please eat. You have grown far too thin," Rayven urged.

Her mother opened her mouth for another spoonful.

A soft knock came at the door. Rayven cautiously looked outside before opening it. A messenger stood on the other side with a folded note in his hand. She opened the door and read the message. She was being summoned to Miranda immediately. She looked back at her mother and the unfinished bowl of soup.

"I will be right with you," she told the messenger and closed the door. She fed her mother a few more spoonfuls and set the bowl aside, gently kissing her mother on the forehead. "Mother, I have to go... Grace? I will be back soon, I promise." She brushed strands of hair from her mother's face and leaned in to whisper in her ear, "I love you, Mama."

With those words, Rayven left her mother and headed towards Miranda's castle.

# Chapter Seventeen

Emily walked slowly through the grove before her. It was a warm day and the wildflowers were in full bloom. A gentle breeze blew through the trees around her. She could hear a man and child laughing. She followed the sounds of their voices. She stopped to watch through the trees. They were playing happily with a ball and some wooden hoops, as a small dog barked nearby. A modest manor house stood behind them made of red brick. Smoke billowed out from one of three chimney stacks. A well-manicured garden surrounded the home and bordered a stone pathway leading up to the front door.

She watched as they stopped what they were doing and played with the small dog. The dog jumped on the boy, knocking him backwards to the ground, and proceeded to lick the boy's face repeatedly. The boy giggled with delight and the man laughed heartily at the sight. The father threw a toy. The little dog jumped off the boy and ran after the toy, tail wagging happily. The boy ran after the dog and both came back to play near the man. They tumbled and tussled with the toy, clearly enjoying each other immensely.

The man stopped and turned towards Emily's direction. He took a few steps towards her and then stopped, straining to see, as if sensing her presence. Emily knew the man at once. It was Martin. He was a little worse for wear, but still had rugged good looks and the unmistakable silver blue eyes. Convinced there was nothing to see, he turned his attention back to the boy and his dog.

Emily smiled to herself. Martin had finally found peace and happiness. He reminded her so much of the way Merrick used to be. He picked up the boy, held him high in the air and then spun him around. He placed him on the ground and the boy cheered for more. The little dog yipped at their feet. Martin was truly content.

Martin looked back towards Emily again and then returned his attention back to the boy playing with his dog. Emily felt good inside. She knew how hard Martin's life had been after he lost his mother and sister.

Emily also knew this was but one possible outcome… She knew that fate was not set. Although, she hoped for Martin's sake that this dream would come true.

The boy jumped up and waved at a woman walking around from the side of the manor. She was carrying a bunch of flowers in her hand. Dark hair flowed around her shoulders. The little boy ran to her and threw his tiny arms around her neck in a warm embrace. The woman laughed lovingly and whispered something sweet to the little boy that garnished her another hug.

She walked over to Martin and gently kissed him on the cheek. They smiled at one another and watched their son play with his little dog. The boy's laughter was matched only by the dog's playful barking.

Martin hugged the woman and looked longingly into her eyes. They kissed. The woman squeezed Martin's hand and turned to walk up a dirt path to the left of the house. She waved at the little boy completely engrossed with the small dog.

Emily wanted to continue watching Martin and his son, but decided to follow the boy's mother instead, wondering what kind of woman had won his heart, hoping for a closer look at her. Emily followed the woman quite some distance to a private cemetery. The woman sniffed the flowers in her hand as she walked towards one of the graves. She stopped to kneel in front of it. She lowered her head momentarily and placed the flowers gently on the ground in front of a stone grave marker. Emily saw her wipe away a tear, stand up and walk back to the manor house.

The woman walked right past Emily as she left the cemetery, brushing her dark hair out of her face. Emily immediately gasped in shock. She saw the scar on the woman's face, recognizing her instantly as the woman who was going to have a hand in trying to murder her own family, one of Miranda's brutal raiders.

How could this be? This woman was a cold-hearted killer! This had to be a mistake! And, yet… she was obviously Martin's wife and they were very much in love. Something must have happened to bring the two of them together. She was no longer a raider, nor was she living on the dark side. She was here…with Martin.

They had started a new life together. Emily was floored… This complicated things, Emily thought to herself. She watched the woman walk slowly back to the house where Martin and their son awaited.

Emily walked into the cemetery to look at the marker where the woman had just laid the flowers. It read:

## GRACE
### Beloved Mother
3023-3072
*May you always feel the warmth of the sun upon your face.*

Emily sighed deeply. So, you understand how it feels to lose someone you love? You lost your own mother. Then, Emily recalled seeing this same woman kill her mother back in their Glendale home. I wonder how many other mothers you have killed as a raider, she said to herself. I won't let you take mine away from me.

~~~~~~~~~~~~~~~~~~~~~~~~~~~~~

Emily slept motionless on the ground with Martin sitting beside her, adding more wood to the fire. The snow flurries whipped around them.

"I know who you are…," the boy from the clinic whispered in her mind.

Emily grew restless and began thrashing in her sleep.

"I know who you are…," the boy repeated, laughing sadistically.

Emily opened her eyes and grabbed Martin's arm, startling him. "The boy from the clinic – he knows who I am," she told Martin, visibly frightened. "We have to save them!"

Martin was confused, "Save who?"

"My family. He knows who I am. He's going to tell Miranda. He probably already has," Emily told him, panic in her voice. "We have to do something. If we don't, she's going to kill my family!"

Martin held up his hands, "Whoa, slow down. What are you talking about?"

Emily told Martin about the vision she had earlier regarding the raiders murdering her family. She explained to him that they were sent back to find her and the keystone. They would use Miranda's powers to track her down and her family was killed in the process.

Martin asked, "But, you are here."

"I know I am here, but they go back in time and try to kill me and steal the keystone to prevent me from getting here at all. Understand? My family just gets in their way. We have to stop them," she explained.

"And, how do you propose we do that?" he asked.

"We use this," she said, holding the keystone in front of his face. It was the first time she had acknowledged its power to Martin. He looked at the necklace and then back at her. The deep purple keystone was glowing.

"Mira said I am a descendant of the bearers of the keystone and I can yield its power," she told him.

Martin eyed her curiously but listened carefully. "And, you know how to use that?" he asked, pointing to the necklace.

"I think so, yes, if I do as Mira said. Look," she argued. "The boy was at the castle with me when Merrick was beating me up. The boy was there."

Martin's eyes narrowed at the mention of his father. Now he knew who had hurt Emily. Martin felt anger flare within him. His father had nearly killed Emily. What would compel a man to strike a young girl so brutally? It was despicable. Just one more thing his father would have to answer for, Martin concluded.

Emily continued, "The boy from the clinic just stood there and watched Merrick hitting me. The boy was enjoying it. He was smiling. He must have ratted me out to Miranda. How else could they have known? There was no trace of me anywhere on your world, but somehow, they found out about me. They will try to go back and stop me from coming here altogether. I can't escape who I am anymore than you can," she told him.

Martin frowned, "And, who exactly do you think you are?" he asked.

Uh oh, she said to herself. She walked right into that question. She hesitated, unsure if now was the best time to tell Martin her true identity. She really didn't have a choice and Mira had left it up to her.

She sighed. "This is going to be hard for you to hear, but you need to know..."

Martin frowned again.

Emily thought about how to tell him... This was a tough one. Just tell him, she said to herself.

"Okay. You already know how everything fell apart after your mother died..."

Martin nodded, unsure of why she was talking about his mother.

"And," Emily continued, "You know that your baby sister went missing..."

Martin sat up straight. "Where are you going with this?"

"Well, she didn't exactly go missing...," Emily said, biting her bottom lip, waiting for Martin to explode.

He looked angry. "What are you talking about?" he demanded to know.

"You need to stay calm," Emily said. "Or I'm not going to talk about this. Promise?"

"I promise nothing. Why are you talking about my sister?"

She twisted her fingers over her lips.

"Stay calm and promise."

She knew she was making him angry and she wasn't trying to provoke him, but she didn't need him losing control either.

He frowned angrily. "Tell me… and yes, I promise to stay calm."

Emily sighed deeply. "Your father was in a bad way and Miranda sorta offered to make all that pain go away in exchange for…"

Martin leaned in, not wanting to believe what he was hearing. "In exchange for what?"

"You promised to stay calm – in exchange for your sister."

Martin jumped to his feet, startling Emily.

"What?!" he yelled.

Emily immediately regretted telling him the truth, "You said you'd stay calm."

Martin stomped over to his horse, muttering angrily under his breath, preparing the horse for travel. "I am going to kill him, I swear! With my bare hands, if need be."

Emily yelled at him. "Martin, stop! You have to hear all of the story. You can't just leave. Your sister is not with Miranda! Just stop and listen. Listen!" she insisted.

Martin's shoulders stiffened and he turned back to face her. "Then, talk fast, because I am going to kill my father and that witch he serves."

"Please, calm down," Emily pleaded.

He huffed and came back over to sit beside her, his face red with anger. She gave him a moment to contain himself. She had never seen him this angry, but she didn't blame him one bit. This was a horrible thing to learn.

She continued, "Miranda has brought back this dragon, the worst. She was using children to feed it," she cringed, recalling the vision. "I guess that is how it gains its strength – innocents. I saw your sister in one of my visions – in a cage, deep in a cave."

Martin's mouth opened and his head dropped.

"Please do not tell me that my sister was fed to that creature," he said trying to control his rage.

"No, she wasn't," Emily told him hastily.

Martin was visibly relieved.

"Then where is she?" he demanded to know.

"Mira said knights rescued her and as many children as possible," she explained.

Martin nodded, understanding the gravity of the situation.

She paused for a moment, carefully choosing her words.

"Your sister was sent away," she said softly.

Martin jerked his head up and was about to speak.

Emily held up her hand to stop him from interrupting.

"Just listen… She was sent away along with this keystone I am wearing, for her protection. The keystone was recovered from the water where your mother… well, anyway…Your sister was just a little girl. She wasn't safe here, neither was the keystone. So, she was sent away…"

"Where?" Martin wanted to know, growing impatient.

Emily sighed, "Well, that's the tricky part. She was sent far away and back in time…"

Martin just shook his head, not understanding what she was saying. He had a puzzled look on his face.

"Martin, your sister was my grandmother…"

She let her words sink in.

Martin looked astonished. His hand went up to his jaw, comprehending what she was saying. He looked away and then back at her. Not wanting to believe.

After a few moments of silence, Martin stood up. "You are not being truthful. That is not possible."

"It is possible, and it is true. Mira and the elders saved her. If they had not done what they did, your sister would have been killed. And, Miranda would have taken over this world and others a long time ago. And, we wouldn't be having this conversation right now. The elders bought Aquila time. By hiding your sister and the keystone, they slowed down Miranda. She's been hunting for this necklace all this time. But they couldn't stop her from building an army and bringing that beast back. She must be stopped. It all has to be stopped. Before it's too late."

"Your presence here has played right into her hands," Martin pointed out.

Emily couldn't argue with that.

"Maybe, but the army she has will easily defeat the light side and that dragon of hers will devour everything in its path. She's more powerful now than ever before," she reminded him.

He studied her for a moment, considering her words.

"You have come a long way since that day I nearly ran you over with my horse," he realized.

Emily grinned, "Ah ha! So, you admit it!"

Martin rolled his eyes. "Continue, please."

"That's pretty much it. Miranda is using her power to weaken the mist wall and soon her army will crossover to this side. Then all of this…," she motioned with her hands, "will be gone."

Martin stared at her. "You seem to have accepted your role in this," he noticed.

"Well, I don't really have a choice. I can't go back now. I saw what might happen to my family. Miranda isn't going to just let me go. She won't leave me alone. What other choice do I have?" she asked.

He didn't have an answer.

"I'm scared. I've seen so much. These visions I'm having are terrifying and painful," she said, reaching for her ribs. "I'm trying to be brave, because a lot depends on me now. My family. The people here…Your family…," she said.

"I no longer have a family," he reminded her.

She bit her lip but didn't argue. She couldn't tell him everything she knew, not yet. They sat in silence for quite some time. Emily was waiting for him to ask questions, but she didn't want to press him.

So, she waited.

Finally, he asked.

"My sister…," he said softly. "Tell me about my sister. Was she happy? What was she like? You have the necklace. Does that mean she is dead now?"

Emily had been giving this conversation a great deal of thought, wanting to do her grandmother justice. She deserved it.

"My grandmother, Victoria," she said.

Martin smiled and looked at her.

"Victoria," he repeated, fondly.

"Grandma was happy. She was adopted by a wonderful family and they lived in a place called Washington state back where I'm from." She looked around. "It's actually a lot like here. Tall evergreens, mountains, the ocean. It's beautiful there. She was married and had a family of her own. She lived a very long, happy life. She was beautiful…," she told Martin.

He hung on her every word.

"She was graceful, funny, kind, artistic, warm, caring and had such a beautiful spirit too. She liked gardening, quilting, baking, listening to classical music and big bands. She loved reading books. She encouraged me to be my own person and follow my dreams. She loved taking walks on the beach with her two little dogs, Mick and Baby Girl. When she got older and Grandpa passed away, she moved in with us, in Glendale."

Emily stopped talking. The loss of her grandmother was difficult to discuss. It made her sad.

"Please continue," he said.

Emily sighed. "She had visions too, you know. Like I do. My dad used to give her a hard time about it. He just didn't understand. My grandmother gave me this necklace, like she knew how important it was, and she told me to always take care of it. To keep it safe. I figured it was valuable and special to her, and besides it's so pretty. I've always worn it," she said proudly, touching her necklace.

"What happened to her?" Martin asked. He was comforted somewhat by Emily's kind words about his sister.

"She got old. She got sick. She died," Emily said, eyes tearing up. "She was my friend. I loved her so much. And, I miss her…" She sniffled. "You would have been proud of her. She was a really special lady."

He looked away, trying to maintain his emotions. He was glad his sister had a good life. That gave him comfort, but it saddened him that he never had the opportunity to know her. They both sat in silence for quite some time.

"Thank you for telling me that, Emily," he said.

She wiped away tears.

"So, the good news is…" She looked at him. "You and I are related." She smacked him lightly on the back.

Martin looked at her.

"That is a shocking reality," he joked. "I would like to hear more about her, if that is alright with you, when we have more time."

"Of course," she said. "I'd be happy to."

Martin forced his thoughts back to the present. He told Emily about his own experience, believing he was drowning. Martin suspected the boy played a part in that too. With his ability to toy with people's minds, Martin could see how incredibly dangerous he could be. And, if he was working with Miranda? Well, that was another serious threat to contend with.

"Before we continue, you need to eat. You've been sleeping for quite sometime and need your strength for what lies ahead," said Martin. He stood and retrieved some soup for her that was bubbling over the fire.

She frowned. "Okay. I need to splash some water on my face first. Where can I get cleaned up?"

He pointed to the woods behind her. She stood, a bit wobbly on her feet, but headed towards the water. Martin followed her. She stopped and looked at him.

"Where are you going?"

"To keep watch over you," he told her.

"I need some privacy."

She walked away from Martin and reached the creek. She used a rag to wash some of the dirt off her face from their journey. The water was cool and refreshing. She could see Martin standing by her out of the corner of her eye.

"You're too close," she scolded.

He stepped back a few paces.

"Still too close," she said, continuing to wash.

He backed up a few more paces.

"You're tooooooo close," she said loudly.

He turned and walked into the woods, leaving her by herself. The forest suddenly came alive around her. She heard strange noises everywhere. She stopped washing and looked around. No sign of Martin. No sign of anything. She finished quickly and stood up.

"You're too far away now!"

He immediately reappeared.

"Make up your mind," he said with frustration.

She walked past him, heading back to the fire to eat her soup. Martin waited for her to finish before asking more questions.

"What did she look like?" he asked.

She stopped and mulled over the question.

"She had gray hair by the time I was born, but I've seen lots of pictures of her. She looked a lot like your mother, especially the painting from your castle."

Martin smiled. He was pleased to hear this.

"I see a resemblance in you," he admitted.

"Thanks – Uncle Martin," she smirked.

He cringed. "Do not call me that."

Emily mocked being offended. "Well, it's true."

Martin waved her off. "It might be true, but Martin will suffice."

She smiled back at him. "Of all people you could be related to? Me?" She laughed. "Kind of poetic justice, don't you think?"

He ignored her comment. "The heavens have a sense of humor. I will agree to that."

Martin summoned Thalien again to tell him what Emily saw in her vision. Thalien had warned Doctor Pernell about the boy already. The doctor confided his own suspicions about Donovan and that the boy was definitely more than he appeared to be. They all agreed.

Emily told Martin and Thalien that she wanted to stop Miranda's raiders from hurting her family, thwart their attack before it even happened. Thalien reminded her again that her vision was only one possible outcome. Emily wasn't willing to wait and find out if it came true. Donovan knew who she was now. And, from her vision it was clear that Miranda learned about Emily and where she was from.

"Miranda isn't exactly following any rules," Emily reminded him. "So, why should we?"

Martin raised his eyebrow.

"Are you sure you can even do this?" he asked concerned. "You have never tried to do this before. It is not a walk through the rose garden you are suggesting. A few days ago, you thought this was all a dream and now?"

"But, it's not a dream, is it?"

He shook his head no.

"With this?" She placed her hand around her necklace. "I think I can do it," she told him, trying to sound somewhat confident.

Martin frowned. "I hope you are right, because I am coming with you. I do not want to end up floating through space."

"You won't," she said, frowning. "At least, I hope not."

"Good heavens. That is not reassuring," Martin muttered. He turned and began pacing nervously.

"What is your plan?" Thalien asked.

"I was hoping to surprise them. Ask the keystone to take me back to that moment I saw earlier. I want to get their before they do. Hide and then jump out at them," she suggested.

Martin threw his hands up in the air.

"What could possibly go wrong with that?"

Emily gave him a look. "Ye of little faith," she scoffed.

Thalien expressed his concern. "Mira instructed you how to use the keystone?"

"Yea, sorta…" Emily seemed a bit unsure.

Martin rolled his eyes.

Thalien took Emily's hands.

"Heed my words carefully, child. Know in your heart what you want. Know in your mind where you want to go. Know with your eyes what you want to see, and the keystone will not fail you. See it and it becomes. Do you understand?

"Yes," she said with confidence.

Martin walked over to them and stopped pacing. "We do this my way, if we make it there at all. Understand?"

Emily argued, "That depends. We have to bring them back."

"Bring them back?" Martin disagreed. "We must kill the raiders."

"And do what with them? Leave them at my house? That's not gonna work. We can't leave any trace of them behind."

Martin hadn't considered the problem of creating too many questions at their destination. Thalien nodded in agreement with Emily.

"She is right. They don't belong in her world and must be brought back. Leave no sign. Leave no trace."

Martin knew they were right. "Understood. We must kill them once we bring them back. We definitely cannot let them go.

Emily did not agree, "We have to at least try and talk to them," she insisted. "At least try with one of them."

Martin didn't argue.

Thalien patted Emily on the shoulder. "Be safe and remember what I told you. Trust in the keystone and it will trust in you."

Emily stood by Martin and closed her eyes. A swirling mist began to move within the keystone, followed by a slight humming sound. She concentrated as hard as she could.

"See it and it becomes," she repeated Thalien's instructions.

Emily placed her hand on Martin's forearm. Both could feel the vibrations grow stronger.

Thalien watched closely.

Emily whispered. "Take me home to Glendale. Before Miranda's raiders arrive…"

Minutes passed. The keystone grew louder and louder. It pulsated a brilliant purple light. She heard strange words in her head, reminiscent of the words the dragon had spoken to her. The words repeated over and over again.

Emily repeated them out loud too.

"Alandrien telamunden estelian," she whispered softly.

"I do not think this is going to…," Martin said just as they vanished into thin air. "…work." He finished his sentence, only to find himself in an unfamiliar setting.

They were back in Glendale. The keystone had worked. Emily was breathing heavily and opened her eyes slowly.

"That was unsettling," Martin admitted. "I trust you know how to get us back to Aquila."

She looked around and then back at Martin. "Could you feel it? Could you feel how powerful it was? It was talking to me, communicating with me, sharing information with me," she said excitedly.

Martin looked around at the unfamiliar surroundings.

"Wonderful," he said sarcastically. "I hope it told you how to get us back to Aquila."

# Chapter Eighteen

Her mother stood in the doorway of their home, car keys in hand. "Girls, let's go!" She called out. Sarah hurried down the staircase with her cabbage patch doll in tow, dragging it behind her. Emily soon followed, headphones in her ears, iPod in her hand, grooving her way down the staircase. Her mother laughed at her.

Emily stopped in the foyer and danced in a circle around her mother. "What goes around, goes around, goes around. Comes all the way back around," she sang to the music filtering in her ears. Her mother danced with her too. Emily laughed and kept singing and dancing out the front door. The family dog trotted happily behind Emily, eager for its frosty treat.

Her father stood in the driveway waiting for them. He shook his head as Emily continued to serenade him outside the minivan before hopping into the car. He looked at his wife walking towards them.

"Their music makes no sense to me. Goes around and around and around?" he said.

His wife laughed, "And, our parents said the same thing about the music we listened to, dear. Nothing has changed." She climbed into the passenger seat and made sure both girls were buckled in. The dog jumped in between the girls.

The car windows were rolled down. "Who's ready for ice cream?" her mother asked.

Both girls cheered.

"Mom, can I run over to Suzy's after we get ice cream for a couple of hours? She has a new video game I want to check out. I can walk," Emily asked.

"As long as you are back before dark, yes," her mother agreed.

Her father double checked to make sure Sarah was secured in her car seat before he got behind the wheel. He turned on the radio before backing down the driveway, tuning into an 80's pop hits station. Emily groaned when he turned up the volume to the Phil Collins song, "Sussudio." His mother and father looked at each other and grinned. Sarah clapped happily along with the music, content with whatever her parents played.

"Does it have to be so loud?" Emily complained.

"Our car, our rules," her father said.

He put the car in gear and drove down the road, only making matters worse for Emily when her parents both began to sing along with the radio.

"SuuuSuuuuSssuuudio!" they sang loudly.

"Kill me now," Emily sighed.

~~~~~~~~~~~~~~~~~~~~~~~~

Emily and Martin watched from the shrubs as she and her family left their house. Martin eyed her curiously when she came dancing out of the house, twirling in circles. Emily caught his glance.

"What? You never danced around your front lawn?" she asked.

"No," he confirmed.

"That I do believe. You should try it sometime. Maybe you wouldn't be so…stiff."

He looked at her. "I am not stiff," he said, watching her family from the safety of the bushes.

"Oh geez," she said. "Stiff as a board."

When her family was out of view, Emily and Martin stepped out from their hiding place. Emily was home again. Everything was exactly as it should be. People went about their daily lives. Her neighbor, Mrs. Bauer, was walking her cocker spaniel. She eyed them curiously.

"Hello Emily! Are you in some kind of play?" she asked, looking curiously at Martin and the way they were dressed. Her little dog yipped at Martin.

"Yea, we're in a play. We just got back from rehearsal," she told the woman.

"Sophie – stop barking at the man," she ordered. The little dog stopped barking, walked over to Martin, squatted on his boots and peed.

"Good heavens," Martin said shaking urine off his boots.

"Sophie, don't pee on the nice gentleman," she scolded the dog.

Emily tried not to laugh.

"Well, good luck with your play," she said and continued walking her dog, with a quick wave goodbye.

Martin watched her leave and looked back down at his boots.

"Charming," he shook his head, annoyed.

"Sophie doesn't like you," Emily teased.

"The feeling is mutual."

Emily laughed.

Martin looked back at the little dog.

"You put clothing on your dogs here?" he asked, slightly amused, referring to the pink sweater Sophie was wearing.

"Yea, dogs in sweaters. So what?"

"How strange. We need to get out of sight," he replied.

Emily agreed. "The Dairy Whip is four streets over. They won't be gone long. That was weird – seeing myself." She motioned for Martin to follow her into the house.

"Imagine my own horror," Martin added. "Seeing two of you."

She stopped and turned to look at him.

"Martin, did you just make a joke?"

He smirked.

"Did it hurt? Do you need to lie down?" she teased.

He ignored her. "Let us continue. Now what?" he asked.

Once they reached Emily's front porch, she retrieved the passkey from underneath the decorative squirrel where her parents hid it. She returned the key and the squirrel back to its place. Martin picked up the fake squirrel and examined it.

Emily shot him a look, "Don't ask."

He put it back down and followed her into the house. She locked the door behind them. They waited quietly in the foyer. Martin looked around at the pictures on the staircase wall. He pointed at one closest to his head.

"Is that you?" he asked, suppressing a grin. It was a picture of a little girl sitting in a small turtle shaped pool.

She gave him another look. "Hush. Focus."

The doorknob wiggled. They both looked at each other. Emily nodded and pulled Martin back into the laundry room, just off the foyer. The scene began to unfold exactly as Emily had envisioned it. The raiders forced open the front door lock and entered her home, waiting to ambush her family. They stepped into the foyer, stopping to listen for any sounds or movement from within. Emily and Martin waited for the raiders to walk past before stepping out behind them.

"Are you looking for me?" Emily asked coolly.

Surprised, the raiders spun around, standing face to face with Emily and Martin. They had been caught completely off guard. Martin and Rayven locked eyes on one another. Emily took a vase off the table in the foyer and smashed it over Rayven's head. She collapsed to the floor.

"I always wanted to do that," she told Martin, who dealt swiftly with the other raiders. They were a bit confused by this unexpected turn of events. He rendered the first man unconscious after several hard blows. Emily took a closer look at the woman lying on the floor while Martin wrestled with the remaining assailant, exchanging blows.

"Hurry it up, Martin," she told him.

He looked at her quickly, allowing the raider to punch him squarely on the jaw. Martin stumbled back a step, which allowed the man to charge after him, knocking him to the floor. Emily looked for something to hit the man with and spotted her father's golf bag in the corner of the foyer. She grabbed one of the golf clubs and began hitting the raider with it wildly. Both men stopped fighting momentarily to look at Emily, puzzled by what she was striking him with. They struggled to their feet. Emily swung at the assailant with the golf club but hit Martin by mistake. He put up his arm to deflect the blow.

"Hit him, not me!" he shouted.

The assailant paused to see Emily swinging the club right at his head. He ducked. She missed and hit the staircase railing, bending the golf club. The assailant hesitated long enough for Martin to land an uppercut under his chin, knocking him squarely off his feet. He flew back, out cold on the foyer floor.

Emily waved her arms in the air triumphantly. She felt vindicated and relieved that they caught the bad guys before her family was hurt. Martin looked back at the female assailant lying motionless on the floor. He dragged the three raiders together in the foyer. Emily surveyed the damage to her home. Martin looked around at the damage too.

"Mom's going to be mad. That was her favorite vase I just broke," she realized.

"She will live," Martin pointed out. "And, that was the entire point of this trip. Take us back, Emily." He cautiously peered out the front window.

Emily took one last look around her home. She longed to remain behind but knew that she could not. Now was not the time. She felt a sense of duty to see this out and knew Miranda would not let her return to her normal life. Emily had to help.

Martin looked out the window again. "We must go, Emily. They are returning in that strange motorized stagecoach!"

"It's called a minivan," she chuckled.

He didn't ask her to explain further. His only concern at that moment was not being caught inside her home. Emily held the keystone in her hand. She looked at Martin to see if he was ready. He nodded. Suddenly, she stopped.

"I almost forgot!" she said. "I'll be right back."

Martin looked at her, baffled, and then back at the front door. Emily ran up the staircase and into her room.

"Emily!" he yelled frantically up the staircase. "We have to go! They are here!" He continued to watch out the window.

Upstairs in her room, Emily rifled through drawers, digging into boxes, searching. "I'll be right there!" She yelled back to him.

Martin saw her parents open the minivan door. Her father walked their dog and stopped to talk to a neighbor. Her mother walked around to unbuckle the little girl from her seat and help her out.

"Now, Emily! Now!" Martin said urgently.

Emily tipped over another box and finally found what she was looking for. She shoved it into her pocket and raced down the stairs. Martin turned back to her, pointing towards the door.

"Now, now, now!" he said urgently, in a hushed voice.

She closed her eyes and recited the words she had been given before, summoning the keystone to return them to where they had just come from. They both felt the stirring sensation.

Martin turned towards the door, hearing the voices directly on the other side. Emily kept her eyes shut, repeating the words over and over again, feeling the power grow within her. When she opened her eyes, they were back on Aquila. Thalien was sitting by the fire. He stood up when they materialized. Martin looked at Emily and the raiders on the ground in front of them.

"Young lady, that was way too close," he scolded her.

"I'm sorry. I had to get something from my room." She turned to Thalien and asked, "How long were we gone?"

He scratched his head. "You only just left. No more than a second ago." He looked down at the three on the ground. Martin was binding their hands together. "I will take them to Mira for questioning," Thalien told them.

"Wait," Emily stopped him. She pulled him aside to speak with him in private, motioning to the woman on the ground. Martin watched her curiously. She told Thalien of the vision she had with Martin and the female raider. Emily asked him to share that information with Mira. Thalien nodded. She moved away so Martin could not hear.

"I want to ask you something, Thalien."

"Yes?"

"I understand how powerful the keystone is… Why can't I just go back and stop Miranda from hurting Isabeau at the water that day? Wouldn't that make all of this go away?"

Thalien got noticeably upset and shook his head vigorously. "You must never do that, Emily. To rewrite history to suit your own needs goes against everything the keystone represents. No, not ever." He looked back at Martin.

"Isn't that what I just did?" she asked.

"No, it is not. You saw your family attacked in a vision. It had not happened yet. That was a glimpse into the future. It was one possible outcome and you thwarted that attempt," he corrected.

"So that was all for nothing?"

"No, you captured three raiders. That is helpful. And, you saved your family today. Tomorrow is always uncertain."

Emily said nothing.

"You cannot go back and change the past, Emily. You simply cannot. If you did…think of the repercussions – the ripple effect through time. Who lived, who died, who was born. You have good intentions, but it is impossible. What is done, is done," he said firmly.

She still said nothing.

"Emily, do you realize that you wouldn't even exist if you did that?"

"Yes, I would. I would still be the granddaughter of someone. Just somewhere else and some other time… I think," she frowned.

"You cannot be sure. You could simply be – erased. Changing the past, changes the future. Even the slightest change can make a huge impact on the future. You cannot go back and stop Miranda. That is not what the keystone is for and I am not even sure it would allow you to do that," he told her adamantly.

She sighed. "If I could just warn them…"

Thalien placed a hand on her arm, interrupting her, "Emily, stop. I beg of you."

She frowned at him, "Okay, okay…"

Thalien looked at the three raiders. "I must go. Be safe." He and the raiders disappeared before her eyes.

~~~~~~~~~~~~~~~~~~~~~~~~~~~~~~~~~

Back in Glendale, Emily's little sister Sarah opened the front door and gasped.

"Mommy, Mommy! Look!" she called out.

Her parents raced to the front door and stepped inside. Shocked by what they saw. Their house was in disarray. Emily's father pulled back Sarah and her mother.

"Go next door and call the police," he ordered. They left the house immediately and did as he said.

Emily's father walked through the house, making sure no one was still inside. Finding no one, he went back outdoors where his wife and daughter were standing on the lawn with their neighbor and waited for the police to arrive.

The police arrived and walked through the house. Emily's father and mother walked around but found nothing was missing. Some of the furniture in the foyer had been damaged and overturned. The rug had slid a few feet up the hallway. Emily's father held his bent golf club in the air. Her mother began picking up pieces of the shattered vase from the floor and dumped them in the waste bin.

Emily's father talked to the police officer after filing a report. "I just don't understand it. Why would someone break into our home just to bend my golf club and break my wife's vase? And not even bother to steal anything?"

The police officer shook his head. "Teenagers most likely, pulling a prank. Kids do some really stupid things."

# Chapter Nineteen

Miranda stood at the fortress wall looking down over the ruins of her dark kingdom. Thanks to Donovan, she now knew the identity of the girl and confirmed that she was in possession of the keystone. Everything was coming together nicely. The final piece was in play. She sent out raiders to hunt down and capture the girl. She wanted Martin and the girl both brought to her. She was positive that she could corrupt Martin's mind as easily as she did his father. Men were far too quick to anger, which always left them open to manipulation. Merrick was getting too old, too obstinate. He would get the job done. She did not doubt that fact. However, once the mist wall was down and the world belonged to her, Miranda wanted new blood to stand beside her.

Merrick was…disposable.

Isabeau was…disposable.

The girl would be a tasty morsel for the beast, Miranda thought.

Martin would be a nice replacement indeed… Donovan had shown how easy Martin was to fool. So weak minded. She could make him see anything she wanted him to see.

Donovan, her young apprentice, had proven to be valuable to her arsenal. What a remarkable gift he possessed. He had tried to test that power once on her, but she immediately struck him down. Mind tricks could not work on a powerful sorceress. He took quite the lashing for that misstep but learned a lesson. He understood to do as he was told, or she could squash him like a bug.

For his part, she would let Donovan stand beside her in the new world order. His authority and power would be only second to hers. He would not be an outcast anymore or shunned by the society on the light side. He would be a god among men. She knew Donovan's was a sick mind, devoid of empathy…but to condemn him for his cruelty would be…well? Pointless. She once felt love… love for Merrick, love for their child. However, those emotions did not serve her well.

Donovan never felt such emotions. There was no room for mercy in his heart. He was not capable of feeling remorse. He was born bad, just waiting to be cultivated by Miranda, much in the way the witches shaped her future all those years ago when she was banished to the dark side. Donovan would carry out any order she gave him. She knew she could count on him fully. For that, he would be richly rewarded when the time came.

She lifted her hand to her neck, stroking the place where she intended the keystone to rest upon. Miranda smiled. She was pleased.

~~~~~~~~~~~~~~~~~~~~~~~~~

Martin and Emily continued their journey. He assured her that they would reach the location of the sacred Council of Dragons soon. They climbed higher into the mountains. She had no idea what she was supposed to do or say when she arrived. How was she going to convince dragons to fight against the beast she saw in the cave? What was to stop them from just eating her too? To be a dragon's dinner…

Miranda had an army and the beast.

Emily had Martin…the necklace…the dragons.

At least, she hoped so.

Martin stopped suddenly and dismounted. He walked back to help Emily off her horse.

"Why are we stopping?" she asked.

"We are here," he told her, somberly.

She looked around and saw nothing but ice, snow and glaciers climbing into the sky. A few scattered trees lined the path, weighed down from the snow. Martin immediately began gathering twigs and branches to start a fire to keep them and the horses warm. There was a tiny alcove on the side of the mountain that was tall enough to stand in. Martin moved them into it.

It provided adequate shelter from the elements. Emily helped by bringing stones over for Martin to form a circle on the ground. He placed the wood in the center. She watched him start the fire with flint, which was difficult since the wood was damp. He took out some straw from the horse's feed bag to help get the fire started. It didn't take long before a warm glow illuminated the small cave.

Once the fire was flaming steadily, Martin prepared their meal. He handed Emily a piece of bread and some cheese to eat while the vegetable stew slowly came to a boil.

Neither one of them spoke. Both were fatigued from the long journey. Emily was apprehensive about what was going to happen next. Back home, she had a dog. Going to the zoo was the closest to wild animals she ever got. Now she was expected to converse with dragons and gain their trust enough to ask them to risk their own lives.

The dragons were far removed from the drama of mankind below. They had nothing to gain from helping, yet they had everything to lose. That's not a hard sell at all, is it? She mused.

Men got themselves into this mess. Dragons were supposed to help them fix it.

Mira made it painfully clear that the dragons were needed to level the playing field, so to speak. Miranda had an unfair advantage by awakening the mighty dragon she kept in her caverns.

As Emily watched the embers from the fire billow lightly into the air, she thought of the beast and its hunger for flesh. She saw the river of blood in her mind. There was no denying that men could not defeat it. Might against might was the only chance. She felt that she was an unlikely emissary and the magnitude of this burden was weighing heavily on her mind.

Martin had a bundle in his horse's side bag that he removed and unfolded. She watched him curiously. He brought it over to Emily.

"Stand up, please."

She complied. When she saw what Martin had in his possession, her eyes widened in awe. He revealed a chainmail shirt the likes of which she had never seen. He held it up and looked back at Emily.

"This should fit you," he told her. "Put it on."

He handed it to Emily, and her arms dropped from the weight of it.

"It's heavy," she said.

"Actually, it is lighter than most."

She struggled to put the garment over her head. Martin helped her. There was a small metal breastplate attached to the chainmail shirt. Emily looked at it when she finally managed to get her arms through the half sleeves. She recognized it as the same colors that once flew over Merrick's grand castle. She looked up at Martin. He stepped back to inspect her.

Emily ran her hands over the shirt. He handed her a helmet that went with the chainmail. She took it from him and placed it on her head. It too was heavy. Her bangs hung slightly over her eyes. Martin brushed her red bangs back off her face and studied her.

"It will do," he told her.

"Why am I wearing armor?" she asked the obvious question.

"If you are going to lead, you should look the part," he told her. "This used to be mine when I was about your age."

Her eyes lit up when he said that. "Really?"

He nodded. "Miranda is actively hunting you. You need to be prepared. You cannot fight them off. At least this will offer you some protection."

"I see," she said. "For a minute there I thought I needed this to see the dragons and was worried this was supposed to prevent me from being…a meal."

He grinned. "If they want to eat you, no amount of armor would protect you."

"Is that supposed to make me feel better?" she asked.

"No," he said matter of fact. "I want you to get used to its weight. Over time, you will not even notice you are wearing it. And, I need to show you a few defensive moves."

"Cool," she said.

He frowned. "I said a few – enough for you to defend yourself." He motioned her back towards the rear of the small cave. "This is simple. You are not strong enough to fully deflect a blow, so you must anticipate your attacker's move and sidestep to avoid the hit. Do not just stand there. Use your dagger in a sweeping circular motion to block, as you sidestep," he instructed and demonstrated. "That puts you in a position of power, forcing your opponent to re-adjust their balance." He demonstrated again. "You try…"

Emily frowned, but mimicked what she just saw Martin do.

"Good, good," he said.

"Yea," she said. "Step and swipe, step and swipe…"

"That is correct."

He picked up a couple of branches and stripped them into long sticks. "Let us try it together. I am going to come towards you, and I want you to defend yourself."

Emily steadied her feet and held her stick in a defensive position. "Bring it on, pretty boy," she taunted.

Martin frowned. "Be serious, please."

"I am serious. Look how serious I am," she said, making her best tough guy face.

"Be serious," he scolded her.

He moved slowly towards her and let her walk out the sidestep and swipe maneuver, giving her a feel for the move. Then, he moved towards her more quickly. She immediately side stepped as he charged her and then in a circular motion, she swiped and struck his back. She stood, proud of herself.

"Good," he admitted. "When your opponent turns back to face you. Then, what?" he asked.

She thought hard. "Run? Serpentine, serpentine?" She grinned.

"No, you do this…" Martin walked towards her, stepped to her side and swiped his foot behind her ankle, causing her to fall on her backside. "You knock them down, and then you run. You can not defeat them, at least give yourself a chance. You try it."

She stood up, dusted off her trousers and moved towards Martin. She tried several times to swipe his leg, but he was like a tree planted firmly in the ground. She was getting frustrated.

"Okay, what am I doing wrong?" she asked, slightly annoyed.

'Swipe and push. I am much larger than you. Swipe and push at the same time. Hit me right behind my knee cap."

She concentrated and stepped to his side, immediately kicking behind his knee with the back of her foot and pushing him with her shoulder at the same time. This time it had the desired effect and Martin was knocked off his feet.

He stood up and looked pleased with her.

"See? It is not always about strength. It is more often about leverage and using your mind to anticipate your opponent's move." He moved back over to the fire. "Come, your soup is done. You must eat and rest before you seek out the Council of Dragons."

She did as she was told. "Do I have to wear this to see the dragons?"

He looked over at her from his soup bowl. "No."

She put down her bowl and awkwardly pulled the chainmail shirt off and set it neatly on the ground beside her. "Thank you for that," she said.

He nodded at her. She finished her soup and laid down on the blanket Martin had placed on the ground for her. She stared at the firelight dancing upon the ceiling of the cave and turned her head towards Martin. He was staring intently into the fire.

"Martin, I don't want to go to sleep. Bad things happen when I do," she told him.

He looked over at her sympathetically. "I know. I am sorry. I do not know what greets you when you sleep, but you must rest.

You must be clear minded when you see the dragons. Rest. I will keep watch over you," he said, trying to comfort her.

She nodded and closed her eyes. It didn't take but a few moments and Emily was deep in sleep.

~~~~~~~~~~~~~~~~~~~~~~~~~~

The sound was deafening. She covered her ears with her hands to drown out the sound, but it had no effect. She looked up and saw massive beasts flying in an orchestrated attack on a larger creature. The blood curdling screeches from the battle above her head were terrifying. The smaller dragons were using an attack and retreat method, working in pairs to confuse and disorient the beast.

One of the smaller dragons miscalculated its retreat and the beast snared its wing within its jaws. It immediately ripped off the dragon's wing, grabbed the remainder of its body and flung it violently to the side. The dragon screeched in agony, spinning wildly out of control, unable to right itself before falling to its death. Emily watched in horror.

The larger beast roared in victory and turned its attention to the other dragons. The clashing of body against body from these massive creatures was sickening. They clawed and snapped their mighty jaws at each other, tearing into their flesh. Blood spilled onto the ground below. Emily tried to find somewhere to run from the carnage above her head, but there was no place to hide.

Another dragon fell to the ground not far from where she stood. Its head had been bitten off. Its body slammed to the surface and shook the ground when it hit. The dragon's lifeless eyes were open, and its tongue hung loosely from its mouth. The screeching sounds from overhead were terrifying. She was scared for the dragons who risked their lives to defeat the beast.

The keystone began to hum and glow around her neck. What was it doing? Could it be used to aid the dragons?

Suddenly, the dragons joined in formation around the beast. Their wings were spread wide and beating in unison. They circled the beast, who had been weakened by the constant attacks, but was far from being beaten. The beast's head turned angrily from side to side trying to ascertain what the dragons were up to. It roared its warning to them.

The dragons lowered their heads to the ground and focused their attention on Emily. She realized that their wings were beating to the same rhythmic tone as the keystone. They were connected and working in unison with one another, in a coordinated effort. A light emulated from the keystone, casting a purplish glow upwards, surrounding the beast.

It agitated the beast. It tried to move away, but the light held it in place. It was unable to move out of the keystone's glow. Emily watched in awe as the keystone's humming grew louder. It was hurting the beast. It flung its wings and snapped its jaws in duress.

The keystone reached its crescendo and a powerful boom could be heard in the air. The beast froze, momentarily disabled. The dragons surrounding it immediately rotated their bodies and lunged for their final attack. The beast was powerless to defend itself. Blow after ferocious blow was leveled on the beast by the smaller dragons, tearing at his throat until blood poured to the ground. Its eyes rolled back in its skull just as the keystone stopped its humming.

The dragons pulled back and joined their circular formation once again, as the beast dropped out of the sky, smashing into the ground, forming a crater below its massive body. The force of the impact knocked Emily off her feet.

The dragons lowered their heads in solace to their fallen comrades that were killed by the beast. They formed a single file line and flew gracefully away, back into the clouds.

Emily felt herself being lifted off the ground and placed on the back of one of the dragons. It flew her the opposite direction from the other dragons. She rested her head softly on the back of the dragon, grateful for their aid and sacrifice. The gentle beating of the dragon's wings through the air was serine. She smiled, enjoying every moment.

Emily opened her eyes and saw the ceiling of the cave. She sat up. Martin was watching her. She smiled at him. Her vision gave her a renewed sense of peace and hope. She understood the connection the keystone had with the dragons and how they would work together to defeat the beast.

We are all connected in some way, as Mira had told her.

She stood up and faced Martin.

"I'm ready," she said. "I'm ready to meet the Council of the Dragons."

He stood and nodded, sensing that she had gained some insight and courage while she slept, as was evident by her confident demeanor and calmness.

"Indeed," he agreed. "You are ready."

He turned to leave the cave.

"Wait, Martin," she stopped him. "I have something to give you." She ran back over to her saddlebag and removed something. She walked back over to Martin, stood proudly and stuck out her hand. He looked down at the object she was holding.

"What is this?"

"It's for you," she said, smiling warmly at Martin.

It was a small photo album that she had taken from her bedroom before they returned to Aquila.

He cautiously took it from her and turned it over in his hand.

"Open it," she instructed.

He flipped open the small photo album, seeing a picture of Emily with an elderly lady, arms around each other in a warm embrace. He knew immediately it was Victoria. His reaction was immediate. He gasped and felt tears form in his eyes.

"Is that… is that?"

"Victoria, yes. Your baby sister. My grandma," she smiled brightly.

He looked up at Emily and then back at the album in his hands, flipping through the pages. His hands trembled slightly. It was an album that Emily had compiled of her grandmother over the years.

There was a picture of her grandmother in her garden, proudly holding a freshly clipped pink rose in her hand. A beautiful smile graced her face. Martin held it up, moved closer to the fire for a better look and studied it closely.

He turned to another page.

Emily stood with her sister and grandmother. There was a mound of snow shaped like a man. They were bundled in heavy coats, wrapping a scarf around the snowman's neck, laughing happily at their creation. Martin smiled.

He turned to another page.

Emily was building sandcastles near the ocean shore. The sun was setting behind her. Her grandma stood nearby, smiling. She held a small dog in her arms, and another dog on a leash sat at her feet. Each of the little dogs wore a sweater, pink and blue respectively.

Emily pointed. "See? Dogs in sweaters. Grandma dressed up her dogs too," she grinned.

Martin laughed out loud, letting the tears stream down his face, without shame. He turned to another page and saw Victoria dressed up like a witch with Emily standing beside her in a similar costume, holding a straw broom. Martin looked up at her, puzzled.

"It's for Halloween," she explained. He shook his head in confusion as he smiled. "It's once a year, people dress up, you go house to house and say, 'Trick or Treat' and people give you candy," she explained.

He laughed again. "Yours is a strange but wonderous world," he admitted.

The next page showed her grandmother with her grandfather, holding hands and smiling lovingly at one another.

"Her husband," she told him. "My grandpa…"

He nodded, continuing to look through the album.

There were several pictures of his sister, Victoria, as a young girl herself. She was riding a pony in one photograph and watching the sunset in another, as the sun glistened off her strawberry blonde hair. That face, the hair and those eyes. It was like looking at his mother all over again. He wept quietly and rubbed his finger over his sister's face.

Emily stepped away to give him some privacy. She watched him go page by page, allowing him the time he needed to absorb seeing his baby sister again after such a long loss.

He finally walked over to Emily. Tears still visible in his eyes. "May I keep this?" he asked, tenderly.

"Of course," she said. "I brought it for you."

He gave her a warm embrace.

"Thank you, Emily." He released her and placed one hand on her shoulder, holding the photo album in his other hand. "This is the most precious gift I have ever been given. You have given me my sister and I can see that she was indeed happy and loved. I miss her so," he said.

"You are very welcome, Martin. And, yes, she loved us very much and we loved her too. She was…special…the best," she told him. "I miss her too."

He smiled, holding on to the album tightly.

"You must be on your way now. I will treasure these always," he said.

"I know you will," she said softly, and smiled. Tears formed in her eyes in remembrance of her beloved grandmother. She was happy that Martin was so touched by her gift.

# Part IV

## Requiem

*There are some people that live in a dream world,*
*And, there are some who face reality.*
*Then there are those who turn one into another.*

*You've spent your whole life running, trying to catch up*
*with something that has never been there for you.*
*All you have done is go farther and farther away*
*from the precious love that has been waiting for you…*
*All the time.*

~ Douglas H. Everett

# Chapter Twenty

Doctor Pernell was deeply troubled after his conversation with Thalien. He was pleased that Martin and Emily were making solid progress. The confirmation that Donovan was involved in all this mayhem was not entirely a shock. Doctor Pernell was not, however, prepared to hear that Donovan appeared to be working alongside Miranda, the evil sorceress from the dark side.

An enemy in their mist was one thing, but this enemy was living right under his nose. Doctor Pernell believed that Donovan was somehow responsible for Rebecca's disappearance, but why? The child was harmless. Why drive her away? Unless she saw something, he wondered.

The search party for the little girl had failed thus far. She was far too young to fend for herself and with raiders looming about, he feared the worse for her. He calculated how far she could travel by foot in the time she had been gone.

Was she returning to her home? He suspected that she was returning to the only place that was familiar to her. Doctor Pernell was determined to find out. It was half a day's ride to the farmhouse. He hurried around his office to gather some medical supplies, in case she was injured.

When he turned around, Donovan was standing in the doorway, blocking the exit. He startled the doctor.

"Where are you going?" the boy asked.

"That is none of your concern," Doctor Pernell told him. He grabbed his medical bag and walked towards the door. Donovan did not move. "Donovan, step aside please. I must go."

Donovan eyed him carefully but did not budge. The doctor was not in the mood for games.

"Donovan, move to the side, now," Doctor Pernell ordered.

Suddenly, the boy closed his eyes. Doctor Pernell could feel Donovan trying to invade his mind, tearing apart his thoughts and trying to control him. It was an unpleasant sensation. The doctor turned his back to Donovan and placed his medical bag on the table. He opened a drawer and retrieved something from within it. He slipped it into his pocket and turned to face the boy again.

The doctor struggled to fight off Donovan's mind control. He was powerful, so incredibly powerful. The doctor fought hard. Donovan opened his eyes, clearly frustrated.

"I am a cleric," Doctor Pernell reminded him. "You cannot wield my mind like a toy, child."

He pulled his hand out of his pocket, reached out towards the boy and released a red powder into the air. Donovan inhaled it, coughed and struggled for air, before collapsing into the doctor's arms.

Doctor Pernell called out to a nurse, placed the boy on a bed in the closest room, and gave her strict instructions that no one was to enter Donovan's room under any circumstance. He locked the examination room and took the key with him. The red powder would render Donovan unconscious for a good twelve hours. More than enough time to get to the farmhouse, Doctor Pernell thought to himself.

~~~~~~~~~~~~~~~~~~~~~~~~~

Miranda was interrupted abruptly from the deep trance she had placed herself in. She spent most of her waking hours in this state to travel in her mind's eye among her seekers and communicate with her spies.

Something had happened. She could no longer see her most trusted cohort, Donovan. He was lost to her and that had not happened since she had recruited him. Clearly something was amiss.

Miranda stood and paced frantically around her bed chamber. Had his cover been blown? Had he been killed? She needed him. He had a unique gift and was a powerful tool needed to advance her plans.

She closed her eyes tightly and tried to no avail to reestablish contact with Donovan. She had no one else that close to the clinic, which she considered a central hub of activity. This was a problem. A major vein in her access to the light side had just gone dark, and she needed to ascertain why…immediately.

She called out and summoned her guard standing outside in the hallway.

"Bring Rayven to me at once," she ordered.

The guard nodded and hurried up the dark corridor. He was immediately replaced by another guard to stand in his place. Miranda was seething and anxious.

So close and yet so far. She didn't need anything getting in the way. So much time was spent placing all the chess pieces in position. To lose one would cause a chain reaction.

Where was Donovan? She had to find out.

She walked over to her chamber window and looked out over the scorched earth of the crumbled kingdom she reigned over.

The land was dead.

Its people not too far behind.

She wanted out. She wanted what was kept from them. She wanted her freedom back. She wanted revenge.

She wanted it all.

Moments later, the guard returned with some equally troublesome news. Rayven was missing. She had not returned from her last mission. None of the raiders had returned. They had lost contact with her and her team. Miranda stared at the guard in disbelief. It was way past their time to report back in. No word whatsoever had been received from her. She ordered him to repeat what he had just said.

Upon doing so, Miranda let out a cry of anger that made the guard take a half step back. He made a quick exit and closed the door behind him.

Rayven's mission had not been especially difficult, but it was critical. Miranda had sent her back in time to eliminate the girl and her family, which would have eliminated the threat in her own timeline.

There was always risk, diving into a timeslip. But she knew her calculations were correct and there should have been no issues. And, she trusted the information Donovan had given her. The girl was supposed to be wiped out and the keystone delivered to Miranda well before Emily appeared on Aquila. Rayven was one of her best seekers and an equally efficient soldier dedicated to Miranda.

Had Miranda's over confidence gotten the better of her? She was not prone to making mistakes, yet...both Donovan and Rayven were missing. She was being toyed with. She had all of this planned out so meticulously and now the scales had been tipped. She was off balance and not sure of what to do.

She closed her eyes and slowed down her breathing. She mustered all her great powers and sought out Rayven in her mind.

Nothing...

No contact at all.

Not even a faint glimmer of Rayven or Donovan.

It was as if they had been completely erased. This was something Miranda had never encountered before. She was deeply troubled by this. Suddenly, she felt vulnerable. It was important that she move up her own timeline.

Perhaps, she should enlist Merrick to put a stop to his son's meddling. Perhaps, it was time to unleash the beast. She needed that keystone. She needed its power. The mist wall had to come down.

Too many variables were uncertain, especially now that Donovan and Rayven had gone dark in her mind. Merrick, she thought. Perhaps he could find out what had become of the boy and Rayven. She would solicit his help at once.

~~~~~~~~~~~~~~~~~~~~~~~~~~~

Rayven woke up with searing pain on the top of her head where Emily had hit her with the vase. She was lying with her back on a stone floor inside of a small room, devoid of all furnishings and not even a window to peer out of. She touched the lump on her skull and closed her eyes. She tried to sit up and felt the room spin around her. She moaned from the pain and dizziness. She attempted to sit upright again and clear her head. She took in her surroundings.

Rayven had no idea where she was, but she knew she was being held against her will. She had seen the inside of dungeon cells long enough to recognize when she was in one. Every weapon on her had been removed. She stood and steadied herself before examining the small room.

"There is no door," she said to herself.

She felt along each wall, searching for a hidden latch or release that might open one of the walls. She found nothing. She was essentially inside of a stone box, wide enough to turn around in, wide enough to lie down in, but big enough for little else.

"Terrific," she said rather annoyed at her predicament. She smacked the wall with her hand in frustration.

Rayven sat back down on the hard floor and closed her eyes once again. Concentrating, she attempted to see outside the walls that confined her. Nothing. It was as if her mind was also trapped within the confines of the stone walls.

An unease crept over her. In all her days, she had always been able to project herself beyond her physical location with her mind. It was one of the qualities that made her such a great seeker. She attempted to make contact with Miranda with her mind, straining to project her thoughts beyond the confines of the space that held her captive.

Nothing.

Just a black void of nothingness.

Rayven was trapped both mentally and physically.

She wondered what happened to the other raiders she had traveled with. They had walked into an ambush, she realized, as she recounted the events leading to her capture.

How had Miranda not foreseen this? How had she been caught off guard like this? If Miranda was the most powerful sorceress, how was this even possible? What wasn't Rayven being told?

Rayven had to entertain the possibility that there was much more going on than she was even aware of, and that forces were working against them, just as powerful, if not more so, than the dark sorceress she served. It gave her pause… She liked knowing exactly who her opponents were or what they were capable of.

Obviously, someone had outsmarted them.

The girl was waiting for them. Rayven recalled the smug look on her face and the man accompanying her. His face looked familiar. His eyes were unlike any she had ever seen. She hesitated when their eyes met – that hesitation caused this, she believed. If she had not hesitated, she could have deflected the blow to the head from the young girl and made a better accounting of herself. At least, she could have put up a good fight.

Rayven knew she had failed at her mission. And, failure was not something she was used to. She had to find a way out and rejoin her ranks. She could not remain here in this perpetual emptiness forever…or so she hoped.

Her head was throbbing from the blow. She laid back down on the hard unforgiving stone floor, fighting the pain she felt on her head. She drifted off to sleep with thoughts of the stranger's face still lingering in her mind. It was Martin's face she saw in her thoughts as the darkness engulfed her.

~~~~~~~~~~~~~~~~~~~~~~~~~

Doctor Pernell quickened the pace of his horse over the plains of Aquila. He was uneasy leaving Donovan unattended when it was obvious now that the boy was using his gift to manipulate others in a harmful way. Donovan knew exactly what he was doing, and he was trying to control others with his powers.

As he rode along the path, he recalled what Thalien had revealed to him. Emily had seen Donovan in her vision alongside of Merrick on the dark side. He was one of them, helping Miranda. They had been completely duped by his innocent persona. He knew his spell would wear off eventually and then… what to do with Donovan?

He was locked in a hospital room at the moment, but Doctor Pernell knew he had to find a more permanent solution to the Donovan problem. Mira might be able to help, he thought to himself.

Doctor Pernell's horse came over a ridge and slowed his pace. The modest farmhouse where Rebecca had once lived was looming ahead. A quiet reminder of the tragedy that had unfolded there. Doctor Pernell brought his horse to a slow trot and carefully approached the dwelling.

The front door slightly opened and then closed on its own as the wind blew it. Nothing seemed out of order other than the uncomfortable silence of the once thriving farm. He stopped his horse and studied the scene before him with great sadness. He could envision Rebecca here beside her loving parents with not a care in the world.

He looked down as the wind carried a hair ribbon through the air that had been stuck on the twig of a bush. Doctor Pernell was a healer and could not fathom the blood lust of so many others. He could not justify killing for personal gain in this manner. It was senseless. He had dedicated his life to the protection of living beings, not the destruction of them. He was determined to find Rebecca and bring her back where she was safe and sound.

He looked around before dismounting his horse. The quietness of his surroundings was a bit unnerving. Even the sounds of birds had ceased. It felt as if the land itself was in mourning at this farmhouse. He lowered his head in reflective respect for the loss of life and destruction of an innocent family.

He swung his legs off the horse and slowly approached the farmhouse. He saw no sign of life, no sign that Rebecca had returned. He sighed as he pushed open the front door and entered. He was standing in the front parlor, which was open to the kitchen. He took a few steps forward and immediately noticed the dark stain of blood that covered a large portion of the kitchen's wood floor. It forever marked the location where Rebecca's mother had been slain.

"May your soul find eternal peace in the heavens," he whispered softly.

He continued to the back bedroom and service porch looking for Rebecca. He found no trace that she had even returned. He glanced briefly at the small pile of books that sat on a wooden bench by the front window. He gathered them up in hopes of returning them to Rebecca. He also picked up a small wooden frame on the floor that featured a sketch of Rebecca and placed it with the books he was now carrying.

He searched the entire farmhouse, but did not find a sign of the girl, much to his disappointment. He sighed heavily and headed for the front door only to be stopped by a shuffling noise behind him. He stopped suddenly and turned towards the sound, straining to here its exact location.

He didn't hear anything else but stood perfectly still, hoping the source would reveal itself again. Moments later, he heard another shuffling sound and knew it was coming from inside the bedroom. He walked softly back into the bedroom and looked around but saw nothing. A large wooden bedframe was in the corner, over a tightly woven floor rug. He noticed one of the corners was curled under and he walked over to examine it.

He pulled the rug back further and it revealed a small wooden door, much like a storm cellar. It was cleverly hidden beneath the large area rug. He pushed the rug back further and carefully pulled the round latch up and opened the small door.

Dust bellowed up in protest from its hinges. Light from the bedroom window filtered down within the small crawl space hidden beneath the floor.

Doctor Pernell heard muffled cries and sighed in relief. He had found her. She had burrowed herself deep in this dark hole. He let her know it was him.

"Rebecca, it is Doctor Pernell," he said kindly.

"Go away," she cried.

He carefully stepped down the rickety ladder that was attached to one side and he ducked. It was not big enough for a man of his height to stand up in, but he moved towards the sound and made his way to Rebecca. She had her back turned towards him and was curled up in a ball, crying softly to herself. He sat down on the dirt floor next to her and placed his hand soothingly on her back, trying to comfort her.

"It is going to be fine, child. I promise you," he said softly. "Your mother and father may not be physically here, but they are always with you in spirit. Take comfort in that. They will always watch over you... Come now, let us go. You can not stay here. Come where we can love and care for you..."

She lifted her head and wiped away her tears, "That's not true. You said no one cared about me and told me to leave! Why were you so mean to me?" she cried painfully.

He knew then exactly what had happened. Donovan had cast his net on another victim in an alarmingly cruel fashion. He shook his head and looked kindly into her eyes.

"Sweetheart, that was not me. Unfortunately, that was Donovan playing a cruel joke on you. I would never say such a thing to you. You are always welcome at our clinic and you can stay for as long as you need to. His words had no substance and came from malice. Do not pay attention to anything he says," he assured her.

She looked confused, "But, I saw you..."

"I know, but Donovan can shift into anyone he wants and pretend," he explained.

"But, why? Why would he want to do that to me?" she asked.

He thought for a moment. "Sometimes people are just cruel. It is like a sickness. It is difficult to understand, but true nonetheless," he told her.

She stared into his eyes, trying to process what he had just said. "So, it was all a joke?"

"He was trying to hurt you and obviously he did," he explained. "Donovan used his abilities to inflict pain on you. I will do everything in my power to make sure he doesn't do that to anyone ever again," he said strongly.

She nodded.

"He is not a nice boy," she said.

"No, he is not," Doctor Pernell agreed. "Come, let us get you out of this place and back to the clinic. A nice meal and warm bath should make you feel much better," he added.

She nodded. They made their way back into the bedroom through the opening. Rebecca gathered a few more of her things and mementos from the house. She stopped to look around before they left.

"I don't suppose I will ever come back here again," she said sadly, casting her gaze at the blood stain on the kitchen floor.

"Probably for the best, sweetheart," he said comforting her.

He picked her up and placed her on the back of his horse. He put her belongings into the horse's saddlebag. He gave Rebecca a long moment to look back at her home before mounting the horse and turning it back towards the clinic.

Rebecca looked over her shoulder until the farmhouse grew smaller and smaller and eventually disappeared behind the ridge, leaving her former life in the past. She felt alone and afraid but was comforted by Doctor Pernell's words and their sincerity. She had a safe place to go, the clinic. It would become her safe haven as she faced the future.

# Chapter Twenty-One

Martin led Emily up a slight rise that cut through the icy cliff of the mountain, a short distance from the cave. He had to stop and help her several times, as she lost her footing on the slippery slope. He stopped abruptly at the bottom of a twisting stone staircase, covered with snow and ice, that led further up the mountain. It disappeared into the clouds above. He looked up at it and then back at Emily. She stopped beside him and glanced up at the steep staircase.

"You must go alone from here," he said somberly.

Emily looked at Martin and then back at the path before her. "Alone?"

He nodded.

"I have no idea where to go…," she reminded him.

"There is only one way to go. Up. You go up… It will lead you to exactly where you need to go," he told her.

Emily's face grew alarmed. "I don't think I'm ready to do this alone," she admitted.

Martin smiled warmly at her, "You are."

He adjusted her chainmail tunic and tightened her belt. He pulled her cloak around her and fastened it securely. He sighed. He was worried about her but tried not to let it show.

"You are ready. I know you are. Trust in yourself, Emily. This is the task that has been chosen for you. It does not come lightly, nor does it come without cost. The Council of Dragons will listen to you. There is a strong light that shines within you. Let them see that. Let them see the love you feel for your family and your grandparents…my sister…let them feel that. Be honest with them. Remember, they can feel and hear your thoughts. Do not be afraid. They will not harm you," he sighed again.

She stared up at him, reluctant of the task before her. He sensed this. He saw the look of fear and uncertainty in her eyes.

"I believe in you, Emily. I am not an easy one to sway. Now, you must believe in yourself. Understand?" he asked.

His words comforted her fears somewhat. She smiled at him and stood tall with confidence.

"I do," she told him, trying to be brave.

She leaned against Martin and gave him a warm embrace. He laughed slightly and hugged her back. She turned towards the staircase.

"I just go up?" she asked again.

He nodded. "Up."

"And, you're sure I won't be a dragon's dinner?"

He grinned, "Yes... Well, mostly sure."

Her mouth dropped open and she hesitated. "Mostly?"

He laughed again. "I am teasing you."

"Phew," she said. "Will you be here waiting for me?"

He turned serious and sighed. "I honestly do not know when our paths will cross again. I can not see the future, as you can. Somehow, I suspect we will be united again in this cause, but when and where remains to be seen. Until that time, be well and I will keep you in my thoughts."

She didn't like the idea of not being with Martin. She had grown fond of him and felt safe by his side. It was the moment of reckoning, she knew that. Time to stand on her own two feet and face this task. He handed her a small bag containing food, water and supplies.

"Just in case," he told her.

"In case of what?" she asked.

"One never knows what lies beyond this path. I just want you to be prepared, in case you have to wait," he explained, trying not to be foreboding.

She frowned. "Okay, just in case."

She turned towards the path and began climbing the staircase. She turned back to look over her shoulder and Martin gave a slight wave, turned and headed back towards the cave.

She steadied herself and continued up the staircase. The steps were narrow and slippery, covered with ice. There was nothing to hold on to and she feared she might slip and fall to her death. Martin had given her a pair of gloves with some sort of mesh on the outside. They seemed to help grip the side walls as she made her way up the winding stairs.

The wind was howling and the temperature was frigid. Emily's teeth were chattering. She was so cold. She couldn't imagine how anything could live in these conditions.

She lost her footing several times, looking down at the stairs behind her. It was a long way to fall, she cautioned herself. The stairs continued upward with no end in sight. She lowered her head to fight off the unforgiving wind and forged ahead.

Step by step.

Higher and higher.

She didn't know what to expect. Her legs were growing weak, but there was nowhere to stop and rest. Her toes felt frozen and she didn't know how much longer she could continue to climb upward. She was exhausted and freezing.

Suddenly, without warning, the wind died down. Emily paused and looked around. The wind had indeed stopped and so had the snow. The temperature felt warmer, which seemed impossible since she was climbing higher. Surprisingly, she saw an end to the stairs. She was relieved to have finally reached the top. The staircase behind her seemed to go down forever. However, she was now on level ground. The temperature was invitingly warm, much to her surprise.

She pushed the cloak hood off and shook the traces of snow out of her hair. She looked up and saw that this area was encompassing both the light and the darkness. She saw the sun and the twin moons in the sky, as well as the stars shining above. It was nowhere and everywhere at the same time. She felt the importance of this place, steeped in ancient history, and was humbled by it.

There was an unmistakable calmness about this place. A giant circular gray stone wall stood in front of her. She slowly approached it and stepped through an archway that led into a courtyard that was larger than a football field. The ground within the circular wall was completely covered with shiny stones of various colors. It was strikingly beautiful and reminded Emily of a stained glass mosaic that one might see in a church or cathedral.

The center of the courtyard contained a flat oval shaped stone, pale in color and much larger than the other stones. Her entire house could fit on that stone, she noted. It seemed to be pulsating and emitting a light source.

Emily looked around. She saw nothing and no one. Her footsteps echoed as she crossed the mosaic courtyard to examine the pulsating area closer. She stood in its center, reaching down to touch the stone beneath her feet. It was warm to the touch.

She could feel the vibration beneath her feet and looked around. She was standing in the center of a massive stone structure. Emily looked up and marveled at the thousands of stars that dotted the sky. It looked like the entire universe was dangling over her head. It was glorious!

She felt the temperature drop sharply and rapidly. She could see her breath again. She shivered. Her surroundings were changing. Everything around her was being swallowed by a huge fog bank. It was so thick that Emily could not see through it. The stone beneath her feet began omitting a low-pitched tone, which steadily grew louder.

The odd thing was that the fog didn't cross into the courtyard. It looked like she was standing in the eye of a hurricane. The fog bank reached higher and higher till the mountains disappeared and all she could see were the stars directly above.

There was no sound except the constant humming of the stone she stood upon. The swirling fog surrounded her. The stillness within the courtyard was eerie, yet beautiful.

She heard a loud swooshing noise over her left shoulder and turned quickly towards the sound but saw nothing. She heard another swooshing sound from behind her and spun around.

There was nothing there.

Another swoosh, then another and another from all sides now. She was being circled by multiple sources in the fog bank.

All she could hear was swoosh, swoosh, swoosh.

Her hand lowered to the dagger Martin had given her. She was frightened of the unknown. Emily kept turning towards the sounds. The swooshing was getting closer and louder but remained hidden within the fog bank. She could not see what was making the noise.

Something was happening, not just around her… but to her.

Her necklace began pulsating in unison with the stone beneath her feet. The sound of the vibration grew louder in intensity. It was working in rhythm to the swooshing sounds around her.

The swooshing noises grew faster and faster. Emily felt herself becoming light headed. She was overcome with the sensation of spinning, round and round, with the swooshing noises in the fog bank. She became unsteady on her feet, swaying slightly back and forth. The power surge she felt from the keystone and the stone beneath her feet overwhelmed her.

Emily staggered, looked up at the stars again and blacked out, falling softly to the smooth stone beneath her.

~~~~~~~~~~~~~~~~~~~~~~~~~~~~~~

She felt the tingling in her mind.

*Annadune adelth mirash tonagoden...*

Strange words from a language she did not know.

*Annadune adelth mirash tonagoden…*

Emily slowly opened her eyes. She saw the stars above her come into focus. She stood up carefully. The fog had dissipated. In its place stood eight massive dragons.

The Council of Dragons.

She gasped but did not move a muscle. The dragons formed a perfect circle on the outer ring of the pulsating stone, surrounding her. She turned around and looked up at the majestic creatures looming over her head.

Here stood Emily Richardson of Glendale, California in the company of dragons. It was a wondrous site to behold.

She was in sheer awe.

They stood perfectly still with their massive heads tilted downwards looking directly at her. Their giant wings folded neatly beside them. Sharp claws on their feet and wing tips were signs of just how lethal they could be when provoked. Their tails had long, sharp spikes on the ends of them, reminding Emily of a stegosaurus from the dawn of dinosaurs. Those tails could be a deadly weapon if it were to strike an opponent, she thought.

They were beautiful, despite their size and fierceness. They varied in color from bright blue, vibrant greens, warm reds, yellow and orange. The dragons had glittering scales that seemed to reflect the light. Their scales were almost mirror like in appearance, offering unique camouflage and concealment.

Emily marveled at that feature, realizing that these dragons could reflect the visual pattern of the world beneath them or the skies above as they flew. She could see her own reflection on their bodies.

They were at least three stories tall, muscular, powerful and their eyes had a piercing glare, almost glowing from within. They could see at incredible distances with those eyes. She could understand how easily they could spot their prey.

For all their massive size, Emily thought they were incredibly graceful.

"Wow," Emily heard herself exclaim softly.

*Wow...wow...wow...wow...wow...wow...wow...wow...*

The dragons had mimicked her perfectly. They had the ability to track sounds, echo locate and mimic the captured sounds, even human voices.

Emily grinned.

These creatures were centuries old. They could feel what she felt and hear her thoughts. They had long ago developed the ability to communicate telepathically. They had evolved beyond the mere physical world and had become quiet, gentle spiritual beings, far removed from the madness of the world.

Emily smiled and let their warmth sweep over her. Any fear she felt towards encountering the dragons quickly dissolved.

Describing what she felt at that moment was just not possible. There were not enough words, she realized, to convey the awe she felt for these creatures. Their sheer wisdom penetrated her mind, making her feel welcomed among them.

She didn't have to tell them *why* she was there or explain to them *who* she was.

They simply *knew*.

They knew *everything*.

And, the dragons made that abundantly clear.

Emily found great comfort in this realization. They accepted her, totally and completely, as the bearer of the keystone and knew her heart to be good and true.

The Council of Dragons spoke to her mind and conveyed an understanding of what was being asked of them. They took turns speaking, but seemed to always speak as one voice. The dragons were saddened that the human beings on their world had still chosen a path of destruction and had not transcended to a more peaceful state of mind. It was such a terrible waste.

One should always walk in the light and embrace the serenity that the universe offered – being one with nature, one with all those around you and forever connected. Their wisdom was powerful and moving.

Emily was reminded of her vision in which she saw two of them killed by the hideous beast. She suddenly felt sickened and ashamed. She looked down, not wanting to betray her thoughts, knowing that she was asking these beautiful beings to sacrifice their lives to protect her own kind… She had seen their deaths. She wanted no harm to come to them. This wasn't their fight and to ask them to intervene was…well, wrong, she believed. She wanted to cry. Could men do nothing more than cause misery and death?

*Annadune adelth mirash tonagoden levian destole minirth…*

She heard them whisper in her mind.

She looked up at them, turning to each one as they repeated the words in their own language.

*Annadune adelth mirash tonagoden levian destole minirth…*

277

She understood their words now, as clearly as she understood her own language. They had enabled that gift within her. The keystone continued to pulsate in unison with the stone beneath their feet. Emily noticed that the dragons' hearts were also beating and glowing in time with her necklace and the stone she stood on. The keystone's origins were here in this place and it resonated within the dragons around her.

They spoke to her.

*We are all connected...*

*We do not fear death of the physical body...*

*We are all and we are one.*

*Do not fear our fate...*

Emily closed her eyes. The dragons showed her what must be done. They showed her where she must go and who she must enlist to her aid. They reaffirmed their allegiance to her and her desire to bring about peace on the world. They showed her who would live and who would die in a vast canvas of knowledge that startled and exhilarated her.

The glimpses she was given by the keystone paled in comparison to the knowledge these dragons held about the future of the worlds around them.

They told her not to fear or mourn the losses she was privy to, as this was the way it would unfold, and no loss was too great or too small. All loss served a purpose. She was not to change what would come in pursuit of stability and peace. Things would happen as they were meant to. They assured her that life went on forever in one form or another.

Evil could be conquered, but nothing came without sacrifice. They promised to stand with her to the very end. Aquila was fighting for its existence, to be free of the darkness that threatened to engulf them all.

The dragons asked her to search her heart, reminding her that she still had free will. Even as bearer of the keystone, Emily was free to return to her own world, if she wished to do so, but Aquila would surely fall, as sure as the sun stood watch over them.

Aquila would fall into darkness, forever extinguishing the light and diminishing all hope.

Emily was feeling overwhelmed by the speed of which they revealed things to her. Instinctively, they slowed down, not wanting to overburden her. They knew it was far too much for a young creature as herself but she needed to be prepared for the dangers that lie ahead.

Emily felt them infiltrating her mind, laying the groundwork for her to follow, gently directing her and unlocking her mind to things she never thought possible. They revealed to her the power of the keystone and its incredible abilities if used correctly.

It was a part of them. It was a part of her.

It had been forged by them to bind worlds, serving as a gateway. They conveyed the concerns and risks of anyone with malice gaining control of the keystone and how it could rip the very fabric of time and space, leading to the destruction of all things.

It was no longer a matter of Emily merely understanding the situation before her.

She knew now with absolute certainty.

She understood it to her core.

She felt it.

She was a part of them now... the dragons.

And, they were a part of her.

She trusted the dragons completely and they trusted her.

Emily and the dragons had become one.

~~~~~~~~~~~~~~~~~~~~~~~~~~~~~

Emily spent a great deal of time communing with the dragons, as they shared their wisdom of the ages with her. She suddenly didn't feel like a child anymore. She reached up to touch the chainmail tunic Martin had given her and the necklace from her grandmother, feeling worthy of them in a way she had not felt so before.

Communing with the dragons was like a meditation of sorts. Spoken words were no longer necessary and they talked directly through her mind. It was a new journey she was embarking on and the dragons bestowed in her the courage of the ancients and the devotion of her bloodline. The energy she felt within gave her renewed hope and confidence.

She was to meet Miranda head on, cut off the head of the snake and beat her at her own game before her plan could ever fully be set into motion. This meant beating Miranda on her own turf. This also meant defeating Merrick and the beast as well. Strategically positioning themselves in a way that they had the element of surprise on their side. With Miranda gone the threat would be eliminated. The dragons would handle the beast, even to their own demise.

They had told Emily that she could not change what was to come…

They knew her thoughts and cautioned her again about invoking her own will – the dangers of doing so. To wield the keystone for one's own will was not its intent, they cautioned. The greater good was always paramount.

Emily reached out to touch the dragons, one by one. They were cool to the touch and the scales were as hard as diamonds. She knew her time spent with them was coming to an end and that she must continue.

She did have one favor to ask of them, however. She smiled fondly upon each of them, wished them well and thanked them for their companionship and wisdom. They nodded their heads knowingly at her. She knew she would be seeing them again soon when the time came to fight the beast.

She let her gaze linger on each one of the majestic creatures, in awe of their greatness. Finally, she closed her eyes and asked for her favor. A resounding response of approval echoed back in her mind. She smiled happily.

She had asked for a ride on the wings of a dragon. They were happy to oblige her. The bright blue dragon to her left shuffled forward and lowered its body completely on the ground. Emily touched its snout softly and nodded her thanks to it.

She proceeded to climb onto its back and held on to its scales as tightly as possible. With a slight wave to the other dragons and a farewell in her mind till they met again, she was lifted gently off the ground. With no effort whatsoever, the dragon took flight.

Emily let out a joyous, "Woooohooooo!"

The dragon laughed softly in her mind at her sheer delight. He climbed higher and higher into the sky until she could almost touch the stars. She felt like she was looking over the edge of time. The wind blew against her face as the dragon smoothly rose into the heavens above.

The magnitude of this moment took her breath away. If only it could last forever? She would be content beyond measure. She might never get to be an astronaut when she grew up, but this was as close to the stars as anyone else had ever gotten, she mused. And, riding on the wings of a dragon pretty much tops all else, she knew for a fact. Riding the dragon was like floating on a cloud.

The moons grew larger as they climbed higher into the sky. She reached out her hand towards them, letting a smile cross her face. She marveled at their size and beauty.

"Wow," she said softly.

It was the most beautiful sight she had ever witnessed in all of her young years, more beautiful than she could have ever imagine. She laid her head gently down on the dragon's back, squeezing her arms tightly, trying to convey her thanks to this majestic creature.

She was surrounded by the vast darkness of space and the sheer splendor of the universe lay before her, with a million twinkling lights. The dragon veered left and spoke to her mind, telling her to hold on tight. She did as she was told. The dragon began to nosedive straight back down at incredible speeds, faster than any rollercoaster Emily had ever been on. She screamed out loud in exhilaration.

"Woooooohoooooooo!!" Emily yelled again in delight, as the wind snatched her breath away. Emily started laughing. She was so incredibly happy.

The speed and gracefulness of the dragon was incredible. When it dipped beneath the surface of the clouds, Emily could see Aquila beneath her. The land was dotted with dwellings of all shapes and sizes. Horses and other animals grazed upon the lush green terrain. She saw the mountains before her. The dragon spiraled repeatedly till Emily laughed with glee. She had no idea how she was managing to even hold on. She was firmly locked in place, holding tightly to the dragon with her hands and feet implanted on its scales.

The dragon wove in and out of the clouds, up and down like an obstacle course. It flew lower towards the ground and Emily could easily make out the border wall and Merrick's once grand castle.

"Take me in closer, please," she asked.

The dragon immediately swooped down lower with only the beating of its wings making a sound. It moved its body in line with the river leading up to Merrick's castle and continued its descent until its wing tips splashed the water lightly, sending ripples across the river's surface. It was incredible to witness.

"That was amazing!" Emily shouted out loud.

The dragon beat its wings harder, splashing water on to Emily. She giggled in delight. It circled over head several times to let her get a good view from above the castle and its grounds.

On the wings of a dragon, she soared through the clouds. She didn't know where it was taking her, and she didn't care. Emily was thrilled beyond words.

*It is time...* The dragon spoke softly to her mind.

"I know," she said warmly. "Take me to Mira, please."

The dragon turned its massive body slightly to the left and soared towards Mira's castle in the clouds. It was such a calming experience riding on the dragon that Emily could easily see herself falling asleep from the tranquility of it all. She squeezed the dragon's neck tighter in a show of appreciation for it indulging her. It veered up sharply and barrel rolled upside down over the top of a cloud in response.

Emily burst out laughing.

"That was so cool!" she told the dragon.

It flew into the clouds in front of them, which seemed to stretch on for miles. Emily couldn't see anything, but she knew the dragon saw absolutely everything. It shifted its body and slowly descended, landing softly on the stone courtyard of Mira's castle.

It lowered its body, allowing Emily to slide off its back. It then lowered its head directly to her face. She placed both hands on either side of its massive head and leaned into the dragon until her forehead was touching its nose. She paused there briefly, relaying her thanks to the majestic creature. She kissed it gently on its nose and pulled away.

"What do I call you?" she asked it.

*My given name is Caponeous…*

He spoke to her mind.

"Caponeous," she repeated. "Thank you for everything. May I take another ride one day?"

He laughed.

*You may take as many as you wish, little one. Just summon me and I will be there.*

He assured her in her mind.

She smiled. With that, he rose, nodded his head slightly at her and lifted off the ground effortlessly and disappeared into the clouds. Emily didn't take her eyes off the dragon until he was swallowed up by the clouds above.

"Goodbye, my friend," she said to the dragon, with a warm smile.

She placed her hand on her necklace and closed her eyes.

"Take me to Mira."

With those words, Emily vanished.

# Chapter Twenty-Two

The hooded figure made his way undetected through the forest. He had not been in the light for a very long time. It pained him physically to be here. It left him raw emotionally to be here. If Miranda had not been so insistent that he sought out and recover the boy, he never would have set foot on this side again. He took the southern route to the clinic, which was the last known location of the boy. He didn't dare take the northern path in search of the boy. No – to do so would have brought him far too close to where he last saw her.

He lied to Miranda when he told her that he remembered nothing. He did remember... He remembered all too much about his beloved Isabeau. He didn't think he was physically capable of setting foot on that land again, not after all it cost him. The anguish was still right there below the surface, but he hid it well. It was his pain to bare, and even Miranda could not take that away from him.

He knew these lands better than most. He easily navigated through the kingdom of the light and arrived at his destination well before Doctor Pernell was within range. He watched quietly through the protection of the trees for quite some time and saw no one that remotely constituted a threat to him.

Patients, orderlies, nurses, groundskeepers... A handyman worked to repair the roof of the barn that sat adjacent to the clinic. A handful of visitors wandered about the gardens chatting mindlessly to one another. Mere sheep, he thought.

This is why the light side will be so easy to conquer, he mused to himself. They are far too self-indulgent and oblivious to the real threat at the border wall. While they wallowed away in the riches and fruitfulness of their endeavors, the dark side wasted away and scavenged for every scrap they had. That sheer desperation to escape the endless misery was the single most driving force behind the civil war and ultimate invasion that Miranda had been planning for so long. The beast would clear the light side of any who objected, and Miranda's army would hunt down those that remained. Finally, the light would be engulfed by the darkness.

The irony of his previous life on the light side did not escape Merrick, but he had come to see things differently now. He had no attachment to the light side anymore and believed that its total obliteration would once and for all wipe his mind clear of the excruciating pain he felt every day over what was lost to him.

He approached the clinic from the far side by the creek. Blood would be spilled this day. Merrick would see to it. It was pathetic how exposed this clinic truly was to attack, he mused. Their complacency would be their undoing. No one paid any attention to Merrick as he entered the clinic. Staff went about their business. Patients laid idly in their rooms taking no notice of him.

Locating the room should not be that difficult, he thought. If the boy was actually here, Merrick would find him and kill anyone that got in his way. The doors on the ground floor were all open, except one. Merrick approached and tried to open it. It was locked. He looked around. He had not drawn any attention to himself. He took out a knife from his utility belt and shoved it between the door frame and the door itself. Merrick drove the knife in as far as he could and pushed all his massive weight against it, trying to pry the door open. It made a loud crunching sound as the wood splintered from the force.

A nurse looked up from her desk down the hall and was immediately alerted.

"You there, can I help you? You can't go in there."

She stood and walked towards Merrick. One final shove and Merrick had forced the door off the hinges. The nurse hurried towards the room.

"Stop! Sir, you are not permitted in there," she said loudly as she ran to the door.

Merrick let her get close to him before snatching her and yanking her into the room, placing her in a strangle hold. She grabbed his powerful arm with her hands. She couldn't breathe. She struggled. Merrick tightened his grip on her throat. She was but a rag doll to him. She flailed her arms and legs in a desperate attempt to free herself, but finally went limp in his arms. Suffocated, he tossed her body to the ground.

Donovan was motionless on the bed, still unconscious. A male orderly appeared in the doorway, saw the nurse's body on the floor and shouted for help. Merrick promptly silenced him with a knife to his gut. The man grabbed his midsection and fell back against the broken door as blood oozed from his wound and flowed onto the floor.

Merrick spun around to face the lifeless boy and picked him up. Without so much as a backwards glance, Merrick left the clinic with Donovan over his shoulder and disappeared into the protective cover of the forest amidst the cries and shouts for help from behind him.

~~~~~~~~~~~~~~~~~~~~~~~~~

Mira had summoned Martin to her castle in the sky. He was reluctant to leave the cave where he watched Emily make her way to the Council of Dragons, but he knew that she had to make this part of the journey on her own. He rode fast through the ranges and plains, making good time on his own, with only Emily's horse in tow.

Mira had one of the raiders held captive, while the others were disposed of. Two less raiders in the world were no great loss to anyone, Martin reasoned. But, why keep the third? He didn't expect to get much information from the raider, but he trusted Mira's judgment on these matters.

It was a long way from the clinic and a long way from the medical residency he came here to complete. He wasn't sure how he managed to get swept up in this situation, but ultimately, he was glad he was involved. If he had not nearly ran over Emily with his horse, he never would have learned of his sister's fate.

He reached into his tunic pocket and touched the photo album that Emily had given him. Having it meant everything to him. Now that he knew he was blood related to Emily, he felt even more protective of her and hoped that she was safe.

He stopped only long enough to refresh the horses and rest a moment. Mira had said the matter was urgent, so he wasted no time returning to her location.

When he finally arrived, the mylox brought him to the top. It wasn't his first choice for a mode of transportation, but he appreciated their effectiveness. It was the only way to the castle. Martin was greeted by Thalien and brought to a large chamber within the castle.

"Wait here, please," Thalien said and left Martin alone.

Martin walked around the chamber, occasionally looking out one of the many stone castle windows but saw nothing but clouds. Mira entered the room and greeted him.

"Martin, lovely to see you again. I trust your journey went well?" she asked.

He crossed the room to meet her. "Yes, Emily is with the Council of Dragons. Can you see how she is? Is she well?"

Mira closed her eyes and then opened them again. "Indeed, she is better than well. She has been enlightened and has found the courage to carry on. She and the dragons are as one now," she smiled warmly.

Martin nodded. "That is good. For I know they will protect her far better than I ever could," he acknowledged.

"Do not underestimate your contribution, Martin. Your part in all this is invaluable. Emily will need you by her side before the end of all this…"

"Then I shall be ready for that time," he affirmed.

"No doubt," she agreed. She motioned to a chair in the back of the room. "Would you take a seat please? Help yourself to the food and beverage on the table at the rear, if you wish, but please remain seated back there until I call upon you to come forward."

Martin nodded and moved back to the rear, which unlike the rest of the room, was dimly lit. He was almost completely seated in the dark but didn't question her intentions. He helped himself to some food and took a seat.

Mira watched him. When Martin was seated, Mira moved towards the center of the room and closed her eyes. Within moments, Rayven stood before her, materializing out of thin air.

Rayven immediately was on alert and spun around looking for an exit. Mira put up a hand to calm her, while Martin watched curiously from the back of the room.

"There is no way out from this room, except through me, I can assure you. Please take a seat," Mira said, motioning to a chair that was not there two seconds ago.

*You will release me at once!* Rayven said to Mira with her mind.

Mira laughed.

"We will have none of that mind manipulation that Miranda enjoys so much. You seekers and shifters with all your pesky intrusions. Not here. Not in my home," Mira said disapprovingly.

Mira closed her eyes and envisioned an open door. She inserted the open door into Rayven's mind. With a slight tilt of her head, Mira slammed the door shut. Rayven jumped back. Her intrusive thoughts were immediately shut off. She looked surprised.

Mira wagged a finger at her. "That door will remain closed. You may no longer intrude on the thoughts of anyone on the light side, especially the likes of Emily and Martin. Do you understand?"

Rayven frowned and reluctantly sat down, knowing she was in the presence of a sorceress.

"I am Mira," she told Rayven. "You do not know me, but the one you serve is my sister."

Rayven was surprised to hear this, but sat stoned faced and said nothing. Mira circled Rayven.

"You and I are going to have a long chat," she said.

"I'm not telling you anything," Rayven spat venomously.

"Oh, I think you will tell me everything," Mira smiled warmly. "Martin, would you care to join us over here," she called back to him.

Martin stood and walked across the room. His eyes never left Rayven. He stepped into the light and she saw his face. There was no mistaking that she recognized him from Emily's house. Her face betrayed her feelings. She was surprised and obviously flustered. She stared intently back at Martin, as Mira motioned for him to sit in the chair directly opposite of Rayven, which too appeared out of nowhere.

Martin stared at Rayven, and she at him. Mira smirked. Emily was very perceptive to have told her about the vision she had regarding these two young people. The chemistry between them – good or bad – was palatable in the room. Mira grinned but said nothing yet. She allowed the two to stare at each other, sizing each other up, letting nature take its course.

Who was going to blink first? Mira wondered with amusement. She watched with interest and still did not speak. Moments seemed like hours. Finally, a slight blush crossed Rayven's cheeks and she looked away, breaking Martin's steely gaze.

Mira smiled. And, we have a winner, she thought to herself.

"Shall we begin?" she finally said. Mira placed her hand gently on Martin's shoulder and patted it, before circling Rayven again.

"You were about to tell me everything you know about Miranda's plans…"

Rayven said nothing.

Mira nodded. "I see. Cat got your tongue? Well, let me see if I can help loosen it a bit."

Suddenly, Emily appeared at her side. Both surprising and startling Martin and Rayven. He jumped up and gave her a warm embrace.

"You are back!" He looked in her eyes, saw her new resolve and smiled. "And, you have found the answers you sought."

"It's good to see you too, Martin," Emily told him sincerely. "I have so much to tell you. Guess how I got here?"

He shrugged his shoulders. "How?"

"On the wings of a dragon!"

Martin laughed wholeheartedly. "Did you really?"

She nodded excitedly and proceeded to tell him all about her encounter with the dragon. When Emily spoke of it, her entire face lit up. Martin didn't think it was possible to see someone so elated as Emily obviously was about her adventure. She was positively giddy. He looked down fondly at her and smiled.

"I am happy for you, Emily. I truly am."

Emily returned his smile, before turning her attention to Rayven. "What were you saying?" Emily asked.

Mira interjected, "Oh, she is not in the talking mood." Mira placed her hand on Martin's shoulder again, gently pushing him back down into his seat, opposite Rayven.

Emily stood in front of Rayven, determined to get her point across. "I know exactly who you are and what you have done."

Rayven completely ignored Emily, directing her remark to Mira. "I will not engage in a fireside chat with a child."

Emily leaned in closer and whispered into Rayven's ear.

"I know all about Grace," she whispered, causing Rayven to look into her eyes. "If you want to see her again, I suggest you cooperate."

Rayven was shocked to hear her mother's name.

"Do you understand me now?" Emily asked.

Rayven nodded her head, visibly shaken. Mira and Martin looked at one another and back at Emily. Her time spent with the Council of Dragons had changed her, Martin noted. She now spoke with an air of authority. Emily turned and walked around the room, gathering her thoughts.

Martin watched her and smiled.

She had found her courage.

He was proud of her.

She was so young to carry the weight of Aquila on her shoulders. The new strength she exuded reminded him so much of his own mother. The might of the dragons by her side had served her well. Emily turned to face Mira and Martin.

"We need to go to the dark side. That's where Miranda will be stopped," she told them.

"Miranda will not allow anyone close to her. She has her fortress locked down," Mira told Emily.

Emily looked at Rayven. "There's someone that can help get us inside. And, she knows exactly who I'm talking about."

Rayven stared at her, dumbfounded.

The dragons had shown Emily exactly what needed to be done. "Her brother, Philip. He can get us in and out undetected," Emily told them.

Rayven sat up in her chair and protested. "My brother? How do you even know about him? Leave him out of this. He's not involved in any way," she said angrily.

"He's about to be very involved," Emily told her.

"How do we find him?" Martin asked.

"She's going to take us to him," Emily told him.

"I will do no such thing," she said defiantly.

Mira watched on, listening intently.

"Do you want Grace to walk on the light side? Isn't that what you want more than anything else?" Emily asked.

Rayven was furious that Emily even spoke of her mother. "It is not possible, therefore what I wish is irrelevant."

Emily looked at Mira.

"Oh, but it is possible. You have been lied to," Mira enlightened her.

"What are you talking about?" Rayven demanded to know.

"You have spent your entire life believing that no one can cross through the mist wall, without Miranda's protection, even then only briefly, forcing you to return to the dark side... Yes?"

"No one can crossover," Rayven said forcibly.

Mira frowned. "Really? And you know this to be a fact or is it just a lie Miranda has spoon fed the populace to control them?"

"It is not a lie," Rayven argued.

"Oh, but it is," Mira corrected. "It is true that those with malice in their hearts will be consumed by the wall, unless Miranda places a spell of protection on you, which has allowed you to conduct your raids. However, she may have left out one teeny bit of vital information.'

Rayven looked from Emily to Martin and back at Mira again.

"Which is?" Rayven wanted to know.

Mira took a long pause before answering.

"The kindhearted may cross…" Mira waved her hand in the air. "The mist wall was never supposed to keep out good folk. Oh, I know we all have made mistakes or committed misdeeds of one kind or another, but mistakes and misdeeds do not make a heart dark with malice and cruelty. Kindhearted folk with good intentions? They are given safe passage through the wall," Mira told her.

Rayven stood up angrily and shouted.

"You are lying!"

Martin immediately stood up and took a step closer to Rayven, placing himself between her and Emily.

"Sit down," he ordered her.

Rayven was fuming with anger. "You are lying, nothing but lies!"

Martin stepped closer to her, a mere inches away. "Sit down or I will knock you down," he ordered.

Rayven raised her eyes and leveled her glare at Martin. They stood locked in that position for a few moments.

"Sit down," Martin demanded. "I shall not ask you again."

Rayven blinked hard and sat down, folding her arms angrily.

Emily stepped forward. Martin moved to the side to allow her to approach Rayven.

"We can prove it to you," Emily said.

Rayven shot a glance at her, "How?"

Emily leaned in to Rayven again.

"That thing you want the most… We can help make it happen. Your mother can be safe. She can be free. She can walk on the grass and feel the sun on her face," Emily said with conviction.

Rayven shook with anger, "How do you know these things? How do you know about my mother? And, my brother?" she demanded to know.

Her eyes suddenly fell to Emily's neck and then she understood. She saw the keystone dangling around the young girl's neck. Rayven stared, mesmerized by the swirling purple light within it.

"The keystone...," she whispered faintly.

Emily pulled back from Rayven instinctively. Rayven raised her eyes and looked at Emily.

"You have the keystone," she said quietly.

"Yes, I do," Emily answered.

Rayven let that sink in. This is what Miranda needs... If she could just get the keystone back to Miranda. Rayven's thoughts betrayed her. Mira stepped forward.

"Remove those thoughts from your mind," Mira warned Rayven. "I can assure you that Martin here will strike you dead before he allows you to touch the girl or the necklace that she wears around her neck."

Rayven shot a glance at Martin.

"Gladly," he added, glaring at her.

Emily continued.

"Do you want us to get your mother out or not?"

Rayven shook her head.

"This is all magic. You are just playing games," she insisted.

"We are going after Miranda with or without your help," Martin added.

"Then why waste my time with this dramatic performance," Rayven scoffed.

Mira and Emily looked at each other.

"You are one of Miranda's most trusted seekers, are you not?" Mira asked.

Rayven did not reply.

"I know you are. You can get to her easily," Mira said.

"I will do no such thing and I am sick of your lies."

Emily shook her head. "No, Miranda's the one that's lied to you all these years. And, we can prove it. Do you want your mother out or not?" she asked, repeating her question.

Rayven looked away.

"Do you want your mother out or not?" she asked again.

Rayven glared at her, refusing to answer.

Emily looked at Martin.

"Let's start by getting her mother out," Emily told him.

Rayven stood up again, angrily.

"Wait! Leave her alone. You will kill her if you take her through the mist wall!"

Martin stepped forward again. "Sit," he ordered.

Rayven glared at him but sat back down in her chair.

Mira corrected her. "No, it will kill her to remain behind. Is your mother a good person?" she asked.

Rayven nodded her head yes.

"If we do this...If we save your mother...If we get her out...then will you believe us? Will you believe that Miranda has been lying to you all this time?" Emily asked.

Rayven did not answer.

Emily whispered into Rayven's ear. "I love my mother too and, in my vision, I witnessed you kill her."

Rayven turned her head to look at Emily.

Emily nodded.

"I watched you murder my mother. I should let Martin do to you what you were going to do to my mom, but you can help us. If we're telling you the truth and we can get your mother out safely, to live out her days on the light side? What's it worth to you? Daughter to daughter," Emily asked.

Rayven looked up into Emily's eyes and held her gaze.

"What's it worth to you?" Emily asked again softly.

"Everything," Rayven finally whispered back.

Emily nodded.

They understood each other now.

Some things transcended all else.

Emily turned and walked across the room. Martin watched her and nodded approvingly. She had handled herself remarkably well. Emily had a quiet resolve and new determination that he admired.

He turned back to face Rayven.

"Try anything and I will strike you down without warning," Martin cautioned her.

She ignored his remark, not taking her eyes off Emily. All she could think about in that moment was the very real possibility that this young girl was telling the truth. Perhaps, her mother could finally be free. That was worth the risk to Rayven. She had nothing more to lose at this point. She may have pledged her allegiance to Miranda, but what if she had been lied to and her mother suffered all these years for nothing?

Emily leaned against the wall in the back of the chamber and took a deep breath. She wasn't used to this new role bestowed upon her. She didn't want to let anyone down. She needed a moment to compose herself.

Mira motioned for Martin to step aside so they could talk in private.

"I will send Thalien for Doctor Pernell. He will have to meet you at the wall. If you do get her mother out, she will need refuge and medical attention, I have no doubt."

Martin nodded.

"You and Emily should rest for a while. The days ahead will not be easy for any of you," she told him.

With a wave of her hand, Mira sent Rayven back into her little stone box, unreachable and undetectable by the outside world. Rayven's eyes never left Emily – even as she vanished into thin air.

# Chapter Twenty-Three

Hunger. The insatiable need to feed. The beast grew restless. It was trapped in an underground hell, with heavy chains around its legs and a metal collar around its neck. It grew tired of the tiny morsels it was fed. It needed more. It wanted more. It craved more. The beast was weary of the tiny creatures cowering and whimpering in fear before the crunching of their bones finally ceased their cries.

It didn't want to be fed.

It wanted to hunt.

The thrill of the chase, closing in on one's prey. Swooping down from above with the wind beneath its massive wings. It wanted to feel its weight upon the ground, not this cold slab that had been its prison for far too long now.

The master came infrequently now and as her visits lessened, so did her grip on him. Her spell slowly wavered over the years of neglect and complacency. Miranda was far too overconfident that she held the beast in her grasp. She underestimated the sheer will of its need to be free and its thirst for blood.

The beast tugged at the chain attached to the stone wall, bit by bit, loosening the gravel around the spikes that held it in place. It gave just a little, but a little each time would eventually lead to a lot. It narrowed its gaze to the dim light coming from outside of its cave. Soon, very soon.

The sounds of snapping bones could be heard beneath its weight. It was only a matter of time. No one would be its master. It would be free of its chains, head to the surface and feast on all the glorious morsels it craved and burn everything else to the ground, leaving only ashes in its wake.

~~~~~~~~~~~~~~~~~~~~~~~~

Merrick returned the boy to Miranda on the dark side.

Donovan had not stirred during the entire journey back. Whatever spell had overcome the boy was certainly extremely effective. Miranda would not be pleased that someone had tampered with her little pet.

Merrick cared not for the boy. He thought Donovan was a liability and a nuisance, more than a benefit. The boy was too immature and uncontrollable. However, Donovan's ability to manipulate minds intrigued Miranda. She felt it best to keep oddities such as Donovan close at hand. He was such an easy plant among the sheep on the light side. The poor misunderstood child, whose parents didn't want him – a very clever ploy indeed. Merrick believed, more to the point, that Donovan's adoptive parents knew their son was pure evil and wanted to be rid of him.

Miranda's handmaidens cared for the boy in a chamber not far from her own living quarters. They washed his lifeless form and placed him on a cozy bed. They doted on him, keeping vigil over the boy.

Merrick shook his head in disgust. The boy should be destroyed. If it was up to Merrick, that is exactly what would happen. Donovan would be a thorn in their side and Miranda was foolish to think she could control the boy for long.

He actually thought about killing the boy on the way back to Miranda's fortress and making up a story about his demise. However, he thought better of it and concluded that it was best to keep the boy around until Miranda's plans came into full fruition. Then, he would dispose of the child. Miranda was adamant that she needed the boy. Merrick had other battles to concern himself with. The boy could wait.

He walked away from the chamber where the boy was being fussed over like a little prince much to Merrick's dismay. Maybe the boy would never wake up and that would suit Merrick just fine.

One down, one to go.

Miranda was waiting for Merrick in her meditation room. She was sending him back to find her raiding party. If they had been killed, there would be traces of a scuffle, bodies to recover. Miranda wanted answers. She wanted Rayven back.

Merrick had no idea where he was being sent. He didn't question his orders. He just knew he was looking for the raiders. All he did know was that it would take magic to send him there. This piqued his interest, but still he did not question his orders. He was curious himself, so he did not object. Raiders did not go missing. And, if someone had taken Miranda's seeker captive, Merrick wanted to know who and why. He was prepared for whatever needed to be done to get those answers.

He knew the sorceress had the power to move back and forth in time and place, if need be, but to do so required so much energy and power that it was rarely done. Now was not the time for Miranda to be weak, but this was an exception. Someone was moving her chess pieces around without her consent, and she wanted to put a stop to it.

Merrick stood at the doorway as Miranda and her brood of witches hummed and chanted, swaying slightly over their bubbling brews and incantations. It stunk of rot and sulfur inside the room. Merrick twitched his nose at the offending odor. Miranda's eyes were rolled back into her head and she was mumbling softly. Merrick turned his head from side to side, making his neck pop, bored with the scene before him. He coughed loudly, intentionally being disruptive. .

Miranda closed her eyes and turned her head towards Merrick.

"Patience..." she ordered.

Merrick shook his head in annoyance. "I am not going to stand here all day," he said impatiently.

Miranda frowned, clearly displeased by his insolence. She slowly stood and approached Merrick. He stood up tall, overshadowing her by quite a margin. She stood in front of him and murmured some strange language that Merrick could not decipher.

"Find Rayven," she ordered.

Merrick nodded.

"Find out what has become of her and her raiding party. Do nothing else. Do you understand?" she ordered.

Merrick frowned and nodded. He paid her no mind. If there was killing to be done, he would gladly do it. He wasn't going to lollygag around if anyone got in his way. Her words meant little to him.

She waved her hand in a circle around his head and Merrick felt a strange sensation coursing through his body as the room around him began to fade from view. All turned to silver glass. He felt as if his body was floating. Then, he vanished, leaving Aquila far behind.

~~~~~~~~~~~~~~~~~~~~~~~~~~~~~

The grass beneath his feet was damp from the early morning dew. A bird chirped merrily in the tree above his head. A sun was lifting itself over the horizon, casting a pinkish-orange hue across the sky, as dawn approached. There was a slight chill in the air, but no frost on the ground.

The absence of the two great moons caught Merrick by surprise. There was not a day in his life where he did not gaze upon them in the skies over Aquila. Yet, in this place? The moons were absent. He realized that he was no longer on Aquila.

The surroundings were strange to Merrick. A concrete road was directly in front of him. Houses were lined up, side by side, painted in different colors, but very similar in appearance. He heard a dog barking in the distance. He stepped back into a cluster of trees and bushes that sat on the far side of one of the houses. A metal box resting on a stick had the numbers '903' written on it. He looked back at the dwelling it belonged to and carefully approached. He didn't see anyone outside. He didn't want to linger here longer than necessary and headed towards the house.

For his large frame, he was very light on his feet. He turned the doorknob. It was locked. He took out his small dagger and easily manipulated the lock until he heard a slight clicking noise. The door squeaked lightly as he pushed it gently open. He waited inside the foyer for a moment for sounds of anyone stirring within.

If the raiders were supposed to be here, he saw no sign of them. The bent golf club was propped up in the corner. Merrick eyed it curiously. The remnants of the broken vase were at the bottom of a trash can inside the laundry room to his right. A copy of the police report was left on the dining room table. Merrick glanced at it with interest.

There had been a disturbance reported from the previous day. The raiders, perhaps? He wondered. The report did not say what became of the intruders, he noted. He walked quietly through the house on the ground floor. Running his hand across the back of their couch, staring at the large flat screen over the fireplace, wondering what it could possibly be.

Whatever happened here, he had missed it. He circled back to the front door and decided to head up the staircase. The raiders were obviously here looking for someone or something. The first stepped creaked loudly once it felt his weight. He pulled his foot back quickly, waiting to see if he had disturbed any of the home's occupants. When he heard nothing, he continued up the stairs, shifting his weight carefully to avoid making further noise.

About midway up the staircase, he glanced to his right at a photograph that was hanging on the wall beside him. He stopped abruptly. He knew that face. He was jolted from his mission back to a place when he had often stared upon this face.

It looked just like Isabeau, even down to the red hair and stark green eyes. His mouth opened when he saw the necklace hanging around the woman's neck. It was Isabeau, but it was not. Confusion swept over him. He took the picture down from the wall and examined it more closely. It looked just like Isabeau, except there was a slight scar above the right eye, barely noticeable, but still it was there. He knew every inch of Isabeau's face. She had no scar, no matter how slight.

Is this who the raiders were after? This woman in the picture? The one wearing Isabeau's necklace – the keystone? If this woman had Isabeau's necklace than that would mean…? But

301

no, that was impossible. Merrick had given his daughter to Miranda long ago. Why would she be here in this strange place, far from Aquila? Still there was no denying that face. His heart was racing. Could his daughter be here in this house?

Merrick looked up to the top of the stairs and back at the picture in his hands. His eyes caught the next picture on the wall.

It was Emily.

He pulled it down too. She was also wearing the necklace. He looked back and forth at Emily's picture and the one he believed to be his daughter. Emily had similar features of his wife Isabeau, but she was not the dead-on ringer like the other woman in the picture was…

And, if this young girl was wearing the keystone? What had become of his daughter in this world? If it was in fact, his daughter? Miranda's deceit knew no end, he fumed. What was she up to and why was his daughter sent to this place?

Merrick turned the frames over and pulled at their edges. He managed to pry the backs off and remove both photographs from their frames. He rolled the pictures up, stuck both inside his tunic pocket and returned the empty frames to their respective places on the wall.

He slowly walked the rest of the way up the staircase and saw no signs of anyone. The rooms were slightly opened, and he checked each one to see sleeping people within. He let his gaze linger when he came to Emily's room. He recognized her from the picture. If she had the keystone, should he take it from her?

If Miranda had wanted him to know this secret, she would have told him. There was a reason she kept it from him. Merrick knew the girl lying in the bed was connected to Isabeau in some way. She had to be. The necklace proved that. He would find out for himself. He couldn't trust Miranda to tell him the truth.

He debated what to do at that point. He was there to find the raiders and to determine what had happened to them. He found no answers. He would leave it at that and pursue this revelation on his own time.

An overturned book was lying on the stool next to the door of Emily's room. Merrick paused to glance at it. It had a picture on the soft cover of a small man holding a sword with mountains behind him. It was titled *The Hobbit*. The spine of the book was worn from too many uses. He picked it up, turned it over and read a passage:

*"There is nothing like looking, if you want to find something. You certainly usually find something, if you look, but it is not always quite the something you were after..."*

"Indeed," Merrick said to himself.

He lifted his eyes from the pages and glanced over at Emily, snoring softly as she slept. He pocketed the book in his tunic and headed back down the stairs.

He exited the home and walked quickly around the exterior and still saw no trace of the raiders. He closed his eyes and concentrated. Summoning Miranda to bring him back. The cold silver glass surrounded him again and he was returned immediately to the dark remnants of Miranda's meditation chamber.

She stood eagerly by, waiting for news, disappointed that he was returning alone.

"You have failed?" she asked.

"I have not failed," he replied. "They were not there. It appears there was a disturbance the previous evening, but no one was captured."

Miranda frowned. "Well, that is very odd indeed. They did not summon me to return them either. What could have possibly happened to them?"

Merrick shook his head. "I do not know of their fate."

Miranda looked at Merrick sternly. "Did you uncover anything else?"

Merrick was aware of the pictures hidden within his tunic but had no intention of telling Miranda about them. To do so would be to reveal that he in fact had retained his memory and she had not wiped it clean as she so believed. What she didn't know would not hurt her, Merrick reasoned.

"Nothing of any interest, no," he answered curtly.

She studied him carefully for a few minutes, looking for any trace of deceit, but found none. Merrick knew how to hide his emotions. He would not give her even a hint that he found anything significant. It was his riddle to solve.

She broke her gaze and turned her back on him. "You may leave," she said with a wave of her hand, dismissing Merrick.

"Gladly," he muttered under his breath. He turned on his heel and headed back to his own chamber.

~~~~~~~~~~~~~~~~~~~~~~~~~~~

Doctor Pernell knew immediately that something was wrong. As his horse turned the bend directly in front of the clinic, he saw people running around in a panicked state.

He quickened his pace but stopped short of the clinic. He dismounted and turned to Rebecca, who was groggy after her long nap on the horse.

"Stay here," he said.

She rubbed her eyes and looked towards the clinic.

"What's wrong?"

"I do not know, but I want you to stay right here until I return. Do you understand?'

She nodded yes.

Doctor Pernell ran towards the clinic, casting a glance over his shoulder to make sure Rebecca was obeying.

He stopped abruptly when he stepped inside and saw the carnage at Donovan's room. The orderly had bled out all over the clinic floor. A nurse was slumped over and not moving. Donovan was gone.

A marshal spotted the doctor and ran over to him.

"Two dead, sir. Must have been raiders. They didn't steal anything, but they kidnapped the boy named Donovan," he reported urgently.

"Damn," Doctor Pernell swore. "Any witnesses?"

"It happened very quickly. Looks like the nurse spotted them entering the room and they silenced her. The orderly must have interrupted whatever was going on and it cost him his life too. One of the patients says he spotted a single assailant, very tall, dark clothing with something draped over his shoulders, presumably the boy," the marshal added, looking at the pool of blood in the room.

That caught the doctor by surprise. "A single assailant?"

"That's what they said."

There was a lot of commotion in the corridor. Orderlies were covering the bodies with sheets and preparing to move them away from curious eyes. The custodian was in the process of cleaning up the blood. He had a grim look on his face. Doctor Pernell nodded at him sympathetically. The doctor inspected the doorframe and saw that it been broken off its hinges by a very powerful man.

"Merrick?" he asked himself. "Surely even he would not be so bold." Doctor Pernell turned to the nurses huddled nearby. They looked frightened. He tried to offer them some comfort.

"It is going to be all right. The raiders will not be coming back here. Please help me notify these poor souls' families," he said sadly.

The nurses hurried back to their stations to follow his orders. Doctor Pernell thanked the marshal and headed back out to retrieve Rebecca. She was still seated on his horse. He reached out his arms to help her down.

"Come now, child. I want you to go to your room and stay there until the nurse brings you down for dinner, understand?"

She nodded. He removed some of her belongings from the saddle bag and handed them to her.

"I will have the rest of your things sent up to you, as soon as possible," he offered.

"Thank you. What happened?" she asked.

"Nothing to concern yourself with. An accident," he assured her. "Go around the back and enter by the gardens."

305

She could tell by the commotion that it was more than just an accident. She was certain Donovan was behind it in some way. He was no good. He had hurt her feelings and played a dirty trick on her. She'd never forget that. She didn't question Doctor Pernell. She gathered her things and headed towards the residency portion of the clinic.

He watched her do as she was told. He took his horse to the barn and returned inside to contact Mira and Thalien about what had occurred. They would need to be warned that Donovan was on the loose. There was no telling what the boy was capable of. Donovan was obviously valuable to Miranda or she wouldn't have extracted him so quickly from the clinic. This was troublesome, indeed. He was just another pawn in Miranda's bag of tricks that would have to be dealt with, and fast.

~~~~~~~~~~~~~~~~~~~~~~~

"What on earth? How odd," Emily's mother said, as she came down the staircase later that morning. There were two empty picture frames hanging on the wall. Both photographs had been removed.

Emily came up behind her. "Mom, have you seen my book, *The Hobbit*? I had it on my chair last night and now it's gone. I bet Sarah took it."

"I don't know, dear. Ask your sister. Say, what happened to the picture of you and my mother?" she asked.

Emily looked at the empty frames on the wall and frowned. "Beats me. Maybe the ones that broke in took them, although I don't know why they'd want our pictures." She turned sideways and squeezed past her Mom on the stairs. "Sarah! Sarah? Where did you put my book?"

Her Mom stared at the empty frames, perplexed. When she heard the two girls arguing in the kitchen, she hurried down the stairs to play referee. Just another day on the frontlines for a mother.

# Chapter Twenty-Four

The mist wall reached as far as the eye could see, resembling an ominous grayish cloud bank, churning in place angrily. It gave even the bravest among them pause. It was an effective barrier. One did not tread lightly within it. You could not see beyond it. The only way to know what was on the other side was to pass through it. Nothing lived nor grew near the mist wall. It was a dead zone, avoided by every living creature on Aquila – plant and animal alike.

Martin approached the mist wall with great care. Mira had brought them within a safe distance. They walked the remainder of the way on foot. He was not looking forward to crossing over. In all his years on Aquila, he had never done so. Not even on dares from his youth had he ever stepped foot inside the mist wall. And, now here he was – going willingly. The thought filled him with great unease.

Emily seemed the calmest of all, probably because she had not spent her childhood hearing tales of horror about what lies on the other side. Tales of strange, carnivorous creatures, rivers of blood, death and decay, torture and despair.

Emily looked to her left and to her right, sizing up the massive wall of mist in front of them. Being this close to the mist wall was unnerving. She could feel its energy, pulling them in closer, taunting them to enter.

"Whoever dreamed up this one?" she remarked under her breath. "Super creepy."

Martin sighed. If the dark side was the only world Rayven knew, Martin pitied her for that. He could not fault her for wanting to get her mother out of that wretched place. He looked at her briefly. She was not unpleasant to look at. Emily caught him studying Rayven and smirked.

"What?" he asked.

"Nothing. Nothing at all," she grinned.

Rayven looked at them both and glared at Martin.

Emily leaned into Martin and spoke quietly. "It's that charm of yours working its wonder. That's all," she smiled.

"Stop," Martin said.

"Just saying," Emily teased.

"You know you are not so big that I cannot put you over my knee and give your bottom a proper spanking," he said in good humor.

Emily scoffed. "I'd like to see you try."

She intentionally bumped into Martin. He bumped Emily back and nearly knocked her over. She laughed.

"Would you two stop behaving as children?" Rayven said with annoyance.

"Quiet!" Both Martin and Emily said in unison.

Rayven rolled her eyes.

The mist wall was emitting a low humming noise, making it even more mysterious and haunting. It sounded like a giant tuning fork to Emily. She could feel the vibration of the tone where they stood.

It didn't sound natural to her. It sounded almost mechanical. She had been told that the elders and the Council of Dragons created the mist wall to contain the darkness. But created it how, she wondered? Was there some giant machine underground like in the H.G. Wells classic *The Time Machine*?

"What if we crossover and cannot get back?" Martin asked Emily quietly, concern resonating in his voice.

"The keystone will provide safe passage," Emily reassured him and herself.

The trio stood quietly for several minutes taking in the gravity of their situation. Standing in front of the mist wall was starting to give Emily the creeps. Her imagination was taking over, wondering what horrors awaited within.

Rayven was anxious, trying not to be too optimistic about their promise to rescue her mother, in exchange for assistance. Martin knew what perils awaited them on the other side of the mist wall and was apprehensive. He was concerned for their safety. Emily was growing extremely nervous but took comfort in the words of the Council of Dragons.

She sighed deeply and looked up at Martin.

"Are we ready for this?" she asked.

"Yes," he assured her, only half believing his own words.

Emily inhaled deeply.

"So, we're really going into the mist wall?" she asked absently. "Suddenly, this seems like a really bad idea."

"I tend to agree," Martin echoed her sentiments. He took her hand. "Do not let go of my hand. Understand?"

Emily swallowed hard and nodded her head. Saying you're going to do something and then actually following through with it are two entirely different things.

Martin gave Rayven a gentle push from behind.

"Move."

They cautiously stepped forward into the mist wall together. The effect was disorienting. Emily understood why Martin was holding onto her hand. There were strange hushed voices all around them. One lost all sense of direction. She heard the tormented cries of men and women that had attempted to crossover, only to be forever trapped within, consumed by the wall. It was chilling. The moisture in the air touched her skin like tiny pinpricks.

Something within the mist brushed against Emily. She jumped back, startled. She suddenly felt claustrophobic. The effect was making her queasy. The mist was oppressive, pushing down on her. She started to breathe quickly, feeling the fear rise within her.

"Steady," Martin told her.

They continued to inch forward. Martin had his hand on Rayven's shoulder, making sure she did not bolt and run. He continued to hold firm to Emily's hand, so she did not get lost in the mist.

It was cold inside the mist, with no breeze whatsoever. The humming noise was louder now and starting to make her head hurt. She couldn't see in any direction. She was becoming more frightened with each step they took.

"Martin?" she said softly, the panic evident in her voice.

He squeezed her hand.

"I am right here," he told her. "Close your eyes."

She shut her eyes tightly and grabbed onto Martin's arm with her free hand. An icy hand touched her hair and tugged it. Emily gasped and swiped at the air. She buried her head into Martin's shoulder. It was like being trapped in the worse haunted house imaginable.

"Something just touched me," she said in alarm.

"There are beings in the mist – phantoms," he told her.

"Oh my God," she replied, terrified.

"Keep moving forward," he advised.

She could feel them pressing up against her body, sniffing her, pawing at her, tugging at her clothes and hair.

"Martin?" she said again desperately.

"I am right here, little one," he assured her.

She let go of Martin's arm and shoved her hand into her pocket until it came to rest on the small cross that she always carried with her.

"Our father who art in heaven, hallowed be thy name," she repeated over and over again. Something laughed hideously in her ear and she stopped talking.

Martin pulled her closer to him. Emily felt the keystone beginning to vibrate. She touched it, wrapping her fingers around it. Her hands were trembling. The humming of the mist wall was making her dizzy.

There was nothing more Martin could do. Neither his sword nor his might were of use in this place. You cannot fight the unseen in the space that exists between worlds.

They continued moving forward slowly for several minutes. Suddenly, they broke through the mist wall and were standing on the dark side.

Emily's mouth dropped open and she let go of Martin's hand. She was not prepared for the vast wasteland before her. It looked like the apocalypse had occurred here. It wasn't just dark... It was desolate, a hauntingly dead world. They took a few more steps forward and the ground beneath her feet crunched. She looked down and gasped. She was walking on human and animal skeletal remains.

"What the heck?" she said out loud.

"Try not to look down," he advised her.

She was breathing fast. All she saw around her was a wasteland of bones and ruins – death. What trees were visible were twisted and ugly with no leaves. Contorted branches cried out in agonizing pain.

It was pitch black except for the incredible light cast down by the two moons, serving as two giant light bulbs in the sky. The ground was barren. No grass, no flowers, no life to be seen of any kind. Just endless death and destruction. The smell was putrid. She gagged briefly.

"This is awful," Emily remarked. "I don't understand. How can one side be so beautiful and then there is this? And, people live here?"

"The selfishness of those on the light side make this possible," Rayven said bitterly.

"Of course, the treachery of those on the dark side had nothing whatsoever to do with the creation of the mist wall. You think you are all innocents?" he countered angrily.

Emily ignored them both, stunned by the devastation she was witnessing. "This isn't right," she said to herself. "No one should live like this. On my world, I mean, we have our problems. Bad problems, but I think overall humanity tries to help each other. We don't have portions of our planet that look like this... It's sickening," she added. "I'm not trying to be preachy, but this... this is wrong."

Neither Rayven nor Martin replied.

"Martin?" Emily turned to face him and asked him directly. Her eyes searching his face for answers. "I mean, look at this. Surely, something can be done, right? There are women and children here. I saw them in my visions. You can see that this is wrong, can't you?"

No one had ever asked him that question before. He had never given it any thought actually. He scratched his head.

"It is just the way it is, Emily. It has been this way for a very long time now," he told her, seeing the sad look in her eyes. "I am sorry. It is just…our way."

She shook her head no and pointed to the necklace she was wearing. "I mean, I get it. It's always been this way for you. That doesn't make it right. I can just feel their pain, can't you? I mean it's making me physically ill to be here. I'm not saying let all the bad people take over the light side, but… not everyone here is bad. And, even the bad ones? Well, this is inhumane. I'm not just going to look the other way. I'm going to do something about this," she told him with conviction.

His features softened and he smiled at her.

"I do believe you will," he said fondly, brushing a whisp of bangs away from her eyes.

Rayven stared at her, realizing that Emily wasn't like the others on the light side of Aquila. She was wrong to judge Emily so quickly. She could tell that the girl was sincere in her concern.

A loud shriek could be heard nearby.

"We must be cautious," Martin warned.

They walked upon two humanoid creatures hunched on all fours, tearing apart what seemed to be a rodent like creature, eating it raw. The humanoids looked up at the trio with bloodied mouths and bits of flesh dangling from their rotted teeth.

"Oh my God," Emily gasped, shaking despite the comfort of Martin by her side.

He held fast to Emily's hand and placed his other hand on his sword, raising it slightly to let the humanoids get a good look at it. His way of letting them know to carry on and not to bother them or he would most certainly strike them dead. They looked at his sword and turned their attention back to their meal.

"I'm going to be sick," Emily said. She pulled away from Martin and vomited over a pile of human remains.

"She has no business being here," Rayven commented.

"Did I ask your opinion?" Martin snapped.

Emily pulled a rag from her trouser pocket and took a swig of water to rid herself of the taste. She covered her nose and mouth with the rag, trying to block out the stench around her. Martin approached Emily and put his hand on her back, never taking his eyes off Rayven.

"Can you continue?" he asked, concerned for her wellbeing.

Emily looked back at the humanoids feasting on the rodent and spoke nervously. "There is this book I read in Honor's English class about Hell. It's called Dante's *Inferno*. I always imagined that it looked something like this."

She held on to her stomach, trying not to vomit again.

Martin looked around and then back at Emily.

"The dark side is everything the light is not. This place is death and disease. It is a vile, cursed place. Can you continue?" he asked again.

"Yes, I think so," she said nervously.

Rayven watched them both. The girl was not accustomed to what she was seeing, but it didn't bother Rayven in the least. Seeing a couple of subhumans eat a rodent was nothing compared to what other horrors awaited them.

Emily noticed the silence. No birds or insects could be heard of any kind. Occasionally, she heard the screams of something in the distance, but she had no idea what was making the noise in this bleak godforsaken place. The wind whistled slightly.

"How far?" Martin asked Rayven.

"You brought us in this way to go undetected by the raiders at the fortress. It is a longer journey. If we keep up a good pace, a day or two, depending on what we encounter. Watch your heads for raptors above," she warned absently.

"Raptors?" Emily asked, looking up.

Martin explained, "Raptors are smaller than dragons, but are meat eating predators. Think mylox, but deadlier and faster."

She looked at Martin, trying to make out his features in the dark. The two moons offered light, but not as much as the sun.

"Raptors, huh?" she echoed back.

"And, griffins too," Rayven interjected.

"I know what griffins are!" Emily said, sounding alarmed.

Griffins had the body, tail and back legs of a lion, but the head and wings of an eagle with talons on its front feet. Martin shot Rayven a dirty look, but she didn't see it in the dim light.

"Any other creatures you'd like to tell me about?" Emily asked Rayven.

Rayven obliged her curiosity.

"Giant serpents that can swallow a man whole, womrats the size of a large dog, wolves the size of a horse, carnivorous minions that serve Miranda and pick up strays like us along the border walls..."

"That is enough," Martin silenced her.

"How does anyone survive here?" Emily asked bleakly.

Rayven was quick to reply, "We stay in small villages close to the fortress, under Miranda's protection. Anyone that ventures out too far is going to be some creature's dinner pretty fast."

"Keep walking and stop talking," Martin ordered.

Emily pulled her cloak hood over her head. She kept glancing above and around her for anything that moved. The smell was sickening as they pushed forward through the hellish wasteland. Rayven led the way and she told Martin that she knew how to get them back with the least amount of hazard. He had no choice but to trust her. Emily stayed close to Martin, often holding on to his arm whenever she heard something growl, howl or shriek close by. He never took his hand off his sword.

"This whole place is slithering," Emily said alarmed at how the ground moved with them.

"The snakes feed off the dead," Rayven added.

Martin quickened his pace to stand beside Rayven. He grabbed her arm tightly. "You are intentionally frightening her and if you do not shut up, I will gag you," he warned harshly.

She snapped back at him and yanked her arm free. "Better that she be prepared for this than unaware of the dangers that lurk in the darkness."

Emily piped in, "Hello? I can hear you."

"Stop intentionally frightening her," he warned.

"She needs to know what she is walking into," Rayven argued angrily.

Martin glared at her. He knew she was right but didn't approve of her methods.

"I agree but tone it down. You do not have to scare the wits out of her," he snapped back.

"Again," Emily interrupted. "I can hear you…"

Martin sighed and came back to Emily's side.

"My apologies," he told her sincerely.

"Look," Emily said, taking them both to task, "I'm not a baby. I rode on the wings of a dragon across Aquila and have seen a lot of things since I've been here that well…yea, cut me some slack, okay? I'm not a baby," she repeated, defensively.

"Of course not," Martin agreed. "You are being quite brave."

"Thank you, Martin."

"Big and strong, like me," he joked warmly.

"Yea, big and strong," she said, showing him her muscles.

He smiled and turned his attention back to their harsh surroundings. Rayven listened to the interchange with interest but said nothing further.

They walked for hours and no one spoke. Occasionally, they would stop when something got too close to them and Martin took up a protective stance to fight whatever might endanger them.

Emily could feel eyes watching her in the darkness. More of those creepy evil garden gnomes that she had seen at Merrick's castle, she surmised. Salivating in the dark, waiting to make a meal out of her. She shivered at the thought and kept her own hand close to her dagger, reminding herself of the self-defense techniques Martin had taught her in the cave.

They began to climb a sharp rise and Emily saw a tall mountain in front of them, black as the night. Its location given away by the fire and lava spewing from its top like a chimney.

Its fiery embers slowly pouring down the sides of the mountain, barren of all life. Emily paused to look at it.

"That is where Miranda's fortress is located," Rayven said, breaking the silence.

Martin did not respond. Emily stared a moment longer at the fiery mountain and kept walking. Rayven fell back and walked next to Emily.

"You actually rode on a dragon?" Rayven asked curiously.

Emily looked over at her, "Yea, I did."

Rayven nodded approvingly. "That is quite impressive."

Emily didn't respond back. She didn't trust Rayven yet. She didn't want to share details of something so special with someone that would have easily killed her mother, if given the chance. Martin squeezed Emily's hand again, sensing her unease and unwillingness to talk to Rayven.

They continued in silence, steadily closing the distance between themselves and Miranda's monstrous fortress. The hideous sounds and shrills of the dark pressed in on them with every step they took.

~~~~~~~~~~~~~~~~~~~~~~~~~~

Philip had not seen Rayven come back for quite awhile now. He stepped out from his hiding spot between the crumbling buildings next to the tavern and made his way up the back stairs where Rayven and his mother lived. He let himself in. Grace had fallen asleep in the chair exactly where Rayven had left her. He gently kissed his mother on the cheek, and she opened her eyes.

"Philip, my boy," Grace said in a soft voice, "Are you home for dinner now?" Grace looked at the soup sitting in front of her. It was ice cold, but she offered it to Philip.

"No, Mama," he said. "I brought you some fruit and potatoes. I'm going to make a little salad for you, fresh food and not that slop in the soup bowl," he told her.

He moved her soup bowl away from her and emptied the contents of his bag on the small counter and used the cutting knife to slice up the fruit and potatoes he had brought her. He turned back to her and showed her a small bottle.

"Look, Mama, I brought you some seasoning. The kind you like," he said.

She clapped her hands excitedly, "Oh good, good. That's my boy. Your sister should be back soon, I think. I can't remember where she went." She looked around, confused.

"It's all right, Mama. Let me get your meal ready for you." Philip went to work lighting the small stove and frying the potato for his mother. She sat back in her chair and hummed softly, watching her son.

Within minutes, he had prepared a small plate of fresh greens and potatoes. He sprinkled her favorite seasoning on top and placed the plate in front of her with a fork and napkin. She smiled widely. He put some on the fork for her.

"Oh goodness, this looks delightful. Thank you, my son." With shaky hands, she slowly raised the fork to her mouth. "Mmmmm," she smiled.

He leaned over and kissed her on the forehead.

"Eat up, Mama," he said and turned to clean up the small kitchen area. He brought her some fresh water to drink with her meal. When he was done cleaning, he took a seat opposite his mother and watched her. She was deteriorating more rapidly with each day and it broke his heart. He was pleased to see her eat every bite on her plate.

When she was finished, she looked up at her son and said, "More?"

He shook his head. "There is no more, Mama," he said sadly. "But I have a treat for you," he added with a twinkle in his eye.

She clasped her hands together in eager anticipation.

"Let me see, let me see," she said like a giddy schoolgirl.

He laughed warmly at her and pulled out something wrapped in a cloth, placing it on her plate in front of her.

"I have a pastry for you, with warm honey on it," he said proudly.

Her face lit up. "Oh my!" She picked it up and smelled it. "This is wonderful," she beamed. "Come, share it with me."

"No, Mama. It's for you," Philip insisted.

She hungerly ate her tasty surprise. Pastries were hard to come by in these parts and he had nearly gotten killed stealing it off the food caravan to Miranda's fortress, but it was worth it to see the look of joy on his mother's face. He let her enjoy her treat and walked back over to the kitchen. He took out a few more scraps that he had managed to steal.

The food he brought would hold them over for at least a week. Philip laid a couple of books on the night table by his mother's bed. He had a bar of soap and creams that he placed by the wash basin and a couple of new wash towels. He placed a full box of candles and flint by the stove. He checked to make sure they had plenty of clean drinking water. He was prepared to boil some, if they were low.

When his mother was done eating, he could tell she was getting sleepy again. He walked over to her and reached out his hands, "Come, Mama, please lay down on the bed and get some rest. I am sure Rayven will be back soon."

His mother nodded and allowed her son to help her onto the small cot. He pulled the ragged blankets over her and made a note to himself to try and find a new blanket for her soon. She patted his hand gently.

"You are a good boy, Philip," she said as she closed her eyes. "I love you so much."

"Thank you, Mama. I love you too."

He stayed a few minutes longer until she fell asleep. He took a quick look around the tiny room and headed out, not wanting to run into Rayven.

From the dark street below, they watched Philip close the door behind him. Martin looked to Rayven for confirmation. She nodded.

"That's him," she said.

Emily stepped forward.

"Let me go talk to him alone," she said.

Martin objected, "Alone? I do not think so."

Emily protested, "He's not dangerous. Is he?"

She looked at Rayven, who shook her head no.

"And, you look dangerous," Emily said, referring to Martin. Martin frowned.

"Of the three of us, I'm the least threatening," she concluded. "And, he doesn't even get along with her," she said, pointing at Rayven.

Rayven shot her a dirty look.

"Am I right or not?" Emily asked.

Rayven nodded yes.

"Just stay close by and let me talk to him…"

Before Martin could stop her, she had stepped out into the street and slowly followed Philip. She turned back to Martin and raised a finger to her lips to shush his protest. Emily followed him down the road. She lost her footing on the crumbled rocks beneath her feet and gave herself away. So much for stealth, she thought.

Philip knew immediately he was being followed. He quickly turned the corner and pulled back into a doorway, waiting for Emily to pass. She stopped when she turned the corner and realized that she had lost him. He stepped up behind her and jabbed a pointy object into her back.

"Why are you following me?" he demanded to know.

She spun towards him, "Hey, take it easy with that thing," she looked down and chuckled. "A stick? Your weapon is a stick?"

He dropped it immediately. "I don't believe in weapons," he said in his defense.

"Obviously," she grinned. She pulled the hood back off her head and brushed her bangs back from her face.

Philip was immediately disarmed by her appearance. He thought Emily was beautiful. All the females he saw on this side were scarred or disfigured in some way. Not this one, she was…flawless, perfect. And, clean. He leaned in slightly and sniffed. She smelled nice too – a smell he could not place, fragrant flowers from passing caravans to the fortress, perhaps?

Emily leaned away from him.

"Are you sniffing me?" she asked, frowning.

"I'm sorry," he apologized.

He was gawking at her and it was obvious. He looked up at her hair. It was light colored. The women on this side had dark hair, always dark hair. Emily's hair was like firelight. He couldn't stop looking at her.

"Stop staring at me," she told him, looking at him strangely.

He blinked, and averted his eyes, embarrassed that he had let his gaze linger so long. "You are not from here," he said.

"No kidding, Sherlock," she replied with sarcasm. "I have a lot to say so please just listen…"

He stared at her.

"My name is Emily and I know you are Philip. I'm here with your sister, Rayven, and she's a real peach, that one."

"A peach?" he asked, confused.

"Never mind," she continued. "We need your help."

"Help with what?" he asked.

"We're going to get your mother out of here."

She let her words sink in.

"That is not possible," he dismissed.

"Actually, it is…"

She proceeded to tell Philip who she was and why she was there. She explained that Miranda had been lying to them all, for years about crossing into the light and that some could be saved. He was shocked to hear this and looked at her in disbelief. Emily told him as little as possible, but as much as he needed to know. He was, after all, going to get her inside the castle and help her free Isabeau…a little piece of information she had yet to reveal to Martin or anyone else yet.

He listened intently. Emily motioned for Martin and Rayven to join them. Philip looked apprehensive at the two as they approached. He didn't even acknowledge his sister, nor she him. He did look over Martin carefully.

"You're from the light side too, aren't you?" he noticed.

"Yes," Martin admitted. "Is that a problem?"

"Not for you, no," Philip said. "For us? Yes."

"Do what they ask, Philip," his sister ordered.

He glanced at Rayven but did not reply. He turned his attention back to Martin, noticing his hand resting on his sword. It was finally crafted, not like the crude weapons that soldiers on the dark side wielded. Martin's clothes were finely tailored, as were Emily's. As a thief, Philip noticed details.

"What are you supposed to be? A knight? Or something like that?" he asked curiously.

"Something like that," Martin answered curtly.

Philip just stared at him and then looked at his sister. "And, you're going along with this why? Aren't you one of Miranda's little shield maidens?" he said with distain.

"If it gets mother out…then yes. It is the one thing we do agree on, Philip," she said bluntly.

He nodded. "You do this for us, if it's even possible. We help you in return. Right?"

Emily nodded, "Yes."

Philip stared thoughtfully at each of them.

"A knight, a seeker, a princess and a thief? Ferrying my mother across the dead lands? What could possibly go wrong?" he asked sarcastically.

He turned to head back to the tavern. Rayven followed him. Martin and Emily walked closely behind Rayven and Philip, back to the small room where their mother slept.

Emily pulled Martin aside.

"Did he just call me a princess?" she asked with amusement.

Martin grinned, "I believe so, yes."

Emily smiled, "Well, that's a first."

Martin laughed, "Do not let it go to your head, Emily."

She laughed back. "Me? A princess? Go figure!"

Martin grinned.

"Where is he going?" she asked a nurse passing by her table with a plate of food.

The nurse stopped and looked out the window at the doctor. "He has an urgent matter to attend to and will be gone for a couple of days," she told Rebecca, before heading down the hall with the plate of food for a nearby patient.

"I wonder if this has anything to do with Donovan," she whispered.

On a whim, she pushed back her chair, grabbed her knapsack from under the table and filled it with as much bread and fruit as it could hold. She grabbed a water bag hanging from the side counter of the dining hall and quickly exited by the back garden where Doctor Pernell was readying the wagon for departure.

She waited until he went back inside. She then climbed onto the back of the wagon and covered herself with the stack of blankets that he had thrown in. She kept a small opening to peek out of. Rebecca heard the doctor come back and forth a few more times before he climbed up onto the seat. The wagon rocked slightly back and forth as he positioned himself. He smacked the reins of the horse, causing the wagon to lurch forward.

He was completely unaware of the little stowaway in the back of the wagon. Rebecca pulled the blanket back slightly over her head and watched the clouds go by, eventually falling asleep.

~~~~~~~~~~~~~~~~~~~~~~~~~~~~~

The foursome carefully made their way back to the room above the tavern. Philip looked back over his shoulder at Martin and Emily.

"This is crazy, you know that," he warned his sister.

"She knows things she shouldn't know," Rayven said, motioning back to Emily.

"If they are wrong, mother dies," he said flatly.

"If we don't try this, she is dead already," she snapped back.

"And, if we get caught? We are all as good as dead," he argued.

She stopped in her tracks and raised her voice slightly. "Then go, Philip. Scurry away, back into your hole and be done with it. Be the coward you are. I'm sick of the sight of you!" she said vehemently.

Martin and Emily looked at each other and then back at the family squabble. Rayven shoved her brother out of the way and walked past him. Philip stopped walking. Her words stung. It was an old wound and an old argument, one that had eventually torn their family apart.

Emily hurried to stand next to Philip.

"Sisters… I have a sister too and she's a pain in the butt," she offered empathetically. "She takes my stuff. She tattles on me all the time. Drives me crazy."

He looked at Emily. She could tell by the expression on his face that he was not interested in her sister woes. She shut up and went back to walk with Martin.

"I see your charm skills are a bit rusty too," he teased.

She frowned.

Rayven reached the bottom of the staircase and waited for the others to catch up to her. Philip showed no emotion. He didn't consider himself to be a coward, because he didn't fight. He preferred to talk his way out of trouble rather than get hurt.

His sister, on the other hand, was always striking first and asking questions later. They were just different. She always said he had the luxury of being soft, while she had the burden of taking care of her mother and he as well. He was no coward and resented being called one.

Rayven started walking up the stairs, stopped and turned to Martin. "You saw the route we took. We have a long treacherous journey back to the mist wall. How do you plan on getting my mother back that way? She can barely walk," she wanted to know.

"We need something to carry her on – a wagon or wheelbarrow – something," he suggested.

"Like that?" Emily pointed to a small wagon sitting outside the tavern door.

"Exactly like that," Martin stated. "We shall commandeer it for our needs."

"Great. She will have a lovely bumpy ride," Philip remarked disapprovingly. "Such a brilliant idea!"

"Stop complaining," his sister snapped, glaring at him.

"I will help you bring her down. Perhaps your brother can gather up her belongings?" Martin offered, ignoring the tension between the two siblings.

Philip pushed past them both, brushing his sister aside.

Rayven stomped up the steps, angry at her brother.

"This is going to be a fun trip," Emily said sarcastically.

Martin spoke to Emily privately. "Emily, there is truth in what they say. It is a difficult journey for us, let alone their mother. Can you use the keystone to take us back to the light side, as you did to return to your home?"

She frowned. "I don't know. It was one thing to return to my home. You know? That's my home... But this is Aquila. I'm not familiar with anything here. I might put us inside a wall or a mountain." She thought hard about what he was suggesting. "I'm supposed to think it, feel it and see it in my mind... Going home was easy. If I close my eyes right now? I can see my house. I can smell mom's dinner cooking in the kitchen. I can hear my sister tattling on me. I can hear the kids playing outside. I know where every book or game is on my bookcase... It's me. It's my home. Aquila is so strange to me. I could get us all killed." She looked away, unsure.

He patted her shoulder. "It is quite alright, Emily. If you are not comfortable doing so then you must trust your instincts. This is all new to you. You are correct, of course."

"I'm sorry," she said.

"No need to be," he assured her.

Emily looked around at their surroundings. The structures were crammed together and shabbily built. Candlelight from within lit up the windows in a weird yellowish haze. It was stark, dreary and depressing. She shivered thinking about what was

327

lurking in the dark. As if on cue, she saw sets of beady eyes staring back at her from across the road.

Emily grabbed Martin's arm before he headed up the stairs, "Martin, over there – look."

She directed his gaze to the eyes watching them from the shadows. He bent over and picked up a rock, throwing it in their direction. The creatures scurried away, making shrill squeaking noises as they ran for cover.

"Stay close behind me," he told her.

There was barely space for all of them to stand inside the small room. Philip began collecting his mother's possessions into a burlap sack that sat on the floor. He didn't say a word as he went about his business. Rayven sat her mother up in bed and wrapped her in as many layers of clothing as she could find.

Emily offered to help her, but Rayven waved her away. Grace woke, confused and began mumbling. The two siblings continued preparing her for the journey back to the mist wall. Emily moved around quietly and gathered what she could into her own backpack to help Philip. They didn't have many belongings to speak of, but they managed to collect anything that would fit inside their transport.

They took turns loading the wagon while Martin stood watch outside. It was time to move Grace. She was not steady on her feet so Martin carried her down the dilapidated staircase. Grace kept asking where they were going. Rayven shushed her. Philip had thrown her small mattress in the back. Martin laid her gently down upon it. Rayven and Emily covered her with blankets, enough to keep her warm. Grace laid back peacefully, looking at the stars and asked if their father would be joining them.

"No, mother," Rayven said softly and kissed her cheek.

Martin was surprised at how tender Rayven was with her mother, a stark contrast to her rough exterior. Philip held his mother's hand by the side of the wagon. Martin lifted the handles and the wagon creaked from the weight within. Without so much as a word, they headed out of the dingy village. Grace looked up at their home as she was pushed past it, not realizing that she may never return. Philip did not let go of his mother's hand.

Rayven wiped away a tear. Emily and Martin looked at each other. Martin hoped that Grace would be strong enough to make it across the harsh wasteland. He was concerned that predators would target her, as they often do to those too weak or injured to defend themselves. They would all have to be alert and prepared for anything.

The rickety wagon made a lot of noise, but they really had no alternative. Emily could feel danger closing in around them. They were being followed. Occasionally, she heard low growls and snarls much too close. She would look at Martin. He would nod to her. It was his way of letting her know that he had heard the sound too.

Suddenly and without warning, one of the raptors that Rayven spoke of, swooped down and grabbed Grace with its claws. It clung to the blankets wrapped around her and began to lift her out of the wagon. Emily and Philip immediately threw their bodies over Grace and let their weight pull her back down, but the raptor was not letting go.

Martin swiped his sword through the air with precision, clipping part of the raptor's wing. It made a blood curdling screech. Emily pulled out her dagger and started stabbing at the leg of the raptor, hoping it would release its grip on Grace's blankets and she with it. Some of its blood spilled onto the side of the wagon.

Rayven grabbed a straw broom and began beating the raptor repeatedly. She spun around, eyes glued to the skies for any other raptors approaching. Martin stabbed the raptor with all his strength. He pulled the creature away from Grace, quickly beheading it. Its limp body flopped around on the ground until it was dead.

Rayven and Philip made sure Grace was uninjured. She was not hurt, just confused, which was probably for the best. Martin checked Emily for injuries.

"Are you hurt?" he asked. She had been in close contact with the raptor, stabbing at it with all her might. It had been snapping its jaws dangerously close to her.

"I'm okay," she said, out of breath.

They both looked up and saw silhouettes of other raptors circling overhead.

"We must move quickly," Martin urged. "This dead raptor will keep them busy, but only for a short time. They will smell the blood on the wagon and return for another attack. We must make haste."

Rayven and Philip quickly repositioned their mother back under the covers and walked next to the wagon. Rayven kept the broom in her hand. Philip picked up a large femur bone from the ground, in case he needed to beat something with it. Emily kept her dagger in her hand and walked close to Martin, trying to watch their backs and the skies. They all quickened their pace.

With the scent of blood on the wagon, it didn't take long for another predator to challenge them, believing it had found a wounded animal. The attack came from the side. Emily froze momentarily when she saw the creature charging towards them. It was a griffin, like right out of one of her books. She was transfixed by it. Martin scooped her up and swung her out of the way, before she got trampled to death.

He immediately spun back to fight the creature. The griffin slammed into the wagon and toppled it over, dumping Grace onto the ground. Rayven and Philip pulled the wagon over the top of their mother to protect her from the creature. She was safer under the wagon. Martin struggled with the griffin.

The griffin clawed at Martin with its hind legs and flew off the ground at the same time, making it a difficult target, a danger in the air and on the ground. Emily picked up stones from the ground and pummeled the animal with them. She hit her mark a couple of times, causing the creature to angerly turn its attention towards her. This gave Martin the opportunity to slice at its midsection. The griffin let out a horrific cry and lifted into the air, flying off to tend to its wounds.

Martin and Emily hurried to the wagon and helped turn it right side up. They carefully got Grace back on board. Martin took a sheet from the wagon and tore it into strips. He broke a piece of wooden plank from the back of the wagon and wrapped the strips of cloth around its ends. Martin used his flint to light the cloth on fire. He handed the torch to Philip.

"Swing this at anything that comes near us," he instructed. "Most things are instinctively fearful of fire. Use that to our advantage."

Philip nodded. Martin tore off another plank from the rear of the wagon. He made a second torch and handed it to Rayven.

"Keep close to your mother," he ordered.

Even for the hardened assassin that she was, Rayven was visibly shaken by the predators actively hunting down her mother, sensing her weakness. They could hear the raptors behind them fighting over the carcass of their fallen comrade. They hurried onward.

The eerie light cast by the twin moons revealed serpents shadowing their movements, crawling over and under each other, like sinister waves across the land.

Martin pushed the wagon over the rocky terrain at an incredible pace, never slowing down. It was difficult for everyone to keep up with him, but they managed. Grace mumbled throughout the journey commenting on the moons and the stars, oblivious to the dangers they were facing.

Martin called out. "Emily!"

She ran to his side, clearly out of breath. "Yea?"

"On the ridge to the far left... See them?"

She scanned the area, searching for what he was looking at. Then, she spotted them. Dozens of tiny glowing eyes.

"I see them."

"Make another torch, use Philip's flame to light yours. Prepare yourself. They will come hard and fast," he warned them all.

Emily hastily made herself a torch. She never stopped moving as she did so. She was ready. She wasn't much of a baseball player, but her father made her take golf lessons for three years and she had a heck of a swing.

"Emily, stay close to me," Martin told her.

The eyes glowing in the darkness got closer and closer. She could hear their snarls growing louder. Within minutes the tiny little army of critters charged towards them, believing there was strength in numbers. There must have been over a hundred of the hungry creatures barreling down on them.

Martin stopped the wagon and stood in front of Emily. "Protect your mother," he shouted to Rayven and Philip.

Emily held her torch up, ready to play "Whack a Mole" with the hideous garden gnomes. Several broke off and circled the wagon. Rayven and Philip set the closest ones on fire sending them screaming into the darkness. That did not deter the rest.

It was a frenzied attack of nipping, clawing and biting. Emily wacked as many as she could, sending quite a few of them several feet in the air.

"Four!" she called out and sent one hurdling over Martin's head in a tiny blaze of glory.

Several had attached themselves to Martin's legs, making a ladder of sorts, trying to climb towards his face. He grabbed a few at a time and tossed them high into the air. They made a thud sound when they hit the ground, dazed from the impact. For such close contact, he was using his knife – slicing and tossing, slicing and tossing.

Emily caught one out of the corner of her eye, trying to climb up the back of the wagon, while Rayven and Philip were frantically fighting off the garden gnome horde. Emily stuck her torch under its backside and sent it screaming over the nearest rocky hill. She immediately returned to her golf swings.

The garden gnomes were getting thrashed but kept coming. Philip reached into his pocket and pulled out some of his powder used for magic spells. He quickly poured a circle around the five of them and lowered his torch to the substance. It erupted into a bright blue flame. The creepy garden gnomes halted and jumped back, afraid of this new magic.

They attempted to step inside the circle but got burned trying to do so. Rayven looked at Philip and back at the circle of protection he had just created. Martin picked up rocks and pelted the carnivorous critters, sending them scurrying for cover. They retreated quickly and disappeared into the darkness.

Martin made sure Emily was unharmed and checked on Grace as well. Emily smiled at Philip.

"You're a wizard?" she asked.

"I prefer magician," he corrected. "I know a few tricks. I'm hoping one day to become an alchemist. I'd really like to focus on transforming organic substances into valuable medicines."

"Wow, interesting," Emily said. "That's really cool."

Martin patted him on the back. "Well done, Philip. I am a physician. Perhaps one day you can share some of your ideas on the matter with me," Martin said sincerely.

"You're a doctor?" Philip asked, intrigued.

Martin nodded.

Philip looked at his sister for some acknowledgment. She looked away. Emily saw the hurt expression on his face and whispered to him.

"Don't pay any attention to sour britches there. That was awesome!" she said.

"Thank you," he smiled weakly.

The blue flame slowly died down, but it gave them a chance to rest and hydrate briefly before beginning again. Emily sighed, hoping that the worst was over.

"Time to move," Martin ordered. "Emily…"

"I know, I know… Stay close."

They moved quickly, listening to the creatures of the night shriek and howl. This was their domain, not the humans. They crossed over another ridge, leaving the flowing lava far behind.

Rest was infrequent and brief. There was no safe place to stop, even Martin was exhausted. Emily winced when she noticed that his hands were badly blistered from supporting the wagon's weight for so long by himself.

They kept pushing onward into the darkness. Fatigue had become an enemy. Martin stopped Emily from stumbling a few times. She was falling asleep on her feet. The hours blurred into one another. It was difficult for the wagon to travel over the rocky terrain. They were being hunted from every direction. The fire was a good deterrent but the longer they traveled, the slower their pace.

It was difficult to travel with any degree of secrecy with Grace singing in the wagon. Emily's mind drifted. She looked back at Grace, singing her seventeen chorus of the same song. Emily thought all that was missing was a giant neon sign, pointing at the wagon, saying "Free Happy Meal Here."

Philip and Rayven tried to quiet her, but it was pointless. Grace didn't understand what was happening and had retreated into her own mind.

Martin cast a concerned look at Emily after she fell forward and skinned her knee on shards of rocks jutting out of the ground.

"Great, more blood for them to smell," she uttered under her breath.

Martin set the wagon down and insisted on bandaging her knee, being the doctor. She asked him to stop fussing over her but he refused. She relented and let him wrap a clean bandage around her knee to stop any infection and bleeding.

Emily looked past him.

"I see it," exclaimed Emily. "I see the mist wall!"

Indeed, it was directly in front of them, still quite a distance but they could see the journey's end in sight now. A group of raptors circled overhead, dipping lower to taunt the group.

"Martin...," Emily said alarmed.

"I see them," he replied. He stopped and wrapped more strips of cloth around their torches. "Keep waving those torches. We are almost to the wall."

Emily, Rayven and Philip waved their torches frantically in the air just as the aerial attack began. Martin stopped the wagon and spun quickly around, bringing his sword down on the neck

334

of a raptor as it flew past. He turned back in time to slice open the belly of another raptor hovering nearby.

"Philip, grab the wagon," he ordered. Philip grabbed one handle and Martin held on to the other, freeing up his left hand to defend them with his sword. The rubble was loose beneath their feet making running more difficult. Rayven stumbled and fell. A raptor sped in for an attack as she went down. Martin released the wagon, rolled over the top of her and gutted the raptor in midflight. It cried out in agony as its innards spilled on to the ground. Martin lept up, pulled Rayven to her feet, and took his place at the back of the wagon again. Emily was swinging her torch frantically when suddenly a raptor latched on to her backpack and started lifting her off the ground.

"Martin!" she screamed.

Philip was closest to her and grabbed her leg. He too was lifted off the ground. Martin jumped up and grabbed Emily's leg and pulled down with all his might, stabbing at the creature with his sword. They engaged in a tug-of-war with Emily. Martin struggled to free Emily from its grasp. Philip fell back to the ground. He grabbed his torch, swiping at the beast. He barely missed being impaled by its spiked tail. Rayven ran to help Martin, allowing Philip to protect their mother. She grabbed Emily's other leg and pulled her down too.

With their combined weight they were able to pull Emily back towards the ground, giving Martin the chance to thrust his sword through the creature's heart, killing it instantly. It released its grip on Emily's backpack and she fell to the ground. Martin helped her get back on her feet.

Are you alright? Did it cut you?" he asked frantically.

"I'm okay," she said wiping her clothes off.

Martin turned to Rayven and Philip.

"Thank you," he said sincerely.

"You are risking your lives to save our mother," Philip reminded him. "It is us that owe you thanks."

Rayven met Martin's gaze and turned away.

"Hurry, we are almost there," Martin said.

Martin picked up the handles of the wagon again and made a mad dash towards the wall. Grace continued humming softly, with not a care in the world. Within a few minutes they reached the wall.

It was the time for truth. Rayven and Philip looked at each other and back at their mother. Rayven bent down and hugged her mother, "I love you so much," she told her.

Philip did the same, "I love you, Mama."

Emily spoke up. "You can take her through. Mira said she was protecting you both. How else would you know if we were telling you the truth? Take her through yourself."

They hesitated and looked at Emily.

"It's okay. It has to be this way. You need to see the truth for yourselves. Mira and the keystone are protecting us," Emily assured them.

Rayven nodded and repositioned Grace, making sure she was bundled up nicely before heading into the mist.

Philip looked up at the mist wall. He had never actually been this close to it before. He found the low humming to be unsettling. He looked at his mother and back at the mist wall. He chewed on his lower lip and then looked back towards the direction they had just come from. It was obvious he was nervous and scared. He considered bolting and running away.

Martin discreetly moved closer to him, pretending to check the back of the wagon, and spoke softly.

"Find your courage," he told Philip. "Trust Emily."

Philip looked at Martin and then at Emily.

Emily was standing in front of the mist wall, staring up at it. She wasn't overly thrilled to be stepping into that place once again. It was frightening and something right out of the horror movies she enjoyed watching late at night.

Philip walked over and stood beside her.

"Is it scary?" he asked.

"Oh geez, you have no idea. Things were touching me, sniffing me – things you can't even see! Scared the bejeezus out of me."

Philip looked at Emily. His eyes widened in alarm.

Emily's eyes were fixed on the mist wall. "And, the voices you hear? Talk about scarring you for life! Creepy with a capital C."

She finally looked over at Philip and saw the mortified look on his face. She glanced over her shoulder at Martin. He just frowned at her.

"Oh, um, yea. It's not that bad," she said, trying to back pedal. "I've seen worse," she added.

"Really? Where?" Philip asked. His voice quivered from fright. When he brushed his brown bangs away from his eyes, Emily noticed that his hands were trembling. She looked back at Martin again. He shook his head at her and rolled his eyes. She shrugged.

"Um, yea. Black Friday sales at Walmart?" she offered weakly. "People pushing and shoving each other for a flat screen TV."

Philip had no idea what she was talking about, of course. She frowned, but kept going. She couldn't seem to shut her mouth.

"Oh my gosh, and Christmas dinner with the entire family. Talk about terrifying. Having to hear Aunt Sue's story about the time she had dinner with Warren Beatty. He's an actor. You wouldn't know him. But, the same story year after year. And, Uncle Lyle doing his impressions of Johnny Carson and Sean Connery. You wouldn't know who they are either. Not even good impressions because they both sound exactly the same. We have to applaud and smile. It's insane. And, my cousin, who still lives with his parents, by the way, and he's like really old, like thirty-one or something. Isn't that weird? He always brings his cat to our house. Our dog doesn't like cats. It's such a mess. The barking and hissing. And, there was that year mom overcooked the turkey. It was inedible, like make you gag inedible, but we had to eat it anyway so she wouldn't cry...," she continued.

Martin came up behind her.

"You should stop talking now. You are not being helpful," he whispered to her.

Philip was speechless.

"Am I talking too much? It's the lack of sleep. I get slap happy when I don't sleep. One time I was so sleepy that I put on a Marie Antoinette costume. You wouldn't know who she is either. I mean, I even put on the poofy wig and drew a dark mole on my face. Marie Antoinette had a dark mole on her face, you see? And, then you know what I did?" she asked a dumbfounded Philip.

Martin spoke to her again. "I implore you to stop talking."

She waved him off. "Hush, Martin. Let me finish. So, you know what I did?" she asked Philip again.

Philip shook his head no. Martin rubbed his forehead. Rayven was now staring at Emily too.

"I got my video camera out and put it on a tripod. Then I recorded myself lip syncing and dancing to the song 'Dancing Queen,' get it?" Emily cracked up laughing and began singing. "You can dance, you can dance, having the time of your life, ooh ooh ooh."

"Dear heavens," Martin muttered.

"Get it? Because, she's a queen and she's dancing. The dancing Queen?" Emily cracked up laughing again. She saw the look on Philip's face and Martin staring at her. "I talk a lot when I'm really tired. Sorry."

"I noticed," Martin grinned.

"Well, he asked about the mist wall," Emily said in her defense. "Yea, it's not that bad. It's not like tiny zombie *Phantasm* bad, but… Nice talk."

She smiled innocently at Martin. He chuckled.

Philip didn't know what to say.

A loud screech rang out. The raptors had returned.

"We must go," Martin said urgently.

Rayven glared at Emily, "If you are wrong…"

"I'm not," Emily cut her off.

Philip moved to stand beside his mother by the wagon again, holding her hand. He nodded at Rayven.

Martin lifted the wagon and began moving towards the mist wall. The disembodied voices began immediately. The humming grew louder.

"Keep moving," Martin ordered.

They proceeded cautiously.

"Emily, take my arm. Rayven, Philip – hold on to your mother and do not let go. Do not stop for any reason."

Slowly, they moved forward, trusting Martin to lead the way. Grace stopped singing.

"Am I in the heavens?" she asked nonchalantly.

"No, Mama," Philip said. "Hush now."

She stared up at the mist, intrigued by it. It seemed to be taking longer to get out than it did to crossover.

The wagon rocked back and forth as phantoms within the mist slammed up against it.

"Something grabbed my arm?" Philip said, fear in his voice.

"Steady," Martin said.

Emily had her eyes shut tight, relying on Martin to guide her through. Occasionally, she'd swipe her hand absently in the air to ward off some invisible presence in the mist.

The pitch of the tone suddenly changed. It was higher. Emily found herself having trouble walking through the mist.

"Martin?" Emily asked, growing concerned.

"It is quite alright, Emily…" a voice in the mist wall spoke softly to her.

Emily gasped. "Grandma?"

"I'm so proud of you," the voice said. "You are almost there."

Emily started crying, "Grandma, where are you?"

"Here, always right here with you," the voice said softly.

Martin could hear Emily's words, but not the voice that spoke to her. It was meant for her ears only.

"I'm always with you, darling. I love you," her grandmother said.

"I love you too, Grandma."

He kept walking with Emily gripped tightly to his arm.

Then, he too heard a voice.

"Martin, please keep her safe," a sweet voice spoke to him.

"Victoria?"

"Yes... Please watch over my Emily."

"I will. I promise," he said, stunned to hear her voice.

"I love you," the voice faded away.

Martin fought to maintain his composure. He was navigating their way through the mist wall. It was not the time or the place to get overly emotional. He pushed through the barrier and was greeted by the light side. He continued pushing the wagon away from the mist wall and through the forest, leading them far away from the dead zone. He saw the opening approaching them, leading to a clearing. He and Emily looked at each other and smiled. Both knew what greeted them up ahead.

Emily leaned over towards Grace and whispered to her.

"Here comes the sun," she said to her.

Leaving the dense forest behind, Martin pushed the wagon into the glen with its majestic views of the snowy mountains and valley below.

The sun greeted them triumphantly.

Philip's mouth dropped open. He couldn't believe his eyes. He never imagined that any place could be so beautiful.

They had made it safely. They lifted their hands to shield their eyes from the sunlight. Grace slowly sat up in the wagon. She looked around curiously. The warmth of the sun hit her face. The light reflected in her eyes. Her eyes widened and a smile slowly crossed her face.

Grace's smile was as radiant as the sun.

Rayven and Philip were overcome with emotion and hugged their mother tightly. Grace was safe. The darkness had been lifted from her eyes.

"We made it, Mama," Philip said, tears streaming down his face. "You're safe now."

Rayven wept freely, looking at her mother who was smiling brightly and basking in the warmth of the sun.

Martin helped Grace out of the wagon. She stretched out her legs and gently placed the tips of her toes on the grass, wiggling them. She laughed happily. She shifted forward, putting her weight on her feet. Martin helped her stand. Grace looked up at Martin with the kindest eyes, patting him on the cheek.

"You're a good man," she said softly to Martin.

He bowed slightly at the waist and stepped back, allowing Grace to stand on her own two feet. Rayven and Philip watched their mother find the strength within her that had escaped her so long ago. They held each other tightly, watching their mother blossom in front of their eyes.

Before Grace took her first step in her new world, she looked at Emily. With absolute clarity of mind, Grace spoke to Emily.

"I saw the light in your eyes, like a light in the storm. I knew you would come for me one day. I'll never belong to the darkness again. Thank you, sweet child," she nodded her gratitude and winked at Emily.

Emily felt her eyes filling with tears. It was so moving, seeing this woman transform from a shell of a human being into a beautiful butterfly. Emily walked over to Grace and gave her a warm embrace.

"You are welcome," she smiled at Grace. "I hope you have the happiest life ever."

Grace inhaled deeply, taking in all the aromas surrounding her. She took a step forward, and then another, tilting her face to the sun. Her life had new meaning now. She lifted her arms to her side and began to dance upon the grass. Her dress twirled around her as she spun in a circle. She began to hum a sweet melody, moving freely to the music, swaying from side to side.

She grabbed Rayven and Philip's hands, pulling them forward to dance with her. They laughed with joy. Their mother twirled and rose on her toes, with the grace of a ballerina.

It was a rebirth.

Martin put his arm around Emily's shoulder.

"Well done, Emily," he said proudly. "Well done indeed."

She leaned against Martin, exhausted.

They were witnessing Grace become whole again. The sun was healing her broken soul.

All bad feelings were pushed aside. They were united in this moment of utter joy as their mother, Grace, was finally walking upon the grass with the sun shining down on her face.

Emily smiled.

Today was a good day.

All the years spent suffering in darkness were washed away by the warmth of the sun. Martin and Emily watched the family enjoy a part of life that neither Grace nor Philip had ever experienced before – daylight, sunshine and freedom.

Birds and butterflies flew around them. Grace was delighted. A butterfly landed near her and she stopped dancing, completely mesmerized by it. She began clapping happily, like a small child seeing the world for the first time.

Doctor Pernell was watching from the distance as he pulled his wagon to a halt. He too was touched by the emotional scene before him. Grace was beautiful. Her spirit was lifted. She danced around the green field, full of wildflowers, hugging her children, without a care in the world.

Martin spotted Doctor Pernell and waved to him. He and Emily went to greet him. The doctor climbed down from the wagon. He looked at Emily in her chainmail tunic. Even with dirt smudged on her face, he was stunned by the young girl standing before him. She exuded confidence. It was an astonishing transformation. There was something in her eyes that was not present before.

"My goodness! Look at you!" he smiled broadly. "You look…amazing." He pulled her in for a warm embrace and she laughed. "I am happy to see you," he admitted.

"Thank you," she said warmly.

He stepped back from her and looked into her eyes.

"I feel like I am meeting you for the first time. You're the same delightful girl, but different," he smiled at her. He touched her cheek for a moment. "Good for you, Emily."

Doctor Pernell hugged Martin and they laughed, happy to see one another after such a perilous journey.

"I see the two of you have become close," he smiled, looking fondly at both Martin and Emily.

Martin winked at her.

"She has grown on me," Martin joked.

"Oh please," she teased with a laugh.

She elbowed Martin in his ribs.

He laughed with her.

Doctor Pernell was immensely pleased by the new bond forged between the two. Things had changed between them. They had grown to trust and understand one another.

"How delightful," he said with a smile. He looked at Martin and nodded his thanks. "To see you both now, strong and united? Gives me great hope for what is yet to come," he added, clasping his hands together in front of himself. He bowed slightly, paying his respects. "Thank you, my dear friends."

Martin bowed slightly in return.

Doctor Pernell looked over at the family celebrating in the field. "Is the mother alright?" he asked.

Martin looked back at Grace.

"She is malnourished and confused. I do not think it is anything permanent. She could barely walk a couple of days ago. As you can see, the sun has its own healing powers. I think she will make a full recovery," he assured him.

Doctor Pernell nodded, "That is encouraging news. We will take good care of her. This I promise you. She is safe with us now." He patted Martin on his shoulder and went to introduce himself to Grace and her two children.

Martin and Emily followed close behind. Rayven stepped aside from her mother momentarily after the doctor introduced himself. Grace began dancing with Doctor Pernell. He laughed heartily enjoying her delight.

Rayven walked sheepishly up to Martin and Emily.

"I want to thank you both," she looked back at her mother, dancing merrily with her new friend, as Philip watched joyously.

"I can't thank you enough." She looked at Emily. "This? This means everything to me."

"I know it does," Emily replied graciously.

Rayven looked up into Martin's eyes. She felt her cheeks blush. "Thank you," she said sincerely.

"You are welcome," he replied.

She nodded to them both before returning to her mother. She joined the dance under the canopy of trees. Grace would have a peaceful life here on the light side, a chance to start over. It was a dream come true for Rayven and Philip, the happiest day of their lives.

Emily looked up at Martin and grinned.

"There it was," she said.

He looked at her. "There what was?"

"That spark. Did you feel it?" she grinned. "You and her? That spark?" Emily made a crackling noise. "Zap... That spark."

Martin laughed, "You are delusional."

Emily grinned.

"Oh, I think not. It comes from love," she teased.

"It comes from lack of sleep," he laughed.

She began singing and dancing around Martin.

"Love is in the air, everywhere I look around. Love is in the air, every sight and every sound. Love is in the air, in the whispers of the tree. Dance with me Martin," she grinned, being overly dramatic.

"I think not," he chuckled, backing away from her.

"Zap! Love is in the air," she continued singing and dancing, being incredibly cheeky. She pointed at Martin and then pointed at Rayven. "Am I right?"

He shook his head no.

"You are still insufferable," he laughed.

# Chapter Twenty-Six

Donovan's eyes fluttered and he found himself in unfamiliar surroundings. He was covered by heavy blankets that smelled musky. The furnishings were ornate, but dark. The only light came from a large stone fireplace in the corner of the room. He turned his head and watched the flames. He listened to the snaps and crackles as the heat penetrated the logs. His head was throbbing. Whatever Doctor Pernell had done was still affecting him. He could feel it. His mind felt groggy.

He envisioned a spider inside his head, weaving a web, entangling every part of his mind. He closed his eyes. His ears were ringing. The spider in his mind was crawling from side to side. Donovan tried to push out the thoughts, but when he tried to do so, his head felt like it was going to explode.

He opened his eyes to watch the fire again. He curled his fist into a ball. He was furious. Doctor Pernell was going to pay for this. They were all going to pay for this, he thought. His mind was flooded with thoughts of death and the many ways he could kill someone with his mind. He found comfort in this and smiled. Not even Miranda could tell him what to do anymore. He was better than that. He was better than her. He was stronger than she was… She just didn't know it yet.

Donovan had dreams of his own. He regarded everyone else with contempt. Tiny little ants with muddled minds, controlled by their emotions. Donovan had no such conflicts. He didn't have messy emotions. His was a singular vision. Control. Kill.

He wanted to start with his adoptive parents. They discarded him like garbage. He was different, not the perfect little boy they so desired. Well, they would pay. They would all pay. They would bow to him, bend to his will or die… All of Aquila would belong to him.

He was making a mental list. Donovan's list. And, the many ways each would meet his or her demise. Doctor Pernell would be first for having the arrogance to think he could contain him. He would be put in his place, even if he had to kill every member of his family to prove that point. Donovan grinned. He liked that idea. He liked it a lot. Why kill Doctor Pernell? It would be more enjoyable to break him instead. Take away everyone he cared for. Yes, that was a better plan.

Rebecca… That little pest. She told on me, he realized. The snoop! She would be easy to get rid of. She was such a baby. No one would miss her. He would get rid of her with a swat of his hand, like she was a fly.

Everything was fine until Doctor Stewart showed up. Donovan felt the anger rise within him. He should have pulled him further beneath the water and never let him wake up. He grinned as he thought of Doctor Stewart, bloated and floating to the water's surface, bobbing up and down like a top. He hated men like Doctor Stewart. They were always well liked and so perfect. Donovan didn't care what kind of pain Doctor Stewart might have suffered in his life. As far as Donovan was concerned, Doctor Stewart had not suffered enough. He thought of all the ways he could toy with his mind and welcomed the opportunity to visit him in his dreams again.

The other girl… What was her name? Emily. She was an interesting one. He wasn't sure how she fit into all these latest events. Miranda wanted her. He would have to study this one a bit more. Donovan knew how important she was. Miranda believed that she was the real threat.

This made Donovan mad. Really mad, because *he* was the real threat. Did Miranda think she was his handler? She should be worried about him and the threat that he posed. She would be worried, soon enough.

Donovan was small for his age. He had never fit in with the other children, nor did he want to. They picked on him – called him a freak. He was bullied relentlessly. His dark hair and pale skin made him more suited for a child of the dark side than one from the light. An older schoolboy called him 'dead eyes' once, because Donovan had dark brown eyes and tended to stare endlessly, blinking rarely. It was a pity the boy was severely injured in a fall down the school stairs. Broke both of his legs, with a little help from Donovan.

It was always the misconception of men to think a strong body was a greater threat. Donovan knew that a strong mind was far deadlier.

He wanted everyone to suffer. Their suffering was the only aspect of life he enjoyed. The pain in his head intensified. He closed his eyes and tried to relax his mind. The angrier he got, the more the pain increased. Doctor Pernell? I am coming for you, he said to himself. I'm coming for all of you.

~~~~~~~~~~~~~~~~~~~~~~~~~~~~

Rebecca stuck her head out further from her hiding place, watching the scene below. Everyone was certainly happy. There was a lot of dancing and laughing. The girl Emily was there too. Rebecca liked her. She hoped that when she was a little older that she could be more like Emily. She seemed so brave, Rebecca thought.

The pollen from the flowered tree Doctor Pernell had parked the wagon next to was making her nose itch. She felt a sneeze coming on. She tried her best to stifle it.

"Aaaaachooo," Rebecca sneezed loudly.

She clamped her hand over her mouth and threw her head under the blankets again. It was too late. They had heard her. Martin looked back over his shoulder and walked towards the wagon. Emily followed close behind. They went to opposite sides of the wagon and peered curiously inside of it. Doctor Pernell saw them and bowed graciously to Grace. He headed towards the wagon to join Martin and Emily.

"Is something wrong?" he asked.

"Your wagon seems to have a cold," Martin offered, nodding his head towards the pile of blankets.

"How odd," Doctor Pernell replied.

Emily pulled back the blanket to reveal Rebecca. She had her hands covering her face. Emily smiled at the child's silly attempts to conceal herself. It reminded her of how her own sister Sarah would play "Hide and Seek."

"You know we can still see you, right? Even if you cover your face?" Emily laughed.

Rebecca shyly pulled her hands away from her face and looked around at the three of them staring down at her. She sat up.

"Hello," she said sheepishly.

Doctor Pernell frowned. "Rebecca, I do not recall asking you to accompany me."

"I'm sorry. I thought you might need help, especially if that boy Donovan was involved."

Martin and Emily looked at each other when she mentioned his name.

"Never you mind," Doctor Pernell said. "You are coming back with me to the clinic, young lady."

"I'd rather stay here and help," she said with disappointment in her voice.

"You will be helping me. Grace over there is new here." He motioned towards the woman sitting on the grass, watching the clouds overhead. "You can help get her situated and show her some of your favorite spots at the clinic. How does that sound?"

"I can do that," she brightened up.

Doctor Pernell smiled. "Good. We should really be heading back. I've sent word out to the provinces. Hoping for a show of support along the wall, just in case."

"In case we fail?" Emily asked.

He nodded. Doctor Pernell helped Rebecca climb down and walked her over to meet their guests. Martin and Emily helped transfer all of Grace's belongings into Doctor Pernell's wagon.

Rayven and Philip said their tearful goodbyes to Grace. They had gotten what they wanted. They never thought it was possible, yet here it was. Doctor Pernell assured them that Grace would be well cared for at the clinic.

He let Rebecca tell them about the beauty of the gardens in her own special way. Her enthusiasm was infectious. Rayven noticed the colored ribbons in the little girl's hair and smiled to herself.

"Oh, you will love it," Rebecca told Grace excitedly. "There are so many flowers and there's even a maze made from shrubs." She leaned into Grace and whispered softly. "But don't worry, I never get lost. I will show you the way out," she said proudly.

Grace smiled at the young girl. She turned back to her children. "Come home soon, my loves, won't you?" she said to Rayven and Philip.

"Of course, Mama," Philip said, giving her a long embrace.

Rayven stepped forward and held her mother close. "We will see you again soon," she said, even if she didn't believe her own words.

Rebecca took Grace's hand and led her back to the wagon.

"Do you like pie? The dining hall has the best fruit pies!" she said happily.

Grace smiled, "I'm not sure I've ever had a fruit pie, but it sounds yummy."

Their voices trailed off as they moved towards the wagon. Doctor Pernell watched them and turned to her children.

"I have no doubt that Rebecca will talk your mother's ears off all the way back," he laughed.

Rayven smiled, "That's good. She will enjoy the company. Please, take care of her. We don't know if we will get to see her again." Rayven choked back tears.

Doctor Pernell patted her hand. "Find comfort in the knowledge that Grace will be surrounded with love and light. Never give up hope. Those young people over there?" He motioned to Martin and Emily. "They are going to make everything all right again," he told them.

He nodded to Philip and walked leisurely back to the wagon. He sat next to Rebecca after he and Martin helped Grace onboard. Doctor Pernell wrapped a couple of blankets around them both. He laughed warmly at something Rebecca shared with Grace.

Martin and Emily gathered up the fresh supplies that Doctor Pernell had brought them. They watched the wagon slowly move down the dirt road, taking Grace to her new life.

Emily knew this was a good deed they had all done. She took that moment to ask Martin about something that happened within the mist wall.

"Martin... My grandma? Speaking to me in the mist wall when I got scared?"

"She spoke to me too. Here on Aquila, we believe that when the physical body dies, that we pass on to a higher plain. She watches over you. She wanted you to know that," he smiled.

She reflected on his words for a moment.

"That makes me feel good," she concluded.

She stretched and yawned.

"You are in much need of sleep. I think it is best that we rest awhile before continuing," he suggested.

He turned to walk back towards Rayven and Philip, carrying the supplies in his arms. Emily yawned again.

"Besides, it is best we avoid further tales of this dancing queen you spoke of," he snickered.

Emily looked at Martin and grinned. "Ha, ha. It was actually a very clever costume," she told him.

"I have no doubt. I have seen with my own eyes the manner in which those on your world dress themselves up, even dressing your dogs," he smirked.

She laughed. "This is true."

~~~~~~~~~~~~~~~~~~~~~~~~~

Word spread fast across the land of a possible massive attack from the dark side. Volunteers were asked to join forces along the wall, armed with whatever makeshift weapon they could muster.

It was folly to think these farmers and tradesmen could fend off Miranda's army, but Doctor Pernell offered a compelling argument for the importance of action. Fight or be killed, a simple concept. Fight or lay down and die. Fight for a chance. Fight for survival on Aquila.

Fathers and sons from all corners of the light side made their peace with this prospect. They left the comfort of their homes to begin the journey towards the mist wall. Mothers and daughters joined too, many taking up arms. Others brought supplies and bandages for wounded, doing anything they could to help.

The Marshals were orchestrating the effort between the provinces, per Doctor Pernell's instructions. The ragtag team was assembling along the mist wall, preparing to meet their fate.

They were terrified, but the prospect of letting the scourge of the dark side infest their homeland was enough motivation for anyone. It was allowing the citizens of Aquila to pick their manner of death with dignity.

The aristocrats reinforced their grand estates and asked for volunteers for the frontline. Many dutifully agreed to go join the fight, rather than wait for the battle to come to them.

They had grown accustomed to the raids, but they were generally attempts to steal food and supplies. The realization that this time, Miranda was coming for their very lives had scared them into action.

The time for complacency was over.

The battle for Aquila was underway.

~~~~~~~~~~~~~~~~~~~~~~~~~~~~~~

Martin gathered pine needles for Emily, trying to give her a soft spot to rest upon. She quickly fell into a deep sleep. She snored softly. Emily was so sleep deprived that for the first time since her arrival on Aquila, she actually slept peacefully. Rayven and Philip also slept soundly. Martin fought to stay awake, but he too soon drifted off to sleep.

Martin woke suddenly and sat upright. He had not intended to sleep as long as he did, but his body had other plans in mind. He looked over at Emily, still snoring with pine needles stuck all over her hair.

He tended to the fire and filled the water bags. Before Rayven and Philip opened their eyes, Martin had a nice stew boiling over the fire for everyone to eat. They joined Martin at the fire and helped themselves to some soup.

Emily rolled over and started snoring again. Martin looked over at her and grinned. He knew she would not be pleased when she saw the pine needles protruding from her hair, like a thorny crown.

A log on the fire popped loudly and Emily slowly opened her eyes. She threw her blanket over her head and rolled back over. Martin walked over to her.

"Emily, I am sorry to wake you, but we need to continue," he said softly.

She waved him off with her hand, swiping in the air.

"Go away," she mumbled.

Martin smirked. "I am afraid I can not do that. We have much to do and the fate of Aquila awaits," he reminded her.

She pulled the blanket off her face and looked at Martin. "That's like seriously the worst wakeup call ever," she frowned. "Why don't you just say that the lives of everyone on Aquila depend on me?"

He grinned. "They do."

Her eyes opened wider. "Oh geez."

She rolled back over, collecting more pine needles in her hair. Martin nudged her gently with his boot.

"Let me sleep," she protested.

Rayven and Philip watched with interest.

"I wish I could. However, we must go," Martin admitted.

She rolled back over to look at Martin. Her eyes were heavy and bloodshot. She was not ready to continue their journey. She yawned and looked past him. Rayven and Philip were watching her. She rolled her eyes and pushed herself upright.

"There you go," Martin smiled. "I will get you some soup and water."

Emily grumbled and buried her head in her hands, rubbing her eyes. She gathered her blanket and stood up slowly. When

Martin turned around with a soup bowl in his hand, it was all he could do to contain his laughter.

He leaned in and whispered to her. "You might want to do something about your hair," he grinned.

"Huh?" she yawned. Emily grabbed her backpack and pulled out the compact mirror she kept inside. She winced when she saw herself. Dozens of pine needles were stuck in her long red hair, protruding out in every direction.

"I look like a human porcupine!" she complained, plucking pine needles out of her hair.

Martin held the soup in one hand and reached over to pull out pine needles with the other. He accidentally yanked a section of her hair.

"Ouch!" she said out loud. "That's attached."

"My apologies," he grinned.

Philip walked over to help too, pulling pine needles out of the back of her hair. Emily raised her hands to stop them both.

"Okay, I can do this," she frowned. "Thanks, but stop pawing at my hair."

Martin laughed and stepped back.

Emily removed all the pine needles, brushed her hair and pulled it back with her hair band. She looked at her mirror, snapped it shut and stuffed it back into her bag. She gave Martin a curious look and took the soup bowl from him.

"Show's over," she said with a touch of annoyance, realizing that everyone was still staring.

Martin sat across from her. "You look lovely, with or without the pine needles," he teased.

"I agree," added Philip shyly.

Emily made a face and rolled her eyes.

Martin lifted his hand to his mouth, pretending to cough.

"Zap, zap," he muttered, disguised as a cough.

Emily shot him a look.

"Did you seriously just zap me?" she asked.

He laughed out loud, a deep baritone heartfelt laugh.

Emily picked up a twig and threw it at him, which made Martin laugh even harder.

~~~~~~~~~~~~~~~~~~~~~~~~~~~~~

The crossing through the mist wall was every bit as unsettling as the previous experiences. She wondered what nightmares the elders must have had as children to create such a terrifying barrier. Was a stone wall out of consideration? What about a giant wood fence like on Kong Island?

They made their way back across the barren wasteland, walking for hours. Conversation was sparse. Emily was feeling fatigued and grouchy. She didn't get enough sleep. She was drowsy. She dozed off when she was walking, stumbling, causing Martin to come to her aid.

It was crazy to her that this was the way things were on Aquila. Two sides, polar opposites of one another, like that was perfectly normal. She envisioned herself back in Glendale with her friends, junior activists that they were, donning t-shirts that declared "Save the Dark Side." Something howled in the distance, bringing her attention back to her surroundings. She shivered. The putrid smell was making her eyes sting and that wasn't helping her ability to travel safely.

The dark side lacked suitable accommodations for weary travelers. Quite frankly, it was unaccustomed to travelers of any kind, unless they were on a suicide mission. Few made it across given the numerous predators waiting to devour them.

Rayven quickened her pace to walk beside Martin.

"She needs to rest," Rayven pointed out to him.

"I am aware of that fact. Where do you suggest she does that here in this place?" he wanted to know.

She had no answer.

Martin looked at Emily, who kept lagging behind. She had gone too long on too little rest and it was taking its toll on her. He spotted the remains of large wooden crates a short distance from them.

"There," he pointed. "We can construct a makeshift shelter from that, build a small fire and let her get some rest. She needs to be clear headed for what lies ahead."

He walked towards the broken crates and began bracing pieces of wood together to make a lean-to for Emily to rest under. Philip and Rayven helped by gathering whatever pieces of wood they could find to help with a fire.

Emily sat down on a boulder close by and fought off sleep. Her head dropped down. She could no longer fight exhaustion. She slumped over. The frightening noises around her faded away.

She dreamt of bloodshed and slaughter. She heard the terrible screams and shrill cries of innocent people, as Miranda's army crossed through the mist wall and cut down anyone in their path. The once green grass of the light side was now soaked with blood. Those that turned and ran, hoping to escape the slaughter, were snatched hungrily off their feet by Miranda's beast. The sound of crunching bones and agonizing cries came from overhead as the dragon feasted on Aquila's citizens.

The villagers and farmers never had a chance. They were outnumbered a hundred to one. In one resounding moment, hundreds lost their lives. The carnage was sickening. The canvas that made the light side of Aquila a beautiful haven had been forever altered. Miranda's army moved inward, consuming all in its path, like locust. Burning and pillaging towns along the way.

It was the total annihilation of the light side and all within.

The dawn of a new era was upon them.

Miranda rose from the ashes, no longer held back by the mist wall or Mira's spell. She walked among the bodies littered on the ground with nothing but zeal for the bloodshed at her feet. Her long black robe moved like a tidal wave over the broken bodies beneath her. She stopped to look up at the sun and let its warmth penetrate her. She laughed maniacally.

Emily's eyes fluttered and she moaned in her sleep.

Martin picked her up from the rocks and placed her under the makeshift shelter they had built The small fire would deter predators, but he was keeping watch, nonetheless. They could not remain in one place long, but it was evident that Emily was not physically capable of continuing without more rest.

Rayven watched Martin doting on the girl. He would die before letting any harm come to her. That much was obvious. She wondered what their connection was, and found his devotion to her admirable, almost fatherly. Her thoughts drifted to her own father and his cruelty towards them. He would have never been that kind to her.

Martin was different than other men she had known. Words like dignity and honor were not labels she would associate with anyone on the dark side. Her mother often spoke of such qualities when she shared stories from her books or tales that had been passed down to her. Chivalry was a characteristic she was not familiar with. She watched Martin remove his cloak and cover Emily with it, ignoring his own discomfort from the cold. Was this the chivalry her mother had often spoke of? It was not displeasing to Rayven, just unfamiliar.

Martin looked up and saw that Rayven was watching him. He nodded at her and returned to his duty of watching the surroundings for any threats. Philip was watching them all as he sat silently beside his sister.

"He's different than most, isn't he?" Philip stated, agreeing with her silent assessment of Martin.

Rayven looked at Philip and back at Martin.

"Yes," she agreed, saying nothing more.

In the distance, the piercing cry of some creature shattered the silence. Martin kept his hand resting on his sword, while Emily slept near the warmth of the fire. The rest stop gave Martin time to reflect on his own thoughts. They were getting closer to Miranda, and closer to his father.

Martin knew the time was approaching when he would have to confront the past that haunted him. If his father got in their way? Or tried to harm Emily? Martin would kill him without thought or reservation. It had been far too long, and he felt nothing for the man. His love for his father had been buried long ago. Martin felt the rage building towards the man he once held in such high regard.

The loss of Isabeau was a family tragedy, yet his father had behaved as if it only affected him personally. He cast aside the children, as if they meant nothing to him. Thanks to Emily, Martin had learned what became of his sister. He remembered that fateful night all too vividly – the abductors, the cries, Victoria's tiny arms reaching out towards him, his bloody fists pounding on the door... And, he remembered his father's lack of concern and sheer apathy to her demise. There was no excuse for it. He abandoned his children when they needed him most.

The boy had become a man, ready to face his father. You don't abandon your children, no matter what the circumstances. Martin would make sure his father was held accountable for his actions. His hand tightened over the hilt of his sword. He tried to calm himself. He could not let anger and hatred cloud his judgment, but he would not leave this dark place until his father was no longer breathing. He owed his sister and mother that much...and himself.

Martin looked at Emily – his sister's granddaughter. So much time had been lost. He was robbed of watching his sister grow up, but he could not deny that it was ultimately best that she be sent away. As a boy, Martin was in no position to fight Miranda or his father.

As for Emily, she was a special young girl. She was a part of his sister... And, she was a part of him. He felt blessed to at least have this chance to get to know her. He would sacrifice his life for hers, if need be. He would die for her in a heartbeat.

He pulled out the photo album from his tunic and opened it again. He leaned in slightly towards the firelight to see better. He smiled fondly at the photograph of Emily and her grandmother standing in a kitchen. Emily had flour on her nose while her grandmother held up a tray of freshly baked cookies.

He turned the page. The next picture featured Emily and her grandmother smiling happily and sitting in a boat, with rocky

357

cliffs behind them. They both wore shirts that read "Save the Whales" on the front.

On the next page, his sister's dogs sat in front of a fireplace. Each wore matching red and green sweaters with the words "Naughty" and "Nice" on their backs. He grinned, closed the album, and put it safely back into his pocket.

He sighed and stared off into the distance. It had been such a hard life, driven by anger for so long. He had shed so much blood to protect the light side from those on the dark side. He looked down at his hands, bandages wrapped over the blisters from pushing Grace's wagon. These hands were supposed to be used for healing, or so he thought.

It troubled him how easily he slid back into the role of a killer, how empowering it felt to hold the sword in his hand, and how little he felt for the blood he spilled. Was this who he really was? A killer of men? He thought he had buried this part of himself to become a doctor. Then why did it feel so natural for him to take up arms and kill?

Was he his father's son? Or had he evolved beyond that sort of barbarism? His father – once a respected and trusted ruler – turned into a monster. Given the ease with which Martin had become a killer once again, he worried if the same fate awaited him. He knew the argument. He was protecting Emily. No harm could come to her. And, he would do everything within his power to honor that pledge. Yet, the concern lingered.

Spending time on the dark side had done nothing but allow his own darkness to grow within him. While they trekked across the barren terrain, his thoughts were preoccupied with the many ways in which he wanted to hurt his father for all the years of pain and suffering he had inflicted upon them. And, those cages Emily spoke of? The unspeakable horror of it all.

Would he become a monster to stop another monster? Martin did not relish the thought and feared he might get lost in his own hatred. If it had not been for Emily, he feared that would indeed be the case. They believed that he was protecting them on this quest. Martin knew the truth of the matter. Emily was the one guiding him. He believed in her. She had an unbridled innocence far removed from Aquila. He hoped – his belief in her – would be his saving grace, lest he too be consumed by the darkness and suffer the same tragic fate as his father.

When would all this pain end? He looked at the bleakness around them, realizing that Emily was correct. They had no right to claim all the riches of the world for themselves. She had a way of making him see things differently, and that was a good thing. The wrongful needed to remain where they could do no harm, but she was correct in her observation that things did not need to be so disproportional and harsh. Perhaps, the notion of "humanity for all" was a better path, a more noble endeavor.

He looked at Emily and smiled.

So wise for one so young.

They could all learn a lot from her.

Martin heard scuffling behind the rocks nearby. He watched as a set of tiny red eyes peered at him before ducking for cover. He would need to wake Emily soon. It was time to continue.

~~~~~~~~~~~~~~~~~~~~~

Miranda's tiny minion watched Martin carefully. When the tall one looked its direction, the minion ducked down behind the rock and raced back to the fortress. It had important news to share with its master and hoped it would be rewarded for doing such. The strangers were approaching and one of Miranda's seekers were accompanying them.

It was insistent that it speak to Miranda directly and told her about the humans it saw traveling with the seeker – two males, with a younger female. Miranda was angry that her seeker had been detained in this manner. Was she with the others willingly or by force? It did not matter. If the seeker was compromised, she was of no use to Miranda anymore. Now that she had been located, she would send Merrick out to retrieve the girl and the keystone. Both were within her grasp.

She paced the room and devised a trap to ensnare them as they approached her fortress. What a stroke of luck! The enemy was nearing her gate and it was time to make her move. She ordered the sergeant at arms to bring Merrick to her at once. There was no time to waste. She would have the keystone in her possession before long.

Miranda grinned. Her spies had done well. Once she had the keystone, Merrick could dispose of the girl. This was turning out to be a glorious day indeed!

~~~~~~~~~~~~~~~~~~~~~~~~~~~~~

Martin woke Emily and helped her to her feet. They had to continue. She thanked him for the rest but didn't bother to tell him of what she saw. They ventured on towards the fortress with its jagged mountain in the background, spewing hot lava onto the petrified land. Dim lights from a small village loomed in front of them. Martin and Emily pulled their hoods over their heads to conceal themselves. They were out of place here and did not need to draw undo attention.

It was a dismal place. Several villagers were walking in the streets, stopping to stare at the newcomers. Children wore torn and dirty clothes, playing on rock piles. Small fires lined the main street, with the occasional roasted rat on a stick dangling over the flames. Others that saw them, stepped back into their homes, closing the doors and shutters. Those that remained looked at them with suspicious eyes.

As they approached the village center, several people stood with their backs to them, clad in heavy robes, facing the fires for warmth. Martin was getting an uneasy feeling. To Emily, this scene was all too familiar. She recognized this village from one of her visions.

Without warning, four of the robed figures jumped out and circled Martin, striking him hard on the back of the head with a blunt object. Martin's knees buckled beneath him. He struggled to stand and staggered forward. He quickly began to defend himself. Several others moved out from the shadows, wielding weapons and moving towards Rayven, Philip and Emily.

It all happened so quickly.

Martin shouted to Emily. "Run! Hide!"

She turned on her heel and ran for cover, as did Philip. Rayven looked for something to defend herself with, but found nothing. She resorted to hand-to-hand combat. She managed to get in several good blows before they grabbed her and roughly dragged her out of the village.

Chaos erupted around Emily.

This was her vision.

She had seen this before.

To force her out into the open, the raiders began tearing apart the village piece by piece, stone by stone. They set homes ablaze, driving frightened villagers into the street. Fear engulfed her. People were running frantically to escape the flames. She heard screaming and children crying out.

Emily hid behind the wood pile, watching Martin fight bravely, woefully outnumbered. She could see blood dripping down his forehead. They had wounded him. Through the smoke and flames, she could see villagers being brought down swiftly by swords driven into their bodies. The raiders did not seem to care who they killed.

The thundering sound of horses approached from behind her. Dust billowed up into the air. Riders on horseback, dressed in black, stampeded around the frightened villagers. The ground shook and trembled beneath her feet. The sense of panic was overwhelming. Dirt clung to the sweat on her face.

A dark rider spotted her and turned his horse towards her, digging his heels into the poor beast's side demanding it charge faster. She turned and ran, weaving in and out of the flames, stumbling over fallen bodies and debris. She was running blindly and wildly, desperately trying to stay out of his reach. The burning flames of the tiny village lit up the night.

He still pursued her despite her best efforts to elude him. From behind, she felt herself lifted up and into the air. She was violently thrown to the ground, knocking the wind out of her. She struggled to stand up, trying to catch her breath. The rider dismounted his horse and moved towards her. She stumbled to her knees and crawled forward, digging her nails into the ground, until she backed into a wooden animal pen. She was cornered and had nowhere to run. She bravely brought her dagger in front of her and held it steady.

She could hear Martin's frantic calls in the background, shouting her name and searching for her. The dark figure pulled her roughly to her feet. She swiped at him with her dagger, slicing into his arm briefly. He struck her hard across the face. Her lip split and began to bleed.

The dagger fell out of her hand. She struggled to get free, but she was no match for him. His hands were like a vice.

"Let me go!" She struggled to speak.

He tightened his grip around her throat and lifted her until her eyes were level with his, examining her facial features. He knew she was the young girl he had seen pictured on the wall – the one Miranda sought. He wondered who she was, but did not let his thoughts betray him.

Their eyes locked.

Merrick! Emily stopped thrashing for a moment, terrified that she was standing face to face with the brutish man from her visions. He was even taller than Martin.

She began to struggle and gasp for air, digging at his fingers to no avail, feeling her lifeforce leaving her. She couldn't breathe. He was choking her to death. Her eyes began to roll back into her head.

Merrick ripped off her necklace and tossed her aside. She landed hard against a pile of timber. Her limp form wracked with pain. He looked back at her lying on the ground and then turned his attention to the keystone.

He held the necklace up to a nearby flame and watched the light swim within it. This was Isabeau's necklace. He could feel its power. He put it inside his pocket and turned back to the girl.

The sound of Martin frantically calling her name began to fade. She drifted in and out of consciousness.

Merrick looked back and saw his son fighting several attackers at once. He let his gaze linger for a moment, studying Martin. He had not seen him since he was a young boy. He looked strong, with much of his father's build. But there was no mistaking that his son had his mother's striking features as well. Merrick felt a momentary ache in his dark heart but then snapped his attention back to the girl lying motionless on the ground.

Merrick's strong hand grabbed her hair from behind and lifted her off her feet. She awoke and cried out in pain. He bound her hands and placed her on the back of the horse. She was being held so tightly that she could barely breathe. She gasped for air. He was crushing her. She tried desperately to free her arms, but he had her completely pinned down. She tried biting his hand to gain some leverage. He struck her hard on the back of the head.

"Try that again and I will snap your neck like a twig!" he growled angrily.

He whistled three times loudly, summoning the other raiders to follow him. They had bound Rayven and threw her over a horse to be returned to Miranda. They were unable to acquire Martin. He killed all that approached him. Hearing Merrick's signal, they stopped their attack and retreated.

Martin chased after the raiders but then turned back to search for Emily, as the village burned to the ground. Meanwhile, Merrick rode off into the night, towards the dark fortress. Emily could make out the occasional lit torch. The sounds of screaming from the village eventually faded away. The horse slowed down. The rhythmic *clip clop* of hooves landing on stone were replaced by thundering sounds on the dirt path.

She turned her head to look at the sinister fortress. He stopped the horse, dismounted and pulled her roughly off the animal. Without a word, he dragged her inside and down its dimly lit passageways. He opened a massive wooden door and forcibly shoved her inside, slamming it shut behind him. She was locked within.

She shivered from the cold and from the fear.

She knew what was coming next…

~~~~~~~~~~~~~~~~~~~~~~~~~~~~

Martin was beside himself. He had lost Emily. They had been ambushed. How could he have allowed this to happen? He cursed himself for letting his guard down while he was lost in his own thoughts. He should have known better.

Martin found Emily's dagger lying on the dirt. He repeatedly yelled out her name, but she was not there to answer. He searched everywhere, even among the dead, but he knew the truth.

Emily was gone.

She had been taken to the fortress.

Philip stepped out from his hiding place. Martin spun around and stopped himself short before striking Philip with his sword.

"They are taking her to the fortress. I'm sure of that. Come! Hurry! Perhaps, we can catch them," Martin said desperately.

"I know the way in," Philip said frantically. "They took Rayven too."

Martin spun around to face him. "Did they take her or did she join them?" he asked angrily.

"They took her. I saw with my own eyes. She wouldn't betray you and Emily after what you did for our mother. I swear to you," Philip assured Martin.

Martin glared at him.

"I can get you inside and help you find Emily. That's why she sought me out, remember? It's what I do," Philip explained.

"I have no choice but to trust you," Martin replied. He was terrified for Emily and angry at himself for failing to protect her. "Lead the way," he ordered. "Quickly!"

Martin and Philip ran down the path the raiders had taken. Martin cursed himself again for failing Emily. If any harm came to her? It would be his fault.

"Damn this place," Martin swore angrily.

"It's not your fault," Philip tried to reassure him.

Martin glared at him again.

"Just get me into that fortress," Martin ordered vehemently.

"I'm good at what I do. We can rescue her. I know we can. I sneak in all the time and steal things. For my mother... We can get her back," he said confidently, yet with a trace of concern.

Martin remembered when Emily was beaten in one of her visions, and he knew that beating came at the hands of his father.

And, now? His father had her...

Martin feared for her life.

"Faster," he urged Philip, "We must move faster!"

They ran towards the fortress. Sweat poured off Martin's brow. Philip handed him a water bag. Martin took a drink. His head was throbbing from the thrashing the raiders gave him. He was exhausted, but pushed through the pain and fatigue, focusing his energy on reaching Emily. He summoned Thalien with his mind, asking him to protect her from the beating he knew she was about to face. Hoping that Thalien could shield her in some way, until Martin could save her from Merrick.

Martin was scared...

He hadn't been this scared since he was a little boy. He was scared for Emily. He felt helpless, much like he did when they dragged his sister away. He was not about to lose Emily too, not like he lost his baby sister.

Not this time.

Not now.

Not ever...

This time he would not fail.

# Part V

## When Worlds Collide

*Grief is the price we pay for love.*
~ Queen Elizabeth II
1926 – 2022

# Chapter Twenty-Seven

Merrick locked the door with Emily inside and made his way to Miranda's meditation chamber. She was not there. He walked through the darkened hallways in search of her. He saw activity near one of the bed chambers and headed that direction. He found Miranda inside fussing over Donovan.

Merrick scowled at the boy and ordered the handmaidens to give them privacy. Miranda turned to face him, annoyed by his intrusion.

"Merrick, where are your manners?" she asked harshly.

"Spare me, Miranda," he looked at Donovan with contempt. Donovan eyed him curiously.

"Were you successful?" she asked.

He looked at the boy and then back at Miranda.

She waved her hand, dismissing his concern. "It is perfectly fine. You may talk in front of Donovan. He is one of us, after all."

She stroked the boy's hair, like she was petting a dog. Donovan's expression changed and he stepped slightly to the side to pull himself away from her touch. Merrick noted his distain.

"I have recovered the girl, yes," Merrick told her.

She smiled wickedly. "How utterly delightful!"

Merrick wrapped the necklace's chain around his hand, debating whether to hand it over to Miranda or keep it for himself. She closed her eyes and grinned. She walked towards Merrick and placed her bony fingers under his jaw, pawing at his face playfully.

"Come now, my dearest Merrick," she cooed. "Do not try anything foolish. Hand it over," she said slyly, with her hand extended.

He hesitated, wanting nothing more than to wipe that grin off her face. She narrowed her gaze at him and raised her hand into the air, palm upward. A swirling ball of fire rose from it and levitated above her hand.

"Do not make me ask twice, dearest," she said, leering at him, pressing her body against his.

He recoiled in disgust and she laughed hideously.

"Do not play hard to get in front of the child," she teased sadistically, quickly glancing at Donovan.

She repulsed Merrick. That much was obvious to Donovan. Merrick slowly pulled the chain from his pocket and let the necklace dangle in front of Miranda's face. The keystone pulsed and hummed slightly, seeking out its proper keeper – Emily.

Miranda's eyes widened and her face changed to one of pure wonder as she leaned in to examine her prize. The purplish light within the jewel of the necklace grew brighter. Donovan stepped in for a closer look too, intrigued.

The keystone had a dizzying effect. Merrick could feel its power surging through his hand as he held it up for Miranda to look at.

"Have you ever seen anything so beautiful in all your days?" she asked to no one in particular.

Merrick did not respond. Miranda pressed her hands together in a prayer like motion and smiled – an evil slow smile. She looked past the necklace and directly into Merrick's eyes. She quickly snatched the necklace from his hand and held it up to the firelight to admire its beauty.

Merrick hated her. He hated everything about her. He wanted her dead. Donovan stared at him, reading his thoughts and then he too smiled wickedly at Merrick. He shot the boy a threatening glance and turned his attention back to Miranda. She had not taken her eyes off the keystone. She was completely memorized by it.

"And, you are sure you can bring down the mist wall now?" Merrick demanded to know.

She nodded without looking at him.

"Shall I prepare the army for battle? We will wait for your order to proceed," he said.

She nodded again. He turned and left the room. Miranda placed the necklace on the dressing table in front of her and turned back to Donovan.

"When we have wiped the light clean of its inhabitants, you may kill Merrick. Make it a slow, agonizing death," she sneered.

Donovan smiled and nodded, saying nothing. He left and followed Merrick.

Miranda sat at her dressing table and admired her trophy. She did not doubt she could wield its power. The thought of unleashing the beast and her army exhilarated her. She felt a sense of euphoria. The despair she was about to inflict upon Aquila gave her great pleasure. First Aquila, and then on to other worlds.

*Mistress Miranda of the Universe* – she fancied the title and laughed out loud. She had waited so long for this moment, since the day Merrick had cast her out. She was about to savor her sweet revenge upon Aquila. She placed the keystone in her hand and held it close to her heart. Finally, she would be free.

~~~~~~~~~~~~~~~~~~~~~~~~~~~~

Emily paced around the room and looked out the window. It was too high to climb down from. She heard a steady stream of footsteps outside her room, but none stopped. She dreaded what was coming through the door. She felt it. She had already experienced Merrick's senseless beating in her visions. She braced herself for the worse.

She caught her reflection in the pane of glass that covered the small window. She looked haggard. She barely recognized herself. She touched her lip where he had hit her. It stung, but she knew it paled in comparison to the pain he was about to inflict on her.

Emily's keystone had been taken, ripped from her neck. She needed to get it back, desperately. She felt physically weakened without the keystone around her neck.

Did Mira know what was happening? Thalien? Could they help her? She wondered.

She tried the door again. It didn't budge.

"Blasted!" she said in frustration.

She doubted she even had the ability to summon the Council of Dragons, without the keystone. She was useless now and it was not a good feeling. She weighed all options. She had none. She knew that somewhere within these walls, Isabeau was being imprisoned. But where? How could she get to her? And would it make a difference to Merrick if he learned that his beloved Isabeau was still alive? Or was he too far gone to care? She was willing to bet that seeing Isabeau would make Merrick turn against Miranda... At least, that was her hope.

Hope was pointless if she couldn't get out from this room.

~~~~~~~~~~~~~~~~~~~~~~~~~~~~

Philip raised his hand to slow Martin down. They stopped running. He pointed towards the base of the fortress, at a culvert. Martin shook his head and saw nothing. Philip moved closer and pointed again. Martin finally saw it. A metal grate, small but leading to the underground tunnels and bowels of the fortress. He looked at Philip.

"The drainage system?" he asked.

"I didn't say it was going to be pleasant. It's the only way in. It runs the entire length of the fortress and empties into a river." Philip explained.

"Where does the river go?" Martin asked.

"I don't know. I've never dared to venture that far," he admitted. "But we can access the interior from any number of junction points by using this system."

Martin studied the small metal grate and had doubts that he would even fit through it. "And, you think you know where Emily would be taken?" he asked.

"Yes, she's either in the living quarters area or the Keep," he said pointing to the massive bunker rising into the darkness.

Martin seemed defeated.

"That is a great deal of ground to cover. Finding her would be…," his voice trailed off.

Philip interrupted him. "Look, I've been sneaking in and out of this place for most of my life. I can find her. I know I can. One of the things I do is camouflage myself, a lovely little magic trick I learned early on. They won't even be able to see us, as long as we keep quiet," he assured Martin.

Martin was skeptical but had little choice than to trust the young man. "I'm not sure I can even fit inside that hole," Martin told him.

Philip frowned. "You're going to have to. I might be crafty, but I'm not a fighter. The most I can do is distract and confuse with potions. If a fight breaks out or we meet resistance? That is your area of expertise, not mine."

Martin nodded. "Fine, we must hurry."

"Follow me," Philip told him.

They made their way carefully down the rocky cliffside. Thankful for the cover of darkness. High above, guards stood watch over the fortress but did not notice them. Philip leaned back against the exterior wall, next to the metal grate, and dug deep into the bag slung over his shoulder. He mixed two powders together and mumbled an incantation over his hands.

Martin watched the young magician work his wonder. Hoping, he knew what he was doing. Philip opened his hands, releasing the powdery substance into the air. Martin coughed slightly. A guard above looked down but saw nothing. The spell had worked. Martin and Philip were now concealed from prying eyes.

Philip began to pull the metal grate back.

Martin stopped him. "Wait! If they cannot see us? Then, how is Emily going to?" he asked.

"You can be seen by whoever you wish to be seen. It's the way it works. I do not have time to give you a lesson in magic spells," he frowned.

Martin nodded and helped Philip remove the metal grate. Philip easily fit through the small opening. Martin passed their bags to Philip, including Emily's backpack. Then, he handed his sword and utility belt to Philip.

Martin lowered himself into the opening, struggling to get through. Philip tried pulling on his legs to no avail. Martin grunted and groaned, trying to squeeze himself through the small hole. His shoulders were too broad. He feared he would get stuck halfway.

"Think small," Philip suggested.

"Think small?" Martin snapped back.

Philip kept tugging on Martin's legs.

"Wait, give me a moment," Martin said, exasperated.

He closed his eyes to relax his breathing, focusing on his diaphragm. Shifting to the left slightly, Martin slammed his shoulder into the stone wall, intentionally dislocating it with a loud crunching sound. He fought the urge to cry out in pain.

Philip winced loudly, "Oh, that must have hurt!"

Martin shot him a look. He shifted back and pulled himself through the opening, with his arm dangling at his side. He leaned forward in pain and then moved over to the wall, steadied himself and twisted his body hard into the stone. Another loud crunching sound forced his shoulder back into place.

Philip winced again. "Oh, heavens."

Martin grimaced and breathed heavily. He massaged his shoulder and moved it in a circular motion, trying to manage the pain.

Philip stared at him. "That looked wickedly painful."

Martin frowned. "It was. Let us get on with it."

Philip turned towards the underground drainage system. The viaducts beneath the fortress were full of water, sewage and a host of other vile things that Martin did not even want to think about. Rats scurried along the ledges as they made their way through the waist deep muck and water. To say it stank was an understatement. They held the bags and cloaks over their heads to prevent them from getting wet.

"You wade through this all the time?" Martin asked with disgust.

"I do what I have to do," Philip admitted. "There are large barrels at each junction used to haul water to the upper levels. There is plenty of freshwater underground. I suggest you make use of it or they won't need to see you. They will smell you first," Philip pointed out.

Martin nodded. Lit torches could be seen along the way through small openings overhead. Something bumped up against Martin beneath the water and he jumped slightly.

"Probably just a snake," Philip offered.

Martin stepped carefully through the smelly liquid. There were footsteps and hushed voices overhead. He could not make out their words. Philip led them further into the belly of the fortress, until the drainage tunnel opened into a small set of caves with wood platforms to stand upon. Martin was happy to climb out of the putrid water.

"You are correct, Philip. They will smell us long before they see us," Martin frowned.

He walked over to the water barrels and rinsed the slime off himself, as best as he possibly could. Philip did the same. The odor was overwhelming. It burned Martin's nostrils and eyes. He searched in their bags for some soap. All he could find were the fragrant bars that Mira had given Emily. He used one to rid himself of the stench of the dark side. Martin changed into fresh clothes and tossed a set to Philip. The clothes were woefully too large for Philip but he was happy to discard the smelly ones. Philip ran his hand over the fabric. He had never worn such fine garments before.

Martin glanced at him. Philip looked like a child wearing his father's clothes. "Roll up your sleeves and tuck your cuffs into your boots. I am sorry but that is all I have for you. And, I do not think Emily would be pleased if you showed up wearing her clothing."

Philip agreed and made due with the oversized tunic and trousers that Martin had given him to wear.

Philip turned to Martin. "I must warn you. You will see and hear things within these walls that will not bode well with you. Horrible things."

Martin nodded. They both stepped into a small cave nearby. Philip pointed to a spiral staircase leading upwards. They would have to cross the cave to reach it, but only one guard was inside, fast asleep next to a small fire pit.

"What is he guarding?" Martin asked.

Philip didn't answer. Instead, he moved towards the stairs.

Martin stopped him. "I asked you a question. What is he guarding?"

Philip lowered his head and pointed towards a cave across from them. Martin edged himself closer to the opening and peered inside. He looked in shock at the site of filthy cages chained together. The cages were full of children. He snapped his head back at Philip in pure horror. Philip would not meet his gaze. Martin looked back into the cave.

He leaned further in, and saw a large cavern on the other side. Piles of skeletal remains littered the ground outside the opening. He saw nothing through the darkness. A river of blood flowed through the center of the cave.

The beast raised its head and sniffed the air. It could smell Martin. It growled from the deep recesses of the cave. Martin felt the bile rise in his throat.

Miranda's beast.

The one Emily spoke of...

This is where it was being kept.

This is where his sister was caged all those years ago.

The beast sensed his presence and let out an awful roar, waking the guard from his slumber. The guard stood and walked straight towards Martin, but thanks to Philip's potion, he couldn't see him. The guard looked inside the cave and saw nothing out of order. He yelled back at the dragon.

"Keep it quiet you filthy beast. I'm trying to sleep out 'er..." He spat on the ground and returned to his chair.

Martin was mortified. He hoped that Emily's time with the Council of Dragons had shown her a way to destroy that monster. Philip motioned for Martin to follow him. Martin looked back at the children. His heart anguished for them. When this was over, he vowed to return and save these children.

They made their way up the winding staircase. Philip motioned for Martin to wait while he quickly checked the corridor. He went room to room but found no sign of Emily. He motioned for Martin to follow him. They moved into another corridor.

Suddenly, Martin stopped dead in his tracks.

He spotted him.

Merrick.

He was walking up the hallway directly towards them. Martin immediately reached for his sword, but Philip stopped him and shook his head no vigorously.

He mouthed the words "not now" to Martin.

The two stood motionless as Merrick came within inches of Martin in the narrow corridor. Martin wanted to kill him, then and there, but he knew Philip was right. They let Merrick walk past and continued their search for Emily. Philip tried every door in several corridors to no avail.

Finally, he tried a door at the end, near the rear staircase, that didn't open. He rattled the lock. Emily jumped up inside, ready for Merrick to enter. Ready for her beating to start. She looked around for anything to defend herself with. The room was empty. She braced herself.

Philip motioned for Martin to hurry over. He fiddled with thin slithers of metal and shoved them into the lock. Without any effort at all, Philip rotated his hands slightly and the lock clicked open. He pushed open the door carefully and looked inside.

Emily stood tall ready to fight, with her fists up in front of her. Philip pulled Martin inside and closed the door behind them, allowing Emily to see them through their camouflage spell.

Emily's expression changed immediately.

"Martin! Philip!"

She ran to Martin and hugged him tightly.

Martin was relieved that they had found her. She appeared unharmed, except for a swollen lip. No doubt the work of his father. She pulled away from him and gave him a weird look. She sniffed Martin.

"Why do you smell like flowers?" she asked.

Martin frowned. "Do not ask."

"No, I am asking. Why do you smell like flowers? You smell better than I do," she frowned. "How is that even possible? Did you stop by a beauty spa before you came here to get me?" she asked with a grin.

Emily turned and looked at Philip.

"And, what happened to your clothes?" she asked curiously. "Are those Martin's clothes you're wearing? I'm separated from you guys for a few hours? And, this is what happens? What on earth," she chuckled.

Emily sniffed Martin again.

"Please stop sniffing me," Martin asked politely.

She leaned in and sniffed Martin again.

"Emily," Martin said sternly.

"You do smell lovely," Philip added.

Martin gave him a dirty look.

"We came through the sewage system to get here. We had to wash up and change clothes before walking the corridors or they'd be able to smell us," Philip explained.

"I found a bar of soap in your bag," Martin told her.

Emily grinned and nodded. "The ones from Mira? Oh, so that's why you smell like a bouquet of flowers and Philip looks like Oliver Twist, wearing clothes five times bigger than he is?" she laughed.

"That is a fair assessment," Martin replied.

"Who is Oliver Twist?" Philip asked.

Emily ignored his question. "I agree with Philip, though. You do smell lovely," she teased.

"Stop," he grinned.

They heard footsteps outside.

Philip shushed them. "We must be quiet."

Martin lowered his voice and nodded towards Philip. "Our resident wizard here got us in undetected."

"Magician, not wizard," Philip corrected.

She thanked Philip.

"Merrick took the keystone," she told Martin with alarm.

Martin looked at Philip. "How good of a thief are you?" he asked.

"The best," Philip answered without shame.

"He would have taken it to Miranda. Do you know where to find her in this place?" Martin asked.

"Yes," Philip said without hesitation. "She could be in any number of places, but I know where she generally goes," he admitted.

"We need that necklace," Martin stressed to Philip. "Do you think you can get it back?"

Philip thought for a moment. "I think I could take it right off her neck and she wouldn't even know it," he said confidently.

"Good. In the meantime, Emily and I need a safe place to hide."

"I know of a place. No one hardly goes there. I can take you there and come get you once I have acquired the necklace," he suggested.

Emily looked at Philip. "What makes you think you can just walk up and take it from her?" she asked curiously.

He smiled. "Folks like Miranda think they are untouchable. So much so that they can't even see what's happening right under their noses, literally. She won't be able to see me. She isn't expecting anyone to walk up and grab it, assuming she is wearing it," he added.

"Bold move. I like it. But what if she can sense you? Then what?" she asked.

"Well, then this will be a really short trip, won't it?" he admitted.

Emily looked at Martin. "We don't have a choice. We need the keystone back," she said.

They followed Philip out into the empty corridor. He closed the door gently and locked it behind him.

"There's an old supply room close by, judging by the dust inside, I don't think anyone's been in it for years," he told them.

They hurried to the room, careful to avoid detection. Emily stepped inside. Martin stood by the door, sword ready.

Philip whispered to Martin. "Remember, the spells don't last long, so don't do anything foolish. Stay hidden till I return."

"Be careful," Emily said.

Philip nodded and hurried back up the corridor to find Miranda and the keystone.

~~~~~~~~~~~~~~~~~~~~~~~~~

Rayven was taken to the fortress. She was being held until Miranda had a chance to question her. Rayven was no longer a disciple of Miranda, not after what she had witnessed with her mother. She knew they had been lied to all these years and that her mother had suffered needlessly. She felt like a fool for never questioning the validity of Miranda's rhetoric.

For the first time in her life, she felt hope. She saw the joy on her mother's face and understood with absolute certainty that there was more beyond these walls. And, it wasn't just for those on the light side. The abuse they suffered from their father all those years could have ended abruptly, if they had known they could pass through the mist wall and survive.

Rayven thought about how different their lives could have been. The stories her mother told her were true. It wasn't some fairy tale for only the elite on the light side. That could have been their reality too. She could have worn ribbons in her hair like the little girl. Rebecca talked of flowers and fruit pies. Rayven grew up hunting for rats, fighting for scraps, learning to kill or be killed in this bleak wasteland – all because

Miranda told them they would be consumed by the mist wall. The deceitful sorceress convinced them all that they were doomed to live in the darkness forever.

Unless, they waged war against the light side. Rayven now knew that Miranda was the one that couldn't crossover. Miranda was the one that was forever doomed. Her lies and trickery condemned generations upon generations to live at her feet, never knowing the warmth of the sun.

Miranda fabricated this entire lie – an illusion with no substance. She didn't want to be alone with the undesirables – the murderers, the thieves, the abusers of women and children. They were the ones that were stuck here until they took their last breaths.

Kindhearted folk like her mother, and even Philip, could crossover. Rayven wondered if her sincere change of heart would be enough to allow her past deeds to be washed away and forgiven. Would she ever be able to join her mother in the light? Would she get to help her mother tend to her garden, like she always talked about? Would she ever know love?

Rayven's thoughts drifted to Martin. She wondered if he had found Emily and Philip. The last thing she saw during the ambush at the village was Emily being dragged off on horseback by a dark rider. Rayven had to free herself and find the others. She had to help end this tyranny and make sure that Miranda could no longer deny others the opportunity to see the light of day.

The guards outside her door were not even remotely at her level of fighting experience. They were raw recruits, stuck with walking the perimeters and standing outside of doors, like doting sheep. They would be no match for her superior skills.

She started coughing loudly. The guards outside looked at each other and back at the door, hearing the noises inside.

"Guards! Guards!" she cried out.

They looked back at the door.

"Help me. I need water!" she gagged loudly.

One of the guards grabbed the ladle and dipped it into the water bucket, while the other guard opened the door. They both entered the room. Rayven was bent over at the waist, making heaving noises, feigning illness. One guard walked to her side as

Rayven stretched out her hand for the ladle and the other reached out to hand her the water.

Without so much as a blink of the eye, she elbowed the guard to her side in his throat. He staggered backwards, gurgling for air. She grabbed the ladle from the other guard, jabbed him in the eye with it and kneed him in the groin. Both fell to the floor writhing in pain. She grabbed the key from the guard closest to her and relieved him of his weapon. She ran out of the room, locking the door behind her. No one paid any attention to her as she passed through the hallways.

She moved unchallenged searching for Miranda. If she could kill her, she could end all of this. Rayven took a hard left in the labyrinth of the fortress and headed down to where Miranda spent most of her time – the meditation chamber.

~~~~~~~~~~~~~~~~~~~~~~~~

Martin secured the door behind them. Philip moved swiftly and quietly through the passageways to retrieve the keystone.

Emily was worried. "Martin, we have to get it back. If we don't, then all of this was for nothing. She wins. Everyone else loses."

He nodded. "I understand. Merrick? Did he harm you?"

"Other than the busted lip? No. He just threw me in a room and took off."

Martin frowned. "I will deal with him, rest assured."

She saw the intense hatred in his eyes.

He turned away from her.

"I'm sorry," she said softly.

She was worried about him. She was young, but she knew enough to know that blind hatred was never a good thing. Martin had every right to feel the way he did, but that was the problem, wasn't it? Martin felt too much, while Merrick felt nothing. Bad people used that to their advantage. Bad people had no conflict of emotions.

Then, there was the matter of Isabeau. Neither Merrick nor Martin knew she was even alive. What impact would that have on their lives? Emily wasn't leaving the dark side without Isabeau, of that she was certain.

Martin sighed heavily, deep in thought.

"I knew this day would come. The day when I would finally make him pay for what he has done... He has been a monster since my mother died. He sent my sister to be eaten by that thing in the cave... I will kill him," Martin said coldly.

She saw the tension in Martin's shoulders. He wanted revenge. But Emily doubted it would be that simple. She didn't want to see Martin get hurt. Sure, Martin was big and strong. And, of course, he was younger than his father. But Merrick was bigger than Martin and strong too. Merrick was evil – devoid of all honor, and those were the worst sort of enemies, the ones with no mercy in their hearts.

Martin looked at Emily and lowered his head.

"Emily, on our way to find you, Philip brought us up through caverns beneath the fortress," his voice trailed off.

Emily knew where this was leading.

"You saw them?"

Martin's head remained lowered. "Children..."

Emily could hear the sorrow in his voice. She put her hand on his arm.

"I did not know. I give you my word. I would have done something," he looked at her. The pain was evident in his eyes.

"I know, Martin. That's why we can't give up. We can't lose. There is so much more at stake here than just walking in the sunshine. Did you see it? The beast?"

He shook his head. "No, but I heard it..."

Emily sighed.

"That was where you saw my sister, yes?"

She nodded.

Martin looked away. "It is unthinkable. Depraved. She was fortunate to be rescued from that hellish place. We must save those other children, all of them," he said with anger and conviction.

"We will," she agreed. "The keystone and the Council of Dragons are connected. They can kill that thing. It's why I was brought here. Miranda is going to set it lose on Aquila. The mist wall is weakening. Eventually, it will fall. If Miranda has the keystone, she can use that power to destroy everything," she explained.

Martin listened intently. "You were brought here to stop her. Yet, by doing so you bring the keystone right into Miranda's hands, do you not?"

Emily frowned. "I mean, yes. But the alternative is she just keeps growing stronger, doing whatever she wants. Either way, we still need the keystone to summon the Council of Dragons. We can't stop that thing without them. You didn't see it. I did. It's ten times the size of the other dragons," she said, sadly. Her eyes glistened as she recalled the fight with the dragons, seeing their majestic bodies fall out of the sky to their deaths.

Martin patted her hand. "I am sorry. I was not trying to upset you. I was merely thinking out loud at the irony of all this. I chose to be a doctor. To save and heal. The manner in which Miranda and my father conduct themselves? It turns my stomach."

"I think Miranda keeps these people here on the dark side to feed her own misery," she said absently.

Martin frowned. "Then all of our hopes, at this moment, rest in the hands of a young thief."

Emily sighed. They both looked at the door, clinging on to hope that Philip would be successful in stealing the keystone from Miranda. Emily closed her eyes. She hoped that Doctor Pernell and Mira were readying themselves and the citizens on the other side – in case they failed.

# Chapter Twenty-Eight

The meditation chamber was Miranda's inner sanctum. It was a circular room with torches several feet apart, protruding from the walls. Black wrought iron wall sconces held fat candles, forming a waxy waterfall beneath them. Shards of colored glass were hung from the ceiling on thin strings, occasionally bumping into one another making a slight clinking sound. The colored glass reflected the light from the flames, creating a kaleidoscope of colors on the chamber walls. The effect was one of a fluid motion of color, quite the optical illusion.

In the center stood a wooden platform upon which Miranda and her three witches sat crossed legged on the floor to commune and conjure up their black magic. The walls were crammed with ill fitted shelves full of glass bottles and vials containing every substance one could imagine, ingredients for their many potions.

Another wall was brimming with scrolls and ancient writings. They had either created, stolen or unearthed these to help them with their incantations and summoning of dark forces from places best left forgotten. These ancient evils and spells granted Miranda unnatural powers.

Miranda and her witches swayed back and forth, with their bottles and bowls spread out before them. It was time to bring down the mist wall. Miranda hoped that the keystone would give her the power to do so. It was not meant for them and did not yield to their will. But they persisted in their efforts to gain control over it.

Miranda grew frustrated by their efforts and pushed herself into a deep hypnotic trance, drawing on all her strength to bend the keystone to her will. Her eyes rolled back into her head and she muttered incomprehensibly.

Philip quietly entered the meditation chamber. Everyone was good at something, he told himself. He was good at this – being invisible. Stealing. Sneaking. Eluding. It was his calling and he did so effortlessly. He could snatch a piece of fruit from Miranda's plate, right in front of her, without her even noticing. He enjoyed making a game of it. Or move a chair from one part of the room to another without the occupant noticing, only to watch them scratch their heads in bewilderment. A dangerous game, but a game he was good at, nonetheless.

This would be no different, he believed. The sorceress and her crazed den of witches were engrossed in their chanting. He could have paraded a heard of goats through the room and they would not have noticed. He counted on the individual's tendency to be oblivious and overconfident. They failed to discover his sleight of hand and little bag of tricks. Miranda was no different.

He stood inside the chamber, observing for a few moments. The keystone was sitting on a base directly in front of Miranda. It was omitting a purplish light and humming rather loudly. Philip circled the platform undetected. He stopped with his back to the door so he could make a clean exit.

Without the slightest hesitation, he reached over and snatched the keystone right out from under Miranda's nose.

Philip smiled to himself, pocketing the keystone. He nodded his thanks to the foursome on the floor in front of him and turned to leave but stopped abruptly.

Donovan was standing directly in front of him, blocking his exit, taking Philip completely by surprise.

"I can see you," Donovan said with a sinister grin.

Philip looked past him. Rayven was standing behind the boy.

"And, I can see you too," she said.

Rayven struck Donovan on the back of his head with the hilt of her sword. He immediately collapsed to the floor.

Philip looked down at him. "I guess you didn't see her, did you? You little creep."

Miranda stirred and opened her eyes towards the sounds. She saw Philip and Rayven standing over Donovan, who was lying motionless on the floor. She looked down and noticed that the keystone was missing. She let out a blood curdling scream and rose off the platform. She was screeching like a banshee with her hand outstretched towards the keystone, which was pulsating and humming inside of Philip's pocket. The other three witches joined her screeches, forming an unholy chorus of banshee cries. The sound was deafening.

"I have the keystone, come on!" Philip yelled to his sister.

They turned to flee, but Miranda thrusted her hands forward, slamming the door shut in front of them. She began throwing debris their direction, blocking the exit.

Rayven spun back towards Miranda and raised her sword. She charged towards Miranda, but the sorceress easily lifted her off the ground without even touching her. She tossed Rayven against the wall. Her body slammed into a shelf full of bottles, sending broken glass and liquid to the floor. Rayven moaned and tried to stand back up. Philip ran to her aid.

Rayven pushed herself up. Miranda rose higher and higher above the floor, screeching, hurling fireballs from her hands towards them.

"Get the necklace back to Emily. Go! Run!" she said weakly to her brother. He hesitated but then ran for the door.

Rayven stood and leaned back against the wall. Miranda was enraged. Rayven's sword was no match for her dark powers, but she could at least cause a distraction long enough to allow her brother time to escape.

The other witches stood and charged Rayven. She pushed them back one at a time and drove her sword into them, striking them down easily, as they clawed at her with their bony fingers, digging into her flesh.

Miranda thrust her hands forward again sending Rayven flying to the other side of the room, slamming her into another shelf. The shock from the impact knocked Rayven out. She slumped to the floor, unresponsive.

Philip pushed and pulled the debris away from the exit and squeezed through the door as Miranda hurled a fireball at him, narrowly missing his head. He ran as fast as he could down the darkened corridors to reunite with Martin and Emily. He hoped his sister would be all right. There was no turning back now.

Miranda stormed through the halls, searching for the thief and her precious keystone. When she left the meditation chamber, both Rayven and Donovan were motionless. Servants and guards quickly stepped out of her way as her rage was evident. Merrick approached her.

"What has happened?" he asked.

She violently grabbed Merrick by his cloak and pulled him in closer to her, screaming into his face.

"Release my army," she ordered.

He pulled his cloak from her hands and stepped back.

"Take your hands off me, Miranda. The mist wall? Is it down? We cannot send them into the mist if it is not down yet, you know this!" he shouted at her.

"It was nearly down before some vile creature stole the keystone from me!" She shouted angrily.

"Who?" Merrick asked.

"A thief!" she screamed, practically frothing at the mouth.

Merrick took another step back from her.

"You wielded its power then?" he asked, skeptically.

"I drew from its power, yes." She was growing annoyed with his questions. "Do as you are told, Merrick. Stop asking me to explain myself. Know your place!" She shoved past him.

He watched her storm down the corridor. Merrick headed back to where he had left the girl. If the keystone had been stolen from Miranda, the thief would be trying to return it to its rightful owner. He quickened his pace.

Miranda felt a rage that she had not experienced in years. After all of her planning and scheming, she was not about to be blindsided by these intruders. She would deal with Rayven later. If she was not dead, she would wish she was dead soon enough. Miranda would tie Rayven to a stake outside of the fortress and let her minions feast upon her slowly, until she was completely devoured.

How dare Rayven betray her! After all she had done for her. She gave her a way out from that wretched existence in the village to be one of her seekers. She should be grateful. She should be loyal. Yet, Rayven had joined forces with the girl and Martin. She was present when the thief snatched the keystone. She was protecting the thief. Miranda seethed with anger. Her betrayal would not go unpunished.

Miranda slammed her hand against the wall and screamed at the top of her lungs. She tried to reach Donovan with her mind, but he was not responding. He was still unconscious in the meditation chamber and of no use to her now.

She screamed in anger, grabbing guards as she stormed by, demanding that they track down the intruders in her fortress. They ran in every direction in search of the culprit. She smashed ceramic vases on the floor and overturned service carts as she walked past, in a fit of rage, sending servants scurrying for cover.

She tried to track the thief with her mind, but could not find him. Something or someone was blocking her vision. Someone extremely powerful. It was infuriating Miranda. This was her dominion. How dare anyone interfere!

Meanwhile, Merrick hastily made his way back to where he had left Emily. He hoped to catch the thief in the process of returning the jewel to the girl. He removed the key from his pocket, unlocked the door and stepped inside. Emily was not immediately in his view. He checked behind the door quickly, thinking she may be hiding behind it. He stood in the center of the room and looked around.

Nowhere to hide.

Nowhere to run.

Yet, the room was empty.

She was gone.

Emily had vanished into thin air. Merrick grabbed his sword and spun around to guard his back. What strange magic was this? How did she disappear inside a locked room?

He ran back into the darkened corridor and began searching for the girl. He realized that they were one step ahead of him. He and Miranda were both being bested. Was his son involved too? Merrick slammed the back of his fist into the stone wall, knocking one of the wall sconces onto the floor. The embers scattered across the stones, causing a basket of linens to catch fire. Servants rushed to douse the small fire with water. Merrick paid no attention to them whatsoever.

He swore to himself. This cannot be happening. Miranda wanted her army unleashed? Then so be it. He found the commander in charge and gave him the directive to assemble the troops, armed with swords, metal tipped spears, battle axes, bows and arrows. It was time to make their way to the mist wall. The blood lust among the ranks was strong. They had been waiting for this day to come, and they wanted their pound of flesh.

Miranda would not be pleased that Merrick was not leading the assault himself, but he could care less. He had more important matters to attend to.

Somewhere within their midst was the girl…

She was the one to concern himself with.

She had help and so far, they were outsmarting both Miranda and Merrick. He had not had a challenge this satisfying in a long time. He relished the opportunity to stand before a worthy opponent. If that happened to be his son? All the better.

Merrick had questions he wanted answered. The pictures he saw on his scouting mission were clearly descendants of Isabeau. There were missing pieces of a puzzle. Without answers, he was unsure of how to proceed. He questioned Miranda's ability to succeed. She was obviously not as all seeing as she believed herself to be, because she certainly did not anticipate this.

"Arrogant witch," Merrick swore under his breath. He could feel the tension in his muscles and the anger rise within him.

Merrick's heavy footsteps thundered through the corridors and up the narrow stairwells, hunting for his missing prey. The fortress was in complete chaos among a flurry of activity. The warning had been issued that there were intruders within, and orders were given for the army to assemble. Soldiers and guards raced from one place to another, some preparing for war, others searching for anyone that did not belong in the fortress. Merrick stopped and observed his surroundings, looking for any signs that might lead him back to the girl and her allies. So far, he saw none, much to his frustration.

~~~~~~~~~~~~~~~~~~~~~~~~~~~~~~~

The beast from the fiery chasm below the fortress sensed that something was amiss. It roared angrily to be let out. It dug furiously at the dirt, making deep trenches with its claws. It tugged at the chains for more give, enraged that it was still captive. It slammed its body against the walls in violent protest.

The guards ran to the cave opening. They were fearful that the beast might break free. There was little they could do. If the chains did in fact break, they would be powerless to stop the beast from making its way to the surface.

It sniffed in the air – sensing danger, sensing chaos, sensing death. It roared, wanting to satisfy its thirst for blood. It tilted its head to the side, letting its tongue flick out into the air.

It could taste the fear.

It craved the fear.

It hungered for their fear...

It shifted its head back and roared, a deafening roar.

The children in the cages whimpered softly, huddling as closely together as possible. They too sensed that something bad was about to happen to all of them and soon. They pulled at the cage doors trying to free themselves. The guard smacked a stick on the cages, forcing the children to pull their hands back inside.

~~~~~~~~~~~~~~~~~~~~~~~~~~~~~~~

Emily and Martin heard the commotion, followed by footsteps running towards the doorway. Martin pushed Emily behind him, in case it was not who they were expecting. Philip flung open the door, necklace in hand, clearly out of breath. He had a cheeky grin on his face.

"She's one ticked off witch right now," he said and handed the keystone back to Emily, triumphantly.

She and Martin smiled, relieved that he was successful in his mission. Martin patted Philip on his back.

When Emily put the necklace on, the keystone's pulsing subsided, only the swirling light within remained. She felt dizzy for a moment and put her hand against the wall to steady herself.

"Are you all right?" Martin asked.

She closed her eyes and then opened them again. She inhaled sharply and held on tight to the keystone.

"It's guiding me, growing stronger," she said. She looked at Martin and Philip. "Miranda and Merrick are both hunting us."

"Then we must make haste," Martin said urgently. "We must strike first."

"Yes," Emily agreed.

"My sister is injured," Philip said.

"We will go back for her, as soon as possible," he assured Philip.

Emily moaned and grabbed her head. In her mind, she saw Miranda charging towards Isabeau's chamber. In a fit of rage and with one swift stroke, Miranda slit Isabeau's throat. Her lifeless body collapsed to the floor in a pool of blood. Vacant eyes stared up at Miranda, as her lifeforce slowly left her body.

"No," groaned Emily.

Both Philip and Martin tried to steady her on her feet.

"Martin, please get Rayven. We need her help," she asked.

Martin shook his head no.

"Absolutely not. I am not leaving you again," he protested.

"Philip and I have something we must do," she told him.

"Then, I will accompany you," he argued.

"There's no time to explain. We have to go now. Get her and meet back here," she said.

Martin wasn't convinced. "I lost you in the village. I am not willing to risk that again."

Philip looked from one to the other. "Maybe, I should go get my sister and you stay with Martin," he suggested. "To be safe."

"No," Emily said quickly. "It's not something Martin can help me with."

Martin didn't like the sound of that. "Emily, I do not agree. I do not think we should split up," he said with grave concern.

"Martin, trust me. I know what I have to do," she urged.

It was obvious he could not change her mind. He resigned to trust her judgment. He looked sternly at Philip.

"Keep her safe."

Philip nodded, "I will."

"Get back here as soon as possible," he said to Emily.

"I will," she said and gave him a warm hug. "Please, be careful. Merrick is out there...so is Miranda."

"Agreed. You as well," he added.

There was so much bustle at the fortress at that moment that they easily blended in with the activity. Martin followed Philip's directions to find his way the meditation chamber, while Philip and Emily headed the opposite direction.

"Would you mind telling me where we are going?" he asked, after they watched Martin leave.

She looked at Philip. "The Keep," she said soberly.

"The Keep? Are you mad?" he asked a little bit too loudly and quickly lowered his voice. He didn't want to draw attention to them. "Why would you want to go there? No one goes there unless it's to die."

"We have to rescue someone," she said urgently. "We have to hurry. Do you know your way around it or not?" she asked.

He hesitated.

"Well, do you?" she pressed.

He frowned. "Yes. Sneaking around is second nature to me."

"Good, let's go," she said.

He shook his head but didn't question her further.

"Follow me," he said, quickly moving down the long passageway to a small enclave that led to an outer bridge.

"Who are you looking for?" he asked over his shoulder.

"A person of great importance," she said.

"In the Keep?" he asked in disbelief.

Emily saw the towering structure of the Keep in front of them. They quickened their pace to get inside.

"You're just going to walk right in?" she asked, surprised.

"If we aren't in shackles, they assume we are servants or workers. No one cares. No one stops me, ever. The guards look up and barely notice you. Although, they're looking for intruders. That's us. So, it's not going to be as simple as all that," he pointed out.

"Great," she sighed.

"Come on," he urged, stepping into the Keep. "No matter who speaks to you, don't answer. Let me handle it, understand?"

She nodded. Emily let out a deep breath, steadied her nerves and followed Philip inside.

The Keep was not someplace that anyone went voluntarily. It was without a doubt the loneliest place in all of Aquila. There was no reprieve. No second chances. No forgiveness. No mercy. No justice. Only total isolation followed by death.

The first thing Emily noticed were the sounds echoing from within, cries of despair and pain. The occasional scream pierced her ears. She heard a whip crack in the air, as it tore into flesh. Someone was being flogged nearby. Their screams of agony gave her chills. Overhead, the remains of men, in various stages of decomposition, were crammed inside human sized bird cages, metal rods pierced their bodies. The stench of death permeated their senses.

Emily gasped. Philip reached back and took her hand, sensing her repulsion and unease at the horror around them. The floor was slippery from bits of flesh and blood. Emily's left boot slid to the side. Philip grabbed her arm to steady her footing.

Numerous torture devices littered the area. To Emily, it looked like something out of the infamous Tower of London and the Spanish Inquisition in their treatment of prisoners.

Winged carnivorous creatures, resembling the Nyctosaurus from Cretaceous period, hovered over rotted corpses, picking at their flesh. She was astonished at the living conditions or lack thereof. She tried not to look into any of the cells by keeping her eyes fixed to the floor. She saw enough in her peripheral vision to last a lifetime. It was beyond barbaric.

The Keep was like a stone beehive, with row after row of tiny cells, dark and cold. The occasional filthy hand would force its way through a small opening begging for food or water. It was an endless loop of suffering and misery.

Emily was having difficulty controlling the dizziness she felt from the keystone. She fought hard to keep her head clear. The closer they got to Isabeau, the stronger the keystone seemed to pulsate.

Philip stopped and turned to her. "Please tell me who you're looking for. From here on, the Keep spans in many directions, like a pinwheel. I need a point of reference to follow," he told her.

She understood. "It's a long hallway, far from the others here," she explained. "Kept hidden, secret. Only two guards. There is a large chamber inside. A prison cell, like none of these," she said, motioning to the tiny holes in the walls that held lost souls waiting to die.

Philip bit his lip and concentrated. "Two guards? Hidden hallway?"

She nodded.

"I saw a place such as that once, but didn't dare explore further," he paused. "The place you speak of felt mournful. I can't explain it, but it was not someplace I ever wanted to revisit."

"Can you get us inside?" she asked.

He looked at her.

"I can. Getting past the guards will take a bit of a trick," he admitted. "If I'm right about where you need to go, then we must head upwards, towards the far corner of the Keep."

"Okay," she said.

He quickly made his way across the passageway and up a winding staircase. Philip weighed his options on the best way to sneak past the guards. Maybe they wouldn't have to, he thought to himself. A sleeping potion? They wouldn't know what hit them. He swung his bag to the front and rifled through it without even skipping a beat. Emily stayed close on his heels.

When they reached the top, he paused.

"Does this look familiar?" he asked.

Emily peered over his shoulder and nodded. It was exactly as she had seen in her vision. No sign of Miranda. Good, she thought. We were ahead of her so far. At least, she hoped so.

Philip held up his hand to show her a pink powder and shushed her with a finger to his lips. He held up his other hand motioning for her to remain where she was. He casually walked up to the two guards.

"You there," the one to the left of the hallway spoke first. "You don't belong up on this level," he said.

Philip raised his hand slightly. "Sincerest apologies, my dear friends," he said and blew the powder into their faces. The guard that spoke fumbled for his weapon but slumped to the ground before being able to remove it. The other guard fell asleep with his mouth opened, as he was about to cry out a warning. Both guards were sound asleep on the floor. The one that spoke to Philip had begun to snore.

Philip motioned for Emily to join him. She hurried over. They stood looking down the long dark corridor where only a faint sliver of light could be seen beneath the heavy door frame. It certainly had an ominous feel about it, Emily noted to herself. The sound from the levels below were muted here. Emily looked around, straining to see their surroundings.

"Allow me," Philip said. He reached into his bag and threw a fine dust into the air. The dust erupted into a blue luminescent light source, which lit up the area a good thirty or forty feet deep. There was nothing there. No other doors. No windows. Only the one long dark hallway with a single door at the end. A fine layer of dust could be seen upon the polished stone, with not one footprint among it. No one had walked across the floor in a very long time.

Sounds from the Keep did not reach this place. All traces of the outside were muted here, furthering the feeling of isolation.

"Odd," Philip said. "Who could be so dangerous that an entire level of the Keep was devoted to them?"

Emily didn't answer him. It made her heart sink to think of all the years Isabeau had spent locked away in this awful place, a fate worse than death in many ways. Slowly wasting away mentally until your body was finally spent. To go from the beauty of their castle to this? With no birds, no trees, no sun or warmth. Emily was glad that she would be there to release Isabeau from her forced damnation at Miranda's hands.

"You sure about this?" he asked.

"Positive," she said. "Open it, please."

They moved down the hallway. The lock was lit sufficiently enough from a torch right outside the door. Philip took out his slivers of metal and went to work on the lock. It was almost rusted shut from lack of use, and the air this high in the Keep was damp. A smaller door about a foot high was at the bottom. Emily suspected it was where food was shoved in. It looked like a pet door to her. How awful, she thought. Philip worked feverishly on the lock. It seemed like it was taking far too long.

Finally, Philip heard that familiar sound. Click. Philip pulled back the latch and pushed the door open slowly. It creaked loudly in protest. Philip and Emily stepped inside.

~~~~~~~~~~~~~~~~~~~~~~~~~~

Donovan stirred. His head hurt. He sat up slowly, annoyed that he did not see the seeker in his mind, before she hit him. He was focused on the one stealing the necklace from Miranda. He allowed it to cloud his vision momentarily.

Seeing the necklace in Miranda's possession excited him. Then, the thief snatched it without Miranda so much as flinching. Donovan found that to be extremely interesting. How could such a simple trick fool Miranda so easily? Donovan questioned her abilities. Once again it demonstrated how easy it was to fool those around him. Donovan chuckled. The thief reminded him of himself. Everyone tended to underestimate him as well, until it was too late.

He looked around the meditation chamber and saw bodies of witches thrown about, barely alive. He hated them. He didn't think they had any real power, only power they created with their potions. They were fakes, in his opinion. He was the one with the real power.

Donovan closed his eyes and let his mind drift across the room. It settled upon the witch lying closest to him. He entered her mind and let her body fall deeper and deeper into a black pit below. She cried out, flailing her arms, trying to fly. He let her fall to the bottom, until she impacted, crushing every bone in her body. The witch heaved and then lay still, blood gushing from her mouth.

Donovan smiled and turned towards the other witch lying against the wall. He entered her mind easily and lifted her up in her unconscious state. He sent her further and further up into the sky, towards the stars until she could no longer breathe. Her face contorted in pain. She floated aimlessly into space. Back in the meditation room, he stared at her, knowing her mind had just shut down and her heart had stopped beating.

One left, he mused.

*You really are a sick little monster, aren't you?*

He heard a voice in his head and looked around the room. He spotted Rayven pushing herself up against the wall. She was talking to him with her mind. She had invaded his personal space and only Miranda was permitted to do that. Rayven must be a strong seeker, he realized, not at all pleased with this intrusion.

Rayven was weak and sore, but her mind was strong. She stared directly at Donovan, taunting him.

*What's wrong? Didn't your Mommy love you enough?*

That made Donovan angry. He flinched and she saw it.

*Struck a nerve, did I?*

Rayven continued her taunt.

Donovan refused to answer.

398

*Well, I can't say that I blame her for sending you away. No one wants a freak for a kid, right?*

She laughed in his head, playing on the boy's emotions or lack thereof.

*Shut up!*

He snapped angrily in his mind.

She smiled. So... He did have a weak spot. No one liked to be unloved and unwanted, not even Donovan. She stored that information away, knowing it might come in handy.

*You don't suppose Miranda regards you as her own child now, do you? Boy, you sure drew the short end of the Mommy straws, didn't you? Honestly, from what I've seen? She treats you more like a pet.*

She chided him.

*Stop that!*

He shouted in his mind. He stood up and stomped his foot.

Rayven smiled again.

*Are you going to cry?*

She laughed in his mind.

*Get out of my head!*

He ordered, smacking his hands on his temples.

*Not so fun when someone does it to you... Is it?*

She teased.

He was getting upset.

No one had ever gotten into his head and made fun of him before. His mind was his safe place. And, she was ruining it for him. His immaturity was showing itself. He was letting her get to him. He wiped a tear from his eye.

*Stop it or...*

He said angrily.

*Or what?*

She snapped back.

*I'll kill you!*

He yelled at her in his mind.

She stood up to face him.

399

"You have a lot to learn, little boy," she said to him just as Martin rushed into the room.

He saw Donovan and Rayven faced off with one another. He immediately drew his sword and swiped it in the air as he approached the boy. Donovan's eyes widened with fear when he saw Martin coming towards him. Martin was an intimidating figure and Donovan instinctively took a few steps back.

Rayven shot her hand up to stop Martin.

"It's all right, Martin. The boy and I were just having a little chat to get acquainted," she said.

Donovan took another step away from Martin.

"I ought to wring your neck," Martin said, glaring at the boy.

Donovan was sniffling. He had been completely disarmed and caught off guard by Rayven's assault on his mind. He didn't have the maturity to deal with this situation. He was used to lurking in the shadows of people's minds. He wasn't equipped to handle this type of confrontation mentally from Rayven, nor the physical threat from Martin.

A puddle formed at Donovan's feet.

He had wet himself from fear.

Martin looked at the stream of urine coming down the boy's leg and snickered.

"Not so tough after all, are you?"

Donovan said nothing.

Martin spoke to Rayven. "We have to go. Can you walk?"

She nodded and gave Donovan a warning.

"Watch your step, little boy…"

Donovan just stood in his puddle of urine and watched them leave. His face flushed with anger.

*No, you watch your step!*

He screamed with his mind. He was too afraid to move and she had already closed herself off to him.

Donovan's words were heard by no one.

# Chapter Twenty-Nine

Isabeau sat in a chair by the small window, staring blankly out into the darkness at nothing. She did not bother to raise her head as the door scraped across the floor. Philip and Emily looked at one another. He closed the door behind them and stood guard by it. He cautioned Emily that the sleeping spell would only work for a short period of time and that whatever she planned on doing, she had better do it fast.

She understood. She slowly approached Isabeau. Emily glanced quickly around the room as she crossed its interior. These were certainly far better accommodations than the others in the Keep. The stillness within the room was chilling. The only sound was made from the wood crackling in the fireplace.

She wondered why Miranda had bothered to accommodate Isabeau in the manner that she did. Guilt, perhaps? Or was it Miranda's way of gloating? Emily decided that it was probably Miranda's way of keeping a trophy of her grand trickery. Isabeau was that trophy.

A loud horn blew outside, startling Emily.

Isabeau did not move her head even slightly. She continued to stare into the darkness.

"I am so glad you have arrived, sweetheart," Isabeau spoke in such a soft voice that Emily could barely make out her words. "Those are the sounds of battle. The horns of Miranda's army have been blown... I feared this day would come."

Emily stopped and stood still, facing Isabeau. She looked back over her shoulder at Philip but could barely make him out in the darkness.

"You were expecting me?" Emily asked, surprised.

"Oh, yes, for quite some time now," her voice trailed off.

Isabeau slowly turned and faced her. Emily was taken aback by the face that greeted her. She looked so much like her grandmother that it was unsettling yet moving.

"Isabeau," Emily whispered, as if she didn't really believe she was finally standing face to face with the woman in her visions. She was older but still as graceful and beautiful as she was in her younger days. Isabeau was regal and radiant even as a prisoner in this place.

From the back of the room, Philip gasped. He understood now why it was so important to come here. This was Isabeau from the House of Stewart – Queen of Aquila – on the light side. Merrick's beloved wife. Everyone knew their tragic tale and here she was, locked away in Miranda's Keep. He was stunned.

Upon hearing her name from Emily's lips, Isabeau smiled softly and looked up at Emily with the kindest eyes.

Emily spoke softly. "You look just like my grandma," she said, trying to maintain her emotions.

Isabeau nodded knowingly. "My darling Victoria...Your grandmother," she smiled warmly. She reached out her hands for Emily to take.

Emily moved forward and knelt on the floor by Isabeau's chair. She took her hands and lowered her head out of respect. Isabeau squeezed Emily's hands lightly.

"It's an honor to meet you," Emily said as she looked into the woman's green eyes. It was almost like looking into a mirror, an older version of herself. "Excuse me, but what do I call you? My lady?" Her face blushed from embarrassment.

Isabeau's smiled grew wider, "You may call me Isabeau," she told Emily. "Although, I am your great grandmother, my dear."

She cupped Emily's chin in her hand and studied her face. "You look just like my baby daughter," she remarked fondly.

"I'm here to save you," Emily said, feeling a bit silly after she spoke those words.

The smile never left Isabeau's face. "You already have, my darling child." Isabeau's eyes glistened over slightly and she sat up straight in her chair, regaining her composure.

"How did you know I was coming?" Emily asked.

Isabeau looked at the necklace around Emily's neck and explained. "The keystone never leaves you. It is always a part of us, always connecting us. You have always been a part of me, even if you were unaware of this fact. I could always sense you, your mother and my Victoria. Sometimes I could even see you when my visions were strong, but mostly I could just feel you. I have known you were on Aquila since the moment you arrived. I have been waiting for you."

Emily let her words sink in. "My mother? She never wore the necklace," Emily told her.

Isabeau nodded. "She is a descendant too, but not all of us have the calling. Victoria knew you were the chosen one from the moment of your birth. She kept it safe until it was your time to wear it. She chose wisely, do you not agree?" Isabeau smiled at her fondly.

"I hope I can make her proud," Emily said sincerely.

"My dear, she has always been proud of you…"

Emily looked away. She was crying. Isabeau ran her finger down Emily's cheek, wiping away her tears.

"So much for such a young one to endure, is it not?"

Emily nodded.

"I'm so sorry this happened to you," Emily said.

"It was not of your doing, sweetheart," Isabeau said sadly.

Emily looked into Isabeau's eyes.

"Merrick is here. So is Martin," she told her.

Isabeau nodded.

"I am aware of this. I am glad you are here with me, to whatever end awaits us all," Isabeau said warmly.

"I'm afraid things have been set into motion now, terrible things. Miranda is coming for you. We must leave. Are you able to travel?" Emily asked.

Isabeau weakly stood up. Emily held her arm to offer support. "I am ready to be rid of this place," Isabeau said defiantly. "Miranda has gone unchecked far too long. I hope today will be a new beginning for us all."

She looked up to see Philip standing by the door.

He approached them and bowed slightly.

"My lady."

"And, you are?" she asked.

"I am no one," he said.

Isabeau took his hand. "Everyone is someone, young man."

Emily answered for him. "Philip – his name is Philip. I couldn't have gotten to you without his help."

Philip stared down at his boots, embarrassed. Isabeau was now the second most beautiful woman he had ever seen.

"Philip – I am eternally grateful for your assistance," she said graciously.

"We must go now," Emily said.

Philip went to stand on the other side of Isabeau to support her from her left. She was a bit frail but otherwise in good health.

"You will have to forgive my slowness," she said. "I have not been outside of this room in years," she told them. "My legs are not cooperating as they should be," she admitted.

"We've got you," Emily told her.

Emily took a blanket from Isabeau's cot and wrapped it around her for both warmth and concealment. They slowly made their way back into the hallway.

"Philip?" she asked, concerned for their safety.

"I know, princess," he said. "I don't have much powder left, but it should be enough to get us safely back to Martin," he told her.

"I'm not a princess," Emily corrected him.

"Begging your pardon, miss, but I do believe you are," he said looking from her to Isabeau.

Isabeau smiled and looked at Emily. "He is correct."

Emily shook her head. "Try telling that to my teachers and my parents," she smirked.

Isabeau stopped briefly and swayed. "I need a moment," she said, already fatigued.

"Of course," Emily said.

"I have not been this close to the keystone in quite a long time and its power can be overwhelming," she admitted to Emily.

Emily reached up to remove the necklace. "Here, do you need this back? It does belong to you…"

Isabeau stopped her immediately.

"No, my dear. It belongs to you. You are its bearer. It is your time now." She patted Emily's hand.

Emily lowered her arms and continued to assist Isabeau.

"Do you have a plan?" Philip asked Emily.

"Get Isabeau to safety," she said. "I only see things in short bursts, so I'm kind of winging this," she admitted.

"Winging it?" he asked, not understanding the analogy.

"Making it up as I go along," she explained.

"Oh, grand," Philip frowned.

"I do not think I can walk much further," Isabeau told them.

Emily realized that she would have to use the keystone to transport them to safety. It took so much out of her to do so, but she had no choice. If she retraced their steps back through the Keep – in her mind – back to the storage room, she believed she could use the keystone.

"Close your eyes," she told them.

"Why?" Philip asked.

"I'm going to use the keystone to move us," she said.

"Why didn't you do that to begin with?"

"I've only done it once. And, I have to know exactly where I am going, from point A to point B, in my head. You don't want to end up inside of a wall, do you?"

Philip winced. "Um, no."

"Back to the storage room," she said. "Both of you please close your eyes and hold hands."

They did as she asked. Emily closed her eyes and pictured the storage room in her mind. She followed the path she and Philip had taken to find Isabeau. The keystone began to hum and pulsate with light. Emily concentrated harder.

"Why is this taking so long?" she asked out loud.

"You are in Miranda's kingdom. She uses dark magic to control this world. You can do it. Patience, my dear," Isabeau said assuredly.

Emily took a deep breath and let her mind drift further away, calling upon the keystone to take them back to the storage room. She felt the strange sensation take over her body, like she was floating. She heard a loud ringing in her ears. When it stopped, she opened her eyes and found the three of them standing inside the storage room, unharmed.

Philip smiled, "Impressive."

They helped Isabeau sit down in a chair. Philip noticed that Emily's necklace was humming again.

"Why is it doing that?" he asked.

"It's like a beacon, growing stronger. It's sharing things with me," she said. She closed her eyes. "I can see the army marching towards the mist wall. Miranda is searching for us. I can see Martin. He's heading back this way." She opened her eyes abruptly. "Oh no," she said with alarm.

"What is it?" Philip asked with great concern.

"Merrick! He's found them! I have to go!" she said urgently.

"What? Wait!"

"Philip, stay with Isabeau. Keep her safe here."

"Now wait a minute, the big guy gave me strict orders to keep you safe, remember?" he protested.

Emily frowned. "You don't understand. Martin is in danger. Keep Isabeau safe. Protect her. I have to go. Now!" She turned to Isabeau. "I have to help Martin. I'll be back. I promise..."

"Take care of my son," she nodded, understanding the gravity of the situation.

"I intend to," Emily said. She gave Isabeau a gentle hug and left quickly, racing down the hallway.

She let her vision guide her through the fortress. A wagon full of weapons was sitting in a hallway. Without the slightest hesitation, Emily grabbed a sword. It was heavier than she expected, but she continued.

In her vision, she saw Martin – covered in blood, with Merrick over him. Both badly beaten. And, she saw Donovan, torturing Martin's mind in horrific ways. She watched Martin die in her mind, at the hands of his father. Her heart raced. People rushed past her in the darkened corridors, preparing for battle. They did not deter her. She had to get to Martin, before it was too late.

~~~~~~~~~~~~~~~~~~~~~~~~~~~~

The face from his past jolted Merrick to a halt. There was no mistaking that it was his son. He watched Martin and Miranda's seeker, weaving in and out of the crowded hallways, bound to some unknown destination.

Merrick studied him, momentarily surprised by mixed emotions. They were on opposite sides of this fight. Too bad for Martin, Merrick concluded. He quickened his pace to shadow the pair. He drew his sword effortlessly, following them closely. Probably heading back to the girl, he deduced. Good. He would have them all. He wanted to be done with it, and finally close this chapter of his life once and for all.

It sounded like a good plan were it not for the nagging feeling in the back of his mind that there was something he was not seeing, something he was missing. Something was being kept hidden from him. He could feel it.

The faces in the pictures haunted him. There was no denying it. His hand absently touched the photographs he had stuffed into his cloak pocket. He just couldn't rid himself of the belief that they were connected to him, connected to his past and his present. Merrick was conflicted and that displeased him greatly.

He pushed those thoughts to the back of his mind. The task at hand was to deal with his son and the seeker, collect the girl and the keystone, and then move on. He had plans of his own that did not involve Miranda and her deranged schemes.

The halls were congested, full of servants gathering supplies of all kinds for the impending battle. It was a long trek across the wasteland. Soldiers would need water and supplies along the route. The first wave of the army was closing in on the mist wall, preparing to crossover.

Martin and Rayven were caught in the flow of a passageway. They had to step aside as carts were pushed down the hallway.

Merrick seized on the opportunity to close the distance between them. They were not far away from his own living quarters. He pulled the dagger out from his belt and moved on Rayven quickly and without warning.

Before she knew it, there was a dagger to her throat with such force that it broke her skin. Merrick was too skilled a fighter to let Rayven break free. He bent her arm behind her back with such force that he almost dislocated her shoulder.

Martin spun around and locked eyes with his father.

Merrick showed no emotion.

He glared at Merrick. The pure hatred for his father was revealed in his eyes. Martin's hand dropped to his sword.

Merrick pressed the dagger harder against Rayven's throat.

"Move or I cut her throat," he ordered, motioning to the corridor on their left.

Martin hesitated. Merrick pulled her arm up further, popping her shoulder from its joint, dislocating it. She cried out in pain. Martin took a step towards Rayven. As he did so, Merrick pressed the dagger against her throat with more force. Blood began trickling down her neck.

"I would not do that, if I were you," Merrick warned.

Rayven fought the pain, trying not to lose consciousness. Martin looked back and forth between his father and the blade. Weighing his options and calculating his odds. Merrick grinned wickedly, seeing his son trying to maneuver his way out of this situation.

"I suggest you move, at once," Merrick ordered again.

Martin turned and followed orders.

"Second door to the right. Get inside," Merrick commanded.

Martin opened the door, stepping inside Merrick's expansive living quarters. It was sparsely furnished but adequate for Merrick's needs. He closed the door behind them. Upon doing so, he wrapped his forearm around Rayven's neck, squeezing the life out of her. She fought, gasping for air and passed out. When Martin turned around, Merrick tossed Rayven's lifeless body to the floor. Martin looked at her lying motionless. He found his son's concern amusing.

"She will live, but I can not say the same for you, boy."

Martin seized on that moment to charge his father. He used his head and body like a battering ram and slammed into his father's chest, knocking the air out of Merrick and crushing his body against the wall.

Merrick clasped both of his hands together and brought them down repeatedly on Martin's back with crushing blows. His son cried out in pain, backing away.

He faced his father. He had waited all of his life for this singular moment. To finally hurt the man that had caused him so much pain. Martin's thoughts raced. He fought to regain his composure.

Martin was a tall man, perhaps 6'4" in height, but Merrick was taller, almost 6'7" and bulkier, outweighing Martin by a good 40 pounds. Martin had youth and stamina on his side. Overall, evenly matched as father squared off against son.

They sized each other up. Merrick had a mental advantage at the moment, because Martin's hatred and rage towards his father was impairing his judgement. He knew better than to blindly attack someone.

He had told Emily as much... using your head was just as important, if not more so, than using your might. Martin tried to calm himself down and rely on his training. The range of emotions displayed on Martin's face in such a short span of time intrigued Merrick.

"Have you learned nothing, boy? Are you just going to stand there and stare? Or are you going to show me what you are capable of?" Merrick scoffed, baiting him.

Finally, Martin spoke.

"I think you will find me a worthy opponent, Father," he said with contempt.

Merrick laughed, "I am not yet impressed."

Martin shifted his weight from one foot to another. Merrick snickered and did the same, mirroring his son's moves. Martin was facing his past and emotions were getting the better of him. A lifetime of buried memories came crashing to the surface.

His father, his nemesis, was standing directly in front of him. All Martin wanted to do was tear him apart limb from limb – for Victoria, for his mother, for his childhood and for Emily.

Merrick seemed to surmise Martin's predicament.

"Do you have something you want to say, boy? Say it and be done with it. Either you are going to fight me like a man or stand their quaking in your boots. I recall the last time I saw you. It was the night your sister disappeared. You had a similar expression on your face...confused...and...pathetic."

Merrick was taunting him.

With those words, Martin struck his father again, delivering blow after blow, which Merrick deflected. He ducked and Martin punched the wall hard, breaking the bones in his right hand. He cried out in pain.

"Tsk, tsk...," Merrick said circling behind Martin. "It seems you have forgotten all I have taught you. Still have not mastered your emotions, I see."

Martin cradled his right hand. It was useless to him now. He tucked it close to his body and faced Merrick.

"I have not forgotten anything you taught me," Martin shouted. "Betrayal, failure, abandonment...weakness," he added.

Merrick frowned at him. "Weakness?"

They slowly moved around the room, both in attack stances, ready for the next onslaught.

"Only a weak man lets his grief consume him so much that he turns his back on his own children!" Martin said vehemently.

Merrick did not like that remark. "Do you take me for a nursemaid? What use do I have for little ones after your mother died?" he asked curiously.

"What use?" Martin asked, shocked by the remark.

"Yes, what use?" Merrick asked again.

Martin wanted to rip out his tongue. "You are a monster!" he yelled, trying to control his rage.

Merrick mulled over that characterization and nodded.

"I can accept that. We are what we are…"

Martin was struggling with his emotions as they continued to circle each other.

Merrick grinned wickedly. "I am many things, but weak is not one of them. You on the other hand? Here with that girl on some grand crusade? It is laughable," Merrick added.

"You used to believe in something once upon a time!" Martin scoffed.

"I did. I believed in your mother, until she was taken from me. Now I believe in power, absolute power."

Merrick took a step closer to his son. Martin instinctively took a step back, which did not go unnoticed by his father.

"Still a child afraid of his father? Here, I will give you an advantage," Merrick grinned.

He took his dagger out and flipped it over in his hand. Merrick leaned over and held it out for him to take. Martin smacked it away with his left hand. The dagger went flying across the room.

"You sent Victoria to her death!" Martin yelled.

His father nodded without emotion.

"Oh, you know about that? It matters not…"

Merrick picked up his dagger.

"She was just a baby!" Martin shouted angrily.

"She was of no consequence to me. Is this hard for you to grasp?" he asked.

"You were our father," Martin said, eyes pleading, looking for some glimmer of the man he once knew and loved.

Martin was exasperated. He shook his head and looked down momentarily, giving Merrick leverage he was waiting for. He tackled Martin, causing them to topple over the table and crash to the floor.

Merrick immediately grabbed Martin's injured right hand and twisted it backwards, until he heard the bone snap, breaking Martin's wrist. The pain was excruciating. Martin cried out.

He began punching his father on the side of his head, with his left hand. But Merrick punched back, using his body weight to hold Martin down. He grabbed Martin's only good hand with both of his arms and pinned it down effortlessly.

Once his son was rendered defenseless, Merrick used his free hand to punch him. The first blow sent blood flying from Martin's nose. Merrick punched him again, squarely in the face, cutting above his eye. Martin blinked hard trying to clear his vision. Merrick delivered blow after blow.

Martin head butted his father, sending him staggering backwards. Martin stood up, cradled his broken wrist, and wiped blood from his face. He wasted no time drawing his sword and moving on his father. Merrick drew his sword too. The sound of metal hitting metal rang out, as their blades struck one another.

"Surely you do not think you can win?" his father asked.

Martin wiped more blood away from his eye. He could feel it swelling up rapidly, obstructing his vision.

"If it is my time to leave this world, I intend to take you with me!" he said angrily.

He swung his sword in a move easily deflected by Merrick. They circled one another. Martin was nursing his right hand and wrist, forced to hold his sword with his left hand. He could fight with both, but his right arm was his natural choice. He would be at a disadvantage using his left.

Merrick continued to taunt him. "You could join me. We could conquer this world together."

Martin spat on the floor in contempt.

"I would rather die!" He shouted back.

Merrick frowned. "Tis a pity then, as you wish."

He charged Martin, metal hitting against metal, parrying about the room, deflecting each other's blows. Occasionally locking arms and swords, only to have Merrick shove Martin back, preparing for another attack. His blade lanced Martin's left shoulder. The wound wasn't too deep, but deep enough to slow Martin down.

Merrick smirked at his son's predicament. Martin's left arm dropped for a brief second as he readjusted his sword, accounting for the injury to his shoulder. His father took that moment to swing his sword with expert precision, lancing Martin's right shoulder, in the same manner as his left.

Martin winced and staggered back. Both shoulders were injured, making fighting with the heavy sword increasingly more difficult. But that was Merrick's intent – to slowly wound his son and render him defenseless, so he could be killed at his leisure.

Martin's nose and upper eye were bleeding profusely. He wiped away blood with the back of his gloved hand, angry that his father was getting the better of him.

Merrick sneered, circling his son like a predator ensnaring his prey, a feeling Martin was not accustomed to. Martin backed up closer to the fire, looked down and quickly picked up a burning log from the fireplace and tossed it at his father's head.

Merrick threw up his hand to deflect the log, but not before hot ash fell into his eyes. It was his turn to wince. He wiped his eyes rapidly, giving Martin a fraction of a second to reposition himself.

"That's the spirit!" said Merrick. The ash left gray smudges across his face, like he was wearing a mask. Martin thought if his father was going to behave as a monster, then he might as well look the part.

The pain in Martin's shoulders and wrist intensified. Merrick dropped his sword and charged, pushing his son against the wall. He shoved his thumbs deep into Martin's open shoulder wounds. Martin grimaced and pushed him away with all his might.

Merrick laughed. "Are we having fun yet?" he asked.

Martin was hunched over, breathing rapidly. He tried to push the pain to the farthest recesses of his mind. He raised his sword once again. Merrick chuckled, bowing slightly at the waist, mocking his son's bravery. He raised his sword too.

"I am going to kill you! You sick bastard!" Martin shouted.

Merrick laughed at the insult. "Sticks and stones, my boy. Sticks and stones."

Merrick began poking Martin's legs with his sword, causing Martin to jump back, making a game out of it.

"Know your opponent, little boy," he said with contempt.

413

Martin rebounded and swiftly smacked Merrick's sword away. He brought his blade down on his father's arm, connecting slightly above the elbow, slicing into Merrick's flesh. He winced and pulled back.

"Know your opponent, old man!" Martin replied angrily.

The two men charged each other, again and again, throwing punches and swiping with their swords. They were locked in mortal combat, both inflicting bodily harm upon the other, in a fight to the death.

# Chapter Thirty

The pain in Emily's head intensified. She stumbled and leaned against the wall. Her visions seemed to be taking over. The screams she heard in her mind were making her dizzy, blinding her. She felt their pain. People being slaughtered. Martin being killed. She shook her head, trying to clear her mind. She had lost sight of him. She had lost his location. She looked around in the vast fortress unsure of which way to turn now.

She headed back to where she was held captive by Merrick, hoping that he would have returned there in search of her. She had to start looking someplace. Emily found the door ajar. Merrick or someone had come looking for her. She stepped inside to search for any clues they might have left behind. She found none.

She turned around and saw Martin slumped in the doorway, bloodied and bruised.

"Martin!" she gasped.

She ran to help him, but he put out his arm to stop her.

"Please do not touch me. Miranda is about to unleash the beast. We must stop her," Martin said urgently.

Emily stopped approaching him.

"But you're hurt. Let me help you," she said, visibly upset by his condition.

"I said no," Martin waved her off, blood dripping down his face.

"Where's Rayven?" she asked, looking past him.

"Dead," he replied somberly.

"And, Merrick?" she asked.

"I killed him. The only thing you need to concern yourself with now is getting to the caverns to stop the beast. Hurry, before it is too late," he urged.

He stepped aside from the door to let her exit. She was confused, but did as he asked.

"Okay," she said. "But I don't know how to get there."

"Keep going straight, turn left and down the staircase till you reach the end," he instructed.

"Okay," she said, hurrying down the corridor with Martin limping behind her. She looked over her shoulder. "Let me help you," she offered again.

"No," he snapped. "Keep moving. We must hurry."

She faced forward and kept going.

A heavy-set man carrying baskets of food came towards them. "Step aside! Step aside!" he ordered, shoving them out of the way.

Emily moved aside to clear his path. She stopped next to a stain-glass window and pressed against the wall to let the stout man get past her. She caught her reflection in a mirror hanging on the opposite wall. Martin was behind her.

Then, she saw it.

The evil grin…

It wasn't Martin at all.

It was Donovan!

She raised her sword and spun around to face him once the man had moved past.

"You?" she said angrily.

Martin's image vanished before her eyes. In its place stood Donovan, smiling wickedly.

"Give me that," he said, pointing to her necklace.

"Over my dead body," she snapped back.

"If you wish," he said and closed his eyes.

Emily immediately felt an intense pressure in her head and sensed Donovan's intrusion into her mind.

She was outside the fortress now in a world created solely by the boy. Strange creatures circled her. They were snapping at Emily. The sky was on fire and molten rock pellets rained down upon her, burning into her flesh. Her skin started to bubble from the heat. She assumed this was another trick he was playing on her, but the pain she felt was real. She was powerless to stop the scene unfolding before her.

He was in total control of her thoughts. It was an unsettling feeling and she fought hard to regain control. She looked down and watched her flesh burning.

*Now you understand my power, don't you?*

He spoke to her mind.

"Stop it!" she screamed.

No one heard her in Donovan's world.

She couldn't even move. Her will had been completely stripped from her. Donovan forced her to take out her dagger and turn it towards herself. Her body shook in violent protest, fighting his efforts to cause harm to herself.

He was so powerful.

The tip of her dagger pricked her flesh. She winced from the pain. Donovan grinned, pushing further into her mind.

Suddenly, Emily was back home in Glendale, standing in her kitchen, listening to her parents talk about her.

*"She's always been such a disappointment,"* her father said. Her mother nodded.

*"She's never going to amount to anything."*

*"Maybe we should send her away?"* her father suggested.

*"Send her away?"* her mother asked.

*"It might be for the best,"* he added.

*"Get rid of her?"*

*"Yes, get rid of her,"* her father agreed.

He was invading her thoughts, trying to learn everything he could about her, to use it against her. She could feel him rifling through her mind, compartmentalizing her memories at rapid speed. Emily pushed back.

"Stop! I know what you're doing!" she yelled at the boy.

He was trying to weaken her. The dagger broke her skin. She felt the warmth of her own blood running down her neck. He had total control over her.

Suddenly, she felt another presence in her mind, warm and comforting. It was protecting her, pushing Donovan back, strengthening her mentally and physically. She relaxed her mind. It surrounded her with energy.

417

Emily opened her eyes. She was floating above the ground, moving towards the clouds. One of her dragon friends flew by. She waved at it. Another dragon circled overhead. She felt the beating of its wings. A cool breeze blew through her hair. She felt a calmness wash over her.

The look on Donovan's face changed. He frowned angrily and tried to regain control of her again, unsure of this new power she was exhibiting.

The dragons spoke to her mind, calming her thoughts and steadying her hand. They shielded her with their power. Emily let her mind release itself to the keystone. She let herself be guided by the dragons to push Donovan out of her mind.

She found herself hovering in a black crevice with a door in front of her. A bright blinding white light was shining through the door, representing freedom. Donovan was still lurking in the dark recesses of her mind. He was trying to pull her back into the darkness.

Emily resisted. She slowly floated towards the light. She was completely absorbed by it. She turned and faced the door. She watched her hand reach out and slam it shut, closing her mind off to the intruder.

Donovan was locked out. The force of the keystone lifted him off the floor and propelled him violently back against the fortress wall. He opened his eyes, surprised and stunned. He looked at Emily, furious that he had lost his toy. He stood up and glared at her.

Emily was equally furious that he had invaded her mind. She wasted no time whatsoever. She walked up to Donovan and smacked him across his face, causing his head to snap back. His face flushed with anger.

He flew into a rage and tried to grab her throat. She easily defended herself. He was small and no physical match for Emily. She smacked the boy a second time and he fell down.

"Stay down," she ordered.

He looked shocked.

He didn't listen.

Instead, he stood up and lunged at her. Emily remembered Martin's training and stepped quickly aside. Her actions infuriated Donovan. The more frustrated he grew, the more reckless he became. In stark contrast, Emily remained calm, deflecting his slaps.

"Stop it," she shouted, as he tried to scratch her face. "What is wrong with you?"

He yelled angrily, "I'm going to kill you!"

Emily frowned. "I don't think so."

She pushed him away and he fell on his backside. Donovan jumped to his feet and charged at Emily. She stepped to the side before he could impact her body.

He plunged headfirst through the stained-glass window. Colored glass shattered everywhere. He grabbed the window ledge, clinging for dear life. Dangling high above the ground, he struggled to pull himself back up.

"Help me!" he called out.

He looked back at Emily and down at the dark depths below. His face registered fear. Emily grabbed him and started pulling him back inside. Donovan grabbed her wrists. But instead of allowing Emily to pull him in, he attempted to pull her out of the window. She planted her feet firmly and tried to get him to release his grip.

"Get off me," she shouted.

He used both of his hands to pull her over the ledge, digging his nails into her flesh. He locked eyes on her and grinned. He tried to enter her mind again. She felt a stabbing pain in her head. The dizziness was creeping back in. Emily's eyes fluttered and she felt like she was losing her balance. She was leaning perilously out the window.

His hand reached upwards, trying to grab the necklace dangling precariously between them. The keystone pulsated brightly and hummed in protest.

"Let me go!" she shouted.

Emily pulled back with all her might, using her legs as leverage to brace herself, struggling to bring herself back inside the fortress window. She let out a fierce battle cry, often used in the forest when being chased by her imaginary dragons.

With one final tug, her hands broke free of Donovan's grasp. He lost his grip and plummeted downward, bouncing off the side, and screaming in terror. His eyes wide with disbelief.

Emily watched his body tumble and fall, until she could no longer see him. Donovan disappeared somewhere below, falling into the dark river that ran next to the south side of the fortress.

"I'm sorry," she said sincerely.

Emily had not intended to kill the boy. She was trying to stop him from pulling her out the window. She was trying to save him. She turned back in search of Martin.

~~~~~~~~~~~~~~~~~~~~~

Isabeau had been resting, deep in quiet reflection. They were waiting for Emily to come back. She was overcome with a strong sense of dread. She knew not of its origins but sensed that something terrible was happening. A wave of nausea crept over her. She closed her eyes trying to see with her mind. She was not as strong as she used to be, and the visions were faint. She gathered all her remaining strength and brought them into focus.

She saw Martin and Merrick embroiled in bitter combat with one another. Death for one was close at hand. She turned to Philip.

"Please take me to Merrick," she urged.

He looked at her, "What? I can't do that. Emily said…"

Isabeau interrupted him, "I am aware of what Emily said, but I need to leave now. Do you know where Merrick's living quarters are?" she asked.

He stared blankly at her.

"Yes…yes, I do."

She stood slowly, holding the chair for support.

"Take me there at once, please," she asked politely.

He didn't want to argue with her. He held her elbow for support. He didn't like this at all. Not one bit. They were supposed to be hiding from Merrick, not going to him. He sighed and helped Isabeau navigate the hallways towards his Merrick's quarters.

~~~~~~~~~~~~~~~~~~~~~~~~~~~

,

Emily was getting frustrated. She couldn't find Martin. She saw a small crowd gathered outside of a closed door. She hurried towards them and heard the commotion inside. She reached for the door and pushed it open.

She was not prepared for what she saw. Emily put her hand over her mouth and gasped. Merrick and Martin had beaten each other to a pulp. They were barely recognizable.

"Oh my God," she said under her breath.

Martin couldn't feel his wrist anymore. His body was racked with pain. One of his eyes was swollen shut. He didn't even have the strength to defend himself. Merrick faired only slightly better. He was attacking Martin wildly, like a rabid dog.

Emily held her sword by her side, unsure of what to do. It made her physically ill to see Martin this way. She suddenly felt small and useless. A million thoughts came crashing down on her all at once. She wanted to protect him, save him. He was her friend. But more than that, he was family. She loved him.

Hatred brought Martin and Merrick to the brink of insanity, with neither yielding, despite their broken bodies. It only spoke to the strength of hatred. But wasn't love equally as strong?

Aquila was a paradox – the best and the worst colliding together. Emily was overcome with emotions. She was oblivious to the tears streaming down her face, unaware that she had been holding her breath – frozen, as she witnessed father and son literally beating each other to death. It was heartbreaking.

Her mind flashed to when she first met Martin in the clearing – warning her of becoming a dragon's dinner. Standing outside of the clinic – poking him. Staring at his back for hours, walking to Mira's castle. His unrelenting tolerance at how obnoxious she

421

could be. Attacks by the raiders. Saving her life, multiple times. Learning he was her grandma's brother – her great uncle. Her newfound respect and admiration for him.

The scars on his back… Scars from battle and scars from abuse. His unwavering protection of her. The chainmail tunic she now wore that once belonged to him. The photo album and his raw emotion at seeing his sister's image. Dogs in sweaters. Zap. Riding on the wings of dragons. Saving Grace. Saving Isabeau. Saving Aquila. Could she save Martin?

How much blood needed to spill before enough was enough? This is not the outcome she had hoped for. She knew Martin wanted revenge against his father, but this was pointless violence.

In her mind, she spoke to him, trying to reach him.

*Martin, please stop.… He's not worth dying for.*

She thought of the boy Martin held in the air, his son. He looked so happy. She wished he would just walk away – concede – live to fight another day and find happiness, before it was too late. She wished she could take away all his pain.

But she couldn't open her mouth to speak. She couldn't understand all this hatred. Certainly, there was a better way? She called out to Thalien in her mind. Maybe he could help?

It was obvious that Martin wasn't going to last much longer. He was dying. She couldn't conceive of a world without him in it. What could Emily Richardson of Glendale, California, do to stop any of this?

Martin and Merrick were so focused on killing each other, from the hatred that consumed them, that they didn't even notice Emily was standing in the room, watching.

Emily closed her eyes, calling out to Thalien again. Isabeau said Miranda's dark magic controlled this world. Was Thalien even hearing her desperate plea? She had to find her courage. She couldn't just stand by and watch Martin die.

She had never known fear like this before. She looked back at the door behind her. For a second, she thought of fleeing. But just for a second.

She touched the keystone hanging around her neck.

Be worthy of it, Emily.

Be worthy of it…

She turned back to face them. Merrick struck his son again. Martin staggered backwards. Seeing him so broken, emotionally and physically, was too much for Emily. The only thing holding Martin upright was his hatred for his father.

He had saved her so many times.

It was her turn to save him.

Find your courage…

She closed her eyes and took a deep breath, wiping the tears from her eyes. She wanted Martin to see her strong, not scared.

Find your courage…

"Martin," she said, barely a whisper.

He turned his head towards her.

Their eyes locked.

Emily fought back tears again. Unspoken words were exchanged in that glance. He wiped blood away from his only good eye. She smiled weakly at him, trying to be brave, bringing her sword to the front. Her hands were trembling.

Martin understood her intentions to fight Merrick, on his behalf. He shook his head no.

"Emily… no…go now…for me…," he begged, coughing up blood as he spoke. He pleaded with her. Hearing him struggling to speak, gutted her. She glared at Merrick and felt anger rise within her.

She shook her head no, refusing to leave.

Merrick turned to face her.

Emily brought her sword up higher, struggling to support its weight. She pointed it towards Merrick and moved closer to Martin. She placed herself between the two men. She summoned her courage and shouted at Merrick with fierce determination.

"Get away from him!"

Her heavy sword shook nervously in front of her. Merrick spit blood onto the floor and looked at her with amusement. She was way out of her depth. She could barely hold her sword off the ground.

"Get away from him!" she shouted again.

"Surely you are joking?"

"Get back!" she ordered, jabbing her sword at Merrick.

He scoffed at her, with blood dripping down his chin. She barely came up to his chest. The idea of this girl trying to fight him was absurd.

"Is this your reinforcement?" he chuckled, directing his insult to Martin.

Emily let out her battle cry and ran at Merrick, with all the strength she could muster. He moved slightly and caught her wrist before she made contact. He responded by backhanding her so hard that she dropped to the ground. She tasted blood in her mouth. She looked up at Merrick and glared at him.

Martin reached out for Emily, but she was beyond his grasp. "Your fight… is with me…not… the girl," he pleaded with his father. Each breath he took was difficult. Martin tried to come to Emily's aid, but his knees buckled beneath him.

Merrick laughed hideously.

"Em…, please…go," Martin begged of her. He gurgled as he spoke. Blood had entered his lungs.

Merrick noticed the chainmail tunic she was wearing and recognized its insignia.

"Was that not yours?" he asked Martin with a chuckle. "Nice touch, but it will not save her."

"Leave… her…alone," Martin begged.

Emily stood up and charged Merrick for a second time. Her sword was far too heavy to be of any use to her. She could not wield it.

Merrick easily moved aside. He grabbed her by her hair and yanked her off the ground. She pulled out her dagger and swung it wildly in his direction. But his reach was far longer than hers and she hit nothing but air. He flung her to the side and sent her crashing into the firewood, knocking the wind out of her.

Merrick walked to Martin and kicked him. Emily stood up quickly and picked up her dagger, which had fallen out of her hand.

"I said, leave him alone!" she demanded, waving the dagger in his direction.

Martin pushed himself up.

"Emily…stop…please stop…," he begged, barely audible. He didn't want Emily to get killed because of him. He slowly stood, holding on to the table for support.

"Touching." Merrick sneered.

Merrick turned his attention back to his son, ignoring Emily. He did not regard her as a credible threat.

Emily picked up her sword. She swung it like a golf club and lanced the back of Merrick's leg. He cried out and fell to one knee. He stood up and faced Emily. He grabbed her chainmail tunic and lifted her off the ground again. Her sword fell out of her hands. He held her inches away, studying her face.

"That was quite rude, child," he spewed.

Emily clawed at his hands, trying to free herself.

"You're like the worse father ever," she snapped. "I can't believe I'm related to you." She regretted saying that as soon as the words left her mouth.

Merrick's eyes widened. So, it was true… He had suspected as much from the images he found on the wall.

"Behave yourself or…," he warned her.

She cut him off. "Or what? Monster!" she yelled.

He frowned. "So I have been told."

"Well, it's true."

Merrick was distracted by Emily, verbally sparring with her. He had his back to his son. Martin staggered across the room, reached down and picked up Emily's sword. He plunged the weapon into his father's back. He pulled out the sword and let it drop. Merrick immediately released Emily and fell to the ground, grimacing in pain. It was a mortal wound. Martin grabbed Emily's arm and pulled her away from Merrick, before he too collapsed to the ground.

Emily started tugging at Martin. "Come on, let's go," she said. "We have to get out of here."

He shook his head no. "This...ends today," he said, barely getting the words out.

"No, not like this. I can't do this without you. Can't we just go?" Emily buried her head in his chest and started to cry. She didn't understand.

Martin tried to comfort her. But every move he made was agonizing. He reached into his tunic, pulled out a bundled cloth and passed it to Emily. She opened it. The photo album she had given him was wrapped inside of it.

"Thank you," he whispered, trying not to lose consciousness. Martin was wheezing from a punctured lung.

Emily called out to Thalien again.

"Hang in there, Martin, please," she begged him.

Merrick was lying on his back, near death. He turned his head to look at Martin.

"Son... Forgive me," he whispered.

Martin stared at him.

"Son...please. I'm dying," Merrick moaned, reaching out a bloody hand to Martin, hoping his son would take it.

Martin blinked hard, struggling to breathe. He pulled himself closer to his father. Emily grabbed hold of him.

"Martin, no," she pleaded, trying to pull him back.

Martin squeezed her hand.

"Martin, don't," she urged.

He dragged himself closer to his father, trying to reach his hand. When Martin was within reach, Merrick swiftly plunged his dagger into Martin's body.

Emily screamed out loud. "Nooooooo!!!!"

She started kicking Merrick with her boot to get him away from Martin. She pulled Martin away, by sheer will alone. Blood poured from Martin's wound, spilling onto the floor. His father's dagger was still embedded in his chest, puncturing his other lung.

"Thalien!" Emily screamed.

He struggled for air. Martin's strength was gone. He fought to stay awake amid Emily's cries, clinging to the sound of her voice. She was frantic. She didn't know what to do. She screamed for Thalien, while crying for Martin. She held him tightly, cradling his head. If fallen tears and love were enough to save Martin? He would have lived forever.

"Martin," she cried, "Please, stay with me. Martin?"

He looked at her face and squeezed her hand.

"No," she cried.

She shook him repeatedly, sobbing. Emily's cries faded away. He felt cold and the sounds around him went silent. He could no longer hear Emily crying out for him.

Martin's mind floated back to the grove and his 10th birthday party. He saw his mother and father holding his baby sister. They were happy. He was happy. His mind continued to float back to that moment. All else around him was fading slowly to black. He felt his feet upon the grass outside of their castle and heard the sounds of merriment around him.

He was home… finally home. It was fitting that this was where he would meet his end. His mind had taken him back to the last time he had felt true happiness, sparing him from further physical pain.

Merrick swung his dagger blindly in the air, attempting to strike Emily. He was trying to kill her too. Emily kicked away his hand, while clinging to Martin's lifeless body.

"Go away!" she screamed at Merrick.

Suddenly, the door burst open.

"Merrick, no!" Isabeau shouted with all her might.

Both Emily and Merrick turned their heads towards the door. The light from the hallway illuminated Isabeau's pale gown in such a way that Emily thought for a moment that she was an angel.

Isabeau stepped into the room.

Emily turned her attention back to Martin. He was no longer responsive. She listened for a heartbeat, but there was none. Emily put her head on his chest and began to sob, begging Martin to come back, shaking him gently.

Martin was dead.

Merrick dropped his dagger, stunned by the vision of his beloved wife standing in front of him – alive.

"Stop, I am begging you," Isabeau pleaded.

Merrick blinked hard, unable to fathom what he was seeing. He dragged his battered body to Isabeau, wrapped his arms around her legs and let out an ungodly cry.

"Isabeau?" he sobbed uncontrollably. "How…how can this be?" he asked, sobbing at her feet. "How can I be looking upon your face again?"

Isabeau reached out her hand to Philip. He helped her kneel. She raised her husband's head and took his face in her hands.

"You have been lied to for far too long, my love. I have been imprisoned here all these lonely years. This young girl and boy set me free," she told him softly, using her long robe to wipe the blood away from his face.

Philip ran to Emily's side to help with Martin, but it was too late. Martin was gone. Emily was holding him, weeping. Philip ran to his sister. She was lying motionless against the wall. Her breathing was shallow, but she was still alive.

Merrick locked eyes with Isabeau and touched her face softly with his mangled hand, "I do not understand," he said. He buried his head at her feet, in shame.

She looked down at her husband and then at her son lying dead on the floor. She lowered her head, crying silent tears.

"Miranda poisoned your mind and blackened your heart," she wept. "You abandoned our children, Merrick. How could you do such a thing? They needed you."

Merrick looked back at Martin's body lying on the floor, motionless and then back at his wife.

"I have killed our son," he wept uncontrollably, releasing years of pain and anguish. The monster within him was swept away at the realization of his wrongful deeds. "I am so sorry," he said repeatedly. "Forgive me…"

Isabeau did not reply. She stroked Merrick's hair and looked upon her son's lifeless body.

Emily was crying uncontrollably now. Miranda's hold over this world was strong, but Emily knew that the keystone was more powerful. She held on tightly to the keystone and slowed down her breathing, trying to summon the healer to her side. The keystone pulsated and hummed loudly, drowning out the cries she heard from Merrick and Isabeau.

*Thalien...Thalien...Thalien...*

Emily summoned him desperately with her thoughts. She felt herself floating, reaching beyond the borders of the dark side. Her mind finally broke through and Thalien responded instantly.

*I am here...* the voice in her head spoke.

Emily gasped and opened her eyes.

Thalien was kneeling beside Martin, deep in concentration. A bright light emanated from his palms. He placed his hands over Martin's body. The light grew brighter, engulfing Martin's body.

Emily lowered her head in prayer, holding on to Martin's hand, waiting for some sign that he could be saved. Somewhere beyond the darkness, Emily sensed Mira's presence too. She was using her powers to shower Martin in a healing light, penetrating Miranda's magic. Isabeau and Merrick watched silently at those trying to save their son's life.

Emily concentrated her efforts on the keystone, channeling its energy to breathe life back into Martin's battered body. It hummed and grew brighter with every breath she took.

When she opened her eyes, she was standing in the clearing where she had first met Martin. She heard the sound of horse hooves pounding on the ground. She turned to see Martin pull back on the reigns. His horse bucked and threw him to the ground. She smiled. He stood, brushed off his trousers, scolded his horse and glared at her.

"Hey, sorry about that," she said. "I should have watched where I was going."

His anger subsided. "Yes, well in the future be more careful."

"I will," she smiled at him.

A dragon's shrill cry echoed through the valley. They both turned towards the sound.

"You best be off. You do not want to become a dragon's dinner now, do you?" he warned, while mounting his horse.

"It was nice seeing you again, Martin," she said.

He gave her an odd look.

"How do you know my name?" he asked.

"It doesn't matter. Have a nice day," she waved.

"You as well," he nodded.

"Martin?"

He turned back to look at her.

"Come back, please..."

He stared at her for a moment before pulling on the reigns of his horse and riding down the path. She watched him go and put her hand around her necklace and closed her eyes.

"Come back, Martin...please..."

Minutes seemed like hours.

She opened her eyes when she heard Martin gasp for air.

"Martin?" she cried. Her eyes widened.

Thalien continued moving his hands over Martin, engulfing him in a healing light. Martin's eyes fluttered momentarily and he stared blankly at the ceiling. The wounds on his body healed right before Emily's eyes.

"Martin? Say something," she asked, watching him breathe slowly, but steadily.

"Am I dead?" he whispered softly.

Thalien smiled, "No, not yet."

Emily grinned and hugged Martin tightly, relieved and grateful. Martin grunted at the brute force of her embrace.

"I thought we lost you!" She hugged him again.

He groaned loudly.

"You just might, if you do not stop squeezing me so hard," he told her, a faint smile crossed his face.

She laughed through happy tears.

Martin looked up at Emily. "I dreamt I met you in the glen," he recalled. "You all but admitted fault at my horse throwing me." He winked at her.

Emily laughed and hugged him again.

"Thalien, thank you," she smiled up at him.

"You are most welcome, my child," he motioned towards Martin. "He will need time to fully heal," he advised.

Philip and Emily helped Martin sit up.

He was alive. Stiff and sore, but otherwise in good condition. Only then did he see his mother kneeling beside his father's broken body. There was no mistaking the shocked expression on his face.

"Mother?"

"Yes, my son," she said softly, overjoyed that he was alive.

Martin shook his head.

"This is a trick. It is that boy... the shifter. That is not my mother," he protested angrily, not believing his eyes.

Emily interrupted him.

"No, Martin. Donovan's dead. I watched him fall to his death. It's really Isabeau. She's been alive all this time. Miranda kept her prisoner here. She didn't die. It was a lie," she explained, trying to reassure him.

Martin searched Emily's eyes for the truth. He reached out to touch his mother's hand. It was all too much to comprehend.

"Mother," he said through tears of joy.

She looked lovingly into her son's eyes and gently touched his fingertips. "My son..."

Thalien moved to Merrick and began to heal him.

"Thank you," Isabeau said sincerely.

"Lovely to see you again," Thalien smiled.

"Well, well, well... This is quite the happy family reunion," Miranda's voice boomed from the doorway.

All eyes turned towards the door.

# Chapter Thirty-One

A heavy fog stretched out like fingers, slowly covering all the land on the dark side. The vast army moved across the dark land. The mist wall was weakening, with only a thin veil between the dark and light sides. The soldiers grew restless and eager once they got their first glimpse of the other side. They were not facing a mighty army as many had feared. But instead, rows of farmers and ordinary folk awaited them, armed with shovels, brooms and pitchforks, ten deep in some spots. Several women and children were spotted among the ranks.

A rumor spread among the army that this was just a ruse, a deception on the part of the powerful sorceress of the light side, to lure them into a false sense of security. The army grew weary and nervous of this trickery. They believed that their eyes were deceiving them, as surely this was in no way an army worthy of defending the light side.

The captain of the guard gave the order and the army stopped moving forward. They marched in place and made battle cries in unison for several minutes. It was their way of warning those on the opposing forces that they were preparing to attack.

"Halt!" The commanding officer ordered.

A few of the villagers turned and fled into the forest at the sight of the army coming towards them from the dark side.

The Marshals cried out, "Steady, hold your ground."

They could see the fear on the villagers' faces. They were not soldiers, but they were willing to risk their lives to protect their homes.

"Volley!" shouted the captain of the guard from the dark side. The first row of soldiers raised arrows to their bows.

"Release!"

The sky filled with arrows, but they disintegrated the moment they hit what was left of the mist wall, giving the villagers a slight reprieve. Relief flowed like a wave among the townspeople.

The army on the dark side shouted in anger. They were tired of waiting. They taunted and hurled insults at the frightened people in front of them. Their vile threats fell on deaf ears. The sound was muted, lost in the mist wall.

Several soldiers ran into the mist wall, swords raised. The villagers in the front took a few steps back, bracing for the attack. The soldiers never appeared on the other side. The mist wall had absorbed them.

~~~~~~~~~~~~~~~~~~~~~~~

Miranda stood in the doorway looking down at its occupants with fiendish glee. Even she could not have orchestrated such a splendid performance with all the players assembled together.

Yet, here they were…

All of them – Merrick, Isabeau, Martin, the seeker, the thief, the girl and yes, the keystone.

She bowed slightly with her hands behind her back, as giddy as a young school girl.

"How absolutely delightful!" she said.

Martin stood slowly, moving Emily behind him. His eyes scanned the floor. The nearest weapon was several feet away. He inched towards it.

Miranda snapped her fingers at him.

"Do not do that," she ordered. "Stay put."

Martin and Emily glanced at each other. Merrick was not yet fully healed. He tried to stand, but his legs gave way beneath him.

Everyone froze in place and watched Miranda.

She glided further into the room and stopped in front of Isabeau, regarding her with great interest.

"The two lovers reunite, I see. How quaint," she hissed.

Isabeau raised her hand towards Miranda, trying to be diplomatic. "It does not have to be this way," she said softly.

Miranda immediately slapped Isabeau across the face, causing her to cry out in pain.

"Silence!" She hissed at Isabeau. "Do not think for one second you have permission to address me!"

Martin moved towards his mother. Miranda snapped her fingers at him again.

"I said stay put, did I not?" she warned.

Merrick reached up and took Isabeau in his arms. Objects began to levitate and move around the room under Miranda's control. She was using her black magic to manipulate her surroundings and those in it.

Thalien stood and took a step back from Merrick. Miranda caught his movement.

"And, you…you do not belong in my world!" she said to him with distain. She pushed her palm towards him, encasing Thalien inside a clear liquid substance. He could only move his eyes, helplessly watching the scene before him.

A dark mist rose up from beneath Miranda's feet and swirled angrily around her. It spread across the ceiling, until the entire room was surrounded by dark energy. Miranda had them trapped inside the room. Her eyes glowed crimson red, and darted quickly from person to person, assessing the situation.

"Shall we play a game?" she sneered, showing her rotted teeth. She looked down at Isabeau. Merrick pulled his wife closer to him, trying to protect her.

Miranda scoffed. "I am glad you could all join me to witness the birth of my new world. We have indeed come full circle."

She sighed deeply and leered at Isabeau. She lifted her hand towards the vaulted ceiling. Isabeau started to rise off the ground. Merrick grabbed her legs, but Miranda snapped her head sharply, breaking his hand in the process. He lost his grip on Isabeau.

Philip looked on in horror. To use magic in this way appalled him. His own parlor tricks were harmless. This was – madness. He thought desperately of some way to combat Miranda's black magic, but possessed no such skills.

Miranda fixed her gaze on Emily, lifting her off the ground like Isabeau, finding cruel amusement in their predicament.

"Martin, I can't move," Emily told him.

He reached back to grab her.

Miranda huffed, snapping her fingers more aggressively at Martin, annoyed by his disobedience.

"Exactly what part of staying put are you having difficulty comprehending?" she asked him. "Honestly, it is quite a simple request. Allow me to help you," she decided with a wicked grin. She waved her hand in the air.

Martin sunk into the floor. He tried to move, but the ground beneath his feet had turned to quicksand.

"I do not take orders from witches. You have me confused with my father," he said angrily.

Miranda snapped her fingers again to silence him.

"I will remove your mouth if you utter one more word," she warned. She looked at Merrick and Isabeau. "Have you taught your son no manners?"

Martin glanced at Emily. There was a sword floating directly in front of her, stopping short of impaling her. He glared at Miranda.

"Kindly stop glaring at me! Do not even blink. You do not scare me, son of Merrick. Behave yourself or I will eviscerate that child behind you!" she grinned sadistically.

He looked back and forth between Emily and his mother. Merrick continued to reach for Isabeau, to no avail.

"Miranda, stop," Merrick said weakly.

"Stop? Surely you jest. You want me to stop?" she asked, sneering at him.

Merrick nodded, never taking his eyes off Isabeau. Miranda saw the love in his eyes for his wife. The love he had never shown her. It was more than she could stand. It was Isabeau again. It was always about Isabeau. Her mere existence cost Miranda everything – Merrick, her child, her freedom. Miranda could control many things, but she could not control her jealousy.

"Look at me, Merrick," Miranda ordered.

He refused. He would not take his eyes off Isabeau. Husband and wife had their eyes locked on one another, as if they knew what was to come next. They held that moment for as long as possible, exchanging unspoken words. Conveying their love for one another with a knowing glance. Their loving gaze enraged Miranda.

"You want me to stop?" she asked again. "As you wish…"

She nodded and brought her other hand from behind her back, revealing a long decorative blade. Without taking her eyes off Merrick, Miranda plunged the knife deep into Isabeau's back.

Isabeau screamed out in pain. Merrick and Martin cried out. Miranda was intoxicated by their anguish, inhaling deeply with satisfaction. She lifted Isabeau higher, as blood flowed down to the floor beneath her feet, staining her gown dark red.

Merrick immediately tried to stand, but Miranda flicked her wrist and the sound of his ankles breaking followed. He fell back down, unable to stand, pulling himself desperately towards his wife. She was bleeding to death.

"No, please no!" Merrick cried out in anguish.

Martin and Emily watched in horror, as Isabeau's head slumped forward. She was losing consciousness. She raised her head and looked lovingly at her son and husband.

"I love you both with all my heart," she whispered.

"No," Emily whimpered.

Isabeau turned her head slowly towards Emily. Their eyes locked.

"You have the power…Do not be afraid," Isabeau smiled weakly at Emily, before closing her eyes and succumbing to her wound.

Both men called out to her, but she was gone. Lost to them once again. Merrick lowered his head and sobbed. Miranda watched the entire exchange with delight and amusement. She brushed off her hands triumphantly.

"I have been wanting to do that for a very long time," she sighed, referring to killing Isabeau.

Martin was sinking deeper into the floor. It was almost covering his legs now. He was totally powerless. Merrick was sobbing, unable to save himself or his beloved wife.

Miranda moved closer to Merrick, stroking his hair, much to his chagrin. He swatted her hand away. She laughed hysterically at his puny attempts to cast her aside.

"Oh, Merrick," she teased. "You always did play hard to get, my dear."

Merrick cursed at her.

Emily looked on in horror, letting Isabeau's words sink in.

*You have the power...*

*Do not be afraid...*

Miranda's dark energy swirled around the room like a toxic fume. Emily could feel it slowly draining the life out of her.

*You have the power...*

Isabeau's words echoed in her head.

Miranda raised her hand and lifted Isabeau's lifeless body to the top of the vaulted ceiling, propping her up like a decoration. She stood back to admire her work. She savored the sobs around her and fed off their torment. Miranda sniffed the air like a crazed animal, as if she could literally smell their pain. She was exhilarated by it. The wicked grin never left her face.

This was her moment. She intended to enjoy it.

Emily struggled to move, but she had no control over her body. The sword teetered inches from her midsection.

*You have the power...*

Those words had meaning. Emily closed her eyes and let her mind drift far away from Miranda's fortress. She found herself surrounded by dragons. The stone beneath her hummed loudly.

*What can I do?*

She asked the Council of Dragons. They lowered their heads and moved closer to Emily, until their wing tips were touching her. The dragons spoke to her, repeating Isabeau's words.

*You have the power....*

In her mind, she saw the birth of stars and the death of them. She saw the explosion that happens right before their light was extinguished and the shockwave that followed. That power resided within her. The power of the stars and all the cosmos. The power to pass through time and space. The power to harness energy and the elements that surround them.

*You have the power...*

The dragons told her again.

*The power lies within you...*

All this time she believed that the necklace was the source of the power, but it was only one link in a chain. The keystone was a mere conduit. She touched the jewel resting gently on her neck. She was connected to everything around her, and the dragons helped her fully realize this fact.

The true power resided within her.

She lifted her hand to touch each one of the dragons, grateful for their friendship and guidance. Emily returned to the chamber where Miranda was acting upon her vengeance, bringing about her self-proclaimed prophecy.

Emily slowed down her breathing, drowning out the noise around her. She focused her attention on the keystone and the power it granted her. She reached deeper within herself, letting the energy flow through her body.

Her eyes rolled back into her head. She allowed the keystone to consume her lifeforce. It bonded with her on a cellular level. She became one with it, in mind, body and spirit. She felt the knowledge of space and time flowing through her mind. She could feel the energy coursing through her veins. Emily and the keystone merged into one and she gave herself willingly to it.

It was exhilarating and terrifying at the same time. A sense of utter peace and calmness crept over her. Gone were the self-doubts of her childhood. She had transformed into the young warrior princess that she had always envisioned. It was no longer a necklace that she wore around her neck.

She understood Isabeau's words.

She did have the power.

Emily *was* the keystone.

# Chapter Thirty-Two

Emily's entire body flowed with energy. A door to a whole new world had opened up to her. This is who she was. This is who she was always meant to be. Emily smiled. She was a songbird, finding her wings to fly for the very first time. She felt stronger now than ever before.

She opened her eyes and looked around. It was a chaotic situation. Miranda's black mist was swirling around them all. Isabeau was displayed on the ceiling like a Christmas decoration. Martin was slowly sinking into the floor, while being struck by objects flying around the room. Meanwhile, Miranda was toying with Merrick in some macabre lover's quarrel. She bent over to kiss his forehead. He violently shoved her away with his forearms. Miranda picked up the bottom of her robe and danced around the room, euphoric in the belief that she was victorious.

Martin looked back over his shoulder at Emily. He saw her eyes beginning to glow, in a piercing purplish hue. For a brief moment, he thought Miranda was doing something to hurt her. But then Emily glanced at Martin, for a flash of a second, and grinned. He knew that grin.

Emily turned her palms outward to face Miranda and pushed both hands forward. A purple energy pulse, like a lightning bolt, erupted from her hands, striking Miranda with such force that it knocked the sorceress square off her feet.

The shockwave broke Miranda's spell immediately. Emily was no longer floating off the ground, nor was Martin sinking into the floor. Thalien was free from his liquid prison. Isabeau floated gently to the ground and into Merrick's arms.

Martin looked at Emily in astonishment.

Dazed, Miranda scrambled to her feet, looking for the source of the attack. She was infuriated. Miranda pointed an accusatory bony finger at Emily. Her mouth opened to speak, but Emily was having none of it. Before Miranda had a chance to utter one word,

Emily thrust her hands forward again. This time with more force. She hit Miranda with another energy pulse so strong that it sent shockwaves across Aquila. Miranda was thrown clear out of the room and smashed into the corridor wall. She ran back into the room, screaming hysterically, practically frothing at the mouth.

Miranda raised her palms and hurled fireballs at Emily. Without so much as a word, Emily instantly froze Miranda's fireballs in midflight and redirected them back towards their master. Miranda was pelted with ice, shattering against her body.

The sorceress cried out in pain but sent more fireballs towards Emily, hoping to hit their mark this time. Emily looked at the fireballs spiraling towards her and lifted her hand. The fireballs looped in the air and sped back at Miranda. She had to swerve and duck to avoid being struck by her own magic. The top of her head started smoking. She'd been hit by a fireball. Miranda frantically swatted her hair, extinguishing the flame.

Martin grinned and cheered Emily on. She was fighting Miranda with a power she had not previously possessed. There was no need for Martin to intercede. Emily was handling the situation masterfully all by herself. He was grateful and proud, doubting very much that she would ever need his protection again. He was happy that this power was bestowed upon her.

Merrick was holding his wife's lifeless body, watching Emily defeat Miranda. Thalien continued his efforts to heal Merrick. But Merrick pushed him away, not wanting to live without his beloved wife.

Thalien looked back over his shoulder for a moment to witness the young girl discover her true self.

"I never had any doubt," he said to himself. He found great comfort knowing that she was the bearer of the keystone and knew she would always use her power wisely.

Miranda stumbled around the room, unwilling to concede defeat. She was disheveled and crazed, screaming like a banshee.

Emily was perfectly calm, eyeing the sorceress curiously, wondering what trick Miranda was going to try next. Miranda raised her dagger high and charged towards Emily. She looked at the dagger Miranda was holding and focused on it. Suddenly, the blade glowed a fiery red, searing into Miranda's flesh. She screamed and dropped the blade immediately, nursing her severely burnt hand.

Miranda snarled and ran at Emily with her bare hands, like a raving lunatic. Emily frowned and hit the sorceress with another burst of energy. Miranda tumbled backwards several times and slammed into a wall. She struggled to get up.

The sorceress leaned on the doorframe and yelled at Emily. "You think you can stop me, child? Think again!" she bellowed, laughing hysterically. Miranda fled down the dark corridor.

Emily turned to Thalien.

"Please, take care of them," she asked, motioning towards Merrick, Isabeau and Rayven.

He nodded. "I shall do my best," he promised.

"They'll need you at the mist wall," she told him. "Please get there as soon as you can."

"We will be ready," he assured her.

Emily needed a moment. She took a deep breath to steady her nerves. Everything was happening so quickly. She had a sense of urgency to stop Miranda and protect those on the light side, but she needed to catch her breath first. Did I really just do that? She asked herself. Cool. Emily turned her attention to Martin.

"I think I made Miranda mad," she grinned.

"Indeed. There are no words for what I just witnessed," Martin said to her.

He took a step back, studying her carefully. She had come such a long way since they first met in the glen. He was trying not to get emotional, but could not help it.

Facing off against his father like she did? Showed a bravery that most men lacked. She mastered her fear instead of running from it. That took courage. She risked her life to save him. No one had ever done anything remotely like that for him before. How could he ever adequately express his gratitude for the sacrifice she was willing to make for him?

She stood there in front of him, wearing the chainmail tunic he once wore as a young boy, with her red bangs falling into her eyes. He smiled warmly at her.

"What?" she asked. "You're looking at me weird. I didn't grow a horn on my head, like a unicorn, did I? From the power?" She absently touched the top of her head. "Nope, no horn." She looked around at her backside. "No tail either. So... what's up?"

Martin cleared his throat and took a deep breath, choosing his words carefully to convey his deepest gratitude and sincerity.

"You saved my life. I want to thank you for that. You risked your own life in doing so. I want you to know that you will never stand alone. I pledge my life to you."

He bowed his head and placed his hand over his heart.

Emily's eyes widened. "Oh Geez, don't get all serious. It's me, okay? I'm still – me," she assured him.

He lifted his head and looked into her eyes, like he was looking directly into her soul. His unwavering gaze was making her nervous.

"Um, okay. So, am I supposed to tap you on your shoulder with my sword or something? I can tell you right now, you're going to have to kneel for that. I can barely lift that thing, but I suppose you noticed that. Or is there like a secret handshake?" she asked.

Martin grinned. "A secret handshake?"

"I don't know. I'm new at this," she reminded him.

He smiled at her fondly.

"You are truly one of a kind, Emily Richardson of Glendale," he said.

"So are you, Doctor Martin Stewart of Aquila," she smiled back at him.

The smile left her face and she grew serious.

"Look, you'd do the same for me. I was scared, okay? I've never been that scared before, ever in my life. Scared of losing you. Scared we were both going to get killed. But I had to protect you. And, I'd do it again, if I had to. Because you know? You're Martin. And, we're BFFs."

"BFFs?" he asked.

"Yea, BFFs – Best friends forever."

He saw her eyes tearing up. She stared at her boots, not wanting him to see her cry. He pulled her close, putting his arms around her. She leaned into him, letting the trauma from the past hours subside. He heard her muffled cries buried into his chest. She was so young, Martin reminded himself. It was a lot for her to contend with, and a heavy burden to carry.

"It has been quite a day, has it not?" he finally spoke, releasing her.

"Yea," she agreed., wiping her eyes.

He leaned over and kissed her on the forehead, brushing the bangs away from her eyes.

"Thank you, Emily," he said sincerely. "I am very proud of you."

"Thanks. That means a lot coming from you," she replied. Emily reached into her trouser pocket and handed Martin his photo album back. "This belongs to you," she said with a smile.

His eyes brightened and he smiled widely. He nodded at her and looked fondly at the album, before placing it safely within his pocket again.

Emily called to Philip. He hurried over, carrying their gear. He nodded to them both. His face blushed when he looked at Emily. Martin raised an eyebrow and grinned at Emily.

She stopped Martin before he opened his mouth.

"Don't even say it," she teased.

Martin laughed. Philip dropped the bags at their feet. Martin discarded the shirt he was wearing, torn and covered with dry blood. He dug into his bag for a clean tunic.

Emily grinned. "You're not going to smell like flowers again, are you?"

Philip reached down into the bag and grabbed a few of the fragrant bars Mira had given Emily.

"Smell this one?" He held it towards Emily.

Emily leaned forward and sniffed. "Oh, kind of smells like mint. Try this, Martin."

She poured water in her hand, dipped the soap into it and rubbed it on Martin's arm. Emily and Philip sniffed Martin.

"That's nice," Philip agreed.

Emily picked up another bar of soap and repeated the process. Then, she rubbed the soap on Martin's arm.

Martin looked at them both in astonishment.

"Oh wow, try this one," she said to Philip.

He sniffed Martin. Emily and Philip looked at each other.

"Vanilla." They said in unison.

"Heavens," Martin shooed them both away, "Kindly stop sniffing me. I am quite capable of bathing and changing myself, scoot!" He chuckled.

"Well, hurry it up. We have an invasion to stop," Emily said. She and Philip smacked a bar of soap into each of Martin's hands. Emily reached down into her own bag and pulled out her gray hoodie. She zipped it up and put the hood over her head. Martin read the back of it as she walked away – Unicorns Are Real.

He smirked, lifted one of the bars to his nose and sniffed.

"I saw that," Emily yelled back to him.

He grinned.

Martin glanced over at his father, still cradling Isabeau in his arms. Thalien worked tirelessly to heal him. Pathetic, Martin thought to himself. He glared at Merrick. He did not wish to be near his father any time soon. He despised the man. Nothing had changed that fact. He had tried to kill him and Emily both. As far as Martin was concerned, he wished his father dead. Martin's eyes dropped to his mother. Knowing she had been alive all this time was difficult to understand. Losing her again? There would be time to mourn later.

He joined Emily and Philip at the door.

Emily leaned in slightly towards Martin and sniffed.

"Vanilla," she whispered to Philip.

Philip chuckled.

"Stop. You are exhausting," Martin teased.

Martin stepped out into the darkened corridor and looked both ways. He walked over to an unattended cart and examined the various weapons piled within it. He picked up a sword and returned to Emily and Philip. He motioned for Emily to step towards him.

"Take this," he instructed. He handed her the sword.

She looked at him curiously. "I don't think I really need that anymore," she told him.

"That may be, but I would feel more comfortable if you were in possession of one. You do not have eyes in the back of your head and..." He sighed. "Do this for me, please."

She shrugged. "Sure. I don't really know how to use one," she reminded him.

"You made an admirable showing of yourself, Emily. When this has passed, I would be happy to teach you how to use the weapon properly," he offered.

She liked that idea.

"Cool."

She took the sword from Martin, turned it over in her hand and held it at waist level.

"How does it feel?" he asked.

"Better than the other one. That's for sure," she admitted.

"Good. It must become an extension of yourself. Feel the weight of it and the length. It is a good blade. It will do, until I can get you a more suitable one. Arms up," he told her.

She lifted her arms while Martin secured the sword to her side. "I'm left-handed," she pointed out. "I mean, I use both, but I'm more comfortable using my left."

He nodded and reversed the sword to the other side of her waist. "Much better," he said.

He rested his hand on the hilt of his own sword. Emily mirrored his movement. Martin smirked. She may not need a sword but he certainly felt better with her carrying one.

"Miranda is going to release the beast and send it to the light side. She's already conjured up a spell to control it. That bought us some time," she told them.

"Can you stop her from here?" Martin asked.

447

"No, from what the Council of Dragons told me, only they can stop it. Well, actually, I'm helping. I have to use my powers to contain it, while they kill it," she explained. She frowned, recalling the horrible vision of the epic battle in the sky. She knew it was about to come true.

Martin sighed. If that creature from the caves reached the outside? The unspeakable horror it would unleash was beyond comprehension.

"The mist wall is almost gone," she continued. "When I used my powers, the shockwave affected everything across Aquila. Martin, we need to go to the light side and help them defend themselves or a lot of people are going to get killed."

He nodded.

"Philip, I need you to save the children. Get them out."

He was somewhat taken aback by this responsibility.

"Me?"

"Yes, you. Use your magic to take care of the guards in the caverns. You have to get the children to safety," she urged.

"And, exactly how am I supposed to do that?" he asked. "You saw what was across the wastelands. If those monsters out there don't kill them, then the journey will," he reminded her.

"Free them. Reach out to me with your thoughts. Safe passage will be given," she explained.

He stared at her dumbfounded and looked at Martin.

"Philip, you have to trust me," she told him.

"I do," he admitted.

"Then, go!"

He hesitated, then quickly made his way to the bowels of the fortress on his rescue mission.

Emily put her hand on Martin's arm.

"Are you ready?" she asked.

"I am," he assured her.

"Close your eyes."

He soon found himself drifting into nothingness.

Miranda had never seen such power before. Certainly, none greater than her own. She raced down to the lower level with the potion she created. It would control the beast once it was beyond her borders. It was time to set it loose on Aquila.

The guards moved quickly out of her way as she entered the caverns. She stood in the entrance where the massive beast was imprisoned and looked up at it.

She uncorked the bottle in her hand and let its vapors filter into the air. The beast sniffed at it curiously. Miranda closed her eyes, claiming the beast's free will as her own, demanding that it do her bidding beyond the dark side.

"Go to the light. Devour all until the ground turns red," she ordered.

With a flick of her wrist, she removed the heavy metal collar around its neck. The beast roared triumphantly. The rest of its shackles fell to the ground.

It was free.

Free to feed.

Miranda waved her hand above her head and opened a huge grate running horizontal in a shaft above the creature's head. The beast looked back at her and roared again. It scampered and clawed its way up the walls of the shaft, until it was free from its prison.

Finally, able to spread its massive wings, it blocked out the moonlight for those standing beneath it, causing a moment of absolute darkness. It rose higher into the sky, spewing fire from its mouth and roared furiously with all its might. It banked left and headed north towards the mist wall, ready to feed at will. Ready to feast on flesh.

Miranda watched it disappear into the darkness, knowing full well what horror she had just unleashed on the inhabitants of Aquila's light side. She smiled at this accomplishment and took pride in the knowledge that many lives would be lost this day. She closed her eyes and sighed deeply. In her mind, she watched her beast fly towards its destination, and her army prepare to cross into the mist wall to slaughter all in their path.

# Chapter Thirty-Three

When Emily first unleashed the power of the keystone, the shockwave of energy was so intense that it immediately brought down the mist wall. Cheers and shouts from the army rang out and the order was given to advance. They marched towards the frightened ragtag force on the light side with no restraint.

The villagers and farmers fought bravely, but their crude weapons were ineffective. They were no match for trained soldiers. Their deaths were swift and merciless. Screams and cries filled the air, as Miranda's army brought down every man, woman and child that stood in their way.

An endless wave of soldiers crossed over where the mist wall once stood, undeterred and unstoppable. The ground soon turned red from the blood of innocent lives.

Emily and Martin materialized in the middle of the slaughter. Bodies were strewn around them in an ungodly carnage. Men, women and children tried to flee.

Martin immediately drew his sword and engaged in battle. Thalien had healed him, but he was not yet fully recovered. He felt sluggish, but his skills still far surpassed those of Miranda's army. He shielded Emily with his body, giving her time to act.

Emily stood motionless. She stared at the blood-soaked ground. She knew what she had to do. She closed her eyes and opened her mind, letting her power guide her.

The keystone around her neck glowed. A purple light swirled within Emily's eyes. She thrust her hands forward. An energy wave shot across the land towards the opposing army. A loud boom followed. The shockwave lifted the soldiers off their feet and knocked them to the ground.

Confused by this new threat, some turned and fled back to the dark side, while others stood their ground and charged towards her. She directed another powerful burst of energy towards them. It knocked the remaining soldiers down and sent them hurtling backwards towards the mist wall. Every time they stood up, Emily hit them with another powerful energy wave until they were all, once again, standing behind the mist wall.

The commander shouted orders at the men to rejoin the ranks and attack, sending a volley of arrows flying into the sky towards Emily and whatever townspeople remained.

She lifted her eyes at the arrows heading towards them and held her palm upwards. The arrows immediately changed course. To the dismay of the soldiers, their own weapons were used against them. They were showered with their own arrows, bringing the vast majority of them down. More soldiers turned and fled. The commander ordered his men to stand their ground and fight.

Emily focused her efforts on creating an energy barrier to surround the army, one that extended the entire length of the mist wall, circling Aquila, and trapping them within. They could not escape from any direction. If they tried to pass through the energy field she created, they simply bounced back like ping pong balls. The remaining villagers jumped up and down in excitement, cheering for Emily.

Then, they heard it.

The mighty roar coming from the sky above.

Miranda's beast had reached the mist wall.

The villagers screamed in fright and turned to run.

Emily closed her eyes and summoned the Council of Dragons, but they were already on their way. She felt their presence before she even heard the beating of their wings. She felt their strength flowing through her.

*We are with you…*

The voices of the dragons spoke to her mind.

Miranda's beast spit fire towards the retreating villagers, setting the trees ablaze. It circled above them, swooping down to grab tasty morsels below. It was a horrifying site. Villagers hid behind trees, trying to escape its massive jaws, only to be forced out into the open when the dragon set the forest on fire with its breath.

Martin stood firm by Emily's side with his sword drawn.

"Emily, we must take cover!" he insisted.

She placed her hand gently on his arm, lowering his sword.

"The dragons are here. This is their fight now," she told him. Her eyes were fixed on the sky. Martin followed her gaze.

Flying in a tight formation from the northeast, the majestic Council of Dragons soared towards them at incredible speeds. The sun was reflecting off their scales. They looked like brilliant lights sailing through the sky. As they approached Emily, the dragons broke rank – four by four. They came at the beast from both sides and formed a circle around it.

Emily smiled when she saw another formation flying close behind the Council of Dragons. The other dragons of Aquila had come to join the fight against Miranda's beast.

"There must be hundreds of them!" Martin said excitedly.

The beast stopped its pursuit of the tiny morsels below, and turned its attention to the enemies in the sky. It was outnumbered, but its sheer size alone made it far deadlier than the collective force of dragons.

The sound was deafening. People on both sides of the wall covered their ears, but it had little effect. They tried to find someplace to hide, but the beast had turned the trees to ash. They were terrified.

The dragons launched an orchestrated attack on the larger creature. The blood curdling screeches from the battle being waged above their heads was terrifying. The dragons took turns rotating their bodies, allowing their scales to reflect the sunlight directly into the beast's eyes with great intensity. This blinding effect greatly diminished the beast's ability to see clearly. It continually moved its head to avoid the blinding light.

The dragons were using an attack and retreat method, working in pairs to confuse and disorient the beast. It lashed out at them. Its heavy jaws snapping at the dragons as they flew past.

One of the smaller dragons miscalculated its retreat and the larger beast snared it within its jaws. It immediately ripped off the dragon's wing and flung it violently to the side. The dragon screeched in agony, unable to right itself. It spun wildly out of control, before falling to its death. Emily felt the pain within her mind, as one of the dragons paid the ultimate sacrifice to help the people of Aquila.

The beast roared in victory and turned its attention to the remaining dragons. The sound of these massive creatures slamming into one another was deafening. They clawed and snapped their jaws at the larger creature, tearing into each other's flesh.

It was raining blood.

Dragons against beast.

Good versus evil.

Emily kept her eyes peeled to the sky as the battle continued above them. She and Martin darted out of the way, just in the nick of time, as another dragon fell to the ground not far from where they stood. Its head had been bitten off. Its body slammed to the surface and shook the ground on impact. The dragon's lifeless eyes were open, with its tongue hanging loosely from the side of its mouth.

Emily closed her eyes and tilted her head back towards the sky. She let her mind and body feel the power of the keystone. She opened her eyes and faced her palms towards the beast.

Suddenly, the dragons stopped their attack and formed a perfect circle around the larger creature. Their wings were beating in unison with the keystone. The beast had been weakened by the constant attacks but it was far from beaten. It turned its head angrily from side to side trying to ascertain their next move. It roared its warning to them.

The dragons lowered their heads to the ground and focused their attention on Emily. They were all connected and working in unison with her. A light emitted from Emily's hands, shooting a purplish glow upwards. It surrounded the larger beast, encasing the creature within a purple sphere.

The beast was agitated and tried to move away, but Emily's light held it in place. It was unable to move out of the purple orb. The beast roared in protest. The other dragons stayed in a tight formation. Their wings beat in time with the pulsation of the keystone, which was humming loudly, causing a vibration on the ground beneath their feet.

Emily's power was weakening the beast. It flapped its wings wildly and snapped its jaws in distress. Emily pushed harder and the power of the keystone reached its crescendo. A powerful boom could be heard in the air. The beast stopped moving, momentarily disabled, frozen in place.

The dragons immediately rotated their bodies and lunged for their final attack. Strike after strike, hitting the beast from above and below. Dozens of dragons attacked the large beast in a controlled onslaught. The beast was powerless to defend itself. It was held in place by Emily's power. It roared in agony.

Blow after ferocious blow was leveled at the beast by the smaller dragons, tearing at his throat repeatedly until its blood poured onto the ground. Its eyes rolled back into its skull and the red glow within them faded.

The dragons pulled back and formed their circular formation once again. The beast dropped out of the sky, smashing into the ground below. It formed a crater from its massive weight. The force of the impact knocked everyone off their feet. Cheers rang out from villagers still at the wall, relieved to see the beast defeated.

Emily looked back at the army trapped within her energy field. They were afraid. Afraid of her. They climbed over each other, trying to find a way out.

Martin looked at the huge beast lying dead on the ground.

"I have heard tales of that creature my entire life, never believing them to be true. The Hell Fire dragon it was called, an ancient evil. To see it with my own eyes? Truly unbelievable," he said.

She looked at the two fallen dragons and the bodies of the villagers. She lowered her head in respect for their sacrifices. Martin followed suit. She looked up into the sky at the dragons flying overhead. They too lowered their heads in solace for their fallen friends killed by the beast.

The dragons formed a single file line, soaring majestically through the sky. They spiraled over Emily, flying low to the ground and directly above her head. Emily stepped forward and raised her hand towards the sky. Her fingertips brushed the underbelly of each and every dragon.

They spoke words of peace and unity in their minds to one another. Emily smiled and thanked them, feeling their warmth within her. She and Martin watched the dragons fly gracefully away, back into the clouds, moved by their quiet dignity.

~~~~~~~~~~~~~~~~~~~~~~~~~

With their eyes directed on the skies, Miranda moved closer towards Emily. She watched in disbelief as her beast was brought down swiftly by a host of dragons, seemingly at the young girl's command.

Meanwhile, Miranda's soldiers were presently encased in a transparent force field unable to move, trapped by Emily's power. Soldiers were swarming over one another in a desperate attempt to free themselves

Miranda was out of moves and alone.

The anger that coursed through her blood was only matched by her shock and disbelief. Her greatest fear had come true. The very object she sought to obtain all these years had led to her demise. The last time she felt devastation of this magnitude was when Merrick cast her and her unborn child out to the dark side, to fend for themselves in the barren wasteland.

This was not the end she had envisioned.

She looked back towards the direction of her fortress.

She had nowhere to go.

She was clearly no match for the power the girl wielded. Her army was useless, and her dragon had been promptly defeated by smaller versions of itself. This child, from beyond Aquila, had stolen Miranda's world from her, effortlessly. A child, wearing a garment that proclaimed 'Unicorns Are Real' on her back, had made a fool of her. It was an embarrassment. Miranda was shaking from anger.

She took out her dagger and slithered quietly up behind Martin. She moved as a shadow, without making a single sound. She would take his life, even if she could not touch the girl. The death of Martin would hurt her. One way or another. Miranda was not surrendering to defeat without one final blow.

She raised her arm to plunge her dagger into Martin, who was seemingly unaware of her presence. The blade stopped suddenly before touching Martin, less than an inch from his back. Her arm stopped, frozen in place. She couldn't lower it.

Emily moved her head to look around Martin.

"There you are," Emily said with a grin.

Martin turned to see Miranda holding a knife at his back. He removed it from her hand immediately. She was unable to stop him. Emily walked up to Miranda and looked up into her cold, dark eyes.

"You're not a very nice person, are you?" Emily pointed out.

Miranda hissed at her.

"Bad manners too," Emily added.

"Do not speak to me, child," Miranda snarled with contempt.

"Well, this child just kicked your butt," Emily reminded her.

Martin inched closer to Miranda, glaring at her. He slowly raised his sword out of its sheath. Miranda's eyes widened.

"You destroyed my family and our lives. You will die slowly and painfully," he said with deep loathing.

Emily placed her hand upon Martin's arm. He turned his head towards her.

"Martin, she needs to pay for what she's done," Emily said calmly.

Martin shook his head no and looked away. He did not agree, but yielded to Emily's wishes. Martin moved to the side. Emily stood directly in front of Miranda. She noticed the bald patch on top of Miranda's head from where the fireball hit.

"You might want to put something over that, like a bow or headband," Emily smirked. "Maybe a hat?"

Miranda reached up and touched the bald patch, before glaring at her with pure hatred, not appreciating Emily's humor. Martin chuckled.

"There's someone here who would like to speak to you." Emily motioned to her left and released her hold on Miranda. She turned to see her sister Mira standing in front of her.

Mira's hands were glowing white with electrical energy. Tiny sparks could be seen shooting out of her palms. Miranda threw up her hands, producing fireballs to throw at her sister.

"This again?" Emily asked. "You might want to get some new material. Fireballs can be so cliché," she grinned.

Miranda hissed at Emily again.

Emily frowned, "Dear Lord, stop hissing. You're not feral." She pulled Martin back. "You might want to step out of the way for this family squabble," she advised.

He moved back and watched the two sisters square off.

"You and your meddling!" hissed Miranda.

Mira was unphased. "You go too far, Miranda. You've killed so many and for what? Your own selfish desires. No more."

Miranda hurled a fireball at Mira, who easily deflected it with her lightning bolt of energy. The two sisters fought back and forth, using their powers, attempting to hurt one another. Occasionally, they shouted insults at each other.

"How long are you going to allow this to continue?" Martin asked, aware that Emily could put a stop to it at any time.

"I'm waiting for something," she said.

"What?"

"Just a minute," she said and closed her eyes.

Martin watched her expression change and a smile cross her face. She opened her eyes and looked behind her. She walked towards Miranda, still fighting with her sister. Emily raised her hand.

"Stop now," she ordered.

Miranda immediately froze in place, seething that she could no longer move.

"Toodaloo!" Mira waved goodbye to her sister.

Miranda vanished into thin air.

Emily motioned for Martin to follow her.

Suddenly, Philip and dozens of children materialized on the field in front of them. Confused, filthy and malnourished. They huddled together tightly, squinting up at the sun. But they were safe. Safe and free, no longer held in the darkness in the clutches of a madwoman.

"This is what we were waiting for," Emily told him.

Martin saw the children and was overjoyed. Emily nodded to Philip. He smiled back at her.

Doctor Pernell and staff from the clinic arrived to help treat the wounded and care for the children. He waved at Emily and Martin. Villagers and townspeople offered assistance. They rushed towards the children, tending to their needs. Food, water, clothing and medical assistance was provided. Every child had three or four adults surrounding them. Women wrapped the children in blankets and warm embraces. The children cried and shivered, traumatized by their experiences.

"This is a very good thing. You have fixed a terrible wrong," Martin observed, moved by what he was seeing. "Being in those cages is not something they will easily forget," Martin pointed out.

"Well, I am hoping Thalien and Doctor Pernell can help with that. Heal their bodies. Help heal their minds. Speaking of Thalien…." Her voice trailed off.

Emily turned to face the group that had just appeared on the light side. Thalien was walking with Merrick, Isabeau and Rayven. Martin couldn't believe his eyes. His mother was walking among them. He ran towards her. Emily greeted Thalien.

"Thank you for helping them," she said.

"No, thank you for helping us," he said warmly. She gave him a hug. "Come now, you will have me weepy and who wants a weepy whitelighter?" He winked at her.

"Thank you for everything," she told him sincerely.

"I must help Doctor Pernell tend to the wounded," he told her, looking somberly at the bodies scattered around the area.

She looked at the grieving people around her. "I wish we could have saved them all," she said sadly.

"We knew there would be sacrifice. It is an unavoidable fact of life, my dear," he squeezed her hand. "I have much work to do. We will take care of things here and see to it that the children have safe haven among us. Please, take them back to the clinic."

"We should stay here and help," she insisted.

"They are not fully healed." He nodded towards Martin, Rayven and his parents. "It is best to take them to the clinic where you can all rest. When is the last time you've slept or eaten?"

Emily shrugged.

"Go, rest. We will meet you later when our work here is finished," he winked.

"Alright," she agreed,

Thalien nodded and made his way through the dead and wounded. The familiar light from his palms worked quickly to save as many lives as possible.

The mist wall was down. Emily couldn't allow the vicious predators to crossover and attack those on the light side. She used the power within her to reestablish the mist wall once again.

This time, however, all those that could crossover would be welcomed. No one would be forced to live in the dark anymore, unless they deserved to be there. Emily would let the mist wall decide their fates.

Emily did as Thalien asked of her and returned Martin, Rayven, Philip, Isabeau and Merrick to the clinic – away from death, away from the mist wall. She was exhausted but relieved for a chance to rest. It was the first chance any of them had to talk to one another.

She looked over at Martin. He was hugging his mother, looking at her with the warmth of a son's love. Emily was happy for him. He leaned in and whispered to his mother.

They both looked over at Emily. She waved at them. She watched Martin take out the photo album. He shared it with his mother, turning the pages slowly, adding his own narration. Her hand lifted to her face in astonishment, showing both sadness and joy. They both laughed heartedly at one of the photographs. Martin looked over at Emily and tugged on his tunic.

Ah, dogs in sweaters.

Emily laughed with them. She watched from a distance, allowing mother and son to share this tender moment together.

She noticed Merrick off to the side, watching the reunion between mother and son. Thalien had physically healed Merrick after his fight with Martin, but what about his mind and his heart? Martin did not address his father. He gave all his attention to his mother. Martin occasionally looked over at Rayven and smiled at her, happy to see she was unharmed. Rayven smiled back.

Emily noticed this. She walked behind Martin and whispered in his ear.

"Zap!" she said.

He burst out laughing, turned and gave her a big hug.

"You! I adore you, child," he said to Emily, smiling happily. He brushed her red bangs away from her face again.

"You're going to squeeze me to death," she teased.

"Where exactly did Miranda go?" he said with concern.

"Mira sent her someplace," Emily grinned.

"Oh?" Martin was intrigued.

Mira appeared and walked towards the group.

"I've sent her to a cozy windowless room in my castle, far away from everything and everyone. She will have plenty of time to reflect on her misdeeds and cruelty. She won't bother anyone anymore," she informed them.

Mira smiled and began chatting with Isabeau.

Merrick seized on the opportunity to approach Martin.

"Son, I would like to apologize…"

Martin cut him off.

"Do not speak to me," he said. "I am not interested."

He turned on his heel and walked away from Merrick.

Merrick watched him and then turned to Emily.

"I am afraid his hate for me runs far too deep to ask for forgiveness. I am sorry for the harm I have caused you," Merrick said sincerely.

Emily absent mindedly touched her lip, split from Merrick striking her. She remembered the sting of it all too well.

"I make no excuses for my actions, but am grateful to be free of Miranda's grasp. Perhaps, in time, my son and I can rebuild our relationship," Merrick said sadly.

"Well," Emily thought for a moment, as she watched Martin talking to Rayven, Mira and his mother. "He has a lifetime worth of pain he's holding on to. I can't even imagine what he's been through," she said honestly, staring at the ground uncomfortably.

Merrick had spent years inflicting pain on people. It was great that he himself felt remorseful, but that didn't change what had already happened. Emily avoided eye contact with him, standing there in awkward silence.

Merrick studied her. "I will do my utmost best to change his mind about me, and prove my worth again. Hopefully, one day wounds will heal."

Emily was skeptical but said nothing more.

Merrick had an uphill battle ahead, but she knew Martin was a man of honor and integrity. If his father proved himself to be a changed man? Well, perhaps one day, Martin would forgive him.

She looked at Merrick, trying to find some trace of the man she saw in her vision, during happier times. She searched for a glimpse of humanity. His eyes seemed remorseful. The choices he made inconceivable and despicable. Merrick looked at Emily uncomfortably.

"I have no right to ask this of you, but..."

He pulled pictures out of his pocket that he removed from her home. They were tattered and smeared with blood, but their images were still visible. Emily's eyes widened when she saw he was holding photographs of her and her grandmother.

"Where did you get these?" she demanded to know.

"I took these from your home."

Emily was shocked and concerned for her family.

"You were in my home? Did you...?"

He knew what she was going to ask. "No one saw me. No one was hurt. I was sent to find the seeker."

462

Emily was visibly relieved.

"I saw these when I walked up the stairs…"

Martin noticed Merrick speaking to Emily. He saw the look of concern on her face. He excused himself and moved quickly towards her. He shoved his father away from Emily and stood between them. Martin pointed a finger angrily in his father's face.

"You. You do not speak to her. Ever. Do you understand?"

Merrick put his hands up and took a step back from Emily.

"Martin, it's okay. I'll talk to him."

Martin looked at her, "He tried to kill you."

"I know, but I have a few things I want to say to him. Okay?" she told him.

Martin glared at his father. "Utter one wrong word? Touch her in any way? I will kill you," he warned.

"Geez, not this again," Emily whispered. "Is that how you people on Aquila solve all your problems? By killing each other?" she asked.

Martin looked at her. "And how do you solve conflict where you come from?" he asked. "Is there no killing there?"

"Well, yes. I'd like to think we talk first." She pulled Martin aside. "Let me talk to him for a minute… alone."

He looked at her and back to his father.

"As you wish," Martin frowned. "But I will be watching from that spot right over there." He pointed at the ground a few feet behind her.

"Oh, I'm sure you will. Thanks, Martin."

She gently pushed him away.

Martin reluctantly backed away, without taking his eyes off his father. Merrick watched his son, realizing that the hope of rebuilding trust with Martin was slim.

"What was your question?" Emily asked Merrick.

He showed Emily the photo in his hand.

"Is this… Is this…Victoria?" Merrick asked sincerely, barely able to speak the words.

Emily looked up into Merrick's eyes and saw that they were wet with tears. He swallowed hard to maintain his composure.

"Yes. That is your daughter, Victoria. My grandmother," she said somberly.

Merrick looked away, his feelings came to the surface and she saw tears flow down his face. He could not look at Emily, but he asked her a question.

"Was she happy?" he asked with great sadness and regret.

Emily didn't hesitate. "Yes, she was very happy," she told him.

Merrick sniffled. "That gives me great comfort. Thank you." He rifled into his pocket and pulled out her copy of *The Hobbit*.

"My book?" Emily was surprised to see it. "You took my book?"

"From your room while you slept," he confessed.

"Wha....? You were in my room?" she asked with alarm.

"I am sorry." He handed the book to her.

She refused to accept it.

"Emily? Is everything alright?" Martin chimed in from behind her.

She looked back at him. "I'm standing right here," she reminded him. "You can see me."

"I heard your voice raise," he told her.

Emily rolled her eyes at him. "Oh geez, I'm fine. You're such a worry wart."

She turned back to Merrick

"You keep it," she said. "It's okay. Do me a favor. Give it to Martin's children one day. Tell them it's from me."

He looked at her and pondered the prospect of Martin having children, realizing that Emily knew far more about Martin's future than she was sharing.

"I shall," he promised. "Thank you."

Emily looked back at Martin and frowned. He looked ready to pounce on his father, if he so much as moved a muscle.

"There is no excuse for the choices I made and the pain those decisions caused," Merrick admitted. "I gather there is something more you wanted to say to me?"

"Uh, huh," Emily agreed.

She took a deep breath and thought for a moment. Merrick waited patiently for her words. She wasn't in the habit, at her age, of giving adults a piece of her mind. Nor had she ever been shy about giving her opinion. She looked back at Martin, and smiled fondly at him. His protectiveness of her knew no limit. She felt equally protective of him.

She sighed and spoke to Merrick.

"You had no right to do what you did. None," she said bluntly. "I saw. The night you sent my grandma away. I saw it in my mind. Martin doesn't know it, but I was there, in my vision. I saw him beating on the door until his fists bled, screaming till he lost his voice. He cried for days. I saw him begging for your help and you just pushed him away," Emily felt tears forming in her eyes, but fought them back.

Merrick looked ashamed.

"You crushed his soul," she said through tears. "You broke him. You threw him away, like garbage. He loved you so much and you... you destroyed him," she continued. "He's carried that hatred inside his entire life." She felt herself getting angry and took a deep breath.

"And, my grandma? You almost got her killed. She was just a baby. But she had a really good life, without you. She was happy and loved. She was beautiful."

Emily angrily wiped away a tear.

"And, I was there on the day everyone thought Isabeau died. Martin's 10th birthday. I was there. In my vision, you spoke to me. I was just like – wow. I could see why everyone looked up to you. And, Martin? He adored you. You could just see it in his eyes, how happy he was. How much he loved you. Even I was blown away by you. By all of you. You were like something right out of a fairy tale, back then..."

Merrick was visibly shaken. Emily wiped more tears away from her cheeks. She wasn't trying to be hurtful, but she wanted him to hear what she had to say.

"But you know what?" she continued. "Martin's nothing like you. Nothing like you at all. And, that makes me very happy."

Her words stung.

"So, I guess what I want to say is… I don't know what's going on in your head now that Miranda is gone, and I don't care. I think people are good at hiding who they really are. So only you know if you're okay. And, I understand being devastated about the loss of your wife, but your kids needed you too. So, I'm sorry. You don't get a pass from me. You don't get to ride off into the sunset on your white horse to your fancy castle in the woods and live happily ever after. Not with me anyway."

Merrick lowered his head.

"So, I reserve judgement on you," she said with absolute conviction behind her words. "Look, Martin means a lot to me. He's my family now. And, you've hurt him more than you can possibly imagine…"

She looked over at Martin, watching them intently. Then, Emily stepped forward and stood inches away from Merrick. She looked up into his eyes.

In that moment, Emily Richardson of Glendale, California delivered a clear and unmistakable warning to Merrick Stewart – once King of Aquila.

"Don't ever hurt him again," she warned Merrick.

Merrick saw the purple mist swirling in her eyes.

She held his gaze.

"I won't let you – hurt Martin – ever again," she said with fierce conviction. She turned her back on Merrick and walked away.

Merrick knew that she meant every word she spoke. He would answer to her if he ever attempted to hurt Martin again.

Merrick slowly walked back to stand beside Isabeau. The love they felt for one another remained in their eyes, but it too had changed. The years had taken its toll. Merrick had much to atone for. Isabeau would have to decide how much forgiveness she had to offer him and where their future together would lead.

Soon, Thalien and Doctor Pernell returned. They were talking outside of the clinic. When Martin looked at Rayven, Emily grinned. He rolled his eyes. Martin knew she was playing matchmaker and he found her efforts endearing. She pulled Martin away from the group.

"I told you love was in the air," she whispered to him.

"Stop," he laughed.

"Do I need to start singing again?" she asked.

"Please do not," he teased.

"Wait for it," she laughed.

"No," he joked.

"I have just the song for you," she smirked.

"No," Martin chuckled, slowly backing away from her.

She grabbed his arm.

"Wait," she insisted.

Emily cleared her throat and began to sway slowly back and forth, hearing the music in her head. She held an imaginary microphone in front of her face, and batted her eyelashes at him, being as overly cheeky as possible. Then, she clutched her shirt dramatically and began softly singing Elvis Presley's "Can't Help Falling in Love with You."

"Wise men say, only fools rush in. But I can't help falling in love with you. Shall I stay? Would it be a sin? If I can't help falling in love with you?"

Martin smirked. She leaned in towards him and continued her performance.

"Like a river flows, surely to the sea. Darling, so it goes. Some things are meant to be…"

The others stopped talking and turned to face them. Martin looked somewhat uncomfortable now. Rayven and his mother were looking directly at him.

Emily looked over her shoulder and saw she had a captive audience. She smirked at Martin. No mercy, she said to herself, and began the next verse, singing louder this time, making sure that everyone could hear.

"Take my hand – come on Martin, take my hand!" she grinned. He rubbed his temple and shook his head no. "Take my hand, take my whole life too…"

She began thumping her chest, feigning fake emotions. She threw her head on her shoulder and then looked up into his eyes.

"For I can't help, falling in love with you, for I can't help, falling in love with you…"

She grinned at him. Applause erupted behind her. She turned and took a slight bow.

Martin had no words. "I cannot believe we are actually related," he grinned.

"Oh, come on, you love it."

He just shook his head and smiled at her.

She reached her hand out to him. "Dance with me, Martin."

"No," he laughed.

"You know you want to," she said with a cheeky grin.

"I am sure I do not," he chuckled.

"I'll get you to dance one day. You just wait!" she teased.

They laughed together and joined the others.

# Chapter Thirty-Four

Across Aquila the dead were laid to rest. It was a day of mourning throughout the lands. The wounded were moved to various clinics for care. Many lives were lost when the mist wall fell. Tales of bravery spread like wildfires. It would forever be remembered as the day the common folk stood shoulder to shoulder and held their ground against the evil sorceress.

An even greater story was told of a young princess from far away and her unbridled courage in the face of danger. The young children would listen with wide eyes as they were told of Emily's adventures on the wings of dragons.

Ambassadors from every province met to address the issue of power and accountability. With the mist wall restored, there was a great exodus of people crossing over, searching for a better life. They would need food and shelter. Citizens everywhere turned out to lend a helping hand. There was no shortage of space or resources on the lights side. All were welcome. Talk was made of building new schools and places of commerce. A new clinic in central Aquila was proposed with Doctor Martin Stewart as its Chief Medical Officer. Of course, Emily teased him endlessly about this prospect.

There were many prisoners in the Keep. A branch of government would be created to deal with them – humanely. One thing was agreed upon, there would be no more torture. Justice would be served. Those unfairly imprisoned would be freed. The depraved and barbaric practices of Miranda would vanish, just as she had. They could not allow a new threat to rise from the dark side. Order would be maintained on both sides of Aquila. The Marshals would play a large part in this new system of law enforcement.

Merrick was the rightful ruler, but few wanted to return the kingdom to him, given his association with Miranda. No one trusted him. It would take a great deal of time for Merrick to ever regain the confidence of those on the light side.

That he himself was not thrown into the Keep was in large part at the behest of Mira. She had asked for leniency given the power Miranda had over his mind. It in no way exonerated him, but they believed that Merrick was no longer a threat and sincerely remorseful.

It mattered not. Merrick was not interested in being a ruler anymore. He had more than his fair share of power and corruption. He fancied a quiet life with his beloved Isabeau, rebuilding their home, rekindling their love and spending their golden years peacefully among their gardens. He hoped that Isabeau felt the same way as he did.

So much time had been lost, like tears in rain. Merrick and Isabeau walked quietly through the halls of their castle, now in ruins. They were saddened by the painful memories it brought forth. Local villagers had volunteered to help rebuild their home and for that, Merrick and Isabeau were grateful. They walked slowly past women sweeping out leaves and listened to the sounds of hammers repairing the roof above their heads. It would not be long before their castle was a home once again.

Merrick and Isabeau walked side by side in their garden. It was now a twisted mess of thickets and overgrown weeds. There was a heavy and uncomfortable silence between them.

"Can you ever forgive me?" he asked of her, finally.

She sighed heavily. "I do not understand your actions. Our children should have always known the love and protection of their father."

Merrick looked down in shame. She was right, of course.

"You dishonored me by turning your back to them," she said.

"I am sorry," he admitted.

"It will take time to heal," she replied honestly.

They continued walking in silence.

Many suggested that Martin become ruler of Aquila, by restoring the kingdom, and uniting Aquila's realms under one banner. He had proven himself worthy of that title. He was the rightful heir. Martin politely declined. He had other aspirations and they did not include stepping into his father's shoes. He wanted to be a healer – a doctor. He intended to save lives, not rule over them. The previous days had not changed that fact.

Somewhere locked away in Mira's castle, Miranda screamed endlessly. She pounded on the walls of her windowless prison, removed from all life, unable to harm anyone. The isolation was driving her mad. She wept uncontrollably between bouts of rage. She wanted it. She wanted the power the girl had. She had to find a way to make that power her own. Clawing at the walls so much that her nails had been ripped off, raw and bloody. She constantly muttered to herself, but no one could hear her

She would walk around the small confines of her cell, waiting and wondering for her fate to change. Waiting to awake from the nightmare. Wondering where she had gone wrong. She would walk. She would wait. She would wonder. Till the ache from her heart gave way to despair. Her time had passed. She would live out her days alone and in misery for her crimes against humanity. A broken shell until she took her last breath.

Doctor Pernell gave Rebecca a position at the clinic – Goodwill Ambassador of Aquila. She gave tours of the grounds and helped patients settle in. She'd bring them books to read, visits with pets to comfort them, and provide fresh flowers to brighten their rooms, always eager to keep them company.

Doctor Pernell acquired a cottage by the creek for Grace to take up residence. Rebecca visited her almost daily. They had developed quite a bond. They'd take walks together and have long talks. It was good emotional healing for both of them.

Rayven and Philip moved into the cottage with their mother. Any animosity that once existed between them had been resolved. They were happy to see her healthy and thriving. They'd come home from volunteering in the villages and find Grace tending to her garden. Evenings were spent on their porch, enjoying Aquila's beauty. It was a dream come true for them all.

Occasionally, Martin would join them for dinner. He and Rayven would take quiet walks along the river, getting to know one another. Rayven's harsh exterior had evaporated once the possibilities of this new life presented itself to her. Neither one was in a hurry for a relationship, but there was something developing between them. Martin had to admit that Emily may have been right. Zap!

~~~~~~~~~~~~~~~~~~~~~~~~

Emily knew her time on Aquila was coming to an end. Both she and Martin avoided the conversation completely. Neither was ready to say goodbye, but her adventure on Aquila was over. At least, for now. She didn't want to leave Martin or her dragon friends. She had grown to love this place and the people in it.

However, she had family back in Glendale that she loved. She couldn't just disappear forever. No, that would devastate her parents. She was comforted by the fact that with her new power, she could visit her family and friends on Aquila anytime she wished.

The day came for her to say her goodbyes. She thanked Doctor Pernell, Mira and Thalien for their faith in her. They hugged her fondly and demanded she come back soon.

Emily took a walk with Isabeau to talk about her grandma. She treasured the time to learn about her daughter, Victoria. She touched the necklace Emily wore, reminding her that they would always be connected. No amount of time or distance would ever change that fact. She gave Emily a warm embrace, thanking her for giving her life back, as well as her son and husband.

Emily said her goodbyes to Rayven and Philip. Thanking them for their help. When Emily smiled at Philip, his face turned beet red, much to his sister's amusement. Emily knew how invaluable Philip was in the rescue of Isabeau and the children. She was grateful to him. She asked Rayven to take care of Martin. Rayven blushed at the mention of his name. Emily grinned, knowing the sound of wedding bells may soon fill the air.

Emily walked alone through the clinic. She wanted to ask Martin for some time alone, so they could talk. She found Martin tending to patients. When she caught his attention, he could tell from the look in her eyes that she had come to say goodbye. He hesitated and looked down.

"Emily," he smiled at her.

She looked at the stack of folders in his hand. "Hey, can we talk? You know, when you're done here?" she asked.

"Of course," he told her.

An awkward silence lingered between them.

"Okay, great," she said.

"I can finish now, if you need me too," he offered.

"Um, actually, I'm heading to the Council of Dragons to say my goodbyes," she told him.

"Oh, I see," he said quietly.

They both looked at each other.

"So, can we talk after that?" she asked.

"Of course," he smiled weakly.

They had both been dreading this day.

"How about at the glen where we met. You can bring your horse, Thundercat," she grinned.

He laughed. "Thunderbolt."

"Yea, that's what I said," she smirked.

"I will meet you there shortly."

She nodded and gave him a quick hug. He watched her leave the clinic, feeling the sadness fill his heart.

Emily had something she wanted to do first. She found Rebecca with Doctor Pernell and asked if she could borrow the little girl for a few minutes. He winked at her and agreed.

"Where are we going?" Rebecca asked repeatedly.

"Be patient and close your eyes," Emily insisted.

Once Rebecca's eyes were closed, Emily closed hers too. She let her mind take them far into the mountains and to the Council of Dragons.

"Open your eyes," Emily said.

Rebecca opened her eyes and gasped.

"It's okay. Don't be afraid. They won't hurt you," Emily told her. "These are my friends."

She took Rebecca's hand and walked her to each dragon.

Rebecca relaxed and looked at them. Caponeous lowered his head and let the little girl touch his nose. She giggled.

"See, these are good dragons. When I go home, they will be here if you need them, okay?"

She smiled at the girl's look of awe and wonder.

"Do you want to go for a ride?" Emily asked.

"Can we?" Rebecca asked happily.

Emily brushed her hand over the dragon's nose.

"Where would you like to go?"

"Everywhere!" Rebecca said with glee.

Emily laughed. "Climb on!"

The dragon lowered himself to the ground.

"Hold on tight," she said to Rebecca.

Emily whispered her thanks to Caponeous. He gently rose into the air. Rebecca howled with delight. He soared over fields and mountains across Aquila. He flew Rebecca above the clinic. Doctor Pernell looked up and waved at them.

Emily spotted Martin walking to the stable to get his horse. She asked Caponeous to fly over him. The dragon obliged her. Martin heard the sound of the dragon, fast approaching. He had to duck. They waved at him. He laughed. She asked Caponeous to return them to the Council of Dragons. The dragon weaved through the clouds. When they arrived, both girls climbed off. Rebecca was bubbling over with glee.

"I'm going to send you back to the clinic now."

Rebecca nodded. "You're leaving today, aren't you?"

"Yes, I am. The people at the clinic will take care of you. Don't be afraid to talk to them. I'll see you again soon." Emily hugged her tightly.

Rebecca wiped away tears. "Promise?"

"Promise." Emily returned Rebecca to the clinic.

~~~~~~~~~~~~~~~~~~~~~~~~~~

Emily turned to face the Council of Dragons. She sighed heavily and walked onto the center stone. Her necklace was pulsating in unison with the dragons' hearts and the stone she stood upon. No words were necessary. They were joined together as one. Emily sat down, crossed legged on the stone.

She'd spent her entire young life writing fanciful tales of knights and dragons. Countless days were spent being chased by imaginary foes in the forest behind her home. The reality was quite different than she had ever imagined.

She was surrounded by the most majestic creatures in all the universe. She looked up at the sky above her. A brilliant canopy of stars, the likes of which she had never seen before, greeted her. She didn't want to leave, but she knew she had to go home. And, yet – this was her home too. She was so conflicted.

She closed her eyes. Every part of Aquila flowed within her. She felt herself leaving her body and floating higher, until she could look down and see the Council of Dragons beneath her. It was the most tranquil feeling she had ever experienced.

Emily smiled.

She was flying.

And, she was not alone. The dragons joined her. They flew beside her, and circled gracefully around her. Their scales reflected the millions of twinkling stars in space. It was the most incredible thing Emily had ever seen. The entire heavens turned into a giant kaleidoscope.

She could see forever. It was absolutely breathtaking. She laughed out loud, exhilarated by the freedom she felt. She would always remember her time on Aquila – every single moment, especially her time with Martin and the dragons.

She opened her eyes and stood.

A terrifying thought entered her mind. What if they were wrong? What if she couldn't return?

Sensing her fear, the dragons moved close to Emily. They formed a circle around her. Emily reached out and touched each one of them. It was very moving and quite beautiful. Her dragon friends spoke to her mind.

*We are always with you…*
*We are one…*

"We are one," she whispered softly.

She closed her eyes and held the keystone in her hand. Emily was beautifully out of place on Aquila, but she quickly adapted and accepted her place in its future. She would miss their gentle presence when she returned home, but she knew they would keep watch over her while she slept.

~~~~~~~~~~~~~~~~~~~~~~~~

It was another day in paradise, except this was the day that Emily was going home. Home to Glendale, to resume her life as an ordinary girl with chores and homework. Home – to where adventures like this were figments of her imagination or only scribbles on the tattered pages of her journals.

No light side. No dark side. No dragons. No Martin.

Water cascaded down the side of the mountain, spilling into the river below. The peaks of the snowy mountains could be seen above the billowing clouds. The dense forest opened up into the narrow valley.

Martin was waiting for her, in the exact same spot where they had first met. His horse grazed on the grass nearby.

Emily appeared next to him.

"You could not resist, could you?" he teased, referring to the dragon barreling down on him earlier.

"One for the road," she smirked.

They walked in easy silence. It was the kind you share with those you are especially close to. Martin's horse followed close behind. Emily didn't want to rush this goodbye. She wanted to fully appreciate the beauty around her and enjoy Martin's company before she left.

"It's so beautiful here," she remarked.

"It is," he agreed.

She stopped and pointed off into the distance.

"It's getting late. See? The deep purple afterglow? It's very subtle. It's how I judge the time of day around here," she said.

Martin nodded. "Interesting."

"Well, how do you know what time it is here?" she asked.

He reached into his trousers and took out his pocket watch.

"We call them watches," he smirked.

"Oh geez. You've had a watch all this time?"

He gave her an odd look. "Yes."

"And you didn't tell me?"

"You did not ask," he grinned.

She just looked at him dumbfounded. "Wow."

He laughed. "It has not always been this way on Aquila. Before the mist wall was created, we had night and day, much as on your own world."

"I know," she admitted. "I haven't known what time it was, since I got here. My watch is broken. Now I look for the purple afterglow where the light and dark meet."

"Clever. In the future, ask."

"We call them watches," she said sarcastically, mocking his accent. She bumped into Martin with her entire body, making him stumble off the path. He laughed heartily.

They walked further enjoying the peace and tranquility of their surroundings. The wind rustled through the trees, lifting the fallen leaves into the air. The breeze moved across the meadow, bending the wildflowers in playful circles. The skies were empty. Not even a dragon sighting. She would never grow tired of this view. Martin noticed that she was smiling.

"What is it?" he asked curiously.

"I was thinking. I spend so much time back home, playing in the woods, pretending to be a knight, fighting dragons. Now this? Aquila? It's a world right out of my own dreams."

Martin thought about her words.

"Have you considered that your desire to be someone else, in a world full of dragons, may be a result of your connection to Aquila? It runs in your blood, as surely as it does mine."

She stopped and looked at him.

"What you believed to be a product of your imagination, could well be an echo from every bearer of the keystone that came before you. It is entirely possible that you, the Council of Dragons and Aquila have always been as one – but you believed it to be a dream. And, your desire to run through the woods, in pursuit of dragons, was a manifestation of this or a subconscious calling to return to Aquila? Merely an open channel to this world?"

Her mouth dropped open.

"It was just a thought," he added with a grin.

"You're just full of information today, aren't you? That actually makes a lot of sense," she admitted.

He cast her a sideways glance and started walking again. She quickened her pace to walk beside him.

"And, where exactly are we going?" she asked.

He sighed. "I do not know. I am walking, to avoid the inevitable goodbye," he admitted.

"Yea, me too, but if we don't stop soon, we're going to walk all the way to Mira's castle," she pointed out.

He smiled and looked around. They had traveled quite a distance already he noted. A dragon flew in the distance, disappearing into a cloud. Emily looked at the sky for a moment, awaiting its return.

"Do you mind if I ask what you spoke with him about?"

Emily looked at Martin. He wouldn't even utter his name.

"Okay, sure," she said awkwardly.

He put his hand up. "My apologies. I should not have asked."

"No, it's okay. I get it," she hesitated, not sure what to say. She decided on honesty. "I told him how much he hurt you. I told him how much you looked up to him, when you were a little boy and how he...crushed your soul, broke you."

Martin stopped walking and turned to her.

"You told him that?"

"I did," she said truthfully.

He looked away.

She kept talking. "And, I told him you aren't anything like him, and that's a good thing."

Martin looked back at her. She didn't see anger in his eyes. She saw sadness.

"Anything else?"

"I told him that he had no right to do what he did to you and my grandma. And, that I didn't care if he was all better now. Like who knows, right? Look how easily that boy Donovan fooled people?" she said.

Martin nodded.

"And, that he doesn't get to just ride off to his fairy tale castle to live happily ever after," she said dramatically.

Martin sighed.

"Oh, and I may have threatened him."

Martin raised an eyebrow.

"You may have threatened him?" he asked.

"Okay, I threatened him. And, I meant it," she said with a frown. "And, I'm not sorry that I did."

He nodded but said nothing. He leaned against his horse and stared at the ground. She stood beside him. Martin wasn't a man that easily shared his feelings. He shook his head and lifted his eyes to look at Emily.

"How did you know this?" he asked. "I never spoke of it."

Emily's eyes widened and she avoided his gaze.

"I see," he nodded. "You saw with your own eyes, a vision."

She nodded slowly. This knowledge seemed to physically pain him. He exhaled and lowered his head.

"I'm sorry. I should have told you."

He shook his head. "No need to apologize."

He became quiet and stared at the mountains. It was painful for him to think about what happened back then.

"Sometimes when I sleep, I can still hear Victoria screaming. She was frightened. She did not understand what was happening to her, nor did I. I never saw her again, never knew what became of her. She was gone, like a ghost in my dreams," he spoke softly.

Martin closed his eyes.

479

"The more I tried to get answers from him, the more violent he became towards me," he said, lowering his head. "I believed I must have done something wrong. Thinking that if I was better? Perhaps, he would love me again. He shut me out. I was alone. I was tired of being hurt, so I left and never looked back. I wanted the nightmare to end."

Emily listened, because that was what Martin needed the most in that moment – to be heard. He took a deep breath.

"I lost my mother that day. And, my father and sister – my entire world. Everything I had known was gone, in the blink of an eye," he said emotionally.

It pained Emily to see him like this, but maybe it was best that he talked about it.

"I did not realize I kept all the hatred with me. When I was hitting him with every ounce of strength I had? I was that little boy again. When you stood between us? I realized that I was not behaving like a man. I was fighting like a child, angry at his father. I let hatred completely cloud my mind and nearly got us both killed. The sheer pointlessness of it all," he said painfully. "That man? He is not worth dying for..."

"No, he's not," she spoke softly. "You can't change the past. I might be a kid, but I do know he can't hurt you anymore – unless you let him."

Martin looked at her.

"He can't hurt you," she repeated, getting emotional, only wanting to comfort him. "He's just a sad, angry man that let you and my grandma down in every possible way. And, you? You would never do anything like that, not in a million years. When we first met, I did everything I could to annoy you and you still protected me. Because it's who you are. You're a good person. He's not. Don't let him cast a shadow over you. Close that door. You're safe. I'm safe. Aquila's safe. So, don't hold on to the past. Let it go. If you see him again? Just say talk to the paw," she said holding up her hand.

Martin chuckled.

"He isn't worth your time," she added. "Big and strong like me, remember?"

She gave him a cheeky grin.

"Big and strong like you," he replied.

He wiped his eyes and looked at her.

"You are very wise. Are you sure you are only twelve?"

"Almost thirteen," she smiled back.

"Thirteen?" he grinned.

Neither spoke for a few moments.

She sighed and stepped away from him.

"Look at the time?" she said, staring at an imaginary watch on her wrist. "If I only had a watch," she teased.

He laughed and reached into his pocket.

"Here, keep it," he handed his pocket watch to her. "I do not need it anymore."

"Really?"

"Yes. It is yours now."

She took it and examined it closely. There was an inscription on the back of the watch that read:

To my son. Martin
From your loving father
On your 10th birthday

Emily's eyes immediately filled with tears and she looked up at Martin. "I can't keep this," she said, her voice shaking.

He smiled weakly, wiping a tear from her cheek.

"Yes, you can. I want you to have it. Keep it, for me."

Emily stared at the watch and rubbed her finger over the inscription. She gave him a hug.

"Okay, Martin. Thank you."

She pulled away and her eyes brightened.

"I have something for you," she said, reaching into her backpack. She pulled out a small gift and handed it to Martin. He grinned at her and unwrapped it, inspecting it closely.

"What in heavens is this?" he asked with a huge smile.

481

Emily laughed.

"It's a sweater... For your dog," she told him. "I had one of the ladies at the clinic knit one for me."

Martin busted out laughing, "I love it, sincerely I do. You are aware that I do not even own a dog?" He held it up and examined the blue sweater with the bright green trim. "This is wonderful!" He smiled broadly.

"Trust me, Martin. You will own a dog soon. When I come visit, I expect to see your little dog wearing his sweater. Agreed?" She smiled warmly at him.

"Agreed," he smiled, tucking the tiny sweater into his tunic pocket. "Thank you, Emily for the sweater."

"You're very welcome," she replied. "Did you want your chainmail tunic back?" she asked.

"No. You keep it. It suits you," he said fondly.

"I'm not good at goodbyes," she told him.

"Neither am I," he admitted.

"Martin?" she said, trying hard not to cry.

"Yes?"

"I'm going to miss you," she said.

"I am going to miss you too. You have grown on me."

She laughed. "I bet. Thank you for everything. You've changed my life..."

"And, you have changed mine in ways I never thought possible," he admitted.

They continued walking up the path. Martin intentionally bumped into Emily. She laughed and bumped back into him.

"It is not going to be the same around here without you," he told her.

"We're family now," she reminded him.

"This is true. May the heavens help us both," he smiled warmly at her.

"I guess I should go now," she told him. "Promise me you will take care of yourself and be nice."

"I promise, and I am always nice," he protested.

She huffed and rolled her eyes. "Really? The first time I met you, you left me behind to be eaten by a dragon," she laughed.

"Alright, I promise to be nice," he agreed.

"And, be happy," she added.

"Yes, happy."

"I'll come back and talk to you whenever I can. You know, about problems at home, school or boys," she promised.

"Of course. Wait, who said anything about boys?" he asked. "What boys?"

Martin's overprotective nature of Emily kicked in.

"I'm not really comfortable around boys," she admitted.

"There will be no boys," he told her adamantly.

She laughed at him.

"I insist on chatting with these boys. They will need your Uncle Martin's permission before they can even think about calling on you. Do you understand me?" he told her.

"Oh great, you'll scare them off for sure," she laughed.

"Yes, we shall see who is good enough to court you, will we not?" he told her. "And, I will escort you to engagements with boys, of course."

"Yea? No," she grinned.

They both laughed.

"I am here for you, if you need me. Do you understand?"

She nodded.

"…and I expect to see you often. No excuses. As a matter of fact, we should make a regular point of seeing each other. If you do not mind," he suggested.

"I'd like that," she admitted. "Thalien explained to me how to judge time here and there. I can come back as much as I want. It's just gonna be weird, you know. I've gotten so used to being around you all the time."

"I know," he smiled. "How about joining me next week for dinner?"

She brightened up. "I can do that."

"Good."

They stared at each other.

483

"Goodbye, Martin. I'll see you soon."

She trusted in the keystone and knew it would bring her back as often as she wished, but it was still hard leaving Martin and Aquila behind.

"Goodbye, Emily. Behave," he grinned.

She put her arms around his waist and hugged him, fighting back tears. He returned her hug and fought back his own. She pulled back and looked up into his eyes.

Standing before her was a knight, just like the ones she had always dreamed of. She recalled all they had been through together and the unbreakable bond they had forged with one another.

"I love you, Martin," she said.

"I love you too, Emily, more than you could possibly know." He kissed her lightly on the forehead and brushed her bangs away from her face.

She stepped back and smiled at him.

He pulled out the dog sweater and waved it in the air, making her laugh. They smiled at one another one last time, as Emily closed her eyes and let the keystone return her home. Martin watched her vanish into thin air and paused for a moment before returning to the clinic. He already missed her. She had made him a better man. He knew he would see her again soon.

"Travel safe, little one," he said softly, holding his dog sweater tightly in his hand.

# Chapter Thirty-Five

Emily's parents climbed out of their minivan and continued to argue with her sister Sarah about whether to have fish sticks for dinner or mac and cheese. Emily saw them walking up the sidewalk and hurried to light the candles on the dining room table. They walked in the front door and immediately stopped talking.

"What on earth?" her mother said.

Her father's jaw dropped open. Sarah pushed past her parents to get a better look.

"Dinner is served," announced Emily.

She moved to the side. The table had already been prepared with fresh flowers, candles and the fancy china they only used for guests. The napkins were folded neatly in their special napkin rings.

The smell of baked salmon and roasted potatoes filled the air. A fresh salad was already in serving bowls and the water was poured into the nice crystal glasses. Emily had soft classical music playing in the background.

Her father smiled and looked at her, "Emily, what's all this?"

"I just wanted to surprise you, that's all. I've been a bit of a pain lately and this is my way of saying I'm sorry and I'm going to try harder," she said sincerely.

Her parents looked at each other.

"Sweet pea, this is just wonderful," her mother said. She moved towards Emily and gave her a hug. Her father hugged her too.

"I must say this is a wonderful surprise. It smells terrific and the table looks great," he said.

"Come everybody, sit down and eat while it's warm," Emily said. "Oh, and I also cleaned the house while you were out and finished the laundry," she told them.

Her father reached over and felt her forehead. "You're sure you're feeling okay?" he asked with a grin.

Emily smiled, "Yea, Dad. I've never felt better."

They laughed and sat down, enjoying Emily's wonderful home cooked meal. She looked at her family and smiled. She had a new appreciation for them and was grateful they were safe. She was glad to be back home. She reached up to touch her necklace. Aquila was only a thought away. She smiled fondly at that realization.

"I love you guys," Emily said.

Her parents looked at each other and then back at Emily.

"We love you too, dear," they said together.

Her father rose from the table and opened a cabinet drawer. He took out her journals and walked back over to the table.

"Here you go, kiddo. You can have these back now. Go spend some time with those dragons of yours," he smiled tenderly at her, tousling her hair.

She looked at the journals in his hands, full of her previous imaginary perils and smiled fondly. The irony of this did not escape her.

"Thanks, Dad. I think I'll do just that," she grinned, knowing that she had real dragons to visit now, not imaginary ones. The keystone around her neck glowed slightly. She touched it and felt its warmth. She knew more wondrous adventures awaited her on Aquila.

# Epilogue

The small wagon made its way along the winding river road. It was full of baskets from the neighboring market filled with fresh fruits and vegetables. The elderly couple held hands, talking quietly to one another as their horse slowly made its way back to their farmhouse. It was a beautiful day and a cool breeze blew in from the north.

The woman spoke happily of the pie she would make that evening from the fruit she had bought. Her husband teased her that her pies were making him chubby. They laughed lovingly at one another. They rounded the bend not far from their home when the man spotted something lying by the water's edge. He pulled back on the horse's reins and brought the wagon to a stop.

"What is it, dear?" his wife asked with concern in her voice.

"Stay put," he told her and climbed out.

He grabbed his walking stick from the back of the wagon and slowly walked towards the object lying on the grass. His wife scooted over to his side of the wagon for a closer look. He walked cautiously towards the object and saw that it was the body of a small child.

He quickly turned back to his wife, "Martha, come here! Quickly and bring a blanket!"

She did as he asked. He bent down beside the small child and rolled the body over. It was a young girl, perhaps eight or nine years old. Her clothes were soaking wet and she was unconscious. His wife handed him the blanket. He wrapped it around the little girl.

"Oh dear," she exclaimed. "Is she alive?"

She was bruised and had dry crusted blood on her forehead. He wiped her long blond hair out of her face and gently searched for a pulse.

"She's alive, but barely," he told his wife. "We must get her back to the house at once and I will go fetch the doctor!"

He lifted her up in his arms and carried the small child back to their wagon, gently placing her in the back. They climbed into their seat and slapped the reins on the horse. It proceeded down the path at a quicker pace towards their home. The husband and wife looked at each other with great concern.

What was a child doing out here? Where did she belong? She must have washed up from the river downstream. They knew all the families in this area, and no one had reported a missing child. This poor child was not from around these parts, they concluded. The child did not stir on their short trip back. The man carried the girl into their home and placed her on a small cot in their extra room. The wife grabbed some washcloths. She wiped the dirt and blood from the girl's face. She removed her wet clothes and put her in some warm pajamas that once belonged to their daughter. The husband brought in an extra quilt. They covered the little girl to keep her warm.

"Albert," his wife said. "Please start a fire in the hearth. She feels deathly cold."

He nodded and went to collect firewood. Martha set a pot of soup on the stove and began to warm it, in case the little girl woke up and needed some hot food. She hung her coat up and waited for her husband to finish starting the fire. Once he did so, he returned to the kitchen to speak with his wife.

"I will return with the doctor," he told his wife and gave her a kiss on her cheek.

She smiled at him. "Be careful," she told him.

He smiled back and headed out the door. She heard their wagon head back down the road as she returned to keep watch over the child. Martha pulled a chair next to the cot and sat next to the little girl. She stroked the child's hair gently and hummed a soothing lullaby to the child, hoping to offer some comfort.

After a few minutes, the child slowly opened her eyes and stared at the woman.

Martha was surprised, but relieved.

"Oh, my goodness, dear," she said. "You gave us such a fright. My husband has gone to fetch the doctor. Don't you worry none. We will take good care of you. What's your name, dear?"

The little girl paused and looked up at the ceiling.

"Rebecca," she said weakly.

"Rebecca," the old woman smiled. "It's nice to meet you, Rebecca. My name is Martha. Are you hungry?" she asked.

The little girl nodded and licked her parched lips.

"Here, let me fetch you some hot soup and water." Martha stood and left the room. She continued to talk to the girl from the kitchen in an animated fashion, trying to make the little girl as comfortable as possible.

The little girl sat up and looked around the room. It was a charming small space full of toys, books and dolls. A stuffed bear sat at the foot of the bed. Martha never stopped chatting away in the kitchen. The girl turned her head towards a dressing table to her left and caught her reflection in the mirror.

She smiled at herself.

The smile turned into a grin.

The image of the little girl faded.

Donovan stared at his reflection in the mirror. He swung his feet over the edge of the bed and slowly stood up. The evil grin never left his face. He stared at the door as the woman continued her mindless chatter. He closed his eyes and concentrated.

The talking stopped. He heard the soup bowl crash to the floor and break. Then, he heard a loud thump as the woman's body slumped to the floor. He gathered what he could from the room – clothing, shoes, blankets and took some food from the kitchen. He shoved the supplies into a bag. He stepped over the old woman's body and looked down at her with little interest. She was barely breathing, but still alive. He contemplated killing her but decided against it. She was no threat. He would let her live. She had been kind to him. He enjoyed having the power to grant life or take it away.

The grin never left Donovan's face. He opened the front door and looked out at the bright sun. He thought of his list. His kill list. It was time to punish those on that list. It was time to take his rightful place as ruler. Donovan smiled wickedly and stepped outside, towards his destiny.

As he walked down the path, the flowers lining the road and the grass under his feet immediately wilted and died. He was infecting the land with his sick mind. Donovan would have his day. He planned on crushing those that opposed him with just a passing thought. When he was done devouring this world, Donovan intended to take the keystone and move on to the next world and then the next, devouring all in his path.

A dragon flew gracefully in the sky. He paused to look at it. Donovan flicked his wrist slightly. The dragon's neck snapped, and it fell helplessly to the ground.

Donovan had become the evil that all men feared.

May the heavens help them all…

THE WORLD OF
AQUILA

HALL OF ANCIENTS

HAVAMAL

PEDORA

SEA OF ROA

BAY OF ISAJUDA

TOTHAVEN

SEA OF AGEE

BALORA

BRUSTAD ISLE

MIST WALL
The Dark Side

MIST WALL
The Dark Side

SERG ISLES

N
W    E
S

THE NORTH SEA

ELIROSE ISLE

EVERNISS ISLE

MIRA'S CASTLE

ASTRID

LOTHIAN

COUNCIL OF DRAGONS

MERRICK'S CASTLE

MIST WALL

THE DARK SIDE

THE CLINIC

LAKE OF SOULS

WALL

DARK SIDE

THE KEEP

SHADOWLANDS

SEA OF THE DEADLAND

Coming Soon

~Book Two~

On the Wings of Dragons

# Whispers in the Dark

Emily opened her eyes. She immediately dropped her backpack. She could not believe what she was seeing. The wind was howling. The dustbowl she stood in was not the Aquila she had left. Dark ash covered the skies, blocking out the moons and the sun. It was cold and dark. She reached down, fumbling with her backpack, and pulled out her small emergency flashlight. She turned it on. She saw nothing. She put on her hoodie and shivered from the cold.

Her first thought was that she had somehow miscalculated and materialized on the dark side. She saw no signs of life whatsoever. She moved her flashlight around only to reveal mounds of bones and debris littered across the barren wasteland.

*Take me to the clinic…*

She opened her eyes and called out, "Martin!"

Her mouth dropped open and she gasped.

The tranquil place of refuge was gone. The glistening spiral towers of the clinic that once reached gloriously towards the heavens had been laid to waste in a crumbled heap. Its beauty destroyed. The ground it once rested upon was torn apart.

Emily put her hand to her head. The pain was blinding. She fought hard not to lose consciousness. She tried to calm her breathing, hoping to regain control over her body. She raised her hand again to protect her eyes from the dust rushing past her.

"Martin!" she yelled out, desperately hoping to find him.

Her head was throbbing. She spun around, taking in the devastation around her. She used her powers to cast a purple glow to light the way. All it revealed was a land, laid to waste, littered with bones, broken and beaten – a land beyond recognition.

Emily cried out for Martin again and ran to the ruins of the clinic, searching through the rubble for any trace of what catastrophe had occurred.

This was exactly what Miranda, the evil sorceress, had hoped to do – to consume the light and allow darkness to wash over Aquila, leaving death and destruction in her wake. This wasn't right. Emily knew they had defeated Miranda. This? This was something else entirely.

She searched frantically, but found no human remains. She rifled through the debris where Martin's office should have been, calling out to him repeatedly, only to catch a glimpse of blue fabric wedged under the foundation wall. Emily ran over and dug it out. It was the tattered remains of the dog sweater she had given Martin. It was covered in black soot. She shook it off and shoved the sweater into her backpack.

She continued to look around, desperately calling out to him.

"Martin!" she yelled. She rubbed her temple again, trying to shake herself free of the searing pain.

"Martin?" she said again, her voice barely audible.

Nothing.

No one.

She could hear her voice shouting out, lost in the howling wind. She called out with her mind, searching. She couldn't connect with anyone and it terrified her.

It was like they had all disappeared.

Every last one of them – wiped off the face of Aquila.

She was breathing rapidly now, full blown panic consuming her. Emily cried out as loud as she possibly could.

"Hello?! Anyone, please?!" she yelled, turning in a circle, waving her flashlight around. "Can anyone hear me?"

No reply at all.

"Martin?" she said quietly, drawing a sharp intake of breath. The pain in her head was unbearable. She closed her eyes.

She couldn't feel Martin anymore.

It was the worse feeling she had ever experienced.

She refused to believe something had happened to him.

Not Martin – not him.

Yet, the connection was broken.

"Oh my God," she cried in disbelief.

She opened her mind to call upon Thalien.

There was no response.

*Take me to the Council of Dragons…*

She felt the familiar floating sensation. The searing pain in her head intensified. When she opened her eyes again, Emily was shocked. She was standing perilously close to the edge of a cliff – one small step to the left and she would have plummeted hundreds of feet to the surface below. She knew she did not miscalculate again and yet she was not standing where she should have been. The ground had shifted and nothing was where it supposed to be.

She felt her anxiety level rising. The scene before her was gut wrenching. The once grand colored stones that made up the courtyard of the Council of Dragons had been completely destroyed. In its place, there was nothing but broken shards of colored glass. The oval that she once stood upon was dim and no longer emitted sound or light.

"Hello!" she called out frantically, waving her flashlight back and forth, straining to see anything, gagging on the ash. She heard nothing except the wind, which blew the dark ash around. She raised her hand to shield her eyes.

The pain in her head was so intense that Emily feared she might pass out. She felt something wet above her lip. She reached up and pulled back blood. Her nose was bleeding. She wiped away the blood with the back of her sleeve. She didn't care if she got in trouble with her mom right now for ruining the hoodie.

Suddenly, she saw them – the dragons.

She gasped in horror and ran over to them. They were lying on the ground. Their carcasses were rotted. She could tell that each of their necks had been snapped by the unnatural way they were twisted behind them. Every single one of the majestic creatures had been killed. Emily fell to her knees and screamed. She began to cry uncontrollably at the sight of the carnage before her. She was scared.

She couldn't feel her dragon friends anymore.

They were gone.

"Caponeous," she cried out softly.

She couldn't feel anything anymore.

This can't be happening, she thought to herself.

It's just a nightmare! It can't be real!

Aquila was now a dead world.

She was alone.

If there were any survivors left, Emily would find them.

She needed to figure out what happened to her family and friends on Aquila and all its inhabitants. Emily looked around in every possible direction.

Gone were the vast forests of Aquila.

Gone were the abundant waterways.

The rivers and creeks were replaced by hard crusted and dried up riverbeds. The green forest was replaced with blackened twigs, standing like barren toothpicks, bent and warped from some unknown force.

The ground had shifted and split. Large boulders and rocks littered the terrain. Aquila had been shattered into pieces.

"Martin…," she said softly.

# About the Author

**T**errie **M. Scott** currently resides in Ohio. She is a graduate of the world-renowned College Conservatory of Music, (UC) with a Bachelor of Fine Arts degree in Television, Radio and Film. Terrie is a United States Army veteran, who served as Public Affairs Non-Commissioned Officer for several years. She currently serves on the Advisory Committee for the Ohio Department of Veterans Services.

Terrie and her daughters, Ashlee and Rachel, own a film production company called M.A.R.S. Productions. In 2012, Terrie produced the independent film "Through a Child's Eyes" about domestic violence, which was written and directed by her daughter, Ashlee. Terrie has been editing and proofreading manuscripts for other writers for over 30 years.

Her true passion lies in animal rescue. She owns an animal rescue organization called M.A.R.S. Safe Haven. In addition to finding homes for severely abused and neglected animals, Terrie worked with Operation Baghdad Pups and SPCA International to bring soldiers pets in Iraq and other war zones safely home to the U.S.A. In 2007, Terrie's campaign to rescue the dog named "Ratchet" in Iraq gained international media attention. Ratchet was finally released by the Army and is now living with Sgt. Beberg in Minnesota.

Terrie is also the author of several books, including Dark Storm Rising, Prosperity's Princess, Monsters, Shadowlands, Immortals, Frozen, Remembrance, Shattered Rose, Voices, Infestation, Retribution, Soul Harvest, My Soul to Keep and Arctic Fear.

Terrie enjoys traveling and spending time with her family and fur babies. She is currently working on Emily's next adventure, entitled *Whispers in the Dark,* book two in the *On the Wings of Dragons* fantasy series.

Visit Emily and her adventures at:

www.otwod.com

Learn more about Terrie's other books at:

www.terriemscott.com

tms@otwod.com

Scan the QR code for the latest news from Aquila.

# Full Circle

*We are riding on our rainbow*
*It's nearly at an end*
*It was given as a promise*
*To each and every man*
*It's a long time since we started*
*And the days left now are few*
*It seems the words sent long ago were true*

*We are waiting, we're impatient*
*We're unfaithful, we are true*
*There's a lesson in the learning*
*Of the different things we do*
*As it was in the beginning*
*It shall be at the end*
*We will come full circle to begin again*

*Search your heart before you die*
*Is the cost way too high*
*To explain all the tears*
*We have caused throughout the years*
*When everything is finished*
*And we've done all that we can*
*We will come full circle to begin again.*
~Little River Band
Beeb Birtles, Graham Goble & Glenn Shorrock
circa 1981

*I fly through the skies.*
*The wind blows through my hair.*
*I have no worries.*
*This is where I know I am free.*
*Free from all the madness and chaos that surrounds me every day.*
*When I'm on my friend's back, we fly and soar through the clouds.*
*It's magic. If only you knew the feeling.*
*The fighting continues every day, on and on, non-stop.*
*It makes you just want to die to get away from it.*
*If my friend had not been there, I would have died just like the others.*
*On the wings of a dragon, my spirit has flown.*

~Michael Adkins

circa 2007

Made in the USA
Middletown, DE
14 June 2023